Church of Golf

—⚬—

A Novel About Second Chances

By Spencer Stephens

BOOKS FOR ALL
SAINT PETE PRESS

With love to my Mom and to my Dad,
Who both gave everything they had.

"Fall seven times. Stand up eight."
- Japanese proverb

1

New Orleans, Louisiana
January 1, 1952

Donald Gibson knew better than anybody that crazy good luck was a fine thing to have in your pocket.

Donald wouldn't be quarterbacking for the University of Maryland in the Sugar Bowl with a chance for a come-from-behind win and a national championship unless the starting quarterback had gotten benched because he threw two interceptions and fumbled. Plus, the back-up quarterback, a kid from Butchers Hill in Baltimore, had celebrated a little too loudly the night before. The police decided to arrest him for – what else? – resisting arrest. He sat handcuffed in a St. Bernard Parish jail cell.

Crazy good luck. All of it. Donald could think of no other way to explain how a guy who usually covered receivers on defense was now at the glowing center of the most important football game of the entire year.

Late in the fourth quarter, Maryland was down by a point and grinding. Eight times in a row, Coach Tatum had sent running plays into the huddle. None of them produced more than a six-yard gain. From the sidelines, his signal to Donald was for a ninth.

Donald kneeled into the huddle and called a right fullback return pass. It wasn't something he planned. He hadn't liked coach's play and when he opened his mouth, out spilled *right fullback return pass*. Donald would hand the ball off to the running back who would cut right and keep the ball just long enough to let the defense zero in. Donald would run behind the defense and the running back would pass to him.

Running back Eddie Lemon didn't like it. "Coach didn't call that. No way." Eddie was an extra-studious boy from Upper Marlboro with a buzz cut, a black unibrow and a rigid respect for authority that would lead him into a satisfying career as a high school disciplinarian.

"Let go of the goddam apron strings, Eddie." Donald grasped the boy's facemask. "Every time you run right, the entire defense does the same damn thing. They don't even know I'm out here. I'm *wide open*. Just do it. The same as in practice." Donald released and stared him down.

"Coach is gonna kick our asses."

"Don't be a pussy. This is going to win the game."

Right tackle Bob Shemonski, as big as a gorilla, shook his head. "Gibson, this better work or it's your ass that's gonna get kicked." The rest of the huddle grumbled in agreement.

"Guys – have some faith. This will work. *This will work.*"

As Donald predicted, the defensive linemen lunged toward Eddie as soon as he took the handoff. Just like in practice, Eddie cut to his right, ran almost to the sideline and then made a move that convinced the defense he was going upfield. He waited until the cornerbacks and linebackers moved toward him and fired a wobbly spiral.

As Donald watched the ball come to him, it felt as if he was watching himself from above. The Donald up above raised his fists as he watched the real Donald snatch the ball from the air and run for daylight. As the real Donald crossed the University of Tennessee's thirty-yard line, he heard foot stomps from behind and feared Tennessee's defenders were faster than he had expected. The Donald up above told him that worrying never helped anything.

Neither of the Donalds saw it coming. A Tennessee cornerback dove for Donald's right arm, which was dancing around with the ball. It came unstuck and in a jerky move, Donald's palms popped the pigskin four feet over his head. Donald thought he might never touch that ball again. But when he slowed, it fell back against his left shoulder pad and then, as if by a miracle, into his arms. He cradled it tightly against his chest, swearing to never let go.

Even when Tennessee's middle linebacker grabbed Donald by the ankle and even as he hop-stepped the last four yards to the end zone, dragging the defender, the ball stayed pressed against his gut, held in place with both arms, like Coach Tatum had taught him.

When he got to the sidelines, he watched the kick for the extra point sail through the center of the uprights and got delirious. "Coach! We're going to *win*."

"Gibson, you fucking pissant, you had no fucking business calling a fucking pass. I'm the fucking coach. I call the fucking plays."

"Coach, we're up by six points. We're winning. We're going to *win*."

"Gibson, I wanted to use Eddie's fucking legs to eat up the clock four fucking yards at a time. If you didn't see that as the plan, then you are a fucking *idiot*. Tennessee's fucking offense is going to get back on the field with almost four fucking minutes left to play and we've hardly been able to fucking stop them all day. What were you fucking thinking? Did you see how close you came to fumbling away this fucking game for us?"

"Coach, do you have to say *fuck* all the time?"

"Gibson, *fuck* is my release valve. It's the only thing that's kept me from taking your head off for the last four years. Every time you do the shit you do," Coach waved his hands like a maniac, "I end up needing to yell *fuck* to somebody. If I didn't, you'd be a dead man by now."

By the time the clock had clicked down to two minutes, undefeated Tennessee was facing fourth and three on its own thirty-two yard line. Everybody knew the boys in orange had the best running back and one of the best offensive lines in the game. If Tennessee could make one reasonably good push against Maryland's average run defense, they would get their customary five yards and a first down.

Coach Tatum called a time out. Donald, back on defense, was assigned to Tennessee's slowest receiver. The entire defense was advised in stern tones: if the ball gets passed toward you, make the safe play and bat it down. We'll get possession and run out the clock. Tatum knew Tennessee's smart coach wouldn't call a pass play. Even if he did, on fourth and short, the ball would go to Tennessee's faster and more reliable receiver who played on the quarterback's strong side – and he was double-teamed.

On the snap, two of Tennessee's blockers got their feet tangled together. A Maryland lineman blew past them and closed in on the Tennessee running back just as he was due to take a hand-off. His right-handed quarterback withdrew the ball and rolled to his left, the only open space available, and looked for a teammate he could throw to. Just past mid-field, there was Donald, who had stumbled trying to keep up with his man. Eight yards past him was an underused Tennessee receiver looking for a chance to make a name for himself.

The pass was underthrown. Donald caught up with his man in time but had no clue that the heavy tap on his helmet was the ball that had bounced off his crown. A second later, a leather missile fell straight into the arms he had held high, hoping to block the receiver's view. Usually, when Donald had the ball, the world seemed stone silent. The moment had been planned and practiced. There was no thinking, only muscle memory.

This time, the roar from the Maryland fans was disorienting. There was no plan for what to do if you intercepted a pass without meaning to.

So Donald ran like hell.

He didn't notice Coach Tatum slamming his clipboard on the ground. Coach put his hands on his hips and pursed his lips until the bottom of his sour face looked like it was being squeezed by the hand of experience. *Just run out of bounds, you idiot. You've got more fumbles than anybody in team history.* Donald zagged away from the big boys in orange who had bunched along the right sideline, all of whom had seen game films showing how easy it was to strip a ball from Donald Gibson. They also knew Donald was fast. In this case, he was fast enough to beat them to the end zone, where he flipped off his helmet and opened his arms to receive praise from legions of Marylanders who had traveled a thousand miles to fall in love with this handsome young man and his fabulous blonde hair who had just brought their underdog alma mater its first national championship in any sport.

At Sam Lorea's Tavern in Annapolis and at Mikulski's Bar and Grill in Reisterstown and in living rooms in Easton and Havre de Grace and

Crisfield, grown men hugged and kissed in front of televisions. Students in the bars on Baltimore Avenue in College Park chugged beers and screamed. The weekend editor at The Sunpapers set the headline that would cover half of the next day's front page: GIBSON SHINES FOR TERPS.

The Donald above wept and, pretty soon, so did the real Donald, who knew this story would get retold thousands of times. *The first national championship in school history.*

Television sports guys would talk in amazement about Donald O. Gibson for years and they would air film clips highlighting the best moments of his life. *Was he the fastest man ever to play for Maryland? The case could be made, Howard.*

Savvy sports fans would make bar bets over little-known facts related to the 1952 Sugar Bowl. *I got five bucks that says Donnie Gibson knew enough to call that pass play for the go-ahead score even though his coach told him not to.*

Lovely and talented women would want him. Boys playing sandlot football would pretend to be him. He would be invited to play in pro-am golf tournaments with the rich guys who wore alligator shoes and traveled by private airplane.

It was all so beautiful. The seeds for a flowering perennial had been planted in dark, moist soil with a southern exposure. A grown man could cry about this and not feel embarrassed.

Off the field, the defensive coordinator urgently summoned Donald. "Coach wants to talk to you."

Coach Tatum grabbed the front of his jersey and shook him. "Any cornerback with hands like yours and a lick of sense would have batted down that ball or run it out of bounds. Do you have any idea what this game would look like right now if you had fumbled on that runback?"

"Coach, I just scored two touchdowns. We're going to win and ... ."

Coach Tatum shouted as loud as he could: "Gibson, you ninny, they gave this job to an ugly, ornery motherfucker like me because I can get players to follow instructions. *Why can't you just follow fucking instructions?*" He pulled Donald as close as he could, then whispered: "The rest of this team needs to think I'm mad as hell because you're a knucklehead who doesn't listen. You and me are going out after this game and buying lottery tickets. I've never seen a guy who could pull so many diamonds out of his ass." Coach slapped him on the butt and pushed him away.

In the locker room after the game, a gnome-like sportswriter from the newspaper in Annapolis, wearing a moustache nearly as large as a long-haired dachshund, waddled over to Coach Tatum. "Did you hear that Gibson was voted MVP?"

"That Donald is one smart kid, isn't he Joe? He's better at ignoring instructions than anybody else I ever coached."

—◊—

On campus in College Park, when April blooms made the world colorful again, Donald was still watching himself from above. The Donald up above liked it that several national brands were eager to have the real Donald graduate, gain release from the bonds of amateur sport and star in their television commercials.

When the real Donald got a note asking him to visit the Office of the Provost, he did a little dance. It had to be something good. But the man who occupied the office, a brittle fellow in a crisp, blue suit with dime-sized liver spots on his temples, didn't seem joyful.

"Mr. Gibson, the assistant dean of the business school says you're failing his seminar on international finance. Your ability to graduate in June is in serious doubt."

Donald looked at his feet and then at the floor and decided he liked the look of polished red oak covered by antique Persian rugs that were heavy with crimson details. It was regal and tasteful. He would have that in his own home someday. "I'm a strong finisher. It'll be fine. Anyway, isn't this what extra credit is for?"

Donald stood up and took a step toward the door.

The man remained semi-reclined in his mahogany armchair with its upholstered silk seat. He fiddled with the end of his tie and didn't look up. "Mr. Gibson, you've created a serious problem. Do you know what that is?"

Donald thought about sitting back down but resisted. "*Relax*. I'm all over this."

"The Board of Regents wants you to become a stand-out alum and to graduate with your class, but that won't happen if you don't matriculate."

Donald sat back down. "Matriculate? What are you saying? I have to enroll?"

"Graduate, Gibson. It means *graduate*. Did you attend *any* of your English classes?"

"I do not think that word means what you think it means. I think it … ."

"Oh, put a cork in it Gibson. *You know exactly what I'm saying*." The man straightened his leathery spine, leaned forward and put his elbows on his knees. He stared in at Donald. "Perhaps your reputation for insubordination is deserved."

"Insubordination? *Insubor* … ."

"It means you don't respect authority. It means you don't take directions."

"I know what it means. I don't know what … ."

"*Mr. Gibson*, just sit still and shut up. You are going to graciously accept the offer I'm about to make and you're going to agree that you won't ever breathe a word of this to another soul."

Donald cocked his head. *This will be good.*

"Your business professor takes a dim view of an entitled dandy who waltzes across campus all day in pursuit of skirts but never finds time for class. He thinks you are ungrateful – that you don't appreciate being selected for a seminar reserved for the most promising business students. He also thinks the university puts too much emphasis on athletics. He is eager to fail you so he can make a point. I know this because I asked him to find a way to give you a passing grade."

The Provost studied Donald's face. It looked like Donald was listening. "So the registrar is going to cancel your registration for the seminar, even though the deadline for doing so is long past. She's going to insert an extra business credit onto your transcript, which you never actually earned. By the time you finish your three other courses, you'll have enough credits to *matricu* ... uh, to take your bachelor's degree in business."

"So do I have to keep going to the business seminar?"

"No. That's my *point*, son. You need not attend or take any examinations. Have you been listening?"

"All I have to do is finish my three regular courses and I can graduate? On time?"

"Yes, Mr. Gibson. That is correct."

"And you won't tell anyone about this?"

"Yes. The important thing is that *you* keep this confidential."

Donald grinned and shook his head. *Crazy good luck is a fine thing to have in your pocket.*

—⚶—

From the eighth green, Donald scanned the University of Maryland golf course. "Every college campus ought to have a golf course, don't you think, Teddy?"

"If I hang a big sign that says, *Do not talk to me when I'm putting*, do you think that will stop you from talking to me when I'm putting? Because you're not supposed to be talking to me *when I'm putting*. Jesus Christ."

"Well, it is great to have a golf course on the edge of campus. You have to agree."

Theodore Gibson straightened up, his putter and his ball still waiting for action. "I would have agreed even more and felt an enhanced sense of brotherly love if you had waited twenty seconds to say that. Shut up, already."

"Teddy, you would enjoy life a bunch more if you weren't so picky about stuff. Have you ever thought about that?" Ted turned to face his little brother. Donald's face was slack. He was obviously unready for a rebuttal. "What? I thought you were putting?"

"You're serious? You think I'm the one with the problem, don't you?"

"You are the one with the problem, sphincter boy. You get all constipated about the littlest goddam things. Holy shit – *don't interrupt Teddy when he's telling a story and don't dare sneak into his closet and poke a finger into the breast pockets of all his starched dress shirts.* You have this super egotistical streak. You have to have everything just so because you are *the mighty Theodore*, omniscient big brother and future lawyer. You take yourself so serious."

Ted stepped away from his ball and let his putter drop. He chewed on his lip and squinted at Donald.

"Sonofabitch."

"*What?* You can't take a little criticism? Teddy is too cool for that?"

"Donald, whenever you talk like this, it sucks some of the life out of me. One spoonful at a time. Just now, you took the last spoonful." Ted stared in at Donald. "I have lost the will to live."

2

Lanai, Hawaii
April 1, 1973

Preparing for his tee shot on number twelve at the Wakea and Papa Worship Center, Bobby Joe Hu opened himself, his eyes, his ears and even his pores, so that the peace, the evenness and the quiet that surrounded him could find an easy path to his core. His windpipe relaxed and expanded. His pulse slowed.

Equanimity, joy and compassion for all suffering beings, benefits of enlightenment, filled his lungs, grew tendrils and reached for his extremities. His compassion extended even to the dimpled *Top Flite* teed up near his feet, which was about to get spanked.

Two miles downslope, far below the fairway that was Bobby Joe's target, reflected sunshine blinked on and off from the waters of Auau Channel, where female humpbacks liked to nurse their calves. Beyond that was Maui, lovely and bluish-green.

Bobby Joe took measure of his need. He settled into his stance, bending his knees until his weight was divided equally between his feet. He swiveled his hips and aligned his back until the weight borne by each of his feet was divided equally between heel and toe. He adjusted his neck until it felt that his head was balanced on the top of his spine, the same way his ball might have felt it was being supported by the tee. He extended his arms, driver in his hands, and began a sweeping backswing.

His mind and heart were filled with universal love and good will. Nirvana was *so near*.

"Kahuna. *Kahuna*. Oh, thank God. We've looked everywhere. I'm so glad we found you." Tim McLeigh and his half-brother, Jerry, jumped through an opening in a line of Cook pines, feathery and pale green sentries that stood watch over most of the island. Tim was holding a notebook. "Can we talk about the church's finances? We've been looking over things since you put us in charge. We have to make some changes."

Bobby Joe imagined a bird, in fear for its safety, preparing to flee its nest. His connection with tranquility was slipping. He stepped away from his ball. "Y'all fellers need to let me school you some more on the fine points of being good golfers. Tain't polite to interrupt a man who's preparing to hit." The young men's faces remained earnest and expectant. Bobby Joe knew the bird was gone and would have to be lured back.

"There's no stopping you, is there?" Bobby Joe stood at ease, his left palm resting on the butt of his driver. He looked to his friend and golfing companion, Dixie Ray Reynolds, who was suppressing a grin.

Bobby Joe returned his attention to the interlopers. "There wasn't nobody who put you in charge. We only agreed to let you keep the books since you volunteered. Go ahead, now. Tell me what's got you so oiled up."

"Well, the biggest thing, Kahuna, is the trash collection. We're getting slaughtered here. Do you know we pay almost $100 a ton to get our trash taken to the dump? Last year, do you know how much we spent on trash? Just on *trash*?" Tim paused, feeling sure that Bobby Joe would turn eager and inquisitive. He stared in at Bobby Joe, who looked on passively.

Bobby Joe could feel the aura of urban impatience that hung around Tim, radiating heat like an infrared lamp. "Tim, just by the look of you, I can tell. You're getting ready to tell me all I need to know. Go on."

Tim's eyes bugged out. *He doesn't get it. He's soft in the head.*

"Kuh-Kuhuna?" Jerry jumped in, waving around his unnaturally hairy forearms. "Wuh-wuh-we spent over tha-tha-thirty tha-thousand *thousand* dollars last year. Just on trash. On tuh-tra-trash. Tim and I fuh-figured this all out. Fuh-fuh-for a lot less, we could buy our own tuh-tuh-truck. *A truck.*"

"Our endowment needs to last and the garbage fees are quite a hit," said Tim, pointing a finger at Bobby Joe. "And let's talk about how the church's money is being invested. I mean, we have over half our money in short-term certificates of deposit. *Short-term CDs? Hello?* Do you know how much more the endowment spent last year than the interest it took in? This needs to be redone. *Now. Right Now.*"

Bobby Joe allowed a few moments to pass. *It don't pay a fellow to hurry his game along just because another golfer expects him to.* But Tim's face began to turn red and his head began to shake. Bobby Joe decided that the pressure inside Tim's head was building, and it scared him. So he hurried it along.

"I know you nice young men come from the big old city of Chicago and you're still learning that life on the bitty old island of Lanai is a mite different. Have either of you met our trash collector? He's a decent young man named Pat Arakawa."

Tim surged. "*Decent?* You want to spend thirty thousand just because he's decent? Decent doesn't matter when we're talking about *our money.*"

Bobby Joe put up his hand. "Don't go busting a gasket. Pat was a real drinker and was causing problems for almost everybody on the island. He needed something productive to do with himself after he got sober. So the village worked out a deal. We invested in a trash truck for him and put him to work. Pat's more reliable than the municipal service we used to pay for from Lanai City. And, *surprise* – Pat's uncle is comptroller for Maui County, the same guy who decides if our church has to pay property taxes on this land. It's no gimme for a non-denominational church to keep a religious tax exclusion when its primary asset is a golf course. Lots of folks on Maui think we're a country club and they want to tax us like one. That little ticket is worth near about eighty thousand dollars a year."

Tim stared at the ground, looking defeated. "Come on, Jerry."

"Now *wait* just a minute. Just hang on. Don't you boys be running off quite yet." Bobby Joe stood close to the brothers, who were shoulder to shoulder. He reached out and took a hand from each one. They were uncomfortable with the intimacy and Bobby Joe knew it. "You're new here and you have a lot to learn. Here's an important lesson. When somebody's on the golf course, they're seeking peace. You need to treat them like you would if they were in church. We call this a *worship center* for a good reason. Do you read me?"

"Wuh-wuh-we got the picture, Buh-Bobby Joe. Loud and cuh-cuh-cluh-clear."

Bobby Joe hugged each of the brothers, his bald, Asian head coming up only to their breastbones. "You two young men are fine, fine people. You're the kind of people this village needs more of. You both care enough to want to make things here better. You be sure and hang on to that." He waved a finger at a gap between the trees the brothers had come through and watched them use it for their retreat.

Bobby Joe returned to the back of the tee box where he could look ahead of his ball and re-measure his need. He winked at Dixie. "Now where were we, darlin'?"

Dixie's chin was slack and her head tilted to her right. "Must you always be so dang *nice*? Them boys were plain rude."

—⚶—

Dixie and Bobby Joe usually spent Sunday morning on number eighteen taking care of the grounds. On this particular Sunday, they drained rainwater from a cistern into galvanized watering cans. They let heavy spray from the spouts drench the round tee box. Then they took hand clippers from a crooked wooden shack built into a nearby hill and set to trimming rough grass that circled the tee box.

With her clippers, Dixie trimmed and thinned, a few bits at a time. As she was finishing her turn around the grass circle, Dixie massaged her wrist, sore and fatigued, and gazed downhill toward the fairway. "Sugar britches, I had the most lovely visit with the Hagood sisters yesterday. They all three said they had trouble clearing the underbrush on the way to the fairway. And I noticed some Banana Poka taking *ovah* down *they-yuh*." She pointed and motioned downhill. "Do you suppose we could trim it back just a bit?"

The pair pulled wooden-handled hedge clippers, trowels and rakes from the crooked shack and inched down the steep golfers' path where they got busy trimming and digging. Bobby Joe worked on trimming the underbrush. Dixie wrapped a string of the invasive Poka vine around her hand and followed it back to its roots, then attacked with a trowel. She dug until the roots had been pulled up and then she stuffed the detritus into the back pocket of her dungarees, all in the vain hope of keeping the Poka from growing back. As they worked, each occasionally stumbled upon a lost Titleist, a Blue Dot or a Wilson, which was promptly deposited in a basket they carried with them for just this purpose. On an island too small to support a single golf shop, balls were a valued commodity.

"*Punkin' Pie?*" Dixie stared Bobby Joe in the eye to ensure she had his attention. "When my time comes, I would really like my ashes scattered right there." Dixie pointed uphill to the tee box. "Some of my very best moments on this golf course have been on this hole. It would be nice to think of my spirit hovering around *hee-yah* and to know I was making the grass just a little *gree-nah*."

Bobby Joe nodded. "Dixie? Baby? Are you forgetting that I'm older than you? And your parents both made it to their nineties. When she was eighty-five, you could have struck a match on your mama's butt, she was so tight. You're going to outlive me by twenty years."

"Just in case?"

"Yes, darlin'. Just in case."

"Hey down there. I'm going to tee off. *Watch out.* Watch out you two!"

Thirty yards uphill stood a girl, not yet a teenager and not much bigger around than a number two pencil. She was wearing wrinkly pink shorts that she had outgrown a year before. On her shoulder, she carried a grass-stained canvas golf bag that was only big enough to house eight clubs. Hands on hips, she stood tall, trying to imitate adults she had seen at their most commanding.

"Ramona, you'll do no such thing," boomed Dixie. "It's the first Sunday of the season. Put down that bag and make yourself useful. There's work to be done."

"I did my work. I already did my work. Mom said so. *I* wanna *play*."

"Where did your mama get to? Does she know what you're up to, young'un?"

"Mom's on the first fairway, almost finished with her mowing. She told me I was done. I wanna play."

Dixie forced out her frustration with a fast exhale. "Young lady, it's the first Sunday of the spring season. No one plays until after lunch. You could go back and offer to do some mowing for your hard-working mama. Or you could march on over to the pavilion and help with preparing food."

Ramona scrunched her nose and considered it all. "If I come down and help you, will you play a round with me later, Miss Dixie?"

"Oh, you know I will. There ain't nothin' I'd rather do."

Ramona dropped her bag and scurried down. Dixie opened her arms. "Come here child and have you a good hug." The two embraced, wrapping bony arms around one another. Ramona sunk her face into Dixie's cotton jersey and, with complete innocence, pressed into the softest part of the woman's bosom. She looked up at a weathered face framed by silver. Dixie smoothed the girl's fly-away, reddish-brown hair. "You have come so far and learned so much, child. I'm just in love with you. And your Mama and your brother, too. You are some of my favorite people."

Dixie kissed Ramona on her forehead and then handed her a wide trowel. "Here," she said. "See if you can clean up the front edge of the fairway, just over there past all the vines and such. Get to it now."

Ramona kneeled and worked on defining the top edge of the fairway, just below the tangled bed of flowers and vines. She chunked the trowel into the soil, marking a clear edge and pulling out unsightly vines and rough, volcanic rocks with her pale hands. Inch by inch, she worked a clean edge across the bottom of the bed. Every so often, she rose and collected a pile of debris she had accumulated and carried it into an adjacent stand of trees where she spread it evenly. After a sweaty twenty minutes, she meandered back over to where Dixie and Bobby Joe were pulling and trimming.

"I finished the whole front edge, Miss Dixie. I'll help more if you want me to. And here, I found three balls." She plopped her find into the basket.

Dixie looked up and smiled. Then she curled up her lips. "Ramona? Did you put on your sunblock before you came out this morning? You look as pink as a little baby *pee-yug*."

"A little baby what?"

"A baby *pee-yug*. Pee-yuh. Eye. Gee-yuh. *Pee-yug*."

What did she say? I wish the grown-ups didn't have to be so confusing. "Mom said I didn't need sunblock today. It's supposed to be cloudy and foggy." She pointed up at patchy remnants of the morning mist, still skimming the treetops.

"Oh, child. Oh, sugar. We both know she said no such thing. That won't save you from a nasty old sunburn." Dixie pulled off her floppy, wide-brimmed hat and handed it to Ramona. "You put this on right now. It won't do for you to get sun poisoning again and we have to haul you by boat over to the good hospital in Honolulu. Now run on home and put you on some shirtsleeves, some pants and some sunblock. While you're at it, get your big white hat and put it on and bring me back mine."

"Miss Dixie, you're almost as bad as Mom." Ramona skipped up the hill, almost too fast for gravity to reach her.

"That girl is lucky to have somebody so sweet who is so devoted to her."

"Bobby Joe, that little girl has been through so much, losing her daddy and all. God bless her, that little cricket is as good as they come. You remember, last fall she came and read to me almost every day when I was home sick with the two-week flu, and it wasn't because somebody asked her to. How many other ten year olds do you know who would do that?"

Dixie knelt back down to finish her gardening and then sat back up again. "You know, thirty-something years ago I felt the same way about my nephew, Donald. After his mama died and his daddy killed hisself, I was so happy that he seemed to get back on track. It was like magic the way he could bring a group together and make things happen. Since I left the mainland, he's gone off in the wrong direction."

Bobby Joe cleared grass and weeds from the edges of headstones mounted into the slope, just down from the grass circle. He pulled at grassy clumps that had grown over and obscured them and scraped where greenish moss had penetrated the limestone. He took out a pock-etknife and gently scraped gunk that had accumulated inside the letters and numbers carved into the stones.

"Dixie, I'm thinking next Sunday, we should reset a couple of these stones, don't you? Does it feel like twelve years since we scattered Wilbur's ashes here? His stone is settling under along with a couple of others. I'm sure Wilbur would appreciate it if we got him sitting upright again. He was a nut about making sure he was squared up at address."

"It don't feel like 1961 was that long ago. That would be a great project for next Sunday." A *clangety clang* came from far away. "I think I hear lunch calling our names, don't you?"

The pair gathered their tools, the watering cans and their gloves, and stored them in the gardening shack. Then they labored up the steep hill, one considered step at a time, toward Fellowship Pavilion for lunch with the rest of their village.

By the time they passed the front door of the Chapel of Balance, they sniffed out the aroma of roasting meat and wood smoke. Bobby Joe took the handbasket of found golf balls that he and Dixie had collected and emptied it into a large, half-filled barrel at the chapel steps. When they crossed the lawn near the pavilion, they could hear the chatty hubbub of one hundred and sixty some villagers.

"Miss Dixie! Miss Dixie!" blinked Mavis Hagood, looking up through lenses as thick as cheeseburgers. "Will you please come sit with us? We feel so blessed when you share your company." Dixie knew that Mavis was extending the invitation for herself and on behalf of the other two elderly Hagood sisters, Gabby and Mildred.

"Mavis, there ain't nothing I'd rather do," Dixie responded coyly. "Where are you girls sitting?"

Mavis pointed out the table and Dixie nodded. "You go ahead. I'll be right there."

Dixie reached out and took Bobby Joe's hand and leaned toward his ear. "I'll see you after lunch. Can I come over to your place so we can listen to your new Van Morrison record? I'll bring something that'll put a smile on that little round face of yours." Bobby Joe's head bounced up and down.

Before Dixie could turn away, he grabbed her gently by the wrist, pulled her closer, and planted a wet kiss on her cheek. "I knew there was a reason I made you my best friend. You make me feel happy all over."

Dixie meandered over to the picnic table where she sat down with the Hagood sisters. "*Mildred*," Dixie exclaimed, "Don't Mavis and Gabby look beautiful? You did their hair for them this morning, didn't you? And don't it look *fine*?" All three sisters blushed and giggled.

Mildred fingered a disobedient lick of her hair. She imagined that if it she could make it fall into place, she would feel at ease. "Oh, Dixie. You're so nice. And you're definitely smarter than people think."

Dixie laughed. "Thank you for being so sweet, Mildred," she said, reaching across the table to touch her friend's arm. "Sweetie, do you ever think you'll learn to give a compliment with your *right* hand?"

Gabby and Mavis snorted and fell into dry heaves, holding onto one another.

"Dixie, she's been that way since she was old enough to talk," laughed Gabby. "She'll be that way until the day she dies. When we were little girls and played with our doll babies and I was worried about whether I looked as pretty as my doll baby, she used to tell me I shouldn't worry – from far away, I was *very* pretty."

Mildred jumped. "Gabby, I said no such thing."

"Oh sister, yes you did. And I loved you anyway. I still do." Gabby reached her long arm around her sister's shoulders and pulled her close. "You're *special*. Bless your heart, we've always known that."

Bobby Joe stood on a stone ledge just inside one corner of the pavilion, his head above the crowd, and raised his arms, palms up. An orchestra of discordant voices came to an immediate pause.

Bobby Joe spoke in an affirmative voice, loud enough to be heard by all of those gathered in a building that felt cozy even though it had no walls: "Sisters and brothers, we have come together to give thanks for our blessings. And ain't this a day when it is easy to feel divinely blessed simply because you are alive? Together, we have survived another rainy season and we are happier and wiser for the experience. Together, we look forward to another season of fellowship on our village golf course.

Let us make welcome the guest who has joined us today. We have Edna Wood Ferris, a missionary, who has come from Massachusetts to visit her cousin, our friend and neighbor, George Burdell. Please introduce yourself. Make her feel welcome."

He paused and bowed his head. It was time for prayer. The assembled souls bowed their heads, clasped hands with their friends and neighbors, so that they were joined as one in an unbroken chain, and chanted in unison:

Lord, grant us compassion so we may inspire others to contentment;
Lord, grant us the strength and courage to love and to be loved;
Lord, grant us the faith to be optimistic and to encourage optimism in others;
Lord, grant us wisdom so that we may know and speak of what is best.

Bobby Joe and his congregation paused again and they finished the prayer: *Amen.* Then, as was custom, each of the elders arose and lifted a scuffed Masonite plate from a stack, and served themselves some lunch. On a table where the plates were stacked were heaps of warm, brown biscuits and several deep bowls, each bearing a bright, mixed salad of pineapple, lime, papaya, banana and coconut. Near the table, villagers took turns kneeling at a fire pit where they extracted roasted sweet potatoes from the embers. With tongs, they pulled smoky strings and chunks of meat from the neck and torso of a slow-roasted axis deer that had been splayed open. The deer was one of thousands that inhabited Lanai. This particular animal, just the day before, had the misfortune of wandering in front of a Jeep that had been piloted by a hurried, white mainlander – a *haole* – a mile outside the village.

Each of the villagers, as they kneeled by the deer, offered a silent blessing to the spirit of the fallen animal.

—m—

"Oh, I do believe the late afternoon is the very best time of day for a round, don't you?" Dixie wondered aloud. With her were Ramona and Tina, Ramona's mother.

"I like to play anytime!" exclaimed a happy Ramona. "I just like to play."

Tina put her arm on Ramona's shoulder and whispered. "Quiet, now. Give Miss Dixie a few moments to clear her head."

"But she talked to me. I was just talking back."

"When somebody's on the tee box getting ready to hit, it's usually time to be quiet, even if they say something to you. If you talk to them, it gets in the way. It's just like when somebody's praying. Many times, if they're on the tee box, that's exactly what they're doing."

Dixie stood directly behind her ball and stared past it to the fairway, a flat, inviting expanse that started out narrow and widened about 100 yards out. Beyond that, the fairway planed for just over 200 yards before it reached a pleasingly flat putting surface. On this day, the flag was center right, just a few inches above a slope that, in most cases, would carry your ball twenty yards off the green into a low spot where rainwater sometimes ponded.

Dixie fixed her eye on a spot in the center of the fairway and imagined where she wanted her ball to land. She lined up next to her ball and after a waggle of her hips, took dead aim. Her skinny arms with the sunspots all over them started back, slow and graceful, just like the branches of a weeping willow tree floating on a breeze. It wasn't until the top of her swing that her wrists cocked and her club became parallel with the ground. Then her hips began to turn. Her arms started downward and built speed until her hips had turned almost square with her target line. Her wrists uncoiled with a quick flip, coming around her right hip. The screws on the center of her persimmon-headed three-wood smacked her ball and propelled it in a straight line toward her target. The ball started low, suddenly rose high and then dove nearly straight down and popped onto the center of the fairway, 190 yards from where it started.

"Oh, how lovely," remarked Tina. "Your swing is so beautiful to watch, Dixie."

Dixie nodded and grinned. "Oh, thank you. But an awful lot of how I play comes from watching you, Ramona." Dixie looked at the young girl, standing next to her mom. "I wish I'd learnt to hit as well as you when I was just ten."

"*Mom.* She's on the teebox still and you're talking to her."

"Baby, Dixie's done swinging. It's okay now."

"Mom, this game is complicated when you're around," said the youngster. "When Kahuna plays with me, we talk almost the whole time." Ramona yanked fast at her three wood – so fast that its grip got stuck against the other clubs on the way out. She stopped and gave it a little shake and, after a second effort, managed a clean extraction. She hop-sprinted up to the tee box, sank a tee and balanced her ball. After a glance down the fairway, she lined up. With a movement as sudden as a bolt of lightning, she took a whooshing backswing, putting her club head so far back it dipped below her left shoulder. Then, after a shift of weight from her right leg to her left, her downswing began. Her hips began to turn, her club and arms started down abruptly after and then her ball was on a bullet-like path over the center of the fairway, never more than fifteen yards above the ground. It didn't touch down until it was even with Dixie's ball and then it bounce-rolled for forty yards, coming to rest 230 yards away.

Dixie shook her head. "Tina, what have you been feeding that child? I don't believe there's anybody else in the village who can swing as *purty* as that."

"Kahuna has been working with her," said Tina who was talking to Dixie but looking at Ramona. "He says that she needs to stay humble and keep practicing."

Tina slid a five-iron out of her bag and took her place on the tee box. After a brief set up, and no practice, she took a deliberate and stiff-looking half swing that sent her ball on a sky-high trajectory that ended 140 yards out. "I made it straight-out and on the short grass," she gleamed. "That always makes me feel so right." She popped her club back in her bag and the threesome marched up the fairway, ponytails and golf bags bouncing, bouncing, bouncing with every step.

3

Glen Burnie, Maryland
February 2, 1977

Donald O. Gibson admired his own image, naked and majestic, in his bathroom mirror. Vestigial packets of muscle-like flesh decorated his bulky arms and shoulders and conjured images of ancient Roman royalty, tended to by maidens bearing decanters of fragrant oil. With his husky neck elongated and his face pulled tight, the puckered and purplish half moons below his eyes mostly thinned away. With his face held just so, Donald could capture a glimpse of himself when he was twenty-two, perfectly square at the corners and adored as a wholesome national champion. He could also deny what many knew about him: that the years had roped him around the neck, forced him to the ground and pummeled him into a swollen and deluded man of forty-seven.

Even when his face was relaxed, he liked that his crow's feet had settled in gently and that his wavy, golden hair had begun a gradual transition to silver. His eyes retained much of their deepwater blueness. Partly because those eyes were built into a man who stood a remarkable six feet and five inches tall, they still attracted attention from strangers. When he first met someone, a moment of visual contact was typically all that Donald needed to command their attention while he went to work on them.

"The day – it dawns bright with the promise of shamelessness and magical thinking," he said to the Donald in the mirror, watching how his lips moved. "Shamelessness and *magical* thinking." His practiced pronunciation was objectively pleasant and free of any apparent regional influence. This was a skill he had cultivated during his senior year at the University of Maryland with a small-breasted speech coach named Brenda who seduced him during their second session together. Between kisses, he would precisely enunciate words and phrases that she found comical. *Shamelessness and magical thinking.*

Donald's development of neutral speech patterns helped him garner endorsement deals with national brands during the early years of the Eisenhower administration. This skill would have been important for anyone who grew up calling his hometown *Balmer, Merlin,* and who hoped to appeal to consumers in Pocatello, White Bear Lake and Abilene.

Donald shook a patriotically colored can of Barbasol as he prepared for his daily shave. He pointed the nozzle at his palm and hit the button. Out spewed a furious white flurry that scattered bits all over the mirror and even on Donald himself.

"Kimmy, I'm out of shaving cream. I *told* you I needed more," Donald shouted down the hall. "You need to come look at this mess." Donald shovel-passed the empty cylinder over the toilet and into a trashcan, which was scarred with cigarette burns and contained misshapen make-up removal pads covered with shit-colored goo and an empty half-pint of Gordon's gin.

Kimberly Gibson sat silently at the kitchen table, reading an article in the Sunpapers about Al Pacino's plans to film a movie downtown.

"Kimmy, what am I supposed to do here? I can't go to work looking like this."

Kimberly rose, poured herself a second cup of coffee and sat back down.

Donald, dripping wet, marched one heavy step at a time to the kitchen, all shockingly pink and naked with his striated man-boobs jiggling. "What the hell? Aren't you even going to talk to me? Can't I get a little respect around here?"

Kimberly didn't lift her eyes from her newspaper article. "What's wrong? Is it lonely with only your ego to keep you company?" She licked a fingertip and turned the page.

Donald scowled and returned to the bathroom where he lathered his hands with soap and warm water, ran them over his face and restarted his morning ritual. Stroke by stroke, squinting to avoid the eye sting of smoke from the cigarette dancing in his tightened lips, he shaved away the patchy coating of salt and pepper, singing to himself as he went:

Hop on the bus, Gus,
Don't need to discuss much,
Just drop off the key, Lee,
And get yourself free

In his bedroom, he pulled on his uniform: khaki pants, a white button-down shirt, a patterned red silk tie, and a blue blazer with an oval *Ford* pin on the lapel. He examined himself in a full-length mirror. *There's a customer who will fall in love with you today. And who could blame her?*

Two rooms away stood Kimberly Gibson, known to some as Miss Reisterstown 1953, her varicose-decorated calves poking out from beneath a bathrobe that was undone just enough to allow a pendular breast and a freakishly large, heart-shaped nipple to hang halfway out. She palmed her coffee cup and watched out the kitchen window as a squirrel carried a nut through the missing door of the rusty garden shed that Donald had struggled to assemble twenty-four summers ago.

Donald slid out the front door and unrolled a waterproof cover to reveal a 1964 ½ Mustang. When he turned the key, a heavy growl shook the hood coated with an electrostatic mix of crimson and metallic flake. *Oh baby, I love you too.* He sat motionless, willing the oil pump bolted to the bottom of the modified 289 cubic inch engine to gush syrupy streams of forty weight Quaker State past high performance valves, lifters, camshafts and piston rings.

He looked at his house, bounded by a saggy, chain link fence and sheathed in faded bluish shingles that were fading more every year. Was this the same house that had once filled him with enough optimism to believe that the beauty queen he had just married would adore him for the rest of his days? What had happened to laughing with neighbors at summer street parties and the squealing rug rats that used to show up every Halloween? *What the hell happened to it all?*

—ᵐᵐ—

Charlie Chasanow paced before his audience of sales associates, all dressed just like him, in blue blazers and khaki pants, white shirts and crimson ties. He crossed his pudgy arms on his chest, his fingers across the outside of his biceps, the better to display his gold rings. He pushed hot air through stout nostrils, past the coarse, black hairs that grew from the dark and moist mucosa installed in a squared, open nose that gave him a piggish look. He blasted stares at the salesmen seated before him, hoping to leave them uncomfortable. Charlie had learned that a manager who stood only five feet and four inches tall had to find creative ways to be intimidating.

As he paced, his leather soles clicked on an asbestos tile floor that had been installed in 1953 by a quiet man from Linthicum with patchy red hair and skin paler than cigarette smoke. After his death in 1960 from a lung disease, the man was discovered to have nearly two million dollars in large bills stored in suitcases in the house where he lived alone. In drawers, boxes and cabinets throughout his home, he kept an extravagant collection of satin panties and bras.

"Ladies, you've got me disappointed," Chasanow announced. "And if daddy ain't happy, ain't nobody happy. When I look at our lot, do you know what I'm seeing?"

Chasanow gestured behind him with his thumb, testing the strength of his shirt buttons. They were pulled tight by the residue of a life in which glazed doughnuts and prime-time television played a starring role.

"Boss, there are lots and lots of cars back there," volunteered salesman Joe Bean. "They've been selling really slow lately."

Charlie unfolded his arms. "Bean, it disturbs me that you got past the second grade. Did you not get the memo? You are supposed to shut up when the boss is talking." He looked around, hoping he had not lost his momentum. "When I look out on our sales floor, I see the lot of you wisenheimers standing around playing pocket pool."

Hands in pockets, he thrust his pelvis forward and backward for effect. "Ooooh. Pocket pool. 'Yeah, I think I'll put my left nut in the corner pocket. *Wuh-huh. Wuh-huh.*' Pocket pool, children, does not sell cars. It don't do nothin' but make customers want to stare someplace else but at you. It don't make customers want to shake your hand when you're trying to become their new best friend. *Johnny*, I just had my right paw in my pants pocket cradling my dick. Here, shake my hand. Go ahead. *Shake.*" Chasanow reached toward salesman Johnny Devlin. "You ain't touching that hand, are ya Johnny? No fucking way."

Donald slipped into the back of the room nursing a king-size Snickers and a Styrofoam cup of coffee. "Gibson, you shithead, where the hell have you been? How come you can't get here at eight thirty like everybody else?"

"I found God this morning, Charlie. We had a chat. These things take time."

"Gibson, you're really begging to be taken down."

"Go back to nagging the newbies, Charlie. It's one of the few things you're good at."

Charlie took a step forward and in three silent seconds, his pupils bored a hole into the middle of Donald's face. He turned his attention back to his audience. "Spring is nearly here and our inventory report says we got 224 cars on the lot. That's the worst leftover inventory picture in twenty-four years. The old man upstairs is breathing fire. He's looking for ways to make things better, ways that include replacing some of you knob jockeys. The only thing that's going to save you is moving units. Otherwise, we're going to see a bunch of you pussies looking for fire-proof panties." Charlie pointed to the imagined center of his group. He took several moments to scan the room, checking faces. "You are dismissed, children. Except for Gibson and Mazzilli, I need to see you."

He sat and waited for his crowd to clear. "Park your asses over here," he said, motioning to two chairs directly across from him at the small table in the front of the room. "I don't want to yell to have to be heard."

Then he stared in. "You two are the worst of the worst here. Tony, I see you wandering the sales floor like a lost child. Son, you ain't a rookie no more. Your first six months might have been the best six months by any newbie in ten years. Since then, you have lost your way. I want you to call up Hutzler's and put in an order for some confidence, kid."

Charlie stared at Donald. "And you, the magnificent Donald O. Gibson. What in the hell happened to you? Oh, wait. You stopped making an effort fifteen years ago. Go take a look in the mirror, man. Look at what a pathetic sugar-coated turd ball you've become."

"Oh, Charlie, I'd love to see things from your point of view. I really would. But I can't get my head that far up my ass. When was the last time you tried selling one of these stink-mobiles? I was showing this lady a Granada and she bumped her knee against the dash and busted a hole in it. These cars got shiny little plastic pieces on the grille that come off in customers' hands when they're feeling 'em up looking for the hood release. The Japanese are killing us with their Toyotas and their Hondas. *Those are good cars.* Those boys in Detroit had a good deal going. But they're drowning. We sat in this room two months ago and listened to the suits from Ford tell us they planned to rebuild the company on the back of the goddam Pinto. *The Pinto?* The amazing car that won't go any faster than sixty two miles an hour."

Donald put on his fill-the-room voice: "Ladies and gentlemen, are you looking for a cramped American shitbox that's slower than a Honda Civic and gets only half the gas mileage? Come on down and see *the Ford Pinto.*"

Donald stood up, leaned over the table and poked his finger in Chasanow's jiggly chest. "So. Get. Off. My. Back."

"Gibson, the problem here is *you.* Every week when I hand you a paycheck, I wonder why we keep doing you the favor. A history is a nice thing to have, but a present and a future are even more important. Right now yours are looking like they fell in the crapper."

"Charlie, for chrissake. We can't hardly give these things away. The one with no present and no future is the American auto industry. They're turning out crap cars. Those lazy fuckers are the worst thing to happen to this country since pantyhose ruined finger fucking. And here you are making out like it's my fault. *My fault? My fucking fault?* Holy cow. I'm figuring that your balls must really hurt." Donald extended his fist and held it in front of Chasanow's face and turned it slowly. "Because it looks like the old man is holding them in his pliers and is twisting pretty good. The only chickenshit thing you can think to do is yell at the man who put Glen Burnie Ford on the map."

Charlie started turning red. Donald felt like he was just getting rolling. "You know who sold almost half of the cars that *ever* went off the lot in the entire history of this company? Oh, yeah. That would be *me*. You know who managed the team who bought this land and produced designs for the building you're standing in? That would be *me*. I planned this whole place with the engineers and the architects. You know who found this plot of dirt when it was nothing? Hmmm. *Me again.* This company wouldn't exist without *me*. And without *me*, Charlie Fucking Chasanow, you ain't got jack shit. The old man? He owes me. I got half a mind to go tell him what an ass you have been to me." Donald snapped his fingers. "Just like that and you'll be filing for unemployment."

"You don't get it, do you Donald? The day is not far off when the old man does what I been telling him to do for years – to fire your candy ass."

Tony ran his fingers through his black hair and tensed up. "Guys? Guys? Are we done here? I need a cigarette."

"Tony, a good smoke will make everything seem better." Donald offered his hard pack of Marlboros, lid open. A February wind cut from right to left across the parking lot of shiny Fairmonts, Granadas, LTDs and Broncos, generating a cold chorus of flip-flaps from the flags hung above on a network of string. Donald pushed his shoulders deep into his overcoat. "Jeez, do I hate winter. If this was any other time of the year, I could decide I was having a bad day and spend the afternoon on the golf course. But look at this: the ground is colder than Richard Fucking Nixon and we got twenty-knot winds."

Tony looked at his feet. "Donald, is Charlie really going to fire us? This morning, he sounded really, really mad. His disgusting nose holes opened up even bigger than usual."

"Charlie? Hell no. If it wasn't for me, that little naked mole rat wouldn't have a job. He's just screaming because the man told him to scream."

"Donald, I was more worried about me. Is Charlie going to fire *me*?"

"You're worrying too much. Just sell some cars and you'll be fine."

"Donald, I *need* this job. I got a wife and a kid."

"Tony, my high school football coach told me something I'll never forget. He said 'Just live your life in a series of sexy poses and pray every night for nuclear war.'" Before Tony could open his mouth to say *Non sequitirs like that are only funny if you've been drinking*, an officious female voice came to life on the outdoor public address system: "Donald Gibson. Call on line 3. Donald Gibson. Call on line 3."

"Looks like Jimmy Fucking Carter's on the line with news about my Congressional Medal of Honor. See ya, buddy." Donald squished out his cigarette, slid through a pair of glass doors and settled inside a pristine beige cubicle at a pristine beige desk bearing a pristine beige phone. He paused. *Easy and breezy.* "Hello, this is Donald at Glen Burnie Ford. What can I do for you today?"

"Is this Donald Gibson?"

"Celebrate madly, my friend. Your search is over."

"Mr. Gibson, I'm with the collections unit at Citizens Bank. Sir, your payment on your Citizens Master Card is 90 days overdue. I'm calling because we need to know when we will receive your next payment."

"You just called me about this the other day. What the hell?"

"Sir, we last called you 30 days ago when you were 60 days overdue and our records show that you promised to issue payment within 10 days. At this point, I need to find out how soon you can make a minimum payment of $232."

Donald paused. "If you want your money so bad, why haven't you sent me a bill in over a month?"

"Sir, we last sent you a bill on January 15 for a total of $11,450."

"Eleven thousand? *Eleven thousand?* There is no way I owe you that. I hardly even made that much all of last year. Call my wife. There's a mistake here and she can probably straighten it out."

"Sir, it's your name on the account. Only your name."

"Mr. underpaid bill collector, you need to prove that I spent eleven thousand dollars. That's just not possible. There's not eleven thousand dollars worth of stuff in my entire house."

"Sir, I need to get a date when payment will be made if we're to avoid hiring an attorney and starting a collections action."

"Look, dingleberry, I've had your card in my wallet for over fifteen years. I used to do advertisements for you. You guys have made thousands and thousands from me. Do you have any idea how many car buyers I've sent over to Citizens Bank for car loans? *Thousands.* How much have you banked on *that*? Oh, maybe a few *million.* So give me some fucking slack. You guys owe *me*. You should be thanking *me* for all I've done for you. Now stop bothering me. I'm at work and I'm trying to earn a living."

Donald slammed the receiver into its cradle and learned a valuable lesson: pounding a telephone too hard with the heel of your fist will make it break into knife-like plastic shards that can inflict a puncture wound.

Gotta see. Gotta be seen. Gotta see. Gotta be seen. Donald pressed his ham hocks onto the front of a lipstick-red 1976 Gran Torino that had been twiddling its thumbs for fourteen months, hoping to be bought. Slotted magnesium wheels, chevron-style decals and deluxe bumpers could not hide its genetic code. It was a bottom-heavy family sedan with a Cruise-O-Matic transmission. The car reminded Donald of a picture he'd once seen: an East German athlete in a one-piece swimsuit, lounging by a pool. The athlete's gender was in dispute and Donald had always regretted that the photo could not be unseen.

It was library quiet in the automobile showroom, an over-scaled and over-bright memorial to an American industry that appeared terminally ill. Curly bits of dust hung in the atmosphere that was heavy with the crowd-pleasing aroma of polyvinylchloride. From his elevated perch, Donald could efficiently scan the lot, owl-like, and be the first to spot a new arrival. If a prospect surfaced and pointed his face and feet toward the main double doors, Donald's fast legs got working and he could be the first to offer breezy and meaningless salutations. The face and the feet were an obvious *tell*: the customer was asking to be approached by a trained manipulator.

If the body language of a visitor was any less direct, they would waste your time. Those were browsers. A guy like that would have you feeling ebullient with talk of dealer-installed options and the benefits of a double rust proofing. He would have you imagining the number that would show up on your commission check, but then his narrative would grow left-handed and nonsensical and he would usher you onto the deck of his imaginary sailboat for a glide across a wide and beautiful ocean and around the Cape of Good Hope before you realized it was closing time and you had been bamboozled.

How long had it been since he had seen a ready buyer? Donald couldn't say. Would he ever again feel the surge of warmth that started in his gut when he got an eager look upon meeting a prospect for the first time – the look of a man flattered to have a few minutes of attention from a Heisman finalist? Donald held out his large hands before him, palms down, and examined the brown spots and the coarse, graying hairs on his hand backs. *Look at those. Those are aged hands.*

"Mr. … Mr. Gibson?"

Donald turned, his hands still extended before him. At his left shoulder stood an antique woman with a weak chin and an even weaker voice. Her yellow-gray hair was tied up in a bun and she clutched a tattered beige purse like it was a shield. She smelled of rose perfume and mothballs.

"Good morning, ma'am. What can I do for you today?" Donald let a grin spread across his face, until the grin was the only thing anybody would notice. The woman hesitated and appeared ready to take a step backward. Donald reached out and touched her shoulder. The woman shifted her gaze from the floor to Donald's face.

There it was – eye contact.

"Mr. Gibson, I need to buy a new car. Probably a Granada."

"Tony, you ever been to the Honey Bee for lunch?" Donald asked.

"Nope."

"Well, today's your lucky day. Follow me. I'm driving. And, by the way, that means you're buying." They climbed into Donald's Mustang and motored off.

"Donald?" asked Tony, as they waited at a red light. "What was the story with the little old lady who came in? I saw you drive off with her in her car and come back in a cab. Are you boffing her? Please tell me that ain't true. I could hardly stand to think of it."

"Nooooooooooo." Donald laughed and mock-screamed, shaking his head. "Tony, sometimes the worst thing a salesman can have is a conscience. That old gal and her sweetheart husband over the last twenty-some years bought twelve cars from me. Here she is, her husband is dead, she's almost ninety and she's too short to even see over the dashboard. She's driving on an expired license that MVA wouldn't dare renew. Despite it all, she's still so loyal to the Donald that she wants to keep on buying from me. Man, I couldn't sell to her. If I did, I couldn't live with myself."

"Donald, the old fart's probably got a retirement nest egg big enough to buy and sell both of us. What's the harm?"

"Tony, when you get to be almost ninety, you won't want people calling you *old fart* behind your back. And I can't be selling a ten thousand dollar luxury car to a ninety-year-old lady who's not even supposed to be driving. That's just wrong."

"Donald, every single one of our guys would have closed that deal. You got Charlie breathing down your back because he wants to fire you."

"Tony, I can't treat a little old lady like that. Don't even ask me why. If you can't figure that out, you got no morals, man."

Tony stared straight ahead, shaking his head. "This makes no sense. That was a deal you should have *done*."

Donald fumed. "That lady's son is president of the Bank of Glen Burnie and I talked to him on the phone. He now thinks I'm a king among men because I called him, concerned about his mom. That, my young friend, is money in the bank. Do you know how many of his banker friends are going to show up on the sales floor asking for me?

That's how life works. That guy can count on me sending some car loan customers to him. It's money in the bank for him, too."

Donald navigated into the parking lot at the Honey Bee Diner and angled his chariot so that it consumed two parking spaces.

"I haven't seen anybody park like this since high school."

Donald squinted. "My dad taught me to park this way. He was a guy who knew how to keep his cars looking right. They were polished and perfect. I mean *perfect*. This world doesn't have near enough perfect."

Donald put his hands on the steering wheel, tapped the gas and let the vibrations enter his body. "This Mustang, she's an investment. I've got thirteen thousand into her. It's easily worth twenty five. In a few years, maybe forty. Tony, people stop me at the gas station and ask me can I open the hood so they can take a look. They admire her. They even beg to buy her from me." Donald pointed across the parking lot at a gaggle of station wagons. "Those cars over there? They're an expense. They're a drag. They ain't *shit*. They're for people who have no idea what a car like this represents. And let me tell you something else, there's not a state trooper or a meter maid anywhere in the state that would give this ride a ticket. They know a car like this is special. They don't fuck with this car. They don't. People with practical smarts don't fuck with perfect."

Tony stared at Donald, mouth open. "You act like this is all news. Please tell me you're smarter than *that*. Jesus. Come on, let's go in. I'll introduce you around. They just love me in here. You watch. These folks are going to *eat me up*."

Inside the diner, Tony and Donald were embraced by the buzz of two dozen lunchtime conversations and the repeating clank of heavy American porcelain against Formica as dishes and coffee cups were laid on tables. The reassuring aroma of fried onions seemed to reach out and put its loving arms around Donald's paunch. They slid into Donald's favorite booth. Tony grabbed a menu. Donald looked about for familiar faces.

A waitress appeared at Donald's elbow. She had dyed-auburn hair in a tidy bun, a perky, turned-up nose and white, sensible shoes with a few grease stains. There was a little green order pad in the left hip pocket of her apron and a bit of her lace slip showed from beneath the scalloped bottom edge of her uniform dress. A hint of a tattoo on the edge of her left breast peeked out from the deepest edge of her v-neck.

Donald reached over and took her hand, looking adoringly at her face. She yanked her hand back and moved away where she balanced her free elbow on her hip, pad in hand. "How we doin', hon?" she asked, staring at Tony.

"We're doing fine, hon," said Donald, reaching again for her hand. "The question is, how is a gorgeous woman like you on a day as fine as this?"

The waitress took another half-step away from Donald, maintaining her eye lock on Tony.

"Becky? Come on, sister, I'm down here," insisted Donald.

"Our special today is a Salisbury steak with fries and gravy only $2.85. Do you need more time to look at the menu?"

"The Salisbury steak will be fine. And a Coke," said Tony.

"A special and a Coke," murmured the waitress, jotting onto her order pad. "And the married, lying sack of shit here will have his usual bacon cheeseburger, medium rare, with a glass of sweet tea, no ice, and an extra large side of onion rings."

Becky reached out and accepted Tony's menu. She grabbed for the menu just in front of Donald. But just as quickly, Donald grabbed his end, starting a tug of war that lasted until Becky relaxed her arm.

"Aw, Becky, come on. It's not going to be like this – is it?"

The waitress released her grasp on the menu and cast an ice pick stare at Donald. She held out her hand expectantly. Donald and his hang-dog eyes held fast.

"Can't we just talk? Is that too much to ask?"

"Yes, it is too much to ask," she barked. "The only thing you get to ask for is that I don't spit on your food before I bring it out."

She marched away.

Donald hung his head and shook it slowly, his eyes closed.

"What the hell was *that*?" Tony laughed, his thumb pointing in the direction of the retreating waitress. "Oh yeah, Donald. She loves you. She *adores* you." Tony reached across the table and grabbed a squeeze of Donald's cheek. "Oh yeah, she's just *eating you up.*"

"Oh, come on. You know how women are."

"What does that mean, exactly?"

"Just what I said. Women are *women*."

"Meaning … ?"

"Tony, I know women aren't stupid, but … *women are stupid*."

———※———

Donald stood alone on the center of his own stage on the first tee at the Eisenhower Golf Course, his feet just beyond shoulder width. The borders of the first fairway ran long and nearly plumb-line straight. The wind stood still. A rare and unusually warm late-winter sun shone off the bentgrass. All was good and correct. Donald breathed in deeply and slowly, inhaling authority, control and clarity. Was there a better place to be on an afternoon when the dispiriting force of winter had yielded to the gentility of spring?

Donald's hands wrapped around the new and slightly spongy grip on the end of a whisper-thin shaft of graduated steel. His knees were bent slightly and his torso leaned forward. As he shifted his weight toward his right, he pulled his club back with his straightened arms in a slow and wide arc. When his arms and his club were just above parallel, he cocked his wrists and continued his gradual shoulder turn until the club shaft was above his shoulders. Then Donald's hips turned left, toward his target, and his weight began a deliberate shift in the same direction. His arms started their move downward and he laid his club head back slightly, keeping to the inside of his target line. When Donald's hands were almost even with his ball, he released his wrist-cock. The head of his driver *ooshed* through the air and his right hip rotated forward so that he faced the fairway. The head of the driver *panked* the Titleist that had been obediently waiting. Donald's ball soared straight out and up until it came to rest in the fairway, 224 yards away.

Donald held his balanced stance and shot a confident smirk to Ted, his playing partner for the day. "Was that my ball that just took off? *My ball?* Uh, was that MY BALL? Did you see how far I hit that?"

"Yeah, Don. I saw. Maybe now, you'll let somebody else tee off?"

"Yeah, keep your plaid pants on." Donald picked up his tiny white tee, parked it over his left ear and relaxed in the golf cart. As Donald fumbled to light a Marlboro, a wooden *phunk* sounded from Ted' direction.

"Where'd you put it this time, brother?" he queried, as he looked up from the back of the cart.

"Down the center. Out about 170 yards."

"Damn, Ted. You've been hitting the same boring tee shot since you were 15 years old. Why don't you go for a little distance? Put something into it, man."

Ted glanced cold over his shoulder at Donald. "How about this? You play your game, and I'll play mine."

Donald hit the gas pedal in the golf cart and, with Ted inside, zoomed ahead to Ted's ball. Ted grabbed a three wood, set up and swung and put his ball 200 yards away, on the edge of the green.

"Some day you'll have to tell me how you get more distance off the carpet than you do off the tee. It just doesn't seem possible."

"Donald, it's a little like when the missus decides to sleep with a penis-toting cretin like me. I don't know how it happens. I don't know why it happens. It just, you know, *happens*."

Next to Donald's ball, forty-some yards ahead, Donald looked at a nearby yardage marker, pulled out a five iron and surveyed. *In a goddam divot.*

"Teddy? Holy cow! Did you feel that?"

Ted swiveled his head. "Feel what?"

"That earthquake? Did you feel it?" Donald took the nose of his club and slid his ball out of the divot and onto good grass.

"We had an earthquake? Just now?"

"Yeah, no shit. It must have been at least ninety eight point six on the sphincter scale. It pushed my ball right out of this little divot over here."

Ted smirked. "A little self delusion is a wonderful thing. It has done wonders for *your* scorecard, hasn't it?"

"Holy shit, Teddy. I think you just hurt my feelings."

Donald lined up next to his ball and swung extra hard. The bottom edge of his clubface hit the ball on its equator, sending it on a bullet-like ride. It bounced once on the right side of the green and then dove into tall weeds that grew twenty yards behind it. "Teddy, you little fucker. Look what you made me do."

Ted took a slow breath and gathered some peace. "Donald, I hope you don't ever have to golf alone. Who would you have to blame for your problems?"

After the golf cart was parked greenside, Donald manhandled a 64-degree lob wedge and pulled a putter out of his bag and strong-stepped in search of his ball. He found it nestled in some tall grass.

"Donald, uh, I think you're away," said Ted.

Donald looked down at his ball. "Ah hah hah hah," he exclaimed, as if the small, white ball had ears. "You are mine. *All* mine. And you will *pay.*"

Donald practiced an easy takeaway, going back only about halfway, and an easy downswing. He did it again, for confidence. Both times, the curved sole of his wedge brushed pleasantly against the layer of roots at the bottom of the reedy tangle.

Donald set up and took the same easy takeaway to a half-swing. His downswing began strong and fast. He dug the leading edge of his wedge into the ground, leaving a smile-shaped divot. His ball popped straight up and right back down again, only a few yards closer to the flag. Donald's shoulders drooped. He shook his head, staring hard at the ground where his club had wounded the turf.

"Donald, uh, I think you're away," guffawed Ted, relaxing on the green.

Donald slammed his lob wedge into the ground where it had left its mark. He kicked his prostrate putter and set up anew to address his ball, breathing like a sore, old mule. Without a practice swing, he swung again, this time with barely more than a cock of his wrists. He hit the ball thin and it skittered straight at the slope leading up to the green where it plugged into the green-side soil.

Donald wrinkled his face and adopted a loud falsetto. *"Ooooooh. A little self-delusion has really done wonders for your scorecard, hasn't it?"*

Ted doubled over, laughing and pointing at Donald.

Donald dislodged his plugged ball with the toe of his lob wedge, scooted it up to the hairy fringe of the green and prepared to putt. "If the freaking grounds keepers were doing their freaking jobs, I would have been on the freaking green already. This is like playing on a cow pasture."

Donald tapped his ball with a firm stroke of his putter, aiming high at the left edge of a small ridge that ran just above the hole. The ball skirted the edge of the ridge, looking for a minute like it would trickle down to the hole. Instead, it clung to the ridge and stopped, still 15 feet uphill from its target.

Donald looked across the green at Ted, who was preparing for his next shot, taking small practice swings with his pitching wedge. "Gimme a sec, this next shot will just drop in." He set up and tapped his ball which gained speed and ran twelve feet past the hole. He walked over to his ball, picked it up and talked to it as he cradled it in the palm of his hand. "Your mother and I buy you books to take to school and study. We even buy you a donkey to ride to school. And what do you do? You stand on the books and you *screw* the donkey." With a flick of his long arm, the kind you could expect from a former quarterback, the ball was forty yards into the leafless woods.

Ted stood off the edge of the putting surface and considered his ball's likely path. He returned his pitching wedge to his golf bag and retrieved a putter. Ted stood over his ball and rapped it firmly. It traveled up the slope, rolled to the right and stopped about ten inches past the hole.

"Gimme!" said Donald, who tossed the ball back to Ted.

Donald retreated to the golf cart and grabbed the scorecard and a pencil. "Ted? Five?"

"Five nothing. I parred."

"Four for Ted. And a six for the legendary Donald."

Ted stared, his mouth hanging open slightly. "*Six*? Gimme a freaking break. You had your regular drive, a foot wedge outta the little divot, a screaming iron into the weeds, two to the hill, relief from an unplayable lie, another foot wedge up to the putting surface, and then… "

"I shot a six, you sticky little ball of crap. Sheesh. Do you always have to be such a downer?"

Donald maneuvered the cart toward the second tee box. Before Ted could say a word, he strode to the box with his driver in hand and set up.

Four hours later, Donald and Ted meandered to the parking lot, comparing scores. The brothers sat on the back bumper of Donald's Mustang, trunk open, changing out of their golf shoes.

"Donald, how is it that I lend you four thousand dollars for a so-called emergency in October, then you have your Mustang reupholstered in November. And here it's almost March and you're golfing on a workday and not even offering promises for when you'll start paying me off."

"Well, if it doesn't matter whether I pay you, why are you even asking? You remember how back on the first hole I said you were being a downer? Well, you're doing it again."

"It's a fair question. You'd wonder. We both know you would."

Donald took a deep breath and exhaled forcefully through pursed lips. Then he leaned forward, elbows on his knees, staring at his feet. "You know, just because you were a noodge when you were a kid doesn't mean you have to be one as an adult. *Honestly.*"

"Man, look me in the eye. Look me in the *goddam* eye. This is your brother, not some bill collector. Remember me? I'm the guy who loans you money when you're down, remember? The guy who crawls out of a warm bed at four in the morning and comes downtown with his checkbook and bails you out of the drunk tank? Is there anybody else in this world who will do for you what I've done? So don't you go shucking and jiving on me. I'm entitled to a straight answer."

Donald slumped and looked at the sky and then faced his brother. "Ted, I'm sorry. I really am sorry. I'm stuck. I feel totally, totally stuck."

"Stuck? You're stuck? What does that mean?"

"Aw, jeez Teddy. Man, the whole world has gotten screwed up in the head. Nobody wants to give me credit for anything. Kimmy hates me. My boss hates me. My customers don't appreciate me. The bill collectors hate me. Some days it seems like you hate me. Nothing's working. I mean, how did I get here? Everybody used to love me. It used to be that people couldn't get enough of me. And now? All I want is a little appreciation and what I get is trash talk. It did not used to be this way. It was never this hard. The world has changed."

"Donald, news flash: the world hasn't changed. The problem is you. Man, hardly anybody remembers the 1952 Sugar Bowl. You're not a star football player anymore. You're not the golden boy. You are never again going to get paid to let Crown Gasoline use your picture in their newspaper ads. You're just another schmuck from *Glim Burnee* who wants to drink some beers, smoke some Marlboros, play a lot of golf and talk about his glory days. Just be humble about it."

Donald shook his head in disbelief and stared at his feet. "Thanks a lot, Norman Vincent Fucking Peale. Come on. I need help here. What do I do?"

"This is help, Donald. I'm helping."

"Teddy, I'm up to my eyeballs in debt. I'm so bad off at work that I couldn't sell dollar bills for fifty cents. Kimmy would probably like to shoot me and collect the insurance money. And here you are telling me that I'm a schmuck? *A schmuck?* That's not helping. *It's not.* You're just piling on."

Ted stood and looked Donald square in the eyes. He put a hand on Donald's shoulder. "The answer to every one of your problems is simple. Just take a look in the mirror. Take a look and be honest with yourself about what you see."

"Teddy, I've heard all this before."

"When I talk to you, are you really listening? Are you? Or are you just waiting until it's your turn to say something?"

"Teddy, what do I *do*? Just tell me: *What do I do?* Where's the button I push to make things better? What words do I say to make the world love me again? How do I get the bill collectors off my ass? How do I get out of my rut? This is not where I planned to be at almost fifty. I'm the punch line in the cruelest fucking joke you ever saw."

"I can't tell you what to do. It's your life. But it seems like you have to make some changes. *You.* You have to make changes."

"I'm a schmuck? And I have to change? Can you please tell me what all that means? I'm struggling here."

—⋙—

Wind-burned, hungry, dehydrated and squinty-eyed, Donald pulled onto his driveway, worn gray from exposure and age. The late-afternoon sun beat down until his shoulders got round. He turned the key and his engine went silent. He leaned back, his neck pressed against the headrest, and closed his eyes. He took in a full suck of air and held it. *It will be fine. Somehow, it will turn out fine.* He exhaled. *It will get better. It has to get better.*

"Kimmy. I'm home," he announced, as he tossed his keys and wallet on a small table, overflowing with unopened mail, just inside the front door. He paused. He listened. Nothing. "Kimmy? I'm hungry. Can you make me some dinner?" Donald found her, rubbery lipped and asleep, wearing only her panties, the covers a tangled mess between her thighs. Donald pulled off his shoes and padded into the kitchen. He opened the refrigerator door, found a can of Budweiser hiding among a forest of skinny bottles containing aged condiments, and snapped it open.

He closed the door and stood back. It was then he saw the note with Kimmy's childish scrawl, held beneath a magnet on the refrigerator door: *Call Attorney Nakamura. About Aunt Dixie.* There was a phone number. Donald pulled the note from the board, looked at his watch and dialed. A curious series of clicks and hums followed. Then a long pause.

Another female voice came on the line. "This is Karen Nakamura. Can I help you?"

"This is Donald Gibson. I got a message from you about my Aunt Dixie. Dixie Reynolds?"

"Mr. Gibson, I … Thank you for calling me back so promptly. Mr. Gibson, I have been handling your Aunt Dixie's investments and legal affairs for many years. She asked that I call you when … . Well, Mr. Gibson, listen, I'm very, very sorry to tell you that Dixie has passed. Just yesterday, in fact."

"Aunt Dixie? She's dead? Are you sure? I just talked to her on the phone a week ago. She sounded fine."

"I'm sure this is shocking news, Mr. Gibson. My heart goes out to you. Dixie was one of the finest people any of us could ever hope to know."

"What happened? *What?* How did it happen?"

"Dixie had a cerebral hemorrhage. She was out on the golf course Monday afternoon with some friends and they tell me she was walking around fine one minute, and then she complained of a severe headache. The very next thing, she was lying on the ground and she wasn't breathing. Her doctor told me that she would have died even if she'd had the hemorrhage in the hospital. It's been a shock to us all."

Donald's butt hit a kitchen chair. He gripped his forehead. His stomach felt like it was getting small and tight and he thought he might vomit.

"Mr. Gibson? Are you still there? Are you alright?"

"This can't be. It can't be. Dixie has always been as healthy as a horse. Are you sure? Are we talking about the same person?"

"Dixie Reynolds from Lanai, yes. Born and raised near Chapel Hill, North Carolina."

Donald discovered he had a talent he thought he had lost years before: he cried big tears, which streamed down his cheeks and along the curve beneath his jaw line and disappeared into the fibers of his golf shirt. He half snuffled and wiped his running nose with the scratchy hairs on the back of his hand. "That's Dixie. That's her." Donald felt his voice getting trapped. "I should have expected this day would come. I just didn't think it would come this soon. Dixie was hardly even 70. She was like my big sister. She raised me and my brother after our parents died."

"Mr. Gibson, I'm so sorry for your loss. I am. Look, I've known Dixie for nearly 30 years. When I was sick with vertigo, she did my grocery shopping and cooking for me and helped me with household chores. Everybody in the village has a story like that. Our whole church is in mourning."

Donald hesitated, unsure what to say. He regained control of his gut and had to make a conscious decision to start breathing again. Have you called anyone else from the family? Do the cousins know?"

"As far as I know, Mr. Gibson, you are the first person outside of the islands to know. I've not called anyone else. I don't think anybody here knows who to call besides you and your brother, who I'm waiting to hear from."

"Do you know anything about her funeral arrangements? Where she'll be buried?"

"Her funeral will be held here on the island. Her body is due to be cremated and her ashes will be spread at our worship center – well, we call it a worship center. Most everybody else calls it a golf course."

"Wait … what? Spread on a golf course?"

"Those are Dixie's wishes, yes."

"On a golf course. *A golf course?*"

"I realize this may seem unusual to you, but on a small island, open land is scarce. Gravesites are far less common than on the mainland. Most of our church members choose to have their ashes spread on our golf course. It returns us to nature, it enriches the soil and it allows our spirits to remain close to the game and the traditions that bond us together in faith."

Donald shook his head. *A golf course?* "When's the funeral?"

"That's part of why I reached out to you. Dixie wanted to make sure you attended. I'm hoping you can fly out. We will schedule the funeral to accommodate you."

"Holy Jesus, that's a tough one. A ticket out and back must cost over a thousand dollars. I need to look into that and let you know how soon I can pull that kind of money together."

"Mr. Gibson, Dixie anticipated the cost of your travel might be a problem. I can purchase a ticket for you and have it waiting for you at the airport."

Donald sat up straight and stiff. "Ms. Nakamura, wait. Listen, is there something you want from me? Because I really have nothing I can give. *Nothing.*"

"Mr. Gibson, I don't want anything from you. Actually, I have some information to share. Dixie has left a large and unique bequest for you in her estate plan. You need to be on the island to consider it and to accept it."

"What are you saying?"

"It's just like I said. You need to be here on the island to consider whether to accept the bequest."

"Ms. Nakamura, what's this all about? What's going on here?"

"Mr. Gibson, I've told you everything I can. If you would like for me to purchase a round-trip airplane ticket for you, just say so. I'll make the call right now."

4

Lanai, Hawaii
February 21, 1977

The beach at Hulopo'e Bay on a Tuesday afternoon was everything a man could want, especially after twelve hours belted to an airplane seat that had a permanent imprint of somebody else's ass. There was Hawaiian sun and powdery sand. A breeze carrying notes of coconut oil fed his nose. A rainbow beach umbrella shielded his eyes from the sun. Next to Donald, a cooler housed a chicken-salad sandwich, a Tupperware square containing chunks of pineapple and papaya, and six icy bottles of Primo, a Hawaiian beer. There were also thin-hipped women in bikinis so small they would be considered illegal at the Maryland shore. Pacific waves broke every few seconds at Donald's feet. The rhythm stoked a lethargy that was completely delightful.

Twenty yards down the beach, a pair of brown-skinned women in fashionable sunglasses jibber jabbed, sometimes in English and sometimes in strings of words that Donald couldn't understand. Their portable radio was tuned to KONI and was loud enough to be heard up and down the beach.

Thinkin' of you's working up my appetite,
Looking forward to a little afternoon delight.
Rubbin' sticks and stones together makes the sparks ignite,
and the thought of rubbing you is getting so exciting

Sky rockets in flight,
Afternoon delight …

Donald pushed some sand into a pile to create himself a footrest. *Yeah, this will do just fine.* He chugged his first Primo and clicked open a second, casting the bottle cap into the sand. He peeked at the brown women. They turned away. A few minutes later, same thing. Donald picked up his cooler and sauntered over. He rested on one knee next to their blanket.

"The Titanic."

The women looked at each other. *What?*

"Pretty good icebreaker, eh?"

The girls smirked. "Not really," said the taller one. "You should go back to your umbrella and then come back and try again."

"Ovary funny. You must be comedians."

The girls both went blank. *What did he just say?*

Donald extended his hand. "I'm Donald. Can I come sit with you? I'm here for a couple of days and don't know a soul."

The women both giggled and made room on their blanket.

The trio talked of camping at the Pohakulua Point, of dates and day trips to Maui to go shopping and to hear music. Then they talked of their plans for the evening and before Donald knew it, the girls had him over to the home they shared on the edge of Lanai City. He was surprised to learn that their skin showed no tan lines. They were brown all over, just like a pair of French fries. And like all the girls he had known from Baltimore, they were pink where it mattered most.

—◊◊◊—

Karen Nakamura's law office occupied a white-washed bungalow with a peaked, corrugated metal roof on the edge of Lanai City's Commercial Square. Around it were the trappings of a paradise in the tropics: a broad sky of unbroken blue, a thin forest of spired Norfolk pines, and the tangy scent of Dole Fruit's pineapple fields that held most of the island under a ghostly green blanket.

Donald stood back from the trim little building for a minute, wondering what might lie within. The porch was fronted by a row of Japanese banana plants. The elephantine greenery swayed in the wind, looking like an entrance to a jungle where a man might crawl in just to hide and then get lost. Sitting in the driveway was a rusty and dusty four-wheel-drive Suzuki Jimny with a canvas convertible cover. Most anybody around would have called it the perfect island car. But to a man who worshipped the 1950 Buick Roadmaster and its round lines, it looked like a queer toy.

Donald climbed three wooden steps, crossed the front porch and opened the door. "Hello, you must be Mr. Gibson," offered a dark-haired Asian woman in the front room, arising from behind a small desk. "My niece, Jenni, met you at Hulopo'e Beach yesterday and she said the *nicest* things about you."

Donald hesitated before offering a curious, uncomfortable smile. "Your *niece?*"

Before he could decide whether this made him uncomfortable, a tall and tan woman with a wave of dark hair held in place by a tortoise-shell clip glided in. When she stood still, she looked immovable. She reached out and gave Donald an unexpected hug. She ushered him to a conference room.

Karen stepped into the adjacent kitchen and poured a cup of coffee and set it in front of Donald. Then she pulled tight two pocket doors, closing off the kitchen and the adjacent hallway. Every inch of wall space in the small room, from floor to ceiling, was covered with bookshelves, loaded with neat rows of virtually identical law books, every one tan in color and bearing a red stripe at its heel. At one end of the table where they sat was a tidy collection of manila folders, each one marked "REYNOLDS, DIXIE."

Karen pulled at the thinnest of the folders, which held crisp layers of clean bond paper that bore perfectly arranged rows of black text, and laid it open. Donald noticed she was wearing no makeup, no rings and, it appeared, no bra. A delicate silver bracelet on her right wrist settled against the back of her hand. She faced Donald from across the table and he felt pleased when their eyes met. He imagined that she found him remarkable. And then he felt a sensation that he hadn't felt for a long while – that he was outside of himself, watching from above. "Mr. Gibson, I am so happy we finally have the chance to meet and to talk. Dixie mentioned you often and talked a great deal about how much she cared for you. Are you getting along ok?"

Donald nodded attentively, looking directly at Karen, and realized he was unaccustomed to having someone ask a sincere question about his well being. The Donald above believed she was succumbing to his charm. "She was like a really amazing big sister to me. You know, she drove me to my first date when I was fourteen? She was the one who taught me how to tie a tie. I still can't believe she's gone. It hurts to even think about it. She's just ... *gone.*" Donald felt flush and then nauseated. When that passed, his eyes began to fill with salty tears, which spilled down his cheeks. He wiped his face with the back of his hand. "Oh, look at me. This is silly." The Donald above thought the tears were a nice touch; that they were convincing Karen the real Donald was sensitive and worthy.

"Mr. Gibson, it has not been an easy time for any of us. I have trouble accepting that she's not with us any more. I think Dixie sensed she was near the end of her life. She sat with me in this very room just six months ago, planning her estate. Now listen, I need to share with you some of the things Dixie has told me." Karen leaned into the back of her chair and looked Donald straight in the face. "In this matter, context is nearly as important as content. Before I offer you my thoughts, you must know that I'm not here to make any comments or judgments. I am but a messenger. Understood?"

Donald nodded and leaned forward, his focus quickly shifting between Karen's face, Karen's breasts and the stack of papers sitting on the table in front of her. *What in hell is this all about?* The Donald above crossed his arms. He didn't know what Karen was going to say but he knew it was going to be fucking excellent.

"I know that Dixie felt you had great potential and was very concerned about your happiness. She was hoping that with her estate plan, she would allow you to reach your potential and to find happiness. Her plan is one that you can accept or reject. The choice is completely up to you." She paused. To Donald, it felt deliberate, possibly to prepare him for a shock.

Donald, his forehead wrinkled and his eyes drawn narrow, stared into his coffee cup, which sat on the table just in front of him and then looked back up to Karen. *Will you get to the goddam point already?*

"Mr. Gibson, Dixie is offering to give you her entire estate. At the moment, it is valued at just under four million dollars. That includes her house, her car, her... ."

Donald's forehead unwrinkled. "Wait? ... *What?* Say *what?*"

"That she is offering to give you her entire estate and ..."

"Four million dollars? *Four million dollars?*" Donald felt his face turning colorful and smooth. He hallucinated a picture of himself in lederhosen climbing a mountain and standing on a precipice where he could sing *Climb Every Mountain* in a lovely female voice that could span four octaves. Then the image turned into the torso and face of a naked Jessica Lange who was laid out before him and her arms were reaching for him and the voice continued and continued and it became Jessica's voice and she was pleading for him to come to her.

The Donald up above kept his arms folded. *Yup. This is fucking excellent.*

The real Donald shook his head and bonked his forehead with the heel of his left hand and got quiet. The air in the room took on the smell of the paper from all of the books lining the walls – lovely, *lovely* paper. He looked at his coffee cup which he realized was exactly half full. *How much fun will it be to tell Charlie Chasanow to take a flying fuck at a rolling Doughnut?* "You said four million dollars? Right? I'm getting four *million* dollars?" Donald stood up and ran his fingers through his hair. He kneeled small and pounded his fists on his knees. He stood tall and beamed. "Four million dollars? That's what you said, right?" His hands began trembling. "Four? Four million ... ."

Karen never stopped breathing. She expected this response. "Donald, there are *conditions* you must satisfy and you need to consider this carefully. This is not just somebody handing you a wad of cash. This is a big change in your life and lifestyle. *Please*, sit back down." Donald sat and sighed. "For now you can have her Suzuki, which is parked outside. You can have the exclusive use of her house, all of her personal effects in her house, and twenty thousand dollars. You can also start receiving a thousand dollars income every month from her estate. Within the next fifteen days, you need to write me a letter that expressly states that you intend to occupy her home. Also, you need to start living in her home and start doing so less than one month after your decision to accept Dixie's terms. Once you start living on the island, if you leave any time before three years, even one day for a vacation, you must return the house and the car and Dixie's personal effects to her estate or buy them from the estate at fair market value. The twenty thousand dollars, you get to keep. But if you leave the island at any time before the end of three years, for *any* reason other than a health emergency, you lose the right to inherit any part of Dixie's estate. You can't go on a boat or go waterskiing. You can't go on a plane. The point is, you have to stay on the island. Do you understand? *On the island.*"

Donald felt a spasm in his right arm.

"If you stay the full three years, you will inherit Dixie's home. You also inherit all of her investments, which make up the bulk of her estate. If you choose to live in Dixie's home, the estate will pay for taxes and insurance for the first three years. But you must pay for utilities and upkeep. If you don't take proper care of the house, you will be evicted. Also, you will enjoy membership in the Wakea and Papa Church of Golf, which allows you use of the Worship Center, subject to the rules of the church. Every member of the church must contribute to the church, according to their ability to pay. For the first three years of your time here, if you stay that long, Dixie's estate will make the contributions necessary to allow your continued membership."

Donald shifted forward in his seat. He reached for the pack of Marlboros in his shirt pocket and put a cigarette in his mouth. "Hey, you got an ashtray?"

Karen stiffened. "There is no smoking allowed in this office."

Donald recoiled and grabbed the unlit cigarette from his mouth and held it between his fingers. He nodded and fidgeted. "All right. Go ahead. I'm … I'm listening."

"I have keys for you to Dixie's Suzuki and the keys to her house. You're welcome to use both during your stay here before you decide what to do. Also, here are copies of Dixie's estate documents and a map of the island, marked to show the location of her home." Karen slid a manila envelope across the table.

"What about my wife?"

"If she wants and if you want, yes."

"I mean does she inherit anything?"

"Dixie's will does not mention her."

Donald took the envelope, opened it and fingered the keys and the map, and even a copy of Dixie's estate plan documents, one item at a time. "Maybe I'm missing something. Why can't I just tell you that I accept right now? What kind of idiot wouldn't want to live here? I mean, is there some catch I need to know about? I feel like there's something you're not telling me. I can't get the four million dollars unless I give up my little shitbox job in Glen Burnie and move to Hawaii and live in a house that's paid for? And join a golf club? And get a guaranteed income? And a car? And for *that* I have to wait ten days?"

Karen took a deep breath and exhaled with discomfort. "Mr. Gibson, it would be unfair to you if you were to decide too soon. That's how Dixie felt about it. I happen to agree. Life here isn't the same as life on the mainland. It's not even like life on Oahu or the Big Island. There are not but three thousand souls on Lanai and every one of them knows pretty much all the business of everybody else. We have one bank. We have one small grocery store. There are maybe two miles of paved roads. There isn't a single stoplight. We only have about six places where you can go get a bite to eat. There are two bars. And we don't have any movie theaters or shopping malls. We have the Dole Fruit Company that owns almost the whole island and all they care about is harvesting pineapples and having people around to do it. You will really be starting a new life and doing so in a place that is completely different from all that you're accustomed to. And you'll be doing it on an island that's only about eleven miles long. It doesn't take long before you've seen the whole thing."

Karen hesitated, wondering if she had said enough. "There's a rule here that applies to pretty much everything you do. Dixie used to put it this way 'What goes around … "

"… comes around. Yes, I've heard her say it a million times. Maybe *four million* times."

"That rule is pretty important on Lanai. This is not a place for anyone who wants privacy or who needs their space or has trouble getting along with folks. We see a good number of people who move here thinking they've found paradise and then a few months later, they move away because paradise feels like a cage full of crazies."

"Aw, shoot. There ain't nobody old Donald can't get along with." He flashed the grin he used for photographs with fans who visited him at Glen Burnie Ford.

Karen's lips tightened until her mouth looked impossibly small. "Donald, just a reminder. Dixie's funeral service starts tomorrow morning at 10:30. To get there, you just walk out of the back door of Dixie's house, follow the shady trail between the wood roses in her back yard, and you'll find yourself on the second fairway of the golf course. Turn right, cross the footbridge and follow the course a few hundred yards and go past the first tee box where you'll see a pavilion. The ceremony will start there."

"Dixie's house is *on* a golf course?"

"Yes. Most of the members' homes are on the golf course or very close to it. They make up a little village on the southeast corner of the island. Dixie's house is in a unique spot. It sits on a peninsula that's quite removed from most of the village. There's only one other house in that little corner. So unless you get out and around, the only person you're likely to come into contact with is your one neighbor."

Donald brightened. "It just keeps on getting better. Seriously, I can't just decide right now? Seriously? You're teasing me, right? Ten days from now, you're going to tell me this was all a big practical joke, right? Dixie's going to pop out from behind a curtain and you're going to send me back to Glen Burnie and laugh at me?"

"Donald, this is serious." Karen rose and slid open a pocket door to expose the hallway. "You can decide in ten days. I expect to see you tomorrow morning. We scheduled it just so that you and your brother could attend."

Karen paused when Donald reached the front room on his way out. "One more thing. Once you get out of Lanai City, you'll find that the road between here and Dixie's house isn't paved. In some places, the road has deep ruts. It handles two-way traffic even though it's barely wide enough for one car. In rainy weather, it's easy to get stuck. In some places, the road is carved out from the side of a steep hill. And that little Suzuki is very tippy. It can be a little treacherous if you're not familiar with the landscape. Please take your time, at least until you get used to driving on the island."

"There's not a car made that I couldn't handle. Not a one. I know cars better'n just about anything."

Karen watched from the window in the front room as Donald zipped away in the faded Suzuki with the blue and white *Namaste'* sticker on the back that everyone on the island associated with the beloved Dixie Ray Reynolds.

"So?" queried Mazie, Karen's secretary.

Karen turned to face her, quizzically. "What?"

"Oh, come on. You know exactly what I'm asking."

Karen exhaled, stood and stared back out the window, her hands clasped behind her. "A man wrapped up in himself makes for a very small package. But Dixie always said she had the greatest of faith in him. So who knows? Maybe he'll surprise us."

"Already you know this?"

"Well, there was the fact that after he learned about Dixie's bequest to him, he was so caught up in what he would get that he didn't even think to wonder why his brother got nothing. He didn't even ask what happened to the estate assets if he didn't get them."

"He doesn't know?"

"Nope. He's clueless. I think he likes it that way."

"Did you tell him about Alani?"

"I told him he had only one neighbor. I figured he might ask about her. But he didn't."

"Don't you think you should have said *something*?"

"He'll find out soon enough. Maybe at some point, he'll learn to ask better questions."

—◦◦◦—

Donald pulled the bouncy Suzuki from the rutted red-dirt road into a rutted red-dirt driveway and killed the engine. A trailing cloud of red-dirt dust overtook him and swirled in a blinding vortex before subsiding to reveal a polite bungalow. Its front was symmetrical and beige with a plain blue door between a pair of four-square windows. It had a peaked, corrugated metal roof and a small front porch covered with a smaller peaked, corrugated metal roof. Two white rockers, parked on the front porch, were framed by hanging baskets that bore multi-colored flowers. He climbed out of the vehicle and, hands on hips, scrutinized the little building. "Jesus, Mary and Joseph. Is there only one kind of house they know how to build on this island?"

He pulled his hanging bag and his oversize suitcase out of the back of his vehicle and lugged them onto the front porch. Donald fished inside the envelope for a key to open the front door, when he noticed the doorknob had no keyhole. He turned the handle and swung the door open. Inside, Donald met with three unfamiliar faces, each framed with bounds of gray hair.

"Eeeeeeeeeeee!" they squealed together. Donald, startled, stood tall.

"Good afternoon ladies. Very sorry. I thought this was Dixie Reynolds' house. My mistake." Donald backed away.

"Young man. You stop right there. Stop right there. This *is* Dixie's house."

Donald looked around, uncertain. "This is Dixie's house? This is?" He glanced cock-eyed at the visitors.

One of them approached and, for a moment, it appeared she wouldn't stop. She reached her hands up and rested them on Donald's shoulders and held him still. She grasped his shirt with both hands and pulled, forcing Donald to bend over toward her until his face was within inches of hers. She held Donald's face in her hands and moved it from side to side, studying him for several remarkably awkward seconds. "I'm ninety-one years old and I have low vision," she announced. Then she reached around his ample middle and hugged him. "You probably look like a very nice man. I can't tell. But it doesn't matter. Just because you look like a nice man doesn't mean you are. But you probably are."

Donald looked past her to the two other women then back to the woman who was hugging him and raised his eyebrows frantically. "How are you, ma'am? I'm Donald Gibson."

"Mildred, for heaven's sake, introduce your *say-elf*," admonished her younger sister with an exaggerated drawl. "Say hello to the young *may-yun*. Tell him who you *owe-er*."

Mildred stood mute, facing the floor and then inched away from Donald. Then she looked up. "We're from Saxapahaw, North Carolina."

"Well, I'll introduce myself," said the one, approaching Donald. "I'm Gabby Hagood. Please come in and sit yourself down. This nice woman who doesn't want to let go of you is my sister, Mildred Hagood. She's really delightful most of the time." Gabby took Donald's right hand in her own and smiled.

"And I'm Mavis Hagood," said the last, extending both her hands toward Donald and giving him a brief hug. She took hold of his left hand and wrist and held on. "Oh, Gabby, he's even handsomer than Dixie said. I mean, just look at that *hair. Oh, that hay-yer.*" Mavis, cute as a puppy, inched as close to Donald's shoulder as she could get and leaned her neck as far back as it would go so she could look straight up at Donald through her thick, rose-tinted glasses. "Oh, my. He *is* a tall one. I do not believe I have ever seen a man as handsome *and* as tall as this one. Not a one. We really should keep him, don't you think, Gabby?"

"Well, Dixie said she was just in love with him so I'm sure we're going to be in love with him too. Donald, do you mind if we adopt you and make you one of our own?"

Donald laughed. "You ladies can do whatever you want. I'm all yours."

"Donald, we spent some time this morning and got Dixie's house ready for you," said Gabby. She pulled at Mildred who was standing inches off Donald's left hip and looking at the floor. "Give the man some room." She turned to Donald. "We put out some flowers and cleaned up and did some grocery shopping. We also packed up some of Dixie's clothes and all the things she kept in her medicine chest so you would have some room."

"You ladies are so kind, and to a total stranger. How can I thank you?"

"We know you loved Dixie and how much you must miss her and so we wanted to make you feel welcome. The truth is that we all loved her," said Gabby.

"Thank you so much for looking out for me, ladies. Yes, when Dixie died, I felt as if I had lost a big sister."

"Your big sister died? Your sister died, too?" Mildred asked, choking up. "Oh, life is so cruel. You know, I worry about losing my sisters sometimes. I pray and pray because I want to be spared the *pain* of seeing Gabby or Mildred get cancer or maybe an aneurism or pneumonia or get something else horrible and I have to watch them die a slow death and I'll be all alone. It would just be so terrible. I'd be all alone. Can you imagine? You know, I lost my husband twelve years ago. He had polyps and bleeding in his lower intestine and ... ."

Gabby jumped. "Oh, Mildred!" She put her hands on Mildred's shoulders. "Donald's sister didn't die," she said, extra loud and toward Mildred's left hear. "He said that losing Dixie was *like* losing his sister. It was *like* losing his sister."

"Oh," said Mildred, raising her head and turning a slow and stiff quarter turn toward Gabby. "Well there's no need to *yay-yull*. I can hear you just *fine*."

Gabby and Mavis looked at one another and shook their heads.

"Donald, I believe that Mavis and Mildred and I will leave you to get settled," said Gabby. "We would just love it if you would come by our house this evening for some dinner. We're just ten minutes away. *Rat cheer*. Just down the road."

"We love to put on music and dance after dinner. Do you dance, Donald?" asked Mavis ever so slowly.

"I was born to dance. It might be my favorite thing."

"Oh, Gabby. I'm in *love* with him already," cooed Mavis, who closed in on Donald's mid-section and stole another hug. "Can't we just take him home with us? I mean, he is so tall. And look at that *hair*. That *hay-yur*. Honestly, have you ever seen such a fine, fine man?"

—∿—

After dinner with the Hagood sisters, Donald sat and rested. He just sat there. And he rested. Parked in a rocker on Dixie's front porch on the edge of a vast darkness, his naked feet propped on the rail and his hands cradling a Primo, it occurred to him that, except for the glow from an antique reading lamp just inside the living room windows, there was no light. There was no traffic. There were no sirens in the distance to remind him that highly portable idiots were on the move. There were no neighbors watching obnoxious televisions and there were no backyard cats screeching. There was only cool air flowing in from the ocean and layers of darkness that hid virtually everything from view.

The faraway edge of a vast Pacific had turned past the sun and had kept on going. In the middle of that ocean, on the edge of a speck of land, Donald stared at a blue-black sky that twinkled with a hundred thousand stars he had never before been able to see. Removed from the artificial light of Glen Burnie, the simple act of looking up had become a stimulating experience. Streams and ribbons of stars spoke of worlds that were beyond imagination. He sucked hard on a Marlboro and forced out a plume of smoke.

Donald imagined that he could hear footsteps drawing closer. After several moments, he realized the sound was not imagined. They were real footsteps, and they were being made by short legs that were walking with a purpose. They were accompanied by a jingling metallic sound which made Donald think there was a dog approaching, too. Donald pulled his feet off the railing and leaned forward. Out of the darkness emerged a tiny Asian man with wrinkled hands and a bald head that shone, even at night. He was followed by a perky black and white mutt.

"You must be the esteemed and beloved Donald O. Gibson," drawled the man, slowly and deliberately.

"And you are?"

"Donald, I am Bobby Joe Hu. I was friends with your Aunt Dixie." He reached up and slid his hand under the railing. Donald had to put down his bottle of beer and bend low to accommodate him. He took hold of Bobby Joe's hand, which nearly disappeared into his own. "It is an honest pleasure to meet a man that Dixie spoke of so highly and cared for so much. Thanks to Dixie, you were loved by the folks in the village before you even stepped off the airplane. I hope the company of the nice folks here helps you to find peace while you search for a way to accept Dixie's loss."

Donald opened his mouth to speak but could find no words. Every person he met here seemed to have something touching to say to him.

"Donald, do you mind if Beauregard and I come and set a spell?"

Donald waved them onto the porch. Bobby Joe parked himself in the available rocker, a place he had sat many thousands of times while enjoying the good company of his lost friend. He motioned with his hand to the dog. "Come, Bo. Lay down," he commanded. The dog promptly obeyed and laid its snout on its front paws. "So I just came from the Hagood girls' house. They tell me you had a right nice dinner together."

"They lured me over with the promise of dinner and dancing. Only they didn't tell me that dancing meant the *hokey pokey*. We put the one hand in, pulled the one hand out, we put the one hand in and we shook it all about. I didn't know this until now, but really, that's what it's all about. They must have hugged and kissed me fifteen times before I got out of there. They begged me to take leftovers. Man, those girls are *hilarious*. They just totally love me."

"When I left them, they seemed quite pleased that you had been able to join them for dinner."

"You can't blame them, can you?"

Bobby Joe decided to grin without revealing his teeth. "Those women tickle me like nobody else. Even into their eighties and nineties, they still have the spirit of happy little grade school girls with pig tails. Ain't never seen nothing like it. It makes a man feel right good just to be around 'em."

"So Bobby Joe, why is it that almost everybody here speaks with a southern accent? This feels like Mississippi on the Pacific."

"Oh, not everybody does – just the sisters and me, and Dixie too, of course. The sisters and I were members of the same Baptist church in North Carolina in a little, bitty old place called Saxapahaw. For a while, my father was the minister. Mavis was my Sunday school teacher when I was a boy. That's where I first met Dixie."

Bobby Joe looked around and decided it was a good time to get to the point. "Donald, I know the details of Dixie's will and the choice you have in front of you. If you choose to come live with us, you will be making a large change in your life. I moved here when I was in my thirties, almost forty years ago. It was not what I expected in a lot of ways. So if you have any questions about our village or about the church or how the church members take care of the golf course, now would be a good time to ask."

"Karen told me *all* about how things work. Dixie's estate pays for all my dues for three years and I get to live here free. Honestly, Bobby Joe, this might just be the most perfect place on the entire planet. There's no boss, there's no bill collectors and there's no batshit crazy alcoholic wife, *you know what I mean?*"

"Yes, I think I do." Bobby Joe put his hands on his knees and sat up for a moment, straight-backed. "Sometimes, things are not as simple or as clear as they look. And this might be one of those times. Donald, if you move here, you will have responsibilities in the village. Did you know that?"

"Responsibilities? You mean paying dues?"

"Every member of the church is expected to make a financial commitment, if they can afford it. We don't call it paying dues. On top of that, you'll be expected to help with the care of the golf course and church grounds. It's hard, manual labor and you'll be at it at least two days a week."

Donald held his bottle of Primo at eye level and smiled at Bobby Joe. "Honestly, I hadn't heard," said Donald. "Is that all?"

"You'll have to follow the church rules if you want to play the golf course. Do you know about those?"

"I don't go doing stupid stuff like driving on a green with a golf cart, Bobby Joe. You don't have to worry about me."

"Well, the church rules are a little more detailed than that. Like, you ain't allowed to play the course without another church member until the board of elders approves it."

"Well, damn. How long does that take?"

"It depends on the person. Some folks, it takes less than a year. Some folks, never."

"Is this supposed to make me want to *not* move here?"

"Well, you'll also be expected to adopt somebody in the village, probably several somebodies."

"Wait – *adopt*? As in, you know, *adopt*?"

"You don't have to take in small children. But you will have to find people in the village who need your help."

Donald searched the porch floor with his eyes and looked back up at Bobby Joe. He was searching for words and couldn't find any.

"Donald, did you happen to take notice of how the Hagood sisters cleaned house for you before you even arrived? How they shopped for you and prepared dinner for you?"

"Yeah, so?"

"They are probably looking to see if they can adopt you. They want to see if you're the kind of person who will accept their help. The sisters missed out on the genes that allow folks to be subtle. So there ain't no doubt they're wondering if you might adopt them. They're getting quite old and need help with things that Dixie used to do for them."

"Oh, come on. Those old gals were just being nice and fell in love with me. That's all it was."

"Donald, three old gals in their eighties and nineties, gals with sore backs and poor vision and arthritic fingers, spent a whole day cleaning up before they ever laid eyes on you. Dixie was no housekeeper. This place was a mess and they turned it into a place where you could settle in. You won't have bottles of Dixie's menopause medicine in the bathroom cabinet. You won't have to clear out Dixie's underpanties. And lookee here, you got purty little flowers in baskets hanging from the front porch."

Bobby Joe paused. When Donald faced him, he continued. "You see, Dixie had adopted those girls and cared for them for years and they fell in love with her. They haven't even had time to figure you out yet."

"So I have to be nice to people. Big deal. I'm nice to everybody."

"You know, Donald, our village don't have but about a hundred and sixty people living in it. And we're several miles down a bumpety dirt road from Lanai City, which ain't much bigger than a picnic blanket. If you're not totally on board with what I'm telling you, chances are that living here will make you good and miserable. Four million dollars won't do nothing to cure that."

"Can you hear yourself talking? You make it sound like I'm a stupid kid. All I know is that until just now, when you started talking down to me, people here have been really nice to me. This place is incredibly beautiful and it never gets cold. I get a nice house, an income and I get to live on a golf course. In three years, I magically turn into a rich guy. What the hell more is there to think about?"

Bobby Joe leaned back and allowed a few moments to pass. "Donald, have you ever had what you thought was a simple four-foot putt and found out that the ball broke completely the opposite of what you expected?"

"So you're saying this is a tricky four footer? *This?*" Donald motioned to his surroundings. "Bobby Joe, do you have any idea what life is like back in *Glim Burnee*? Do you have *any* idea? Man, this is not even a close call." Donald stared into the dark. "So does everybody in the village adopt somebody else?"

"Typically, yes. Most folks adopt more than one person. It's pretty quiet here and there's not much to do. Tending to somebody keeps folks occupied and happy. If we didn't have that, lots of us would have trouble thinking of a reason to get out of bed in the morning."

"If you adopt someone, do you tell them you've adopted them?"

"Mostly, you let them figure it out if they've been adopted. That way, if it turns out they don't need your help or if you want to quit, it won't get all awkward."

"Do you ever have two people who end up adopting each other?"

"It happens right often. Some folks call that marriage."

"What happens if someone doesn't want to adopt anybody else?"

"What does a body do with hisself if he don't have another somebody to spend time with? If he don't have another somebody to look after?

You can't play golf and swim *all* the time. It gets dull a lot quicker'n you'd think. Donald, listen, there's lots of other people here who have come here and tried that tricky four footer. A few made it. Most of them missed and ended up leaving in a big old hissy fit."

Donald sucked his Marlboro down to the last and then flicked it into the yard. "Bobby Joe, this isn't a tricky four-foot putt. Not even close. This is a tap-in for an eagle on the eighteenth to win the Masters by a stroke."

—∭—

Lanai's airport was a naked strip of pavement carved out of a flat spot surrounded by a chain link fence just tall enough to keep out the deer. At one end of the airfield was a flat-roofed metal building, open on all four sides. Like many public buildings in Lanai, it had no exterior doors or windows. Under the corrugated roof was a ticket counter and a few desks where the airport functionaries toiled. There was also a bathroom, several benches and a handful of crow-like birds that pecked around, looking for bugs and scraps of food. When a visitor from the mainland sat inside and listened to the sound of typewriters and staplers and ringing telephones floating on the air that came in easy from the ocean, he knew he was someplace different.

Donald parked just inside the airfield fence and leaned against the Suzuki, hiding behind a pair of Ray Ban Aviators. Far off to the east, a small dot appeared just above the horizon. Donald watched as it grew bigger against the sky, and as it grew wings and propellers, as it touched down and then as it taxied to a stop, twenty feet in front of him.

A haole pilot with a skinny neck appeared in the window of the fold-down door and pushed it open, revealing a short set of stairs. From within the fuselage appeared a grandmotherly woman carrying two fabric bags heavy with groceries and wearing a threadbare flowered dress that held back rolls of belly fat. Just behind her was her fortyish daughter who struggled with a monstrous box of toilet paper rolls. The oversized box blocked her view of her feet. She touched each step with her toe before trusting it with her weight. From just behind her emerged Ted Gibson, suitcase and suitbag in hand.

—m—

The next morning, Donald awoke, started the percolator on a slow brew and then showered and shaved. After, he took tiny and fortifying sips of his first coffee of the day under the canopy of a banyan tree, just outside Dixie's back door. He sat at a wooden table had been hand carved by a wealthy Brazilian embezzler during his final year of life. The man had come to Lanai in the early 1940s to evade capture and punishment and rented the house that later came into Dixie's hands. To occupy himself, he whittled the table into existence. He was pleasantly surprised to discover that he had a useful and lawful calling. He reckoned that if the lands around Ariquemes, his home town in Brazil, had not been denuded of timber by settlers in need of land, his discovery might have come soon enough to avoid bringing shame to his family.

Donald closed his eyes, and enjoyed the giddiness that came from the warmth of a sunny Hawaiian morning and freedom from work, a mood likely enhanced by the promise of four million dollars and abandonment of a suitcase full of worries. He took in the focused sweetness of the ginger lilies growing in Dixie's garden and the cleanness of a place that had been kissed by a morning rain. He could feel an expanding calm and was sure it came from being removed from the call of the bill collector, from the stink of an angry boss, and from his wife's contempt. Could a world of hurt be made to disappear any faster than by relocation to a spot as fine as this?

After getting dressed, Donald searched in vain through the house for a full-length mirror. The best he could do was a tiny reflective oval, hanging by a pink ribbon above the bathroom sink. No matter; his tailored gray suit, his crisp, starched-white shirt and his patterned red foulard tie fit perfectly and left him feeling trim and prosperous.

Donald and Ted exited Dixie's back door, followed a path leading from the back of her house through an arbor in a hedge of wood roses, and past a line of Cook pines where they emerged onto a fairway so full of light that it seemed unnatural. In their dress shoes, they slipped here and there. As they approached the pavilion, they could see a gathering.

"Who are those people? They look ready for a picnic," said Ted. Most everyone was dressed in floral, open-collar shirts, flip flops and shorts. They chatted happily. Some were pointing down the nearby fairway and motioning with their hands, as if describing golf shots.

Donald and Ted approached and, right away encountered Karen Nakamura. Before Donald could introduce Karen and his brother, Karen took charge. "Good morning, gentlemen. I hope you both are well today." She approached them directly and gave them both hugs they weren't expecting. "I know Dixie would be pleased that you were able to be here. And, heavens, I should have told you: *nobody* wears suits in the islands. Most folks who live here are happy to give up their suits and ties."

The gathering murmured and movement into the pavilion began. Karen motioned and they took seats at a picnic table under the pavilion roof near where Bobby Joe took his place, standing on a ledge built into a corner. In front of him was a round table draped with a white cloth and bearing a decorative metal urn.

"Greetings and welcome. We gather today to celebrate the life of our dear friend, our sister, Dixie Ray Reynolds." Bobby Joe told a story that nobody else in the village knew completely: When Dixie's older sister was killed in a car crash, she left behind a husband and her two young sons. Two weeks later, the husband, crushed by the weight of expectations and grief, took his own life. Dixie, who had already bought her home on Lanai, put her move on hold and moved to Baltimore to finish raising her sister's boys.

Bobby Joe scanned his audience for the faces of Donald and Ted and pointed them out. "Dixie spent eight years getting both those boys through high school and onto college. They both have turned into fine men. The older of the two, Ted, went on to law school and is a successful attorney in Baltimore. The younger, Donald, graduated from the University of Maryland where he played sports and has gone on to a successful career in business. She was proud of their happiness and their successes just like their own mother would have been. Dixie always said that it was her work to make those boys feel loved. I hope you will reach out to them and make them feel welcome."

Bobby Joe picked up the urn containing Dixie's ashes and cradled it. "Dixie's final wish was that her ashes be spread around the tee box on number eighteen, a place she considered holy. Please walk with me so that together, we can honor Dixie's wish."

Bobby Joe nodded and the assembly rose. He walked slowly across the lawn, past the whitewashed Chapel of Balance with its peaked green roof, to the tee box on number eighteen where a small table, a chair and a cello awaited. He placed the urn on the table and lifted its lid to reveal a compartment holding about two pints of granular ashes. When the group had assembled around the perimeter of the tee box, Bobby Joe motioned to Ramona and her brother, Toby, and they joined him. Toby sat on the chair with the cello between his knees, a bow at the ready, Ramona standing next to him.

Bobby Joe nodded and Toby drew his bow and began to play his cello vigorously. Soon after, Ramona began to sing.

And I will stroll the merry way,
And jump the hedges first
And I will drink the clear
Clean water for to quench my thirst. ...

And you shall take me strongly
In your arms again
And I will not remember
That I ever felt the pain.
We shall walk and talk
In gardens all misty and wet with rain
And I will never, never, never
Grow so old again. ...

Oh sweet thing, sweet thing
My, my, my, my sweet thing ...

As the music played, the villagers came to the table by ones and twos, took spoonfuls of ashes and found places around the tee box on number eighteen where they let the ashes fall into the grass. Some kneeled and prayed. Some offered hugs to friends whose grief had turned to tears.

Donald edged behind Ted, hoping his snotty bulldog mug wouldn't be so apparent. "*Donald!* It's alright, man. It's alright." Ted reached out and put an arm around his brother's shoulders.

"Did I ever once tell her I loved her? Did I *ever*?" Donald put the heels of his hands on his knees. "Dixie became our *mother* for chrissake. She put her whole life on hold for us and we never even knew. All I ever did was act like a stupid rebellious kid. I was so, so … stupid. I was such a fucking idiot."

"Donald, don't say that. Dixie knew how much you loved her. She knew. She told us both how happy it made her to do what Mom couldn't. *She knew.* Don't do this to yourself."

Ted grabbed Donald by the loose fabric of his suit sleeve and led him up to the grassy circle. He spooned up some of Dixie's ashes and offered them to Donald. Ted took a spoon for himself and together, they knelt and let the ashes fall.

Ted stood and looked downslope at the fairway, the forest of tapered pines, and beyond to Auau Channel and Maui. He closed his eyes and took in the sacred Hawaiian air. "Bless you, Dixie, and thank you," he said quietly. He felt a pull at his ankle and turned to find Donald laid out on the ground, his knees pulled up to his chest and his hands to his own face.

"Why was I so stupid? *Why?*" Donald began blubbering, sounding like a hungry mountain goat. "She was so good to me. I loved her and I never even *told* her." Ted knelt and grasped both of Donald's hands, pulling them away from his face.

"Hey, idiot, you need to straighten up," he whispered in Donald's ear. "This is not about you. All these people are here to say goodbye to Dixie. This is for *her*. Stand up. Stop being a child."

"Teddy, I can't, I can't, I …"

Ted kneeled and gripped Donald's mouth and jaw, pinching closed Donald's mouth. Donald's eyes opened wide at the sight of his brother's index finger pointed at the center of his face. "All these people came to pay their respects and to have a few moments of peace. You're ruining that. Stand up and be a man. Think of somebody other than yourself for a change."

Donald sat up and then stood up and blew his nose on a handkerchief. He nodded to Ted and they stepped out of the circle and watched as the last members of the group took the last bits of Dixie's ashes and sprinkled them onto a legendary piece of ground that had just become even more so.

—⁑—

The flight from Honolulu to Baltimore lasted longer than just the twelve hours spent riding the clouds. For Donald, it spanned a generation of debt, angst and disappointment that had grown one twelve-ounce can at a time into a fetid pool. As the Pacific expanse passed below, he remembered the feeling he had one Christmas when his parents gave him a book of drawing paper and a box of Crayolas. *Life can be so simple and so easy.* Later, as the craggy Rocky Mountains passed, he took on worries. Would Kimmy stand in his way? Could he clear the hurdles of divorce and stale debt?

"Ted, if I divorce Kimberly, would I have to share the four million I'll get from Dixie?"

"Almost certainly not. You don't own the four million. If you don't meet certain conditions, you won't ever own it. As long as the divorce is final before you actually get your hands on Dixie's estate, it's not marital property."

"She'll be crushed. If I tell her I'm divorcing her, she'll just curl up and die right there. Can you tell her for me? You're a lawyer. You're really good at that kind of stuff."

Ted pulled off his reading glasses and tightened every muscle in his face and neck. Doing so made him look menacing, a trick that he had used on special occasions to get his children to obey when they were acting squirrely. "How about if we pretend you didn't just say that?"

"Oh come on, Teddy. It was just a *question*. Do you gotta take everything so damn seriously? Oh, wait. You're a lawyer. Of course you do."

"Donald, you give yourself too much credit. I think she'll be happy to get rid of you. Just look her in the eye and tell her you want a divorce. *Get it done.*"

"Do you think she would be happy if I just signed the house over to her? The mortgage is all paid off."

"The what? *Paid off?* How in the *hell* could you be living in a paid-off house and you're always asking to borrow money from me? How is that even possible?"

"Kimmy's dad paid it off as a fortieth birthday present to her, but he demanded we put his name on the title so we couldn't get a new mortgage without his say so. He would *never* give us that. What a control freak."

"I'd say Kimmy's dad is a pretty smart man."

"So do you think ten days is enough time to get my Mustang shipped to Lanai? I'm thinking it would be nice if it was waiting there for me when I get back."

"Are you even being *serious?*"

"Wait … *what?*"

"Donald, did you see the roads on Lanai? Did you even bother to think this through? You'd get that little rocket stuck on a dirt road the minute you left Lanai City. Besides, where would you even drive it? Give the car to Kimmy and let her sell it. She *hates* that car. She hates you for all the time and money you've spent on it. It would make her feel so good to get rid of it."

"I can't do that. I love that car. I rebuilt that car with my own two hands. I've put my soul into that car. That's my baby."

Ted sighed. *Donald is leading with his chin again.* "Well, if it's that important to you, maybe you could just stay in Glen Burnie so you could be the one to take care of her. I mean if it's *your* child? If there's really nobody else who could care for her?"

"You just love being right all the time, don't you?"

"You're asking for my opinion, and I'm just giving it to you. If you don't like my advice, just ignore it. You won't hurt my feelings. I promise. That's how we lawyers operate."

Ted stared down at the magazine in his lap and then back at his brother. "If you offer to give both the Mustang and the house to Kimberly as part of a divorce settlement, don't you think it will make it easier for her to accept that you're leaving? She knows how much you love that car and she despises you for it. If you offer both to her, free and clear, she'll be less likely to think you're being spiteful and probably will accept that as a full settlement. Those are the only assets you have here anyway. Give them up and have her sign a divorce agreement that she won't ask for anything more from you. If your divorce is uncontested, you won't have to come back to Maryland for court appearances and depositions."

Donald parked his elbows on his knees. He stared at the floor of the airplane, his head pressed uncomfortably into the seat ahead of him. "Goddam it. God*dam* it. I'm feeling boxed in here."

When the airport cab dropped him at the curb, Donald could hardly bear the thought of walking all the way to his front door. Behind that door waited a haggard wife whose spiteful and needy nature was the springboard for a life devoted to passive-aggressive control. Behind that door was a sticky spider's web of uncertainty and obtuse, illogical refusal. Behind that door was the only obstacle to a clean getaway. *She's going to screw this up for me. Somehow she's going to. I just know it.*

He reached for the doorknob and then retreated. He put his suitcase on the front stoop and stared at his shoes. His breath vaporized in the humid cold then came back and spread across his face where it left a coating of wetness. His fingertips and his ears began to feel numb. He wouldn't miss those things. Not even a little.

He went inside, dropped his suitcase on the bed and pulled off his coat and shoes. He found Kimberly in the kitchen, eating and watching television.

"Hey, I'm home."

"Well, I guess you have to be somewhere, don't you? It's just too bad it's here."

"Kimmy, can we talk?"

"Go ahead. It's a free country. Just remember that I'm free to ignore you." Kimberly stared at a game show and chewed. On the television screen, a large wheel with flashing lights turned round and round.

"Kimmy, come on. We need to talk. This is important."

"More important than whether Mrs. Naylin from Ogden, Utah, wins a washer and dryer? Hmmmm. Probably not." She reached for her bag of Utz potato chips.

"Listen, Kimmy, how would you feel if I just gave you this house and my Mustang free and clear and then left you alone – just completely left you alone?"

Kimberly looked up. She turned off the television. "Are you saying you're ready to do that?"

"Yes. I think I am. I *am*."

"You would just give me the house and the car and you won't ever bother me ever again. *Ever?* Like we're talking a divorce?"

"I would even pay off the credit cards. Yes. That's what I'm talking about. I think that, that … ."

"So where do I sign and how soon until you leave?"

5

Lanai, Hawaii
March 4, 1977

"This is the perfect place to be. I am *loving* this." Twenty yards ahead of Bobby Joe and Ramona, Donald cantered to the tee box and plunged the clean, white tip of a tee into the gristly soil and balanced a factory-fresh Titleist on top. The ball and its slender stand stood out, an upside down exclamation point against a plane of greenness that spread out and out and then out quite a bit more. "Oh, yeah, baby. It's such a great day to be *me*." He looked over his shoulder at Bobby Joe. "You want to be me, don't you? Don't try and hide it."

Before the very first stroke of his very first round of golf on Lanai, Donald took a few moments to take in the very first hole on the Divinely Inspired Worship Center. It was, at 338 yards, a short par four with no sand traps, no hazards and a fairway that, he observed, was as flat as Diane Fucking Keaton. A pathological early afternoon sun beat down and left Donald's crown feeling warm and cared for. Most any golfer could see that the course designer had set up number one as an appetizer. The green on number one was nearly the largest on the golf course and was surrounded on all sides by several yards of even-cut rough about three quarters of an inch deep, all designed to make an up and down relatively easy. Even the trees along the sides of the fairway were set back so that a golfer who duffed his tee shot could hope to rescue his pride with a short approach.

Donald relaxed his shoulders and sniffed. "This will be an *easy* par four." *Easier than Janice Highsmith in her parents' guestroom in the tenth grade.* He took a moment to waggle, balance and settle in. And as he did, he heard heavy feet on the carpet of twigs and pine needles beneath the trees, along the right side of the fairway. He kneeled for a better look and saw a person staring back. "Bobby Joe, there's some wing nut in there watching us."

"Yes, that's probably Bradley. He does that."

"He hides and stares at people? Doesn't that seem a little, you know, *weird?*"

"That's just his way, Donald. That's just his way. He finds it hard to be around people."

"He's hiding and *staring* at people. And did I mention that he was hiding and *staring* at people? Because that's weird."

Bobby Joe smiled and took in a measured dose of fresh air. "Donald, you need to relax. Just focus on your game, my brutha. Go back to thinking what a great day it is to be you. Bradley won't bother you none. Cross my heart and hope to die, stick a needle in my eye."

Donald looked ahead at the woods where he had seen Bradley and then at Bobby Joe and torqued his forehead. "Weird. I tell ya, it's weird. Didja hear me? *Wee. Yerd.*"

Donald then turned his attention back to his Titleist. After a second set-up and a couple of waggles, Donald gripped his club, extended his arms, turned his torso to the right, carried his straightened arms back and around and then cocked his wrists before turning toward his target and releasing his club. At impact, the Titleist obliged with a masculine *pa-whonk.* It lifted off from its launch pad, straight toward the greenness until it skied almost straight up and then plunked down, settling in the center of the fairway almost 230 yards away. Donald sashayed around the tee box.

"My shot is *red* hot. Your shot ain't *doodly* squat." He posed Sinatra-style, arms spread wide, hoping for an audience response. Seeing none, he tried again. "I said *doodly* squat."

Ramona and Bobby Joe stood by, plain faced.

"Man, is this ever a tough room. You guys came here to have fun, right?" He held the handle of his driver close to his mouth, as if it was a microphone, and tapped it repeatedly. "Hey. Hello. Is this thing working? *Hello?*"

"Very nicely done, Donald. Ramona?" He nodded at the long-legged teenager with the braces and wrinkly purple shorts and the oddly shaped ponytail that poked from behind the back corner of her wide-brimmed hat. Ramona slid out her three wood and fumbled around in her pocket, fishing for a ball and tee. Once on the tee box, with her back to her playing partners, she rested the grip of her club in the crook of her arm while she worked with both hands to join the ball and tee together in her developing right palm. She stood tall and then bent at the waist, her legs perfectly straight, and inserted her tee into the ground.

Ramona stood behind her ball where she momentarily closed her eyes. Then she kneeled, chose a line and set up, putting the ball in the middle of her stance. She drew back with a wide sweep until the shaft of her club, hovering over her shoulders, was pointed straight down the middle of the fairway. Her downswing began with a turn of her hips followed by the turn of her shoulders. Her thin torso tightened and she let her hips power the rest of her swing. Her club head was slightly closed and fired at the ball from inside of her target line, heading out. The ball shot out low and to the right and rose gradually. Near the mid-point of its flight, it made a gentle turn to the left, and then landed on the center of the fairway. It touched ground 200 yards away and then bounce-rolled another fifty yards before coming to rest.

Donald slapped his palm to his forehead. "You, kinda hit that one a little thin, eh?"

"Ramona, your swing looks so right," said Bobby Joe. "You have slowed it down just a bit and it looks so much more controlled."

Ramona smiled and retrieved her tee. She toe-pranced down from the tee box, wisps of hair bouncing on the air with each step. "Thank you, Kahuna. You always say the sweetest things."

"Baby, I ain't being sweet. I'm being honest."

Bobby Joe selected a spot on the tee box and set up. He looked to the ground beneath him for several moments, then closed his eyes and smiled. Then he opened his eyes again and took several curious waggles. Once readied, he took an unusually slow backswing until his left arm was parallel with the ground, his wrists were cocked and his club head pointed skyward. Then he turned his hips quickly forward and dropped his arms behind him until it seemed he might topple over. All at once, his hips slid and his arms drew in and he swung the club head forward, looking like a baseball player adjusting mid-swing at a pitch that turned out to be coming low and inside. He made solid contact and his ball flew dead straight and on a flat trajectory. The ball never rose more than about twelve yards and came to rest 240 yards away.

"Oh, that was just beautiful, Kahuna."

Donald stood and stared. *Whatthehell? I just got outdriven by a five-foot-two Chinaman and a thirteen-year-old girl hitting with a three wood.*

Bobby Joe pretended to not notice Donald's stunned look. "Everybody ready?" The golfers grabbed their bags and marched.

"So I don't see any golf carts. Where do you keep them?" asked Donald.

"We don't have any carts. This is a course for walkers," responded Bobby Joe, who noticed that Donald was lumbering along with his over-sized staff bag. "That's a beautiful golf bag, Donald. I like how it has your name sewn onto the side. If you ever decide you want a lighter one, let me know, I think we might have a few lying around."

"No golf carts? How does the cart girl deliver beer? Don't tell me you make her walk, too?"

Ramona laughed and held her hand to her mouth. "Omigosh. That is, like, *so so* funny. Drinking *beer* at worship. Like, who would ever do that?"

Donald's eyes scanned the faces of his playing partners, looking for signs of sarcasm. He found none. "Well, just as long as I can smoke." A nervous pause. "Wait, you're not going to tell me I can't smoke, are you? Oh, come on. You can't tell a guy he can't smoke on a golf course. You just *can't*."

Bobby Joe nodded as he walked. "There ain't never been any smoking allowed on this golf course and I don't reckon there ever will be," he declared. "The only ashes on this course are those of the folks who wish to be laid to rest here." He eyeballed Donald. *I'm not kidding. Don't you dare test me.*

When the trio arrived near Donald's ball, Donald fished for a nine iron and set up. He reared back and swung with the energy of a hungry tiger shark lunging for a baby seal. Donald released his club head early and it dug into the lovely green carpeting. His ball popped up and dribbled twenty-five yards ahead. A meaty slice of turf, the size and shape of the two-dollar bills that Donald used to lose at Pimlico, flopped five yards away.

"Aw, you little mother*fucker.*" Donald bared his teeth and then pounded the ground with his club face, leaving a six-inch incision. He reached for his bag and slammed in his club shaft.

Ramona, standing behind Donald, looked to Bobby Joe.

Bobby Joe tightened his chin. *Let's not overreact.*

"Donald, we need for you take care of your divot. Also, we need you to not slam your clubs into the ground."

Donald laughed. "I didn't come all the way from Glen Burnie to do landscaping. Man, I'm here to golf." He started walking, looking up the fairway to where his shot had come to rest. Ramona and Bobby Joe didn't move.

"Donald?" Bobby Joe waited until Donald had turned around. "You're in new territory, friend. The rules have changed. This is not a muni that does twenty-something-thousand rounds a year."

"What? Gimme a break."

Bobby Joe sauntered over to Donald and grasped the big man's arm with a heavy hand. "Do you see those white markers mounted in the ground on the edge of the forest?" He pointed. "Those are the headstones of four generations of members of the Akaka family. Their ashes were scattered by friends and relations right where you're standing. Some of their descendants still live and worship here. They pray on this ground and believe that the spirits of their lost relatives live here.

You'll see headstones like that on every single hole on this course. When we get to the tenth green, if you want, I'll show you the place where Dixie took her last breath and fell down dead. There's a flower garden there now."

Bobby Joe checked Donald's face. He was being serious and wanted it known. "The flower gardens and the plots of headstones are not overgrown because they're tended to by the nice folks who live here." Bobby Joe turned and pulled on Donald's shoulder. "See the steeple poking above those trees over there? You probably recognize that as our chapel. That steeple is visible from almost every place on the golf course. The chapel and the course are part of a unified design done by our founder. Almost everywhere you play on the course, you have that view to inspire you. Do you see that little shack tucked into the woods back there by the tee box? That's where we keep landscaping tools for this hole. Every hole has one. Almost every Sunday morning, Ramona and her mother and her brother and the Hagood sisters come out here and make sure the first hole looks as nice as it does. Most everybody in the village has a hole or a section on this golf course that's their responsibility. To honor the spirits of the folks who used to play here but have passed on, they put their hearts and souls into caring for this place. Donald, this whole community treats this as sacred ground. So you can't come on the course and take divots and walk away. You can't be mashing the ground with your clubs."

Donald shook his head and blinked.

"You fix your damage to the course or you leave the course. Ain't no in between."

Donald scowled. He picked up the slab of turf he had created and replaced it in the hole from where it came. "There's nothing people hate worse than a nag."

"Donald, there are pieces of your divot you left behind."

Donald's shoulders appeared to accept a burdensome weight. He picked up the bits and pieces and inserted them into the hole in the turf from where they had come. Then he looked back at Bobby Joe. "Are we *good* now?"

"When the village comes out to do gardening and course mainte-
nance on Wednesday and Sunday mornings, why don't you plan on
working the first fairway? Ramona here will be working with you and can
show you how it's done."

The golfers advanced to Bobby Joe's ball and he slid a pitching
wedge from his bag. He looked for a moment to the ground beneath
him, closed his eyes, then stood next to his ball. He made a swift putting
motion with his wedge and his ball popped seventy yards, landed just shy
of the left front edge of the green, then bounced onto the putting surface
where it rolled, curled right and stopped ten feet from the hole.

"Very nice, Kahuna," said Ramona.

Donald set up with his own pitching wedge and took a half swing.
I hate fixing divots. The leading edge of his club, and not the club face,
hit the ball at its equator and it rocketed to a grassy spot between two
trees just past the rough. "Ramona would you look in your bag and see
if there's a mojo in there that I could have?"

"A what? A *mojo*?"

"Yeah, mine has gone missing." He slammed his club back into his
bag and stood, hands on hips, looking up the fairway.

Ramona made a face and looked to Bobby Joe. She whispered:
"What's a mojo?"

"It's a mysterious little somethin' you carry for good luck." Ramona's
childish face remained blank. "It's a *joke*, baby. He's pretending he lost
his good luck charm and that's why he's not hitting the ball so well."

Ramona shrugged, surveyed her lie and selected her pitching wedge.
She held her club parallel to the ground, pointing it to the flag and then
traced a line back to her ball. She set up with the ball back in her stance
and took a half backswing with her wrists cocked only slightly. At the
bottom of her swing, the ball clicked. She watched it come to rest just
three paces away from the hole.

Donald dropped his bag near the green and pulled out a pitching
wedge and his putter. Inspecting his ball, he flung his putter to the
ground as he shoved himself between two close-together trees to set up.
He took one practice swing before attempting to make contact. His ball

launched high and landed on the far side of the green where it rolled just off the edge. Donald grabbed his putter and walked. "I've been working on the railroad," he sang. "All the live long day … ."

He abandoned his wedge, an old friend whose loyalty was now in question, for his putter, even though he was a few inches into the rough. Settling into an awkward stance, he looked like a self-conscious St. Bernard preparing to drop a load. Donald gave the ball a little pop and watched as it flew several inches into the air, landed on the green and rolled sharply to the right, coming to rest about fifteen feet from the hole.

Donald looked across the green to Ramona and Bobby Joe who were relaxing on the ground, next to their golf bags. "Donald, I think you're still away," said Bobby Joe, who rose and removed the flagstick. Donald lined up and putted. His ball came to a stop eighteen inches shy of its target. He reached out and tapped the ball with the blunt end of his putter and it rolled up to the edge of the cup and stopped. He tapped it again and it dropped in. He plucked his ball out of the hole and shook his head.

Both Bobby Joe and Ramona one putted. The trio reached the tee box on number two and Bobby Joe motioned toward the markers. "Ramona, would you like honors, little darlin'?" She smiled, a three iron in hand.

"Who's got a scorecard?" queried Donald. "I didn't see any around the first tee. I need to write down my bogey."

Bogey? "We don't keep scorecards on the course," responded Bobby Joe.

"How do you keep track of who wins?"

"Donald, most of the folks who play this course ain't playing to see who has the best score."

"Wait … what?"

"Donald, thinking about my score keeps me from enjoying good company. It feels like I'm missing the point of being on the course."

Donald tilted his head. "Missing the point? Jesus Christ, man. That *is* the point. Like, how do you know if you're getting any better if you

On the sixth hole, an unusually narrow, medium-length par five, Donald unsheathed his driver and duck hooked his tee shot into the underbrush. Both Bobby Joe and Ramona used medium irons and put their tee shots onto the fairway. The threesome approached the spot where Donald's ball disappeared, dropped their golf bags and began a search.

Donald tromped about, muttering. "They had to put the goddam cabbage right next to the skinny goddam fairway, didn't they? Just plain stupid."

"Here it is!" piped Ramona. She pointed to Donald's Titleist, which had come to rest on the fairway side of a large rock. "Donald, can you swing left handed?"

Donald grimaced. "Well, this is definitely an immovable igneous object," he declared, pointing to the rock. "And under EHGA rules, I can move this ball six club lengths without penalty." Donald picked up the ball and placed it on the fairway grass. He pulled out a three wood and began a practice swing. "You guys comply with EHGA rules, right?"

"EHGA? Donald, what's that?" queried Bobby Joe.

"The EHGA? You're kidding, right? You've *never* heard of the EHGA?"

"Nope."

"The Egregiously Handsome Golfer's Association. I'm president and founder and have authority to interpret the rules as necessary to promote the interests of egregiously handsome golfers everywhere." Donald stepped up, swung and watched his ball take a picturesque arc toward the green.

On the eleventh hole, Donald stood at address and teetered. He swung hard and whiffed and had to take a half step to avoid tumbling over. By the time he reached the eleventh green, he was breathing hard and a whitish film had formed in the corners of his dry mouth. "Man, I *really* need a cig. Wait, what day is this? Ohmigod. I think I'm late for work. What time is it? Has anyone really been far even as decided to use even go want to do look more like?" Donald's legs wobbled and he collapsed to his hands and knees.

Bobby Joe took a close look at Donald's unnaturally puffy and pink face. "Ramona, we have to get him out of the sun. We have to get him some water. *Right now.*"

"We can take him to my house." Ramona pointed to a nearby path between the trees.

"Donald, come on. Come with us." Bobby Joe shouldered Donald's golf bag. "Ramona, take Donald's hand. Don't let him wander away. I don't think he even knows where he is."

The pair escorted Donald through a shady path to Ramona's home, a white bungalow with a forest-colored roof of corrugated steel. They lay him down on the living room sofa. "Ramona, go fetch Doctor Arai. Tell him it's an emergency. *Run.*"

Bobby Joe pulled open Donald's eyelids. "Oh son, look at you. You're as dried out as a little old raisin." Bobby Joe poured a cold glass of water and gave it to Donald and guided Donald's hands as he gulped it, rivulets flowing down his chin and neck, and soaking into his collar.

Ramona reappeared. With her was a dark-skinned man with impossibly slim hips and coarse eyebrows as thick and lively as a pair of caterpillars. He kneeled next to Donald, laid out on the couch, and put his wide-mouthed satchel on the floor. He stared at Donald through his almond-shaped eyes. "Ah, so you Mister Gibson. Most lovely to meet you. I look at you and decide if you healthy. You will please to be still. Yes?"

"Doc, we were on the golf course together and he started getting disoriented and weak. He didn't put on any sunblock. He looked really dehydrated and I just gave him a big glass of water."

Dr. Kazuho Arai extended his pruny, tea-colored fingers and began to probe Donald's face. Donald recoiled.

"That is hurting?"

"Uh, *yeah.* Of course it hurts."

Dr. Arai parked his glasses high on the bridge of his nose and moved his face to within an inch of his patient's and, through the bottom half of his bifocals, began to scrutinize. He saw a spread of red splotches.

"Doc, please tell me you're not going to get any closer. I'm not that kind of guy."

"Hmmmm. Patient quickly upset. Quickly angry." He looked up at Bobby Joe. "Always so?"

"Well, all day today anyway."

"I'm not angry. Don't you dare tell me that."

"Mister Gibson, do you feel sick to stomach?"

"Maybe a little. But mostly because your breath is disgusting. What have you been eating?"

Dr. Arai removed his glasses and put a hand on Donald's shoulder. "You dehydrated, Mr. Gibson and you have severe sunburn. You remain inside. Only inside. No sunshine. None." Dr. Arai wagged his finger. "Take aspirin. Drink water. Wait until feel better. Maybe three days. Then you come outside again and will feel fine."

"Stay inside for three days? Just for a little sunburn?"

"Ah, Hawaii sunshine is strong sunshine. Must be most careful. Sunblock so, so important. You wait here until dark. Then you go home. You stay for three days. Yes?"

"Doc, I can't sit around for three whole days. I'll go crazy. Tomorrow morning, I'll be fine. You watch."

Dr. Arai kneeled, reached out and took Donald's hand. "You on island time now. Mainland time no good here. You relax inside for three days. You get sunblock. You stay inside. Only inside. Then you will be happy. I know this. You will see."

Tina usually came home from work around the time the afternoon sun was spreading tranquility with an orange-pink glow. It was a glow cozy enough to make you remember what it felt like to put your infant head on your mother's shoulder. As she walked past the bend in the road, she saw Ramona and Toby, sitting on their front porch.

"So Ramona, who did you play golf with today?"

"Kahuna and Mr. Gibson."

"Mr. Gibson? He put on quite a display at Dixie's memorial service. So does he seem like a nice man?"

"You're about to find out, Mom."

"What?"

"He's inside, sleeping on the couch."

"What?"

"He didn't wear any sunblock and didn't bring any drinking water and he got cranky because he couldn't smoke his cigarettes and couldn't drink any beer on the golf course. By the time we got to the eleventh green, he was all fried and dehydrated and ready to pass out. Plus he was babbling and acting all wackadoodle so we brought him in here. Doc Arai says he has to stay out of the sun for three days."

"Three days? Wait – does he think he can stay at our house for three days?"

"I think he's planning on going home after the sun goes down. Doc told him to avoid getting any sun."

"Are these his cigarette butts all over the front yard?"

"Yeah. He comes out to the porch and smokes them. I told him you didn't want him smoking in the house. He drank up all four of the beers we had left over from your birthday party and was asking if we had any more. I didn't dare tell him your tequila was in the kitchen cabinet. I think he might have drunk that, too."

Tina tapped her foot and shook her head. "Why the heck is he at our house?"

"Doc Arai said he should wait until the sun went down to walk home, Mom. Doc didn't want Mr. Gibson getting burnt any more than he already was."

Tina and her children stepped inside the screen door. There lay Donald, splayed out and face up. He looked to Tina like a rotting whale shark she had seen beached near Haunama Bay. Only this whale shark had its mouth open, displaying an array of silver fillings mounted in yellowed teeth. It had whitish feet hanging out beyond the end of the sofa, and it snored fitfully, throwing off an acidic perfume one snort at a time. A pale and hairy slab of bellyfat, about the size of a pork tenderloin, hung out from above its belt. Half rings of sweat showed on its golf shirt, just under its manboobs.

"Isn't he just about the pinkest man you ever saw?" asked Ramona. "I mean, that face. It looks like raspberry sherbet that's starting to melt."

"I just think he's kinda *disgusting*," said Toby.

"*Mom*, Toby wanted to shave off one of his eyebrows. He would have if I didn't hide your razors."

"*Toby*. Honestly. Please tell me you wouldn't have done that."

"Ramona said we should paint his fingernails pink to match his face. She's a bad influence. She's not setting a good example for me, like you said she should."

"Mom, what should we do? I mean, just look at him. Toby's right. He's disgusting."

"Let him sleep. If he guzzled four beers, he's probably not very good company. When he gets up, he can be on his way."

"Shouldn't we be a little bit nice to him? Offer him some dinner?"

"We've already given him four beers and a place to sleep it off. That seems plenty nice to me. He should be thinking about being nice to us."

An hour later, Donald was aroused by the smell of biscuits and beans. He rose to his feet and listed to starboard, oblivious to his hosts, who were seated behind him at their dinner table. He shifted and relieved a small obstruction he could sense was plugging the flow of gas through his innards.

"Oh, my God. My head *hurts*." Donald clutched his temples. Just as quickly, he pulled them away. "Oh, my God. My face fucking hurts."

Donald turned and surveyed the room that seemed so unfamiliar and came face to face with his hosts. "Uh, hello."

"I suppose you're the nice man who left his cigarette butts all over my front yard?"

Donald grabbed the edge of the sofa for support. "Can't you see I'm in pain? My entire head is *killing* me." Donald clutched his temples and then, feeling the sting, quickly pulled his hands away. "My *face*. Dear God, why does it hurt so bad?" Donald closed his eyes, braced his hands on the arm of the couch and grumbled like a mad dog. "Oh, this *sucks*."

Tina decided to take charge. "Maybe its time you were on your way, Mr. Gibson."

Donald blinked his pinked-out eyeballs and nodded. Then he headed out the door.

"Wow, mom. That was maybe a little harsh."

"He's a grown man. He needs to act like one." Tina and her kids ate slowly and stared at their plates in silence. Then came a knock. They looked up to see Donald standing outside the screen door. He glanced up once and then looked back down at his feet.

"Can I get my shoes and socks?"

Tina motioned. "Ramona, I think I saw them by the couch." Ramona jumped up and met Donald at the screen door with his shoes and socks in hand. Donald sat on the floor of the front porch to slide on his socks and tie up his golf shoes. He nodded and departed.

Ramona peered out as Donald ambled away. "Mom, that poor man needs help. He's never going to find Dixie's house."

"Come on over and finish your dinner. You let that man fend for himself. He's not a child. Let's not treat him like one."

It was only a few minutes later when another knock came at the screen door. "Can you tell me how to get to my house? Please?"

"Mom?" whispered Ramona. "Can't you drive him? He's totally lost. He'll never get home."

Tina plunked her fork down on her plate and wiped her mouth with her napkin. "Give me a minute to get my keys, Mr. Gibson. Ramona here says I need to give you a ride home."

—⁀⁀⁀—

The front door at Karen Nakamura's house was almost always ajar, which was a Lanian signal. It meant you were happy to have visitors. On an island with only three thousand souls, a visitor was always as welcome as a sand save. Bobby Joe stepped inside and spotted Karen, half-reclined on her linen-upholstered couch, scrutinizing a clean stack of legal-sized papers.

"Hello, dear. How are you?" Bobby Joe reached out for Karen's shoulder and gave a squeeze.

"Oh, I'm better now, Kahuna. Every day you come for a visit is an especially good day." Karen's green eyes peeked over her reading glasses, a pencil held in place by her dense, auburn hair, just above her right ear. "Be a sweetie and give me a refill, will you?" She handed over a cone-shaped ceramic cup that felt quite delicate in Bobby Joe's stubby hands.

Bobby Joe did exactly as he was asked, emptying a small percolator into the colorful cup and returning it to Karen. He sat on the couch, letting Karen extend her legs across his lap. He had admired this woman's beauty for years. She always had her hair elegantly gathered in a tortoise-shell clip, with not a strand out of place. Her pearl earrings on ears no bigger than silver dollars framed a face that had probably broken at least a dozen hearts. She always seemed so composed, so finished.

"And what brings you into this little corner of the village? *Oooh*, rub my feet, will you? I love it when you do that."

Bobby Joe smoothed his warm hands across Karen's insoles and glee-fully watched her beam. "I'm wondering if you have had the chance to spend any time with our newest resident? You know, Donald."

"I knew just who you meant, Kahuna. And yes, I have. Just a little. Have you?"

"Yes, and I'm a little unsure of how to proceed. Ramona and I played a round with him two days ago and he collapsed from dehydration and exposure because he ignored suggestions about drinking water and using sunblock. It's hard to figure."

"*Proceed*? How do you mean?"

"If he's going to settle in here, he's going to have to make some changes. Three years is really not that much time to work with."

"Well, if he doesn't settle in, he leaves. Would that be so bad? It would be better for you, wouldn't it?"

"Dixie made me promise that if this day ever came, I'd make my best effort to help him. She knew it would be an adjustment. She believed that life in the village could save him from the worst parts of himself. She also said that Donald was someone who was worth saving.

She really saw something in him. She made me swear I would follow through on this."

"Kahuna, she shared some of those same thoughts with me. I'm a little surprised she gave her entire estate to Donald, all things considered. Listen, I know that Dixie's passing has been hard on you, but do you have to take it on faith that Dixie was right about Donald? I see him as the kind of guy who would prefer a condo in Vegas over a cottage on Lanai. He drinks. He smokes. He's only been here a few days and he's pacing around like he's in a cage."

"Dixie knew him from the day he was born. She had plenty of chances to figure him out. I think she deserves the benefit of the doubt. And I think you could be just a little more tolerant, sugar. He's only human."

"Put me on record as having doubts. I have a hard time seeing how this will work. To live on Lanai happily, you have to be contented with contentment. That's not Donald."

Bobby Joe moved from motions with his palms and started massaging the spaces between his friend's toes with his fingertips, working one at a time from left to right, devoting time to each. "Karen, I have adopted him and I am hoping he'll prove Dixie's faith in him was not misplaced. I have to assume this will work or I just won't be able to be totally committed."

"Well, bless you for taking him on. I don't think most of us have the patience you do. I'm guessing there's a reason you're here telling me all this, or do you just need someone to listen while you rub their bunions?"

"Karen, how do I help Donald make the adjustment to village life? This is a guy who might drown in a bottle of vodka. I'm fearful subtlety won't work, but being blunt and direct might not work either. Most people, if they have the experience that Donald just had, they make a few changes. Donald seems to think there's no problem."

"I think your fears are on the mark. Donald seems like a man who needs to be carefully led to the water and then told to drink it. Perhaps he needs to be told when to stop, and he needs to feel like it was all his decision."

"You think?"

"Yeah, I do. When I was telling him the details of Dixie's estate plan, he walked right past the big questions. All he cared about was what he would get and when he would get it. Not a word about what happens if he doesn't put in his three years. I don't think he heard anything I said except that he was due to get four million dollars."

"Really? You're serious?"

"As a heart attack, darling."

"So he doesn't know the whole picture?"

Karen shook her head. She sipped her coffee. "If you dangled a ten-dollar bill on a string, he'd walk barefoot across a lava flow trying to get it. He *wants* what he *wants*."

Bobby Joe sighed, setting his hands on top of his head. "I feel a little weary at the thought of it all."

"The feet, love. *The feet.* Did somebody blow the whistle and tell you to knock off? Seriously, even if you don't succeed, he may leave here a better, happier person. Wouldn't that make your work worthwhile? I mean, does he have to find happiness in Lanai? Maybe back home in Maryland, where he's got friends and family, is better for him. It seems like Ted may be the only positive influence in his life right now. Perhaps if they were again living close to one another … ."

"He ain't even hardly unpacked and you sound like you're ready to give up on him."

"My father, the greatest trial lawyer I ever saw, told me that people come in three types. There's the ones who learn by reading. There's the ones who learn by watching. And then there's the ones who have to learn by peeing on the electric fence. Donald is the guy who pees on the fence."

It was a prickly pear cactus summer day on Pratt Street in the center of downtown Baltimore. The four-lane avenue was still and quiet. In the middle of the afternoon, there were no cars, no trucks, no buses. There was only a gush of air, hot enough to roast a ham, pushing paper scraps through the gutters. And where was *anybody*? The sidewalks went unused.

Donald stood in the middle of the road, surrounded by a circle of orange safety cones. He was wearing nothing but high-ankle work boots and a pair of tight, white underpants that were smothering his prize-worthy penis. He had one hand on a jackhammer, which hammered incessantly and uncontrollably at the dark grey pavement – *bakatta-bakatta-bakatta* – chunking it into pieces the size of dinner plates. And with his other hand, he was frantically trying to remove a long-tentacled jellyfish that was sucking at his face. The jackhammer wouldn't stop. There was seemingly no way to turn it off and it had to be held tightly. Donald knew that if he didn't, it would run amok.

The more Donald dug his fingers into the jellyfish, the more aggressively it attacked. The creature was hell-bent on engraving its stinging image into his cheeks, his ears, his nose and even his neck. It had the curious ability to dematerialize and to re-form at will, evading Donald's grip with a demonic form of passive-aggressive resistance.

This thing is a motherfucker. Is it angry? Does it just hate my guts? The sound of the jackhammer faded. Donald could sense a voice and the sound of a heavy, repeat knock at the rickety screen door. *bakatta-bakatta-bakatta.* "Donald! Donald! *Donald?*... Hello?" *bakatta-bakatta-bakatta.*

Donald opened his eyes and found that his own hands were scratching at his fiery face. "Oh, God. Make my face stop hurting." Under Donald's fingernails were clumps of wet scabs. *Bakatta-bakatta-bakatta.*

"Coming! *I'm coming.*" Donald rolled out of bed and pulled on his pants. He slid on a t-shirt, careful to avoid having it touch his face. He stopped in the bathroom to rinse his hands and to inspect his face in the tiny mirror. *I look like a baboon's ass.*

Standing outside the screen door was Bobby Joe and Beauregard, whose stubby little tail was wagging. "Can I come in?"

Donald motioned.

"I'm glad you're still with us." He put a hand on Donald's shoulder and looked him over. "Don't you look handsome today, you old rascal? You look like you was trying to force a pair of pantyhose on a bobcat."

"God, my face won't stop hurting. Shouldn't it be better by now?"

Beauregard sniffed Donald around the ankles and rubbed his face against Donald's calves, looking to acquire some new stink.

"We'll hope there are better days to come. Hey, look. I brought you some aloe vera lotion. It will take away a little of the sting while you're waiting around for your skin to get better."

"Thank you, man," croaked Donald through a bone-dry throat. "Hey, I *really* need some coffee. You want a cup?" Bobby Joe nodded.

Donald set up the percolator and stared mindlessly at it, waiting for action.

Bobby Joe broke the quiet. "So, day four of the big Hawaiian adventure. Having fun yet?"

"Oh, holy shit. You're not setting me up so you can give me more advice that I haven't asked for, are you?"

"Well, skeezix, ain't you a surprise? You near about kill yourself ignoring what people tell you to do and now you want to act like a teenager who thinks he's all growed up and don't need nobody's help. If Ramona and I hadn't taken you inside, you might have died. It was that bad. You put yourself in a spot."

"I got a little sunburned. Big deal. Don't make that into more than it really was."

"Donald, Tuesday afternoon on number eleven, you were broiled and burnt. You don't know how close you came to buying the farm. There wasn't no way you could have even gotten home on your own."

Donald stared. "Why was it, exactly, you decided to come over this morning? So you could give me a hard time? You don't think I've suffered enough? Look at my face. I'm a freak show on two legs."

"I thought it was just a little sunburn – no big deal."

"Oh, come on already."

"Donald, I came over because I was concerned about you. But also, I have an old friend coming from out of town in a few months. I'd like it if the three of us could play a round."

"Bobby Joe, do you know how many rounds of golf I've played with people who wanted the chance to fawn over the Donald? The number of times I've had to pretend to be interested in conversation with people who wanted to tell their friends they played golf with the amazing Donald Gibson? I'm really so past that."

Bobby Joe pursed his lips. *What the hell is he talking about?* "Well, I was hoping you would feel inclined to do me a favor, seeing as how Ramona and I saved your life and all. It would really mean a lot. My friend had a football career and he's struggling to find something to do now that he's retired. I thought maybe you might be able to give him a little advice. I know you played some football. It would mean a lot to him and to me."

Donald looked at the container of aloe vera. "*Fine.* I'll come play a round with him. As a favor to you."

"Well that's mighty decent of you, Donald. George will be here in a few months. Until then, be careful and obey doctor's orders. We want you healthy."

"You're not going to make this a habit, are you? You know, inviting friends to play golf with the celebrity that has moved into your village?"

"Celebrity in the village? You're making no sense."

"The University of Maryland football star who led his underdog team to a come-from-behind victory for a national championship? The Heisman finalist? The handsome guy next door who did endorsements for beer and cars and cigarettes? *That* guy?"

"This is you?"

"Oh, come on, you had to have known. You must have seen me on television."

"The only thing Dixie told me was that you played football in college. I didn't know you had been so successful, and I've never owned a television. Except for watching the Masters and the U.S. Open sometimes, I don't really follow sports."

"Well, anyway, now you know. If your friend plays football and you mentioned my name to him, he knows exactly who I am. That's why he wants to play golf with me."

"I haven't mentioned your name to him, and he hasn't asked to play golf with you. I'm asking you to play with him because I thought you might be able to give him some advice. He doesn't know what to do with hisself. Now that George is retired and has started playing more golf, you two may have something in common. You might actually enjoy meeting him. He's really a great guy."

"Wait, who are we talking about here?"

"Blanda. George Blanda."

Donald's shoulders dropped. His mouth hung open. "George Blanda? You're friends with George Fucking Blanda? Are you kidding me?"

Bobby Joe shook his brown head. "I'm not kidding. Wait, do you know George? Is the world really that small?"

"No, I don't know him. I just know who he is. He's about the biggest football star there ever was. When I was a little fucker and we played football, everybody wanted to pretend he was George Blanda. He was *the man.* So how in the hell is it that you know George Blanda? He's my hero. I've been dying to meet him for years."

"George's aunt, a lovely woman, used to live in the village before she passed. George would come for a visit just about every year. He's a very spiritual man and we have become friends. He's come to me for golf lessons several times in the last few years."

"Why didn't you tell me who it was? Jeez, I woulda volunteered."

Bobby Joe swallowed the last of his coffee and *aaaahed.* "Donald, I need to run. Thank you for the coffee. So you think you'll be into playing shape when George gets here?"

Donald nodded. "I wouldn't miss it."

Bobby Joe put a hand on Donald's shoulder. "I knew I could depend on you."

Donald watched from his front porch as Beauregard kicked along and Bobby Joe trundled down the red dirt road on a pair of legs that, from a distance, looked too short to carry a grown man anywhere. "George Fucking Blanda. I get to play golf with George Blanda."

Donald poured himself a fresh cup and parked himself in a front porch rocker, but only after dragging it out of the direct sunshine. As soon as he got comfortable, the sound of screeching metal made him jump. Next door, his only close-by neighbor was pulling her Jeep into her carport. *Holy Jesus, does she ever need some new brakes.* A swollen woman wearing a scowl emerged from the driver's seat and galumphed, one ham hock at a time, to her door. She spotted Donald, who was staring at her. "What the hell are you looking at?" she demanded.

Donald had nearly finished his coffee when along came Ramona, holding a covered plate.

"Well, good morning Ramona."

"Good morning, Donald. How are you feeling?"

"A little crispy around the edges, and a little stir crazy. It's been three days and I'm not ready to go back in the sun yet."

"Since you might not be able to get to the market, I brought you a plate of sandwiches. I made them all by myself. Can I put this in your refrigerator?"

"Absolutely you can."

After returning from Donald's kitchen, Ramona returned to the front porch and took a seat.

"Mom said I should ask you to return the plate when you're done with the sandwiches. She says that men need to be reminded about things like that. She says that men forget sometimes."

"Tell your mom I promise to remember. And, hey, Ramona, I'm glad you're here. I got a question for you. Why is it that you call Bobby Joe *Kahuna*? Is that a nickname or something?"

"I call him that because he is that."

"Wait. … What?"

"He's our Kahuna. On the mainland, it's probably like being a priest or a pastor. It's not only that, it's partly because he's our leader. People look up to him."

"So are people *supposed* to call him Kahuna? Is it required?"

"I don't think it's actually required. But everybody does."

"If he's the leader, does he give people orders and stuff like that? Does he get to boss people around?"

"He mostly makes suggestions."

"So how did he become the Kahuna?"

"He's not *the* Kahuna. He's just Kahuna. When old Kahuna died a few years ago, people just looked to … to Bobby Joe as *new* Kahuna. Like, you know how if you outgrow your favorite pair of pants and so you look in your closet for some other pants and there's another pair that's nice and then you start wearing them all the time and before you know it, that's your new favorite? Well, it's like that."

"So what does a Kahuna do?"

"Just Kahuna. Don't you hear?"

"What does Kahuna do?"

"Well there's the obvious stuff, like he leads us in prayer. He speaks to the group when we're together. I think he also gives people help with their problems. He's pretty good at helping people figure out stuff. Plus, he gives everybody golf lessons, the same as old Kahuna. I think he likes to use golf lessons to teach people stuff. Not just how to golf but, you know, *stuff*. Like, I used to hurry through *everything*, my homework, my swing on the golf course and even talking to people and I still do sometimes, but Kahuna told me that I needed to slow down my swing and my life and just go one step at a time and it will work better and that's what I did and it turned out he was right. My mom tried to tell me the same thing, but with Kahuna you really feel like listening, you know? He says things that make you laugh like *Ramona, I ain't never seen somebody go so dang slow when they were trying to move so dang fast.* ... He doesn't judge me or say mean things if I don't listen to him like my mom does. I mean, I really love my mom but she can be a little ... . Well, she's my mother and sometimes it's hard to want to listen to her tell me what to do, you know? Have you ever felt that way? You know like when your mother keeps telling you what to do? And you say for her to stop and she keeps telling you anyway?"

"Yeah, hundreds of times. So, Ramona, what was it you said about being at worship yesterday when we were on the golf course? You remember, right after I talked about drinking beer?"

"Oh, yeah. I was just saying that people don't drink beer when they're at worship."

"At *worship?*"

"I mean that when we're on the golf course, we're at worship. Golf is our religion. I mean, some people here are Catholic and some are Jewish and some people are other stuff. So people don't agree on all their beliefs, even though it all seems sorta the same to me. But I think everybody here agrees on golf. That's the religion we all share, and we pray on the golf course. Actually some people call it meditating because when they close their eyes, they don't conceive of, like, a higher power or a god. Didn't you notice Kahuna and me praying? We do it before every shot. So anyway, the golf course is our holy place. It's where we worship."

"Golf is worship? Seriously? *Worship?*"

"When you're playing golf, you are close to God. That's what Kahuna says. He says because you're in a natural place and you are enjoying the bounteous bosom of Mother Nature, like God wants and because of that, golf is holy. Does that sound right? I might have some of the words wrong."

Ramona dug deep into her pocket and pulled out a small foil packet. "Hey, you want a stick of Juicy Fruit? I got two left. You can have one, if you want."

—ɯ—

"Ted? Holy cow. I'm so glad I reached you."

"Donald, what's wrong? Please tell me you're *not* calling to borrow money already."

"That's really a crappy thing to say."

"Donald, you are such a little prick. I dropped you off at the airport hardly a week ago and I dared to ask when you could pay me back some of the twelve thousand dollars I loaned you and you raced off like a track star. Already you're calling and you sound desperate. Something's definitely wrong."

"Well, maybe I did get really fucking sunburned and I've been stuck in a tiny house that has no goddam television set and no goddam beer and my Marlboros are all smoked up and so I'm going stir crazy. Plus, I got this tiny Chinaman who thinks he's the exalted poobah of the Pacific trying to tell me what to do all the fucking time."

"You're not calling about a lousy sunburn. No way. Sunburn is maybe a postcard. *Ted, I'm so glad I reached you?* That's a man whose dick is caught in a wringer."

"You don't get it, do you saucerhead? Man, this is *serious*. I have blisters that are oozing bloody, watery pus. Do you remember those toasted cheese sandwiches that Dad used to burn for us on his nights to cook dinner? Well that's my face. The top of my ears look like undercooked bacon strips. They're *glistening*."

"Why don't you make me really sorry I asked? I could have gone the whole rest of my entire lifetime without knowing all that."

"Teddy, this is *my face* we're talking about, and if you didn't want to know, why did you ask?"

"I was trying to be nice, dickweed. So why are you stuck at home?"

"The doctor says I have to stay completely out of the sun until I feel better, which is taking a long time. The sun here is really intense, so you really got to watch yourself. You have to wear a big dorky hat and cover up with sunblock."

"Don't you remember that Karen Nakamura said that? She warned us not to go out without a hat and lots of sunblock."

"She said that? Where the hell was I?"

"You were standing right next to me after Dixie's memorial service. I think you were staring at her tits. I wouldn't expect you to hear anything under circumstances like that. All of the blood that normally runs to your brain had been redirected to your schvantz."

"Teddy, are you going to say anything nice to me? I'm going stir crazy. I haven't had a drink in days. I'm *dying* inside. Gimme a break, will ya?"

"Give *you* a break? You're living for free in Hawaii waiting on a four million dollar payday. I'm not going to give you a break for the whole rest of your sick little life."

"A little empathy, please. That's not too much to ask. This is your brother you're talking to."

"Did you suffer a closed head wound?"

"Wait ... what?"

"Your memory seems to be failing. Who is handling your divorce for free? Who loaned you over ten thousand dollars in the last four years? Who's the only person who still talks to you like they care? You get plenty of empathy." Donald was uncharacteristically speechless. Ted sensed, correctly, that Donald felt a touch of regret for being thoughtless. "So if you're stuck at home, how are you getting groceries?"

"People keep coming by and bringing me food. I don't have room in the refrigerator for all of it. It's piling up on the counters. It's too much. I can't eat it all."

"The man who ignored advice to use sunblock and burnt himself to a crisp, the man who lives rent free in paradise with a guaranteed income, is the object of sympathy of an entire community? You're killing me over here."

"Teddy, these people love me. They totally get me. They want to *take care* of me. I'm going to love it here."

"Donald, they think you're the kind of person who knows that you're supposed to return a favor and be nice back to them. Don't you ruin this by being an asshole and taking them for granted. Don't you *dare* do that. Because if you can't make it work on Lanai? Then, man, you are totally screwed. You've got no other place to go and no other options. Your brother is never again going to loan you a nickel."

"Ted, is it so hard to be happy for me? You talk like you're all jealous. It ain't my fault you have to work on Saturdays just so you can afford to send your kids to that snotty private school in Severna Park with ivy on the stone walls and buildings named after admirals and shit."

"Jealous? I have my dream job, my wife and I love each other, and my kids are turning out to be nice people. I got no reason to be jealous. Look, Donald, nobody gets to screw up their entire life by being an asshole and then gets a second chance to get it right. So don't be acting all entitled. People will hate you if you do that. Your life will suck just as bad as it did two months ago."

"Teddy, I ... . Hey, listen, tell me something. Like, I'm a smart guy, right? Like, don't you think I'm pretty quick on figuring things out?"

"Oh, good. Now we get to the real reason you called."

"I'm serious here. Don't go screwing with me."

"So what is it you're asking?"

"You don't think I'm the kind of guy who acts like he knows *every*thing, do you?"

"Hmmm. You know, Donald, I believe I hear the sound of you being introspective. I'm not used to this. You must be really sick from that sunburn."

"Oh, come on already."

"Now I hear impatience and insistence. That's more like it."

"Man, will you just answer the question?"

"I'm trying to *figure out* the question, dorkazoid. Where are you coming from, exactly?"

"Look, remember that Kahuna guy? He says I act like the rules don't apply to me and I'm living in a magic bubble where I'm always right and stuff is never my fault. Total bullshit, right?"

"He's exactly right. He's totally nailed you. I can't believe he's figured you out so fast. And he's got guts. He confronted you about it."

"You're *killing* me. You can't be serious."

"Do I sound like I'm joking around? Like, why do you go through life thinking you can borrow tons of money from me and you never have to pay it back? Why are all the problems in your messed up little life somebody else's fault? It's because you think the rules don't apply to you. It's because you imagine yourself as perfect, as if you can't make mistakes. Why is it you call me up at three in the morning and bark at me from inside the drunk tank because I can't come get you for at least forty minutes? It's because you think the world owes you something. When shit like that happens, which it does to you all the time? Well, it's never your fault. It's the cop's fault. It's the Mothers Against Drunk Drivers' fault."

Donald pushed a plume of cigarette smoke into the phone. "Holy Jesus, man. I can't believe you would say that."

"Are you saying you didn't know this? Are you *seriously* saying that? I've told you a thousand times: if it smells like shit everywhere you go, look at the bottom of your shoe."

"Oh, wait. Teddy, I have to go. Somebody's at the door and it looks like they have food."

"Don't you dare miss out on more food. That would be tragic. And by the way, Cathy and the kids are fine. Thanks so much for asking. Dingleberry, you know I love you, right? You know that, don't you?"

"I love you too, Teddy. Bye."

Standing on the front porch, just outside the screen door, was a woman thinner than a soda straw and paler than unflavored yogurt. She had tucked her gleaming auburn hair into a bun and was wearing a high-necked, full-length white cotton dress with royal blue piping. A heavy platter burdened her twiggy arms. When Donald looked her in the eye, she gave him a wobbly curtsy.

"Hi. Can I help you?"

"Welcome to Lanai, Mr. Gibson. I am the Princess Lili'uokalani, sister of the esteemed King Kalakaua. I am here because the King requests the pleasure of a visit with you." She blinked over and over, just enough that Donald could tell she was nervous.

Donald's eyes widened and he briefly studied her chest, which was bigger than he would have expected on such a skinny woman. "Hello, princess. A *king*? A real king? Are you serious? A smart fella wouldn't ever say no to a pretty woman asking him to visit with a king, now would he?" Donald could see the woman studying his unbeautiful face and investing effort to determine what it said about him.

"Mr. Gibson, I believe this would be the appropriate time to invite us in."

Donald tilted his head. "*Us?* Well yes, then. Won't you please come in?" Donald pushed open the screen door.

The woman shakily transferred the weight of the platter from two hands to one and motioned urgently to her left, to someone out of Donald's sight and mouthed words to him. *Come here. Come with me. Yes, now. Right now.*

From the edge of the porch came an olive-skinned man in a morning suit with disorderly sideburns that spread across his cheeks like a pair of tiny bearskin rugs. He stood erect and proud, a topper cradled in one arm. Each of his shoulders bore a gold epaulet. On his left lapel, he displayed dozens of multi-colored medals and ribbons. He carried the unctuous aroma of Vitalis. His shiny, black hair was parted on the left, slicked back and *perfect*.

"Most esteemed greetings, Mr. Gibson. I am King Kalakaua, supreme ruler of the Hawaiian Islands. I am to understand you are now a resident of Lanai, which makes you my subject. You may address me as *your Tremendousness*. You will need to bow at the waist before I enter."

"Well, do come in your Tremendousness." Donald held open his screen door. The king stood stock still. Donald stood, unsure.

"Bow, please. It is customary when royalty enters." Donald smirked and glanced at the Princess. She nodded, eyes opened large. *Yes, you need to bow. He's not kidding.* Donald complied. The king entered. "We come to welcome you to the village, Mr. Gibson. My lovely sister, the Princess Lili'uokalani, has brought you a tray of lomi lomi salmon, and kimchi with pickled Maui onion that she made herself. Do you like the onion?"

"Actually, your Tremendousness, I'm allergic to the onion. I like the chive – er, chives – much better."

The woman quietly passed over the tray with a smile made almost entirely of plastic. "Isn't she lovely, Mr. Gibson?"

"Why yes, Your Tremendousness, she sure is."

"So Mr. Gibson, I come with both official greetings and condolences from the kingdom of Hawaii. Ms. Dixie Reynolds was a treasure to us all."

"Well, thank you."

"Why don't you try some of the food from the tray? Did I tell you that Lili made this herself?"

"Thank you, your Tremendousness. You did mention that she had made it."

"Isn't she lovely, Mr. Gibson?"

Donald's neck straightened. He paused. *This is getting weird.* "She sure is, your Tremendousness."

"So Mr. Gibson, are you single? I notice there is no wedding ring."

"Single? Um, no actually. I'm still married."

"So you are separated then. Perhaps you are waiting to become divorced?"

"What's with all these questions?"

"Mr. Gibson, it is unspeakably rude to question the motivations of the man who is now your king and supreme ruler."

"Really?"

"It most certainly is." The king stared deep into Donald's eyes. He leaned his head forward, looking like he expected something. "When one is rude to the man who is your king, one should apologize. It is customary."

"Apologize? You want me to *apologize*?"

"He wants you to bend down and kiss his royal ass," said the woman from next door who had entered Donald's cottage without an invitation. "He hates it when people refuse to kowtow. He's probably hoping to convince you to marry his manipulative sister." Donald's head swiveled. The woman's first impression was established by her exaggerated oval shape and her hair, which was cut oddly short on only one side of her head. "He approaches every new resident like this. He wants to get to you before you find out from your neighbors that he's a kook. The woman extended a hand toward Donald. "I'm Alani Kahunanui, your new next door neighbor." Donald reached out, expecting to shake her hand. She grabbed his fingers and opened his palm. "These are the cigarette butts you put on my lawn." She released a fistful of ash and nicotine-stained Marlboro filters. "Keep them on your own yard."

The princess began hyperventilating and looked at the king. "David, she's doing it again. She's completely ruining *everything*."

"Ms. Kahunanui, you are showing terrible disrespect for your king and supreme ruler. What do you have to say for yourself? You should ask for forgiveness. It is customary."

"David, you're being a jerk. That's what I have to say." She turned her attention back to Donald. "Most people humor him because they feel it's the polite thing to do. But there's no rule that says you have to. He's just another neighbor. But he happens to be the only one on the island arrogant enough to put his name on the ballot for King when the elections come along."

"These veins carry holy and royal blood," barked His Tremendousness, his chest projecting. "My lineage traces back to the earliest days of Hawaiian recorded history. I am the undisputed descendant of High Chief Caesar Kaluaiku Kapa'akea. I am the *entitled* ruler of the Kingdom of Hawaii."

"David, you're one of those people who make me believe in reincarnation. Nobody can get that stupid in just one lifetime."

His Tremendousness approached Alani and poked the tip of her nose with his own. "You should be thankful it is not one hundred years ago. I could have had a servant separate your head from your body with a shiny, steel axe." He carefully placed his topper on the center of his head. "Lili'uokalani, let us depart. The honor that used to be in this home is all gone."

"Look around you, Donald. You have lots of free space to dump your cigarette butts that don't qualify as *my yard*."

All at once, Donald's living room was silent. He watched the king as he goose-stepped up the dirt road, trying to ignore his sister who was pointing her finger at the center of his face and screaming something that only he could hear.

6

Lanai, Hawaii
March 17, 1977

Donald was alone. On a golf course. On a small Hawaiian island. Just before sunrise. He looked around and decided the picture was as sweet and pure as Brooke Fucking Shields.

He fired up a Marlboro and dragged deeply as he stared out from the tee box on hole number two. He glanced behind him to ensure he wasn't being watched. Layers of still and quiet were his only companions. *I can smoke on the course and pee in the bushes if I damned well please.*

Donald reached for his five wood and teed up his ball and stood back for a minute. He took a deep hit from his cigarette, then a second, and then dropped it onto the turf, and set up and waggled. He reached as far back as his spine would let him and nearly swung himself out of his shoes. *The harder I swing, the more I'll slice toward the green on the far right side of the landing area.* His ball started out straight and then rose hard and right, landing just out of sight on the edge of the landing area closest the green. Donald smiled. He looked behind him again to make sure he was alone.

The Donald looking down from above was completely relaxed. *You deserve this. Enjoy it.*

Donald picked up his cigarette from the grass and let it hang from his lips, slid his club back into his bag and marched. He looked skyward and beamed. *This is just what living in Hawaii should be all about. Good golfing and no assholes.* After he crossed the swinging bridge and reached his ball, he lay down his bag and grabbed a sand wedge. With the wedge, he nosed the ball onto nicer grass and examined the terrain ahead: a sharply elevated green notched into the side of a steep bluff of volcanic rock. Donald swung. He hit his ball thin and it shot like a bullet at the rocky bluff. It bounced straight back and clobbered Donald in the forehead.

Shitdamnhell.

A blast of stars with brocaded trails tracked across Donald's eyes. He dropped his wedge, staggered, lost his balance and dropped on all fours. He put his fingertips to his forehead and massaged the welt that had arisen. If he'd had a mirror, Donald might have admired the tiny dimples on the welt and even the attractive mirror-image *Titleist* logo all of which matched the features of his ball. After waiting for clarity and calm to return, he set up and swung again. *Just pop it on the green. And don't dare hit it thin.* At the bottom of his downswing, a determined Donald released early and the leading edge of his sand wedge dug in and lifted up the square of turf and his ball, which feebly flew about twenty yards – just far enough to bounce off the evil wall of rock. It dribbled back, returning to the spot from which it had begun its two round trips.

Motherfucker.

With a silky flick of his arm, he flung the ball an easy fifty yards into the adjacent forest. He yanked his bag off the ground, shoved in the handle of his wedge and began the hike up the steep hill past the number two green, on his way to the tee box for number three. He stopped for a moment on his way up to catch his breath, bent over and hands on knees. *Goddam that's a serious hill.* He took a last drag from his Marlboro and flicked it into the adjacent stand of pines. As he rose, he felt a stinging pain square in the back of his head.

Cockbastard.

He dropped his bag, grabbed at his head and looked around. Sitting on the ground, just behind him, was the Titleist he had hurled away a minute before. *How could this be?* He rubbed the back of his head and felt where the ball had struck his scalp. A small welt had already formed. Donald picked up his ball and stared into the woods.

"*Bradley!*" he shouted, pointing his voice at the tree tops. "You crazy fuckhead! Leave me *alone!*" Donald stared into the woods where he thought Bradley might be hiding. All was quiet.

Seeing no one, he finished his labored march. Once up the hill, he kneeled and panted like a rabid dog. After a minute, he unsheathed his driver, plunged a tee into the soil and set up. He took a mighty swing, teeth gritted. He thwacked the ball on the center of the club face and watched, with pleasure, as it flew high and long. Then his ball turned sharply right and disappeared into the woods that lined the right side of the fairway. Donald grimaced. He marched up and dropped a replacement about 180 yards from the tee box and then set up, ready to swing. As he did, he felt a screaming pain on his crown.

Assholeturdlicker.

Donald fingered his head and felt another welt that had surfaced. He looked to the ground and spotted the Titleist he had hit into the woods a few minutes before. He stood erect and stared into the dark spaces between the trees.

"You're asking for it, Bradley," he announced.

Donald looked ahead and estimated he had over 200 yards to the green. He selected his three wood and, after toeing his ball onto a nice piece of grass, set up and waggled and focused on simple swing thoughts. *Smooth. Full backswing. Smooth. Full backswing.* His takeaway was smooth. And he took a full backswing. At the bottom of his downswing, he felt a polite *click* and watched his ball go straight and low. It landed in the middle of the fairway about 170 yards ahead and then bounce rolled to a stop just shy of the green.

"Gimme some more of *that*, baby. Oh, yeah." Donald sashayed up the fairway.

When he reached his ball, Donald slid out his pitching wedge and dropped his bag all in one deft move. It slammed against the turf and left a deep bruise. He looked behind him again, concerned someone might see him. He looked ahead to the fourth tee box. All empty. He set up near his ball and stroked the turf. Back and forth. Back and forth. *Stiff left elbow. Smooth. Stiff left elbow. Smooth.*

Then he addressed his ball and waggled. He looked once at his target and then back to his ball. As he began his backswing, he saw a grapefruit-sized missile headed right for him. He turned to avoid it, but too late. A volcanic rock with a surface rougher than a Brillo pad struck his right forearm and dug in.

Titstwatbitchcunt.

Donald fell to the turf and curled into the fetal position, holding his arm. The pain stabbed at him and wouldn't stop. He pressed the side of his face against the cool grass, seeking relief, and rocked back and forth. When the pain subsided, he slowly arose and picked up his wedge, which had fallen beneath him and had pressed a cavity into the turf. He put his wedge back in his bag and inspected his arm, which was oozing watery blood.

Donald picked up the rock, which had bits of his flesh and blood embedded in it and stomped toward the woods. "Bradley!" he shouted. "Your little pink ass is *mine*, motherfucker." But no sooner had he broken the dividing line between the open fairway and the cozy forest when another missile, twice as large as the last, came at him, high and tight. He swerved, just in time to avoid being hit square in the chest.

Undeterred, Donald picked up his pace only to catch another rock on his left knee. He fell backward, clutching his leg and struck the back of his head square on the stump of a long-dead Cook pine.

Motherfuckingshit.

Donald clung to his leg, venting and steaming. He could hear heavy footsteps in the forest, getting farther away. He didn't dare straighten his leg for several minutes for fear of making the pain worse. Eventually, when all was quiet, he raised his head. "Asshole! You are a fucking asshole, Bradley!"

He inspected his knee, which oozed a slick mix of blood and sweat. He snorted twice, rose again and exited the woods. Back at the green, he found his ball. He found a dig in the ground where his wedge had plugged beneath him when he fell. He found the deep imprint left by the heel of his golf bag where he had let it drop hard, but his bag and all his clubs were gone.

Fuckingfuckerfuckityfuck.

Donald stood, hands on hips, and surveyed the grounds in all directions. All was quiet and still. The sun had plenty of time before it would clear the horizon.

Donald hiked with his newly acquired gimp past the second tee box where he entered the woods on the path to his new home. By the short set of stairs leading to his back porch, he found his bag and his golf clubs. He parked on the steps and watched as blood oozed from his leg and from his arm. He sighed and walked back across number two and over the tee box for number eleven and found Doctor Arai sitting cross-legged and bare-footed on his front porch, his hands palm-up on his knees and his back perfectly straight. His eyes were closed. Anyone who might dare to put their face close to his would hear and feel the reassuring vibration coming from his chest.

He arose as Donald approached, limping. "Ah, you have calamity. So, so sorry. We clean and bandage. You will feel better."

"Thanks, Doc. Man, you're a lifesaver."

Donald sat on the porch stairs as Doctor Arai abraded and rinsed the flesh wounds on his knee and his arm and then carefully trimmed gauze which he applied with surgical tape. The physician parked his glasses high on his nose and scrutinized Donald's forehead. "What happen? Look painful."

"Doc, I ... I slipped and fell heading down the back stairs earlier this morning. They were wet with dew and my feet went right out from under me. It happened so fast, I couldn't catch myself."

"Ahhh. Stairs leave Titleist imprint."

"Wait. ... What?"

Doctor Arai produced a small mirror from his satchel and handed it to Donald who held it up to his face. On his forehead were two perfectly round welts marked with perfectly round dimples. Pressed firmly into the center of one was a scripted logo that Donald knew all too well. *Titleist.* In the mirror, the imprint was as clear as grain alcohol.

Donald handed back the mirror and his shoulders slumped.

"You black out?"

Donald shook his head.

"You see stars?"

Donald nodded.

Doctor Arai produced a small penlight, held open Donald's eyelids and flashed his pupils, first the left and then the right, watching them carefully. Then he smiled. "You be fine. You rest for three days. No golf. No hard work. No fast movement. No loud noise. Rest. Stay home. Three days. You be fine. I know this."

"Three days? *Again?*"

—⋙—

"Did you get into a bar fight? It's looking like the bar might have won." Bobby Joe held his wire-rimmed glasses in his fingertips and scrutinized Donald's face. "Seriously, are you all right?"

"I'll be *fine*. Just fine." Donald waved him off, annoyed. "Just leave me be."

Bobby Joe parked himself in a rocker, next to Donald, on the front porch.

"Have you seen Doc Arai? Those wounds look serious."

"*Sree days Meestah Gibson. You stay home for sree days.* Holy jeez. Is everything with that guy three days at home?"

"Well, it's nice to hear that you'll live to play some more golf."

"Yeah, but c'mon. Three more days stuck doing nothing."

"So, have you found your way around the island yet? By now, you must have found your way to the town grocery, at least."

"Pine Isle Market, yes. Purveyor of the finest varieties of Spam and packaged mac and cheese one could hope to find. Oh, and let's not forget the twelve varieties of ramen noodles, including chicken and *roasted* chicken. Honestly, why can't they sell liquor like the stores back home?"

"The Dole fruit folks don't want their folks showing up to work drunk or hung over, so they limit the sale of alcohol on the island. Folks usually make a trip to Maui if they want anything more than a six pack of Primo or a couple of drinks or even if they want fresh produce. I make a trip once a week with some of the other men and we pick up provisions for some of our seniors. I would be happy to pick up things for you too, if you want to give me a list."

"Thank you, Bobby Joe. I just might do that."

An awkward pause followed. Donald looked at his feet as he and Bobby Joe both rocked back and forth in silence. *Does he know I was on the golf course alone this morning?*

"Donald, I'm having a few of the men over this evening to play some poker – just nickel ante stuff, no serious betting. Would you be interested?"

Donald perked up. *I guess he doesn't know.* "That sounds like fun. What time?"

"Oh, around sundown."

"So what time is that, exactly?"

"Donald, do you see anybody around here wearing watches? When you notice that the sky is starting to get dark, that means it's evening. Come on over."

"That sounds fine. I'll look forward to it."

"Listen, don't worry about bringing anything with you. You haven't got a source of food and drinks quite figured out yet. No problem."

"Oh, uh … thanks, Bobby Joe."

Bobby Joe stood and put a hand on Donald's shoulder. "Listen, I've got a few errands around the village to run. I've got to be on my way."

"Thanks for stopping. I'll look forward to that card game tonight."

Bobby Joe hopped down the porch steps, took a few strides toward the red dirt road, then stopped and walked back to the railing. "Hey, do you remember when I said that new residents of the village couldn't play the course alone? Well, I meant it. If you want to go play, there's almost always somebody available who will go with you. All you have to do is ask."

7

Honolulu, Hawaii
May 25, 1977

Tommy Banks rat-a-tatted the eraser end of a freshly sharpened Ticonderoga against the polished granite top of the Dole Fruit Company's conference table. It wasn't helping. From the twenty-third floor, a relaxed mind, stuck on a problem, would have gazed out of the floor-to-ceiling windows that formed one wall of the room. Past the windows were the rooflines of condominiums and hotels that ran the length of the beach at Waikiki. Beyond that was the sparkling Pacific, spread out as vast as somebody else's fortune.

Tommy felt like his gums were going to bleed. He had become fixated on the rows and columns of numbers on the sheets of graph paper spread out before him. He tapped the eraser some more and squeezed a handful of hair.

"Tommy, I been looking all over for you. What you doing in here, bruddah?" Kepa Makalua poked his dark-skinned face into the conference room.

"I needed some clean space to spread out all these papers. Hey, I'm glad you're here. I need some help."

"Help with what?"

Tommy motioned in his friend and co-worker and closed the door behind him. "I'm really freaking out, Kepa. I keep going over these numbers. Man, the carrying costs of the pineapple growing unit on Lanai are out of control, and the Thailand unit is turning out to be tons cheaper than we expected. We've got quarterlies with DeLorenzo scheduled for this afternoon."

"I repeat – help with what?"

"They didn't offer a class in business school on how to tell the owner of the Dole Fruit Company that the operation started over a hundred years ago by his beloved grandfather needs to be shut down. There's just no way we can justify keeping this going. It's losing tons of money."

"So you're scared of the old man? Is that it?"

"Well, I wouldn't say that, exactly. It's more like … . All right, basically, yeah. He intimidates me."

"Is that really such a problem?"

"Kepa, DeLorenzo hates me. Every conversation we have is like the Spanish Inquisition. If I sit in front of all the department heads and recommend we shut down Lanai, he's going to bore me a new asshole."

"Dennis doesn't hate you. He just plays devil's advocate like he really means it. He's a little over the top. Big deal."

"Kepa, you don't know the guy. He goes straight for the jugular every chance he gets."

"I don't need to know him. All I have to do is observe him, which I do all the time. All he wants is for people to explain themselves. The only thing he gets really mad about is when people say shit without really thinking about it. I observe *you*, too. Once you think you've figured something out, you always sit and wring your hands over whether people will criticize it. Bruddah, your instincts are good. Just go with it."

"You think I should just put it out there?"

"A little diplomacy never hurt. Why don't you tell him that the cost of Thai pineapple production is way cheaper than the cost of Lanai production and Lanai is getting more and more expensive? Then let him figure it out. If you're not the one actually saying 'let's close it,' it might not be so hard for him to take. Maybe somebody else at the table will be the one to make the suggestion. Or you can phrase it as a question, as in 'What do you think we should do with an underperforming unit like Lanai?' The answer will probably seem obvious once the facts are on the table."

—⁕—

Tommy was always among the first to be seated at the quarterly meeting of department heads. He imagined that it made him look prepared and professional. He always sat on the same side of the table as the CEO and picked a spot several seats away, hoping that his colleagues would shield him from view. It didn't seem to help.

"Mr. Banks? Let's start today talking about your department. Why don't you tell us why it is we've seen such a drop in profits in the pineapple segment? This has been our cash cow for a lot of years and it's losing some of its heft."

"Mr. DeLorenzo, it's mostly because at our biggest pineapple plantation, the costs of production have grown persistently due to government regulation."

"Is there some reason you're talking about Lanai without naming it?"

"Uh, sorry sir. Uh, no sir."

"So what exactly is the problem, Banks?"

"Well, because of harmful environmental effects, the EPA has banned several of our most economical fertilizers and pesticides, raising costs and reducing yields. The minimum wage has risen twice in the last four years and made labor much more expensive. OSHA has begun enforcing worker safety requirements more strictly and the county supervisors recently raised our property taxes."

"I suppose you're going to tell me that these things are not problems at the Thailand or the Nicaragua facilities?"

"Correct, sir. Both of those countries have relatively little environmental regulation and because both countries have so many unemployed, the cost of labor is substantially less. They've also given us concessions on taxes to keep us there."

"Well, what do you think we should do?"

"Sir, I've been wondering about that. What should we do with an underperforming unit? It's a hard question and there are obviously a number of options, some better than others." Silence, heavy as a rock, hung from his neck while Tommy waited for something to happen.

"Mr. Banks, you're avoiding the question. We need your opinion. Everybody at the table is waiting, especially me."

"Sir, I … ." Tommy felt his windpipe constricting.

An elegantly suited man at the other end of the table leaned forward. The room turned its head. "Denny, give the kid a break. Everybody in the company has known for several years that we need to close down Lanai. We've all been afraid to suggest this because we were afraid it would smack of disloyalty. We all know how much you revere your grandfather and we didn't want to be disrespectful."

Dennis DeLorenzo stroked his chin and enjoyed the feeling of having his head rest against the dense filling of his tall-backed leather chair. "Mr. Banks, is Harry correct on this?"

"Mr. DeLorenzo, well, there are a variety of options for Lanai. We could explore them."

Dennis leaned forward and stared at Tommy. "Does your mother lay out your clothes for you before you go to work in the morning? If not, I have to wonder just how you decide what to wear. Your talent for equivocation is unmatched." Tommy sank into his suit, his shirt collar coming up nearly to his chin. "Mr. Banks, if you see a problem, you need to call it out. If you have an idea for how to solve a problem, you need to call it out, after you have done some research to see if your idea has merit. Sitting on a problem while it festers? You might as well poke a hole in the hull of your own boat. It will sink you every time."

"Yes … yes, sir.

"Harry, your point is well taken. But gentlemen, this is a business. Our business is selling fruit for a profit. If we don't make a profit, none of us have jobs. Are we clear? My grandfather was a stupendous businessman, but if he was sitting with us here today he'd say 'close it down,' which is exactly what we're going to do. If it can't be made profitable, we have no choice."

Dennis looked at his fingertips while waiting for his next thought. "Tommy, I've been afraid this day would come eventually. But the question remains about what to do with Lanai. Can we use it for some other profitable venture? Should we sell it? Can we lease it out? What's your thinking?"

"Well, closing the unit makes sense. My research suggests the costs at Lanai are only going to increase. Thailand, in particular, appears eager to attract new business and is signaling that government regulation will remain at a minimum. Plus, the supply of fresh water needed for cultivation is abundant in Thailand, unlike Lanai. But to liquidate it? To lease it? I haven't been able to come up with a good answer to that. I'm not sure if we should go that far or if we can find an alternative use for the island."

"If we keep the island, what would we do with it?"

"That's the question I keep bumping up against, sir. There doesn't appear to be any use for cultivating alternative crops. The same limits we have with pineapples we would have with anything different we'd want to grow there, plus we'd need to completely retool planting and harvesting, which would be a huge capital expense. I've looked into using Lanai as a staging area for distributions to the North American market, but the airport is too small and nearby waters are too shallow to allow sizeable cargo vessels. It appears to have potential as a resort, sir, but that wouldn't seem to fit our business model. We don't have any expertise in-house that would allow us to do that with confidence."

"Well, look how much progress we can make when you admit the limits of what you know, Banks. Let's work on the assumption we have to liquidate Lanai. If we can't figure out an alternative use, then there's not much sense in carrying it. I need for you to do some research to identify possible uses of the island. What will zoning permit? What sort of uses have people made of similar properties in the Pacific Rim? What will available resources permit? We need answers to those sorts of questions. It will allow us to assess value and to identify possible buyers." Dennis turned to his assistant. "Rees, what does my Tuesday look like next week? Am I open for lunch?"

"Yes, sir. Tuesday is open."

"Banks, come by my office on Tuesday. We can have lunch with a couple of the boys from our legal team. We need to get the ball rolling on logistics. We've got capital gains to minimize and we'll need some advice on how we might structure a deal so large. They got some clever monkeys over there who can figure out how to turn our useless desert island into a modest fortune." Dennis turned back to his assistant. "Put that on my calendar for Tuesday and call Albert Benanua and tell him I need to have him and his best land-use guy join us."

Tommy sank back into his chair, thankful he still had only one anus.

8

Lanai, Hawaii
June 20, 1977

Bobby Joe stood quietly and watched as his old friend, George Blanda, settled into his stance and prepared to swing. George waggled, starting a full-body shiver that started with the dangling of his extra-loose buttocks, worked its way up to his shoulders and then back down. He waggled a second time, shifted his feet and blinked with a purpose. George looked back at Bobby Joe, and pushed out a grim smile. Then he put his attention back to his ball and waggled some more.

He backed away and grunted. "It just doesn't feel right. It hasn't for a long time. I just can't get comfortable over the ball. Kahuna? Why don't you go first? I can tell I'm not ready."

"Georgie, it ain't but a littly old ball," said Bobby Joe. "Just give it a good whack and let's see what happens. Go ahead."

"Donald? Do you want to go?"

Donald opened his mouth but Bobby Joe spoke for him. "George, just hit it."

George settled back in and sucked in some air. His palms, as big as dinner napkins, enveloped the grip of his driver. He set his feet wide apart, his legs perfectly straight. He began his backswing; he brought his arms and his club back until his arms were slightly above parallel with the ground and his club head was pointed skyward. Then his arms began an abrupt downward move. At impact, his feet were still both firmly planted. The center of his club head struck the helpless ball with a *dink*. George's Titleist bolted skyward, heading left, and then swerved sharply right and dove through a line of pines.

Donald winced. "Holy *shit*. I wonder … ." Bobby Joe's hand darted out and grabbed Donald's bicep and pinched. Donald turned to his companion, ready to complain but quieted when he saw that Bobby Joe had crossed his lips with his index finger.

George picked up his tee and inserted it into the crevice above his right ear. "Kahuna, are you seeing this? This is my game for the last year and a half. It's killing me. I've had lessons from golf pros everywhere between Miami and Bel Air and none of them can help. I did an embarrassing pro-am with Kathy Whitworth at Pebble Beach. She couldn't help one damn bit."

"Every problem you have on the golf course has a solution. Every one. We'll get it figured out. Have faith and keep playing."

"*Faith*? In what?"

"What do you put your faith in when you heave a football down the field, expecting your teammate will catch it?"

Donald teed off and bounced joyously as his ball touched down 200 yards away and rolled another twenty yards toward the green. "Oh, yeah. That's how it's done." He lingered and stared down the fairway at his handiwork, admiring how it had turned out for him.

Bobby Joe felt the tickle of impatience while he waited for the tee box to be freed. "You know, the goddess of revenge will punish you, if you stare too long."

"Wait. … What?"

"You done yet, Narcissus?"

Donald motioned with dramatic, wristy flair, like the model on *The Price Is Right* who profited from her ability to make people covet Electrolux washer-dryer combos and Chevy Vegas.

Bobby Joe quickly set up and swung and put his ball 230 yards out, nearly in the center of the fairway. He picked up his tee and moved to grab his golf bag before the ball had touched down. He knew right where he would find it.

George found his errant missile in the woods and stood for a minute with his hands on his hips, considering both limits and possibilities. Bobby Joe watched for several seconds. "George, why don't you just drop it onto the fairway grass, over there where you entered the woods? Hitting out of the woods can be right frustrating, and there ain't nobody keeping score."

George took the drop and surveyed his path to the green – 150 yards up an uncomplicated fairway to a mostly flat green with a front flag placement that looked easy. He slid out a six iron and aimed far left of the putting surface. His shot started left and then dove hard right. It skittered in a line parallel with the front of the green and came to rest in the right rough, thirty yards short of the pin. He exhaled and shook his head. "I bet we can find that one."

Donald's approach shot landed on the far edge of the green and rolled a few inches off. Bobby Joe hoisted his ball high and stuck it just past the front edge of the green, two feet from the flag.

When his turn came, George manhandled a pitching wedge. He stroked the ground with the bottom of the club over and over, each time imagining how much effort would be required to send the ball onto the green. He sidled up and swung. He hit the ball flush but let his arms go limp at impact. The ball popped up and rolled, but was still ten yards short when it came to rest. Another stroke later, George had his ball on the green. He lined up an eight-foot putt and tapped. His ball took a perfectly straight track toward the hole but lost momentum and stopped two feet short. One more touch of the putter and it dropped in.

On the tee box for the second hole, George reached for his four iron. "If I just aim normally, I can slice it over toward the hole." He teed up and swung with the rotational force of a tornado. The face of his club came at the ball low and from inside the target line. And when contact occurred, his ball rocketed out fast, straight and high and after a classic arc that would have made Gary Player proud, it came to rest on the far side of the landing area, as far from the green as it could be while still on fairway grass. George slammed his club handle deep into his bag. "I love this game. It's just so darned … *relaxing*."

After putting out on the second green, the trio made the steep climb up to the third tee box. Bobby Joe walked close to his old friend. "So George, it looks like you don't feel any closer to figuring out life after football than when we spoke six months ago."

"How did you know?"

"Lucky guess. Any possibilities? Any ideas?"

"I had hoped broadcasting might pan out, but nobody wants old George and his scratchy voice, his wrinkles and grey hair. I thought coaching might be the thing, but that's not panning out either. The best offer I got is from a junior college near Yellowknife, Canada."

"That might be a spectacular adventure." Bobby Joe noticed that Donald wasn't laboring excessively on his march up the volcanic hill to the tee box for number three.

"Kahuna, that's almost all the way to the Arctic Circle. They have to practice in a dome. In wintertime it gets pitch black at 2:30 in the afternoon. I couldn't deal with even one dark season in Yellowknife. Man, I just can't figure it out. You know, when I was playing ball, it all just came so naturally and it was so much fun. Every day I woke up and my next step just seemed obvious and easy, but now I don't hardly have a reason to get out of bed in the morning. I need something to do with the whole rest of my life and I just can't find it. I have this big open space in front of me and nothing to fill it with."

"You'll figure it out. I know it, George."

"That's so easy to say, and everybody says it."

"Have faith and keep playing."

"You act like I have a choice."

Bobby Joe put a hand on his friend's arm. "One day at a time. Just one. It works much better that way."

When George's turn to tee off came, he grabbed for his three wood. He set up and drew back only far enough that his arms were pointing at the ground at a forty-five degree angle. He tightened and crooked his wrists until his club pointed almost straight up. Then, at impact, his ball dove down. It wormed a bristly path through the rough grass in front of the tee box and quickly came to rest sixty yards away.

By the time the threesome reached the eighth hole, George had become sullen. Whatever angry thoughts he was having, he was keeping them to himself. When he teed off, his club head struck the ground before hitting his ball. George's shot flew a restrained, but perfectly straight, 150 yards. "Well, there's the key to fixing my swing. I just have to hit the ground first. How could I have missed it?" George planked the head of his driver onto the soft ground. "Godfuckingdammit. I hate this. I can't hit a decent shot except by mistake."

Bobby Joe nodded at his friend. "I'm so sorry you're having such troubles. We'll talk after the round and get it all figured out. By the way, you should watch your language. Donald is easily offended."

Donald looked up. "Easily offended? Shit, piss, fuck, cunt, cocksucker, motherfucker and tits. I can cuss as good as anybody. You don't get good at football unless you can cuss creatively. George knows that. Everybody in football knows that."

"He's right, Kahuna. If you're golfing with football players, you're due for a vocabulary lesson. George Halas told me that a football player who don't cuss isn't trying hard enough. He said a football player who didn't cuss ought to go into something less punishing, like hockey."

"You don't say."

"Fucking ay, I say."

"George, that's the first time I seen you look happy all day. Maybe you should cuss some more."

"Cuss some more? Well, shut the front door."

Donald stood on the tee box for a minute thinking about his next shot. "You know, George, you shouldn't feel bad. This is a complicated course. On most of our holes, you have to hit it straight *and* long."

George cocked his head and whispered to Bobby Joe. "Is he trying to be funny?"

George's tee shot on the ninth hole began its familiar fade and, after it curved right, it struck a blackbutt eucalyptus. It shot straight left and vanished into a rocky chasm on the left side of the fairway – a place where many balls had landed but from which none had ever been recovered. "Well, my game may suck, but at least I'm unlucky." He stared into the dark crevices of his golf bag as he reinserted the handle of his driver. "Kahuna, I'm really not feeling it today. I think I may take a rain check for the back nine."

"George, wouldn't you like to walk the rest of the course? It might do you some good. You could just enjoy the company and the scenery. You wouldn't have to go worrying about a thing."

"Naw. If I'm out here, all I can think of is how bad my game has gotten. I just can't enjoy time on the course if my insides are all bunged up."

"Well, why don't we meet back at my shack later? You know the way from here, don't you?"

George retreated on a nearby path. Donald set up and teed off. He stroked a ball 230 yards down the fairway. When he saw his ball skirting the open canyon on the left edge, his sphincter tightened, and without even asking permission. When Donald's ball came to rest on a flat spot of short grass in the fairway, his sphincter magically relaxed. As he and Kahuna walked toward their balls, Donald stared off to the horizon. Kahuna decided it was time to bring him one step into the tent. "Donald, what do you suppose is causing George so much trouble?"

"Well, he's got a terrible slice. He needs to close his club face or something."

"Really?"

"Well, yeah. Isn't that what causes a slice?"

"I suppose. Anything else?"

"It looked like he wasn't taking his club back far enough, and he wasn't turning his hips enough. Did you notice how his back foot stayed planted through his whole swing?"

"What do you say to a man like that to get him to improve his game?"

"Isn't it obvious?"

"Is it?"

"Tell him to close his club face and to turn his hips. You know, turn his hips and shift his weight like he really means it."

"You think that will work?"

"Why wouldn't it?"

"Well, George ain't no greenhorn. He's had him quite a few golf lessons. I have a feeling he knows about the effect of an open club face and not getting all his weight on his front foot at impact. Those things he could probably fix himself. No, I'm thinking there's probably something else causing his problems."

Donald raised both eyebrows and held them near the top of his forehead where they hovered, suspended by the power of abject disbelief. "Bobby Joe, he's leaving his club face open and he's taking almost no backswing *and* his weight is too far back. It's obvious. Can't you even see that? I mean, are you sure you're the go-to guy in this village for golf lessons? Because this is basic. This is so right there you couldn't miss it."

"Is it?"

"Unfuckingbelievable. There's just no talking to you, Socrates. All you ever do is ask dumb questions. Just one after another. Hey, look, you're away. Why don't you just hit already?"

Karen Nakamura and the remarkable George Blanda were sunning themselves on Bobby Joe's patio when Donald and Bobby Joe approached. "It's lovely to see you, boys. George here is all splenetic about his golf game. He could use some male company." Karen caressed George's knee until George squirmed with discomfort. "You'll find it, George. You will."

"Splenetic? Is that what you think I am? What the hell is splenetic, anyway?"

"Splenetic means peeved and irritated to the point that your spleen is ready to burst."

"Can we make that into a cuss word? Because that's exactly what I am."

"Kahuna, George was telling me about his unhappy day on the golf course."

"Yes, he seems to be going through a rough patch."

"Kahuna, what do I do here? My game is nauseating me."

"Well, I'm wondering if maybe it has a little something to do with what you were talking about on the course today."

"Cuss words? That's ruining my game?"

Bobby Joe filled a glass half with iced tea and half with lemonade. "Actually, those cuss words seem to help a little. I'm talking about you worrying about life after football. It looks like you're a mite tense about the whole thing."

"Who wouldn't be?"

"You don't have to be. You could be happy instead, if you'd rather."

"I can just be happy? It's as simple as that? Really? Have you been smoking that stuff they grow over on Maui?"

"George, you said it yourself: you're looking for something to last you the whole entire rest of your life. If you're looking for something that big and complicated, you ain't *never* going to be satisfied."

"*This* is screwing up my game?"

"Seems like it, Chief. You said you feel stuck and unable to move on. When you swing, it looks like the same thing. You aren't really moving forward. Like, I noticed you're leaving at least half of your weight on your back foot instead of letting your body move toward your target and putting it on your front foot. You've shortened your takeaway. It makes me think you're not gung-ho about taking the next step and then the next step after that."

Bobby Joe sucked on his drink. "You don't want to let yourself move forward without a total life plan. But here's the thing: you have to move forward. You're doing it without even realizing it. If you think about just today, you can more easily have faith you'll find something that works. But for the *whole entire rest of your life?*"

"You're not going to tell me to keep my head down or something? Maybe adjust my grip? Open my stance?"

"We'll get to that. I've seen your swing when it works. It's beautiful. It's just that your head is messing with you – all that uncertainty and all that made-up stuff the city folks call *angst*. Take it on *faith* that something good will come. Think about *now*. All that worrying about tomorrow and next year puts your head in the wrong place."

George let go with a *poosh* and brushed back the stringy grey hair that had dipped into his face. "Faith? Just have faith?"

"You're out there on the golf course to relax and enjoy. All that worrying ruins the experience." Bobby Joe rose up from his seat and patted George's knee. "You have plenty of time to worry *after* your round is all over. I'll sit with you and help you do some worrying if you like."

"If I just believe things will work out, they will? Kahuna, that's complete chickenshit."

"Think about all the people who believe that there is an omniscient God. There's a gray-bearded man in heaven who sent his son to Earth, knowing that people would skewer him with spikes and hang him naked off some burnt logs in front of an ornery crowd of hooligans so he could die a bloody and horrific death. They believe God did that just because people are a bunch of helplessly screwed up idiots and need forgiveness. They believe God watches them and counts their sins against a little list of no-no's and requires them to pledge faith in Jesus. They also believe that God made this special place full of fire and pain and misery and that he sends people there who don't have faith in Jesus." Bobby Joe edged forward in his seat.

"And this is relevant, *because* ... ?"

"Why shouldn't you let yourself believe something simpler, that your life will work out for the best? You've managed to find things that made you happy so far. I mean, has there ever been a time in your adult life when you've been unhappy?"

"Well, I thought I had retired from football once, when I was about thirty. I was pretty miserable until I got back into football."

"So being miserable didn't last?"

"It got better. Only about a year later, I was back in football and having fun."

"Did it make sense that you got all unhappy about being retired?"

"Well, I was miserable. I didn't know what to do next. Of course I was worried."

"It sounds like if you had just decided to relax and enjoy the ride – well, you could have relaxed and enjoyed the ride."

"Kahuna, you try and make it all sound so goddam simple. Life is just not that simple. It's not."

"George, take it one day at a time, my friend. After a few dozen or a few hundred days, you'll look up and realize what it is that you're doing with the rest of your life." Bobby Joe checked Donald out of the corner of his eye. *He's listening. This is good.*

George tilted his head, leaned forward and squinted at Bobby Joe.

"George, you golf the way you live. You do. Most everybody does. If there is a big problem in your life, there's probably going to be a big problem in your game."

"When is the part when you tell me about Jesus Christ becoming my personal savior?"

"I'm not a Christian. I'm a golfer."

"Wait. You're not a Christian?"

"I'm just a golfer."

"Aunt Frances always said you were a God-fearing man."

"Frances saw in me what she wanted to, it seems. Which is fine."

"Well, if you're not a Christian, what the hell are you?"

"My religion is simple. My religion is kindness."

"There you go again with the simple. When I get on the plane and go back to life on the mainland, it's a Rubik's cube. Man, it's a whole world full of colored dots that won't line up."

"My daddy was a Baptist minister from China who grew up in Guizhou Province which, at the time, was a place where they spoke seven different dialects. One group thinks their Mongolian is the Lord's preferred language and two miles down the road, you find another who thinks the same thing about their Turkic. They refused to speak to one another, just on principle, which was ridiculous because they couldn't hardly talk to each other anyway. When Daddy moved us to the big city of Raleigh, North Carolina, to do missionary work, he came home one night after learning that black folks and white folks wouldn't worship at the same church, even though they spoke the exact same language. Right there, he decided America was the most complicated place he'd ever seen."

"See? Colored dots that won't line up. Kahuna, that's what I'm saying."

"Well, my point is that he decided he had to take his job one person at a time. Any more than that and it all seemed too complicated. It just couldn't be done. If he wanted to straighten out a box of rusty fishhooks, he had to do it one fishhook at a time." George sat with his hands on his knees, silent. Bobby Joe watched as George chewed on his lower lip. "Well, none of us can do much on an empty stomach. How about we boil us up some shrimp?"

—⋙—

"He says golf is the embodiment of his religious beliefs. Have you ever heard such a thing?"

"For real?"

"Teddy, he is completely serious. He says golf is how he teaches spirituality. He was selling this to George Blanda."

"What? George Blanda? Are you serious?"

"George Fucking Blanda. Swear to God. Just yesterday morning, I was watching Blanda at six foot four taking lessons from this five-foot-nothing Chinaman. It was all I could do not to laugh. The two of them standing side by side? It's like Ripley's Believe it or Not."

"Are you making this up? *George Blanda?* George Blanda is staying at your village and taking golf lessons? You played a round of golf with George Blanda?"

"He's staying with Bobby Joe at his house. Bobby Joe's got him convinced his lousy golf game is caused by his uncertainty about life after football – like figuring out his life is going to let him improve his golf game."

"You don't say?"

"Fucking ay, I say."

"So is Bobby Joe's strategy working?"

"Are you kidding? The guy's hitting with his weight on his back foot and he's leaving his club face wide open. He looks like a caveman killing his lunch. You think a little pop psychology is going to cure a swing like that? Ain't no way. Somebody needs to tell the guy to stop hitting off his back foot and leaving his club face wide open."

"Really? You think his approach is just completely wrong?"

"Jesus Christ, Teddy. You're getting just like him. Questions. Questions. What's with all the goddam questions?"

—⚇—

"He doesn't believe in Jesus? This is not right. This just can't *be*." Wendy Walker stood bolt upright after she had bent down, looking for a place to sink her tee into the soil. Donald stood by with Jerry and Tim McLeigh, each man waiting for his turn.

"Wendy, I heard him say it point blank. He doesn't believe in God, either." Tim sat by the tee box, his palms resting belly-button high on the butt of his driver. "He's not a Christian. He's just not." Donald interrupted his practice swings, not sure he heard the conversation correctly.

"But his father and his mother were Baptist missionaries. He told me himself. He was *raised* by Baptist missionaries. How could he not be Christian?"

"He tells everyone that story. I'm wondering if it's even true. Kahuna just *wants* people to think he's Christian."

"Well, a man who's not a Christian has no business leading our congregation. He needs to be making sure that our children are brought up to love Jesus."

"What bothers me most is that he keeps the village's finances under his own little lock and key. It's like he's hiding something."

Wendy put her hand on her hip, her blinding blonde hair riding on the breeze. "Do you think he's hiding something?"

"All I can say for sure is that when I suggested some common-sense changes to our bookkeeping and investments, he stonewalled me. It was his way or the highway."

Jerry blinked at the sunlight that shone directly into his watery eyes. "I can't trust a mah-mah-man who wuh-won't listen to rah-rah-reason. Cah-cah-can you?"

Wendy pondered the question as she swung her driver. She watched as her shot soared high and then fell onto the fairway as if dropped straight from the sky. "I can't trust a man who tells me to put my faith in God and doesn't even have faith himself. That's just plain wrong."

Donald squished up one corner of his mouth and considered the grass stains on the toe of his left golf shoe. "Did he really say to put your faith in God? *In God?*"

"He's always telling me to have faith – *have faith, have faith, have faith.* He knows I'm a Christian. I've told him. He's been to my house and seen my antique bibles and the statute of the Virgin Mary in my garden. What else am I going to put my faith in? Face it: he's *pretending* to be a Christian. He's basically lying to us."

"What's so wrong about it? Just to be a person who does good things for others?" Donald asked.

"How could he have any morals without religion? And how moral could he be if he lies about his religion? We need a moral leader. Someone who sets a *moral* example."

"So I guess you would go out and kill people if your Bible didn't spell it out for you? Is that the only reason you're moral?" Donald backed a half-step away. *Holy shit. Did I really just say that?*

Wendy guided the handle of her driver into her bag where it could be among its brothers and sisters. She closed her eyes hoping she could calm herself. "Donald, I'm going to pray for your soul. Because I fear that it will spend eternity in hell otherwise. You don't hardly have a chance."

The foursome played in silence as they finished the tenth hole and turned the corner to the eleventh tee. On the eleventh fairway, just over 100 yards ahead, they could see Bobby Joe and George standing and facing each other. With an iron in his hands, George was in an address position and Bobby Joe was motioning with his left hand, his fingers together as if he was imitating the motion of a club head. George was listening intently.

"Oh, no. This is going to be ugly. I golfed with this guy two days ago and he was spraying it all over the place." Donald stood and watched.

Bobby Joe took a step back. George took a full backswing and a full follow-through and finished with a flourish. His ball shot straight at the eleventh green, bouncing onto the front edge and rolling to the back edge. Bobby Joe rushed in for a hug and George awkwardly accepted it, his arms pinned tight against him. He scanned the horizon to see if anyone was watching. He spotted Donald and his three companions and flashed a grimace and gave his head an awkward tilt. *He wanted to hug me. I couldn't just say no.*

Tim sniffed. "Look at Kahuna, sucking up to celebrity. That's just pitiful. There's a complete lack of humility with this guy."

One hundred yards away, Bobby Joe pulled a ball from his pocket and dropped it and motioned for George to swing again. George's shot soared high and then dropped just shy of the front of the green and rolled to the middle of the putting surface, stopping just a few feet away from his previous effort. Bobby Joe spread his arms with excitement and reached over and hugged George again. George looked to Donald again, as if he could step in and help. *Does he always do this?*

Donald held up a palm and turned it into a slow wave. *That's who he is. That's how he does things.*

—⁓—

It was always a relief when the bell at the pavilion rang signaling that lunch was ready. Donald lifted his wide-brimmed hat and wiped the sweat from his face onto the already smudged Terrapins logo on his t-shirt. "Mavis, can I carry those tools back to the shed for you?"

"Oh, thank you Donald. You are such a dear."

Donald gathered the push lawnmower he had been shuttling across the fairway and several hand tools that Mildred and Mavis had been using on the flower garden and stowed them in a weathered storage shed tucked among the pines. "Come along, girls. Our lunch is calling us."

Lunch this particular Sunday was wahoo, caught just the day before. It was salted, wrapped in taro leaves and roasted on hot rocks.

Donald sat down with George and, as soon as he did, they were approached by the King and his sister, who sat on opposite sides of George.

"Welcome to Lanai, Mr. Blanda. I am King Kalakaua and this is my sister Lili'uokalani. You notice she is most beautiful, yes? Milky white skin, yes?"

"Time out, your Tremendousness. George is married." Donald leaned forward and whispered. "Your Tremendousness, I used to be in sales. Let's get together tomorrow and I'll tell you about qualifying your prospects."

George furrowed one eyebrow at Donald and tilted his head.

Donald shook his head and made his lips small. *I'll tell you later.*

After finishing his fruit salad, Donald excused himself and found Bobby Joe sitting alone. "Bobby Joe, you have to fill me in here. How did you get George's game to improve?"

"I just said if he would agree to not worry for two hours I could solve his swing problems. But if he couldn't do that, his swing problem would never get solved."

"And it worked?"

"I did work with him on some fundamentals. As you saw, he was leaving too much weight on his back foot and he wasn't really turning his hips and committing to his shot. He had grown so cautious, he wasn't really doing a full takeaway, which can kill a swing. Once he gave himself permission to not worry, everything fell into place."

9

Lanai, Hawaii
July 5, 1977

"Can we make this quick?" Donald asked Bobby Joe, as he struggled to keep up with his companion's quick walk. "I don't want to spend all day moving couches."

"You got a better offer from someone else?" Bobby Joe asked. "Donald, you don't have to help if you don't want to. When it comes to manual labor, you're the nearly automatic choice, my friend. You're still strong enough and young enough to get it done."

They turned the corner and came upon a bungalow that seemed, to Donald, standard issue: a peaked, silverish corrugated metal roof, simple rectangular wooden frame, and a perfectly centered front door between a pair of four-square windows. For Barbara Peel's bungalow, the trim was painted a creamy color and was set against a reassuring shade of baby blue. Barbara and her fleshiness sat on her front porch in a rocker, picking out a jerky little song on a ukulele. Just down from the front steps sat an extra-large cardboard box decorated with the ZCMI logo.

"Babsy! How are ya' darlin'?"

"Ooooh, Kahuna, you are such a sweetheart for coming over to help me out. I can't tell you how much I appreciate a generous Christian man coming to my rescue."

"Sister, there ain't no rescue going on here. Just a little help, that's all."

"Nonsense. Jesus sent you to me. I can feel it. And I'm in a terrible spot. Look at this big box. If it weren't for you two, well, I just don't know what I would do. And it's due to rain soon. Just look at that sky."

Barbara rose from her chair and stepped down from the porch. She stared up at Donald. "You must be Donald, our newest friend. I'm Barbara. Welcome. Jesus sent you too, didn't he?" She put the side of her face in full contact with his chest, her eyes closed, and put her jiggly arms around his jiggly middle. Donald hesitated, his arms up. Bobby Joe nodded and motioned with his hands. Donald reached around and hugged Barbara, who kept her head on Donald's chest and kept her arms tight around his middle. "Oh, you're a hugger. I can tell. You feel like a good Christian man. I can tell that, too."

"Barbara, um, very nice to meet you."

Done hugging Donald, she put her arms around Bobby Joe. "You're a hugger too. I love huggers."

"Babsy, when I get one of your hugs, I feel the spirit move within me, and I love it when you have a little something for me to do. It gives us a chance to visit. Tell us what you have in mind for your new sofa."

"Well, I need to get it out of the box and into the living room. The delivery company brought it over by truck and was going to charge me seventeen dollars just to carry it up the front stairs and into my living room. *Seventeen dollars!* I'll pray for those men to find the path to goodness and the benefits of charity."

"Then I'm sure they will find it, dear."

"Oh, you're one of the good ones, Kahuna. The spirit of our Lord Jesus has found a home within you."

"He inspires so many, sister. Like right now, for example, I feel a magical, divine and heavenly power that makes me want to *pick up a sofa*."

Barbara laughed. "Oh, *you*."

Bobby Joe and Donald extracted the flower-bedecked behemoth from its sturdy box and from a sealed cellophane sleeve nearly large enough to use as a hot air balloon. They carried it up the porch stairs, through the front door, and into the front living room where they set it down. Donald wiped off the sweat that had formed on the edge of his chin.

"I had thought it would look best if the back of the sofa were to the window. But now I'm thinking that it would be better if it was on the other side of the room, facing the window. Could we move it across and see how it looks?"

The men grunted and huffed until the sofa was across the room and settled it where it faced the front window. Barbara stood back and looked and then looked some more. "Oh, golly Ned, I think the back to the window was better after all." Bobby Joe smirked, widened his eyes and glanced at Donald. They picked it up and moved it once more and exhaled gratefully as they set it down once again.

"Oh, maybe it was better the other way."

Donald cleared his throat. "*Again*? Are you kidding?"

Bobby Joe clamped a hand on Donald's shoulder. "Babsy, why don't you live with it a few days? If you want to move it again, Donald and I can come back over. It's so hard to tell right away with new furniture."

"Well, alright then. That's what we'll do. Now, why don't you boys come out back? I have some lovely chamomile tea and some sweet potato cookies for you."

The trio sat under an expansive umbrella on Barbara's wrought iron porch furniture under a teak arbor and munched politely on cookies.

"Kahuna, I've been having trouble with my slice again. Everything to the right. You don't have that problem, do you? Your game always seems perfect."

"Dear, we all get there sometimes. A slice is enough to keep folks pacing the floor at two a.m. and taking the Lord's name in vain."

"What's a girl to do? I go out for a round and spend all my time in the woods looking for my ball."

"Babsy, I think sometimes you try too hard and get ahead of yourself. I've heard you say many times that we should have faith and that the Lord will provide. Now, I think you might find an answer to your little problem right there."

"Kahuna, you are speaking metaphorically?"

"Sister, I've watched your swing. When you take your club back, you don't need to use your arms to make it come down and hit the ball. Think of your torso as the power of God. It will do all the work for you. You can rely on it. It will provide. Your arms only need to come down and swing through when the power of God pushes them through. Let the heavenly power of God move your arms. You only need to guide your hands gently in the right direction once your arms start to move. Have faith. It will work. How's that? Better?"

"Oh, certainly. I can't wait to get out and try this."

"Try it lots of times. At first it might not work as well as you want. But with practice, I'm sure it will come to you."

After a few more cookies and some more polite conversation, Bobby Joe excused himself and Donald and they walked together down the red-dirt road.

"So why did you tell me you were not a Christian if you were?"

"Where in hell would you get an idea like that?"

"You just told Barbara you were Christian. That seems pretty dishonest."

"I did no such thing."

"*Let the power of the heavenly father guide your golf swing. Just have faith that God will do it for you.* What the hell was that?"

"What works for her is language and imagery that comes out of Christianity. I was talking to her in a language that works for her. She's better for it."

"You know what I think? I think you're full of shit. That woman thinks you're Christian and you're keeping her deluded. I bet she's not alone. All these people in this village support you and it's all because you delude them, too."

"That's an interesting perspective, Donald. What exactly do I get in exchange for deluding people into thinking that I'm a Christian?"

"You get the support of the village – they do what you want. You get your jollies by being *Kahuna*. They pay you whatever it is they pay you. All that."

"What do I want the villagers to do? That's a curious little question right there, don't you think? And how much do they pay me? I want to know a little more about that."

"Wait. ... What?"

"The village doesn't pay me a salary. It never has. I could save myself a lot of time and peace by not feeling so tied to this little village. Do you know how many lovely Saturdays I've spent with shut-ins reading mail and newspapers from the mainland? And I noticed, you didn't deny it when Babsy told you she thought you were a Christian. Does that make you a con man and a charlatan?"

"But I wasn't giving her spiritual guidance. I was just moving her furniture."

"Donald, the essence of faith is believing in something you cannot ever hope to prove. Babsy is going to believe what she wants and it doesn't matter what I say. So do you have faith, Donald? Do you have faith in anything you can't prove is real?"

"Listen slick, Donald O. Gibson puts his faith in the only man that never failed him, which would be *Donald O. Gibson*. It really bothers me when I see someone pretending to be a religious man when he's not. It's just wrong."

"Donald you misunderstand me and the people of the village, if that's how you feel."

"Well, then what *is* your religion?"

"My religion is a simple. My religion is kindness. I have faith in the power of kindness to move people to accomplish great things and to find enlightenment."

"*Kindness? Enlightenment?* That's salesmanship, not religion."

"If I was not sincere in my belief, and if I was selling something, then you might be right. Look, folks like Babsy, she has God and she has Jesus and the story of the crucifixion. Those are her benchmarks. I have the here and the now and I have golf and I have enlightenment that comes from kindness. Those are my benchmarks. That's my system."

"You can't be serious."

"Yes, I can be." He looked up at Donald. "So, do you have plans for dinner? I've been so busy doing for other people, I haven't been able to get to town for groceries since last week. It's about time you fixed *me* a meal for a change."

10

Lanai, Hawaii
August 1, 1977

"God knows everything about you and he loves you." Wendy Walker's arms were spread wide and her voice sounded like it was powered by electricity. "He knows all the nice things you did for your mother and daddy. He knows all the nice things your mother and daddy did for you. God knows how many hairs you have on your head. He knows *everything*."

In the front rows of pews in the Chapel of Balance, right before her, sat seventeen children, all with skin in various shades of brown. Most of them were fascinated with Wendy's platinum hair, a feature none of them had ever seen before, except in a few of the magazines that came from places on the mainland.

"Does God know your name?"

"Yes!" the children replied in unison, their voices creating a fun echo that bounced off the chapel walls.

"Does God know your birthday?"

"Yes!"

"Does God know what you had for lunch today?"

"Yes!"

"Who knows who Jesus is? Anybody?" Wendy imagined she was looking at seventeen blank checks, each of them waiting to be filled out and signed. "Anybody?"

A small hand went up. Wendy brightened. "Yes?"

"*Hay-soos* is my cousin from Manila. He comes every summer."

"Not hay-soos, honey. I'm asking about *Jee-sus*. Who knows that name? Who is *Jesus*?" Silence. Shyness. "Jesus is God's son. He's God's only son. God's beloved son." Wendy held up a picture book showing the image of a twentyish haole with a beard and long hair. He was surrounded by children. "See? This is Jesus."

"Who knows what Jesus did for us? Who knows?" More silence. More shyness. "Jesus died for us. He died for our sins." She held up an illustration of Jesus attached to a heavy wooden cross by craggy metal spikes that caused bleeding from his hands and feet. "God loves us so much, he gave his only son for us. His son died for us. All we have to do is to believe in him and we can go to heaven." Wendy turned the page and displayed an illustration of a heavenly place.

Wendy's friend, Anita, leaned in close. "We've had them sitting for twenty minutes. They're getting fidgety. Let's take them on the golf course."

—m—

On the first fairway, Wendy had each of the children, spread out in a line, tee up a golf ball and take aim with a nine iron. "Practice hitting golf balls and I'll come by and watch you hit." Small clubs were swinging to and fro.

"Alio, step on up and let's see what you can do." The small boy reared back and flung the club head toward the ball and missed. He flung it back behind him and tried again, this time eyes open with determination. He missed again. "Let's slow down. Don't go back so far." Wendy stood behind him and, with Alio holding the club, pulled it back until it was parallel with the ground. "Here. Take the club back to here and then try and hit. Keep your left arm totally straight – like this. And when you're on the downswing, bring your right elbow in close to your hip." Alio did exactly as he was told and when he swung, he tagged his target and watched it fly high and land fifty yards away.

"I did it. *I hit it.*"

"Alio, that was beautiful. Go get another ball from the pile and try again and think of Jesus every time you try and hit the ball. Every time. And remember: straight left arm."

Wendy moved on to the spot where the tallest girl in the group stood practicing. "Lili, go ahead, darling. Show me your swing."

"I practice with my daddy. I can hit the ball really good. Watch this." The round-cheeked girl set up so that her toes were only sixteen inches from her ball. She slowly pulled her club head back until it was over her shoulders. She turned her weight onto her front foot, kept her arms bent and fluid and flipped them around in a semi-circle that seemed centered on her right hip. All at once, she straightened up and, for an instant, tightened her left arm and brought the club head in with a tight flip. Her ball clicked off the face of her club and flew high and straight. It landed 120 yards down the fairway.

Lili smiled and looked up to see what reaction she would get. "My daddy and I hit golf balls together sometimes in Dole Park. He says my swing is wonderful because it's so different."

"Oh, dear. We need to work on that. Lili, you need to step back from the ball and when you swing, keep your left arm straight and tight the whole way through. Here's another ball. Try again."

Lili took half a step back and waggled. "Farther back, Lili. Take another half step. You need to feel like you're reaching for the ball." Lili shuffled further back and suddenly felt Wendy's hands guiding her arms. "Left arm straight. Totally straight all the way through your swing. And pull your right elbow close to your hip on the way down." Wendy guided Lili's arms to demonstrate. "Go ahead."

Lili did as instructed. At the top of her back swing, she looked wobbly. At the bottom of her downswing, she stumbled and put out a foot to keep from falling. "I missed. I totally missed. It made my shoulder hurt."

"Practice that swing. You'll get it. Left arm straight. Right elbow in. Just remember those things. Left arm totally straight. Every time you hit the ball, think of Jesus. He's guiding you."

11

Lanai, Hawaii
August 18, 1977

Rubber sharks, empty bottles of grape Nehi, a polka-dotted pair of bikini bottoms that looked as if they needed to be laundered, a snow globe from Saskatchewan and a stringless ukulele autographed by Jerry Lee Lewis were all suspended from the ceiling in a broad net. Beneath it, one hand wrapped around a Jack and Coke, Donald focused on his prey.

"The Titanic."

She kept her attention on the television behind the bar, which was displaying images of a man named Tommy John in a Dodgers uniform who was making batters swing helplessly.

"The Titanic."

"I heard you the first time."

"Not a very good icebreaker, is it? Hey, look. I'm Donald. It's nice to meet you." He looked her in the eye. She remained stoic and hoped that by staring at the bar, the awkwardness would disappear. "And you are?"

"Uninterested." She pulled four dollars from her pocket, slapped it down and gave a nod to the barkeep.

Donald swiveled his stool so he could focus on his drink and returned to watching the game.

"Mister Donald, you need to lighten up."

"Huh?"

The barkeep was a motherly woman in a sleeveless, cotton dress which revealed her extra-jiggly upper arms. "You trying too hard with woman you don't know. Nobody on island go for that."

"I've been picking up women in bars for almost thirty years. I *know* what I'm doing."

"Not on Lanai you don't, bruddah. This whole different ballgame."

"Did you hear what I just said? I know what I'm doing."

"Maybe your head too hard. You know, on mainland, woman who wants to get quick sexy time have it easy. Guy disappear next morning. He all gone. Here? Not possible. Next day, quick sexy man just down road or in market or at laundromat. See, except for teenagers, that kind crap" she waved her fingers at him "not fly here."

"For real?"

"For real."

12

Lanai, Hawaii
September 3, 1977

"Those sonsabitches are playing so goddam slow. Can't they pick it up a little?" Donald stood in the middle of the seventh fairway. He had one hand deep in his pocket. The other arm was extended, hand on the butt end of his standing five iron, as he waited for a foursome to finish on the green, 170 yards ahead. "Do they have any idea what it does to *me* that they can't keep a four-hour pace? It's just infuckingconsiderate."

"You might try and be a little more patient, Donald," said Bobby Joe. "Aren't there times when the world has to wait on you?"

"When I'm on the golf course, I'm moving ahead, always moving ahead. I'm keeping up with the foursome in front of me so the foursome behind doesn't have to wait on me. That's common courtesy. *This?*" he motioned ahead "is just plain rude. They're thinking of no one but themselves. Total selfishness."

Bobby Joe squinted and shook his head as he looked at their playing partner, Kia'i Pieper, a gracious woman as slender as a knitting needle. She had never been seen on the golf course in anything but an ankle-length skirt and a long-sleeved, white blouse. "Donald," she said, touching his bicep and looking at him from beneath her straw boater, "that woman in the foursome ahead of us, the one with the turquoise flowered shirt, is Masako Higa. She's just come back from bypass surgery and is moving a bit slower than usual. Give her some time. I think she might need it until she has recovered her strength."

"You guys don't get it, do you? If you can't play the game the way it's supposed to be played, you shouldn't be on the course. How many foursomes are stacked up behind us like planes at O'Hare because of this *one woman*? That's not how it should be. Look at this foursome on our heels. They're sitting back there on the tee waiting to go and they're driving me crazy. I can't stand that they're right behind me. I just can't hardly think about playing right knowing they're back there staring at me and waiting for me move along already."

"It's just too pretty a day to be worried about such things. Don't you think, Donald?"

Donald stared back at Kia'i. "Puh-lease. I'm out here to enjoy myself. How can I do that when I have to do all this standing around? I mean, are you having fun? We should be golfing and all we're doing is talking about this slow foursome in front of us."

"Donald, do you have to complain so much?" Bobby Joe asked. "Some of us might be feeling contented if you weren't."

"I wouldn't be complaining if this foursome in front of us weren't moving so slowly. Which gets me back to my point. They're being rude. Honestly, somewhere out there is a tree, tirelessly producing oxygen so *that woman* can breathe. I think she owes it an apology."

Kai'i looked at the five wood she had planned to use for her next shot and then back at Donald. She stooped down in ladylike fashion, knees and heels together, and picked up her bag from the ground. She slid her club back in with its mates. She walked several yards down the fairway, picked up her ball and then came back to confront Donald. "I'm going home. I will be praying that you find contentment and patience. I'll have to pray I find some too because right now, I'm just about out. I just can't take any more of you today." She walked back to the sixth green and made a left turn into the woods and onto a path that led to her corner of the village.

Donald sniffed. "Who does she think she is, Lillian Fucking Carter?"

"Donald, do you have any idea what you just did?"

"Huh?"

"You might as well have just spit in the face of Mother Teresa. That nice woman up there on the green? Masako? She was a physical therapist in Honolulu before she came to live in the village. She has helped just about every single person in this village recover from injuries at one time or another. Dixie, for example? She injured her back a few years ago and her doctor told her she would never golf again. He gave her some painkillers, told her to just quit and said she would have to get surgery if she didn't. She was devastated. After two weeks working with Masako, Dixie was back on the course, fine as a frog."

"Oh, yeah?"

"Kai'i has chronic problems with her feet. Sometimes, that poor girl can't hardly walk it hurts so bad. Masako gets her back up and running every time. She never asks to get paid. She just does it out of goodness. It don't matter if it's a nice day and Masako could be out playing golf. If somebody needs her help, she's there to give it. That's who she is."

Bobby Joe looked Donald over to see if his words were penetrating. He saw no clues. "She's about the most beloved person in the whole village. She's the one we look to as an example of what it means to be a *good Christian*, and here you went and said that she didn't deserve to go breathing up her share of oxygen. So I'm guessing you made Kai'i a mite peeved."

Donald shook his head. "Life's tough. She'll get over it."

"Well now, let's suppose that Kai'i was bad-mouthing Dixie. Could you look her in the eye and tell her you'd pray that she find patience and contentment? Could you be *that* kind?"

"Like any of that would *ever* happen."

"It's just something to think about. While you're at it, here's another something to think about. Why do you suppose it bothers you so much that you have a foursome on your heels? Why are you so obsessed with what's behind you?"

"Why does it bother me? Holy shit, man. Are you completely thick? It bothers me because *I have a foursome right on my heels.* Why else would it bother me? Why does it bother you?"

"Donald, it doesn't bother me. Look up there on the green ahead of you. Do they look like it bothers them that they have a threesome right on their heels?"

"No it doesn't bother them, and *that's* their problem. Don't you even get it? They're rude as hell. They're dicking around up there while we stew in our own juices."

"Donald, look back at the foursome behind us. Do they look like it bothers them that they're right on our heels?"

"Well, of course it bothers them. They have to do a shitload of sitting around. For all they know, they're waiting on *me*. They're having a shitty six-hour round because Mr. Donald Dorkazoid is farting around on *their time*."

"Do they look bothered?"

Donald looked over his shoulder. He saw four men reclining on the grass around the number seven tee box, using their golf bags as back rests. They were chatting and laughing. As Donald watched, the previous foursome caught up with them, sat down and joined them.

"Bobby Joe, they're idiots. They don't know enough to realize they should be half done with their round by now."

"Donald, do you have to be somewhere by a certain time after your round is over?"

"Give me a break, already."

"What's your hurry? Why are you so impatient with a woman you've never even met?" Bobby Joe motioned up the fairway where Masako and her partners were walking off the green.

"And your point would be?"

"Donald, that is my point. What *is* your hurry? Why are you so impatient with a woman you've never even met? Why do you imagine that these people you've never met," he motioned behind, "are so impatient with you? Why can't you just be content to be on the golf course on a lovely day?"

Donald looked up the fairway toward the now-empty putting surface; the foursome ahead were just off the green collecting their golf bags. "Do you think I should wait to hit until that group gets a few yards past the green? Because sometimes I hit it thin and my shot goes long. I'd hate for them to feel like I was hurrying them along."

"Donald, I think we may have made some progress."

13

Lanai City, Hawaii
September 3, 1977

"Good morning, Donald. It's *lovely* to see you." Mazie Horono, a motherly and thick-waisted woman, pulled off her reading glasses and arose from behind her desk in the front room of the small house that served as Karen Nakamura's law office. She took Donald's right hand and held on with both of her own and didn't let go. Donald resisted the urge to take his hand back. He couldn't avoid the anxiety that came from being close to an unattractive woman who was coming on to him.

Whenever Mazie spoke, her voice sounded quiet and controlled, as if she had trained her incisors and bicuspids to screen out harsh elements that lurked within. The version of Mazie that Donald always saw left him heavy with fear that her true self needed to be concealed from view. This surprised him; it was rare that anyone's mere presence could leave him squirmy. "I so hope you have been enjoying your new home. Yes? You are *liking* Lanai?"

"Well, yes, I suppose. It's very nice here, and the golf is good. Hey, is Karen available? I really need to talk with her."

"We are happy to have you on Lanai, Donald. Why with you here, it feels like a little bit of Dixie is still with us. With you living in her old place, it doesn't feel so much like she has left us." Mazie began massaging Donald's hand. He clenched his teeth and looked down at Mazie's fingers. When he realized she was staring him in the face, he stared back. "I really need to see Karen."

"Donald, you know if you ever need anything, *anything at all*, you can always come to me. I would be so happy to … to give you anything I could. Like, I could come over and cook for you, if you would like."

"Mazie, can you please check? I need to see Karen."

Mazie retreated an inch, but she didn't let go right away. "I will tell Karen you are here and see if she can fit you in." Mazie released his hand. Donald exhaled. He put his hands in his pockets where nobody else could grab them.

Donald stood just inside the front window, staring out at two young women in impossibly tiny bikinis as they flip-flopped past the house. Mazie motioned him back to Karen's office.

"What can I do for you, Donald?"

"Can I speak to you confidentially, you know, client to lawyer? I'm here to ask you something."

"Yes. Everything you say is held in complete confidence."

"Well, instead of four million bucks for three years, can I just get one million for one year? I was thinking you might actually prefer it that way."

"Donald, where is this coming from?"

"Dixie's will says I get four million dollars if I stay on the island for three years. For each year that's well over a million bucks. I'm saying let me just have one million after one year. It's a win-win. See, you only have to spend one million and not the entire four."

Karen leaned back in her chair and dropped a pen on her desk. *Maybe he's finally going to ask.* "Donald, the will says you have to stay three years. It says that in black and white. Plain as day. Have you read it? I can make you another copy if you want."

"All I need to know is you're the one appointed to administer the will, and you're a lawyer. I mean, *you're a lawyer.* You can do whatever you want, right? You can keep three million instead of giving it all away. You only give away one million after I've been here a year. See? Win-win."

"Donald, I can't do whatever I want. I have to do what the will says. It says three years. Three full years."

"There's always a way to work things out. Always."

"Donald, it's a little surprising you're making this request. Dixie told me this might happen."

"She said that? Really?"

"Really."

Donald looked in his lap. "If we did it for just one year and one million, who would know? Dixie's not here to complain about it. Her beloved nephew would still get a large chunk of her estate, which is what she wanted. He would just get it a little sooner."

"Donald?"

"Yes?"

"Three years. That's the deal."

14

Lanai, Hawaii
September 10, 1977

Donald measured the board twice before starting to cut it with a handsaw. He had Ramona hold down one end while he sawed at the other, and as he sawed back and forth, sweat dripped from his chin and mixed with sawdust into a pinkish roux. When he had cut all the way through, he held the board up against the empty space inside of the garden shed and found, as he expected, that it fit perfectly. He pulled nails from his back pocket and began to hammer.

As he measured another board, he interrupted himself. "Ramona? How do you hit the golf ball so far?"

"Ask Kahuna. He's the one who gives golf lessons."

"I'm asking you."

"I don't know if I can explain it very well. Not like Kahuna."

"Give it a try. C'mon."

Ramona wrinkled her lips and stared into the distance. Then she looked Donald square in the eye. "Kahuna told me that everybody is different and that everybody has to golf in a way that fits them. If I tell you what works for me, it probably won't help much."

Donald measured the next board. Then he measured again, starting from the opposite end. He inserted a yellow pencil in the crevice above his left ear.

"So when you hit a tee shot, how do you do it? What's the way that fits you?"

"If you try and golf like me, it probably won't work. You're not me."

"Oh, come on already. Just tell me."

"Kahuna told me that the less I try to do and the slower I try to think about my swing, the farther I can hit."

"Wait. … What?"

"Kahuna says that. Honest."

"Yeah, but what does it mean?"

Ramona shrugged her shoulders. "So are you going to saw this board or what?"

"Yeah, I'm going to cut it. So what do you think about when you hit? What are you trying to do exactly? Just tell me what I should do. I want to hit as long as you do."

"I'm not sure I know you well enough for this."

Donald blanched. "I'm just asking about golf. This isn't personal."

"No. It's not that. I don't know who you are yet. I can't give you golf advice without knowing who you are and how you think."

"Go ahead. Try me. Just tell me what works for you."

Ramona tensed up. "My swing comes from my spirit, which is inside here." She put her hands on her stomach. "My arms just have to cooperate with my spirit. They only do something when my spirit tells them they have to. My spirit moves and I leave my arms back as long as possible until my spirit tells them they have to move. Not one second before."

"That's how you hit it long?"

"That's how I hit it long."

Donald began sawing on his pencil mark. Then he straightened up. "How do you hit it short?"

"It's complicated. I'm not sure I can explain."

"Try me."

Ramona breathed in slowly and then forced an exhale. "Kahuna says I have to treat every short shot like somebody new I just met. I have to get to know them before trying to do too much. You know – examine them. After a while, every shot reminds you of a shot you've already seen. If you take time with each one and examine it carefully, you can remember what worked well."

"Ramona, this isn't helping."

"I tried to tell you. If you want to play better, you should talk to Kahuna. He always seems to know what will work. Really. It's like magic."

15

Lanai, Hawaii
October 8, 1977

Donald realized he was awake but not fully conscious. It felt like he had lit a paper match in the corner of a large, dark room. He opened one eye a little less than halfway. Then he froze. He didn't dare open it any further and he didn't dare close it, either. He was so dehydrated, his eyelid and his eyeball felt like pieces of Velcro stuck together. Donald imagined the skin of a tangerine being peeled off. Then he imagined that happening to his eye.

He awoke a little more and became aware that his tongue felt abnormal. If he could have seen it, he would have said it looked like a Shake 'n Bake pork chop. He took two breaths through his nose, became slightly more awake, and deduced that his tongue was coated with the reddish-brown grit that was everywhere on Lanai. The sensation was not pleasant.

He tried to breathe more deeply and couldn't. He was choking on clods of soil piled up against the roof of his mouth. Urgency and anxiety filled his chest and rose into his throat. His face was pressed into soft dirt and seemed to be held there by dark possibilities.

He tried to get up but could not. His right leg was stuck against the ground like it was a chicken wing pressed flat. His ankle was pinned beneath his overturned Suzuki. His head resounded with the ballpeen thump of a hangover that was wedged tight behind the bridge of his nose. He wondered if he would find words adequate to describe this misery the next time he spoke to Ted.

The morning sun rose just high enough that its rays hit Donald's open eye. He moved an arm to shield his face. A voltaic pain sprinted from his shoulder through his neck and into his ear. It was a bright orange burst that came on so fast that Donald released a girly shriek that, at first, didn't appear to come from anywhere within himself. As he struggled for comfort, he was overcome by the sulphurous stink of a clay-like wedge of shit stuck between the cheeks of his ass. The wedge had saturated the back of his khaki shorts hours ago and had mostly dried, leaving an unreachable and scratchy affliction that stretched from the small of his back down to his scrotum.

Donald began hyperventilating through his nose. Sparkly stars appeared and disappeared that he knew didn't exist.

Oh, holy Jesus. This is not good.

Donald thought of the surfer boy who had drowned at Lopa Beach last week, after he got pulled deep by a plunging breaker. How quickly did the boy go from free and happy, carving a line across a blue wall, to feeling doomed? Could the boy, from the deep, have seen the surface of the water? Did he think he could reach it? Or did he right away realize that his life force would be extinguished? Did he give up and accept death or did he die pursuing more life?

Donald, along with a small crowd, saw the skinny boy's tanned body, a packet of acute angles, eyes open and pupils fixed, when he was brought ashore by the search and rescue motorboat. There was no drama and no grief. There was only a figure, both beautiful and grotesque, wearing knee-length swim trunks and a woven, hemp anklet that Donald figured, correctly, had been a gift from a lovely young woman. A team of EMTs wrapped him in a sheet and carried him away, just as neat as a hunk of beef headed home from the butcher's shop.

The thought of Donald's predicament felt larger than himself and left him looking for the handles that he could grab to reassert control. Donald tried to make himself weep, thinking it would make him feel better. He snorted cool morning air in silence and exhaled with the staccato bursts of a toddler in need of his mommy and a drink of juice. He was so dried out that he could shed no tears. His vocal chords were as stiff as a pair of kitchen matches and after several minutes of whininess, they lost the ability to make any sound more noticeable than a sigh. When he tried to shout, seeking help from anyone who might be able to hear him, out came white noise.

Sunday mornings were supposed to be peaceful affairs that included coffee, the newspaper and a couple of bagels on the back patio. Sunday morning was when you hoped that the young thing who had followed you home the night before would take you back to bed because neither of you had yet gotten enough. That kind of pleasure was not to be found if, on Saturday night, you had pounded down eight mai tais and two coconut rum shooters at John-John's Happy Shack in Lanai City and if you had been foolish enough to get behind the wheel of a tippy little Suzuki, sitting on top of your seatbelt, and had bounced down rutted and uneven Laniola Road where it was notched into the side of a steep hill. If you had done that, you would probably mistake a small opening between some trees for the road home. If that happened, it was nearly certain that you would roll into a ravine, tossing yourself partly out and digging the side of your vehicle into a crystalline layer of soil that was home to ant-like creatures who liked your scent. It was also likely that you would become invisible to any charitable Christians who might happen to pass by in search for a soul in need of salvation.

It was enough to make a man get philosophical and to ponder his future, even to speculate on how short his future might be. When such a lethal and broad array of agonies plagued a man simultaneously, it led him to consider how many fates might be worse than death. Compared to paralysis or to a permanent coma, could death really be so bad? Compared to laying for hours in your own filth, dehydrated, forced to be silent, your face pressed into soft soil, death might be a relief.

Donald winced and blew out a burst of air. He couldn't allow himself to drift into thoughts of giving up so easily. He wouldn't. He *had* to hope for a miracle, for a rescue. Yes, he was trapped in a remote corner of a remote island, out of view of anyone, hidden in a place where no one seemed likely to find him. The grains of sand in his hourglass seemed to have nearly run out. But a well-prepared Boy Scout could hike past, find Donald and summon help with a flare gun. Just as possible, a super-intelligent dog would wander past. In his imagination, Donald knew the dog – it was a Newfoundland, ironically named *Sober* – would recognize a man in distress and run home to its owner. *What is it, boy? There's trouble? No, wait. There's a man in trouble? Wait, he's, he's ... stuck under a car? And he's still alive? Take me to him, boy!*

No Boy Scouts showed up and no dogs. Donald's stomach growled like morning had passed and lunchtime had arrived. Pains that felt like they had been injected on the tip of a rusty ice pick penetrated deeper into his forehead, into his neck and shoulders and kept going, burrowing into his spine. No amount of wriggling made anything feel better.

The thoughts that came in such a moment were the kind that could slice through the heavy, blue veil of a thousand treasured delusions. They were the kind of thoughts that were likely to leave an impression as lasting as the one a disobedient child might get when he reached up, beyond the range of his vision, and touched a hot stove. They were thoughts, Donald believed, he would have to keep to himself. He would not have the chance to share them with anyone. They would leave this world with him. That would be so wrong, and so motherfucking *unfair.*

Hadn't he been a total asshole to Kimmy? Didn't she deserve to hate him? She'd wanted children so much and he had refused her and gotten a vasectomy without telling her. She'd wanted his love and attention and he wanted nothing more than the effusive affection of football fans looking to buy shiny Fords. Shouldn't he have offered her a few words of regret? Of apology? Of appreciation? To let her know it really was his goddam fault?

Had he ever told Ted how good it was to have him as a brother? A guy who would be honest with him and who would help him in his hour of need? And he had never shown Dixie just how much he had loved her – *really* loved her. She had put her whole life on hold for him and Teddy. Who knew? Then there was Theresa, the girl who lived in Annapolis by the library who fell in love with him the summer after ninth grade. Hadn't he permanently hardened that sweet girl's heart by demanding, over the phone no less, that she take off her clothes and let him screw her? For years, Donald shuddered when he thought of it. It was a stinky-ass thing to do and he knew it, even as he was doing it. He could never make amends. Out there somewhere was a woman who was telling this twisted little story about this square-jawed football hero that just about everybody knew of and that nobody seemed to realize they should have been despising all these years.

So many mistakes. So many regrets. So much to atone for. And no time.

Donald forced his half-opened eye closed and hoped for sleep. Could he let everything go dark and drift into death? Wouldn't that be the best way? The easiest way? Was it too much to hope that it could happen so simply?

Oh, dear God, just get it over with. Get it done. I'm ready.

With a speed that surprised even him, Donald's dread transformed to hope by the sound of screechy brakes.

He stilled. *There are rescuers nearby. Oh, dear God.* He tried screaming but could only muster a whisper. He grimaced and tensed his gut and tried to scream again. No luck. He felt around for a rock that he could use to bang against the vehicle frame. Would it be enough noise to attract attention? *How long will they be there? Will they leave me?* He found an orange-sized stone that he wedged between his fingertips. He swung and hit the sheet metal surrounding the rear wheel well. It generated a modest tap. Again, harder. His effort yielded only a slightly louder tap. He reached out and pushed against an electric force that singed his guts as he lifted his chest off the ground, twisted his torso, extended his arm toward the car horn and pressed. Out came a glorious, sustained *whoooooonk.* Then another. Donald collapsed, grunting and inhaling granules of red soil and praying he had attracted attention. *Please come. Oh, Lord. Please.*

"That's Dixie's Suzuki. Dr. Arai, I think we've found him." Bobby Joe, Toby and Dr. Arai raced to the top of a steep slope, about thirty yards above the Suzuki, where they could see ruts dug into the dirt by a car that had slipped off the road and rolled downhill. Tangled in the underbrush, if one looked carefully, was the top edge of a roll bar mounted to a vehicle that had an idiotically short wheelbase and which had been the subject of class-action litigation because of its tendency to flip. They hesitated, unsure of the best way to negotiate the gravelly hill without falling.

Bobby Joe made a megaphone with his hands. "Donald, we're coming. Hang on."

"You will please stay here while look at patient. Picture maybe not pretty." Dr. Arai, remarkably agile and balanced for a man of seventy-five, negotiated his way down the slope. He kneeled next to the vehicle, which was lying on its side, and eyed it cautiously, afraid it might roll some more. He got close and leaned over the car frame, looking into the cavity left by the missing passenger door.

"Ah, Mister Gibson. So lovely to see you. How are you today?"

"Doc," Donald whispered, "Doc, thank God you're here. Get me out of here. I'm stuck and my neck *hurts*. Get me out."

Doctor Arai looked up the hill behind him and motioned for Toby and Bobby Joe to join him. In a moment, the pair was by his side. "Mister Gibson, you can move hands and arms? Yes?"

Donald struggled to whisper. "Yeah, I can move my hands and my arms, Doc. Just get me out of here already."

"Must be most careful, Mister Gibson. Most important not to cause harm. Can you move legs and feet?"

"Doc, my legs are fine." Donald kicked up his free leg. "See? Can you get me out of here now?"

"You have pain? Where is any pain?"

"My neck and my shoulder and my back and my head hurt like shit." He heard Bobby Joe breathing hard. "Bobby Joe, can you just help get me outta here? Just get me out, already. This is killing me. It fucking *hurts*."

"We must have ambulance. But first, Toby and Bobby Joe, please to help me extract patient from car. Mister Gibson, you will pull out ankle when car lifts. But not to move from ground. Please to rest. Just to rest."

Bobby Joe pulled out a pocketknife and cut away most of the vinyl that formed the roof over the passenger compartment, giving the trio the ability to reach Donald, if it proved necessary. The three rescuers kneeled and grunted as they lifted on the top edge of the roll bar, which was uphill from the body of the vehicle. When the vehicle frame lifted just a few inches, Donald pulled out his ankle from the pinch point. He wiggled his foot, happy that he had regained possession and that it moved, even if it moved stiffly. The rescuers let the car settle back against the ground.

Donald started to roll, seemingly ready to stand but quickly found his shoulders pinned by Dr. Arai who was reaching in through the hole in the roof. Donald looked at him with a creased forehead and squinted eyes. *Don't be a jerk. Let me up already.*

"Please to be resting. You must rest. If you rest, you will be fine. This I know." Donald reclined again, his freed foot resting on the inside of the vehicle.

Bobby Joe scampered up the hill and zoomed away in his Jeep to find help. Dr. Arai sat on the ground next to Donald. "We wait. You wait. Ambulance return. You see. This I know."

Within only a few minutes, two EMTs came bounding down the hill with what looked like an orange surfboard. They encased Donald's neck in a clamshell-hinged tube of hard plastic and bolted him to the board with webbed straps.

"Doc, I used to play football. I've had a sprained neck before," Donald whispered. "I know what this is. They don't need to pack me up like a tuna. Just let me up. I just need some Percocet and I'll be fine. Don't let them take me to the hospital. I don't want to go." The four men ignored Donald's plea, picked up the board, hauled it uphill and loaded it into the ambulance. With every bump the vehicle took on the unpaved road to town, Donald tried to scream as his neck spasmed and the pain jabbed him like a steak knife. He tried to cry, too. But out came no tears.

"Drink," he whispered to the dark-skinned EMT seated next to him in the ambulance. "Need drink. Need water."

The EMT broke the cellophane seal on a plastic bottle of sterile saline solution, typically used to irrigate wounds, and he attached a pointy nozzle. He lifted the tip to Donald's lips and squeezed. Unable to turn or move his head, Donald sucked in the slender stream of water with a wide-open mouth. The EMT stared as Donald opened and gulped. Opened and gulped. The flesh around his eyes was unnaturally puffy and pallid. The skin of his eyeballs had turned grayish for lack of moisture. His lips circled wide and round and then closed in a desperate reach for more water. The EMT decided that Donald looked like the crazed three-pound kawakawa that he had recently hooked on a drag reel out near Pailolo Channel, splayed on a boat deck, out of the water for the first time in its life and bewildered as to why all this flapping and wiggling was getting him absolutely nowhere.

No matter how Donald might have been tested, he found it easy to appreciate a community that could be relied upon to bring him baked goods and sandwiches and salads when he suffered self-imposed injuries that made it hard to care for himself. Stowed away in his refrigerator, all compliments of caring friends and neighbors, was a large plate of grilled salmon in a ginger glaze, two pounds of steamed shrimp, three different kinds of fruit salad in decorative bowls and about a dozen baked meat pies stacked in a pyramid and filled with cubed Spam and spices. There were also a handful of mysterious tubular bundles wrapped in moistened taro leaves that smelled so much like heaven, one would be tempted to think that they came from angels who were pleased, solely for your sake, that you weren't yet ready to join them.

"It's a damn good thing you guys found me," Donald squeaked, his voice still hoarse. "I could have died out there. I was pinned down and hurting and nobody could see me. I was starting to feel a little desperate. I mean, my world could have come to an end. A complete end. Can you imagine? I mean, *can you imagine*? Jeez, what if I had died?"

"Let's just think about that we *did* find you. You're safe and sound." Bobby Joe fiddled with the divot tool that always seemed to be in his pocket, thinking he would like to find a way to change the topic.

"Yeah, but what if you didn't? What if I died? A slow, agonizing death from exposure, just yards from help. I mean, I can't stand the thought that you could have just passed me by, you know? So how did you find me, anyway?"

"Mahealani, the polite woman behind the bar who served you all those drinks, called me at home. Do you remember that you refused her offer to sleep in the spare room in the attic space above John-John's?"

"Oh, hell. I can't imagine turning down a woman's invite to sleep over. Holy fucking cow. I must really have been tanked."

"She said you stumbled out to your Suzuki and almost fell out of your seat, just trying to get it started. She tried calling your house late the next morning to see if you got there safely and when she got no answer, she called me."

"How in the hell did she know my number?"

"Do you know how many haoles there are on this island named Donald?"

"How many of us are there? We should form a little club."

"Donald, there's fewer than three thousand folks living on Lanai and almost all of them can trace their lineage to either Polynesia or mainland Asia. Think about it."

Donald made a face. "Seriously. How did you know where I was? There's four miles of road between here and town."

"There ain't but a handful of little jiggety-jogs in Laniola Road, and they're right close together. The rest of the road is mostly straight. If you're drunk and you're driving in the dark and you're going to have an accident on your way home, those little jogs are really the only place to do it."

"You even thought to bring Dr. Arai and Toby. You had medical talent and some muscle to help. That's good planning."

"You know, Donald, quite a number of folks have lost control on those funny little curves. With as many visitors as we get who want to drive like they're on the mainland, you won't be the last."

Donald's eyes got big and he tried to nod. He thought about rubbing his temples but then remembered that doing so would make his shoulder and neck scream at him. So he sat still. Completely still.

"Well, listen, I'm glad you're on the mend, Donald. I've got to go visit with Mildred Hagood. She is stuck at home for a few days after getting surgery for one of her cataracts."

"Good to see you, Kahuna. Really good."

"Uh, Donald? Hey, you're *welcome.*"

"Uh, what? Oh, yeah. Yeah. Look, man, thanks for saving my life. I mean it, Kahuna. You and Dr. Arai and Toby really came through for me. Like nobody else has – ever. I don't think I'd be sitting here if it wasn't for you. Really, I mean it. Thanks. I totally love you guys."

"You're very welcome, Donald. It will be good when you're well enough to get back out on the golf course."

"That just can't be soon enough. I'm dying to get out and play. My game is going to hell. I hate to think how bad I'm going to play once I get out there."

"All things in time. All things in time."

Donald reached out low and slow from his reclining perch on his couch so he wouldn't hurt himself and took Kahuna's hand. His eyes moistened. "Kahuna? I owe you, man. I really owe you. For the whole rest of my shitty little life, I owe you."

"You don't owe me a thing, Donald. I'm just doing for folks what they do for me and for each other."

"Holy understatement, Batman. Kahuna, *come on.* You saved my ass. I was at death's door and it was ready to open when you came along. Seriously, I owe you."

"Donald, don't go saying that. It wouldn't be good. If you want to feel like you owe someone, then think about the village. Mahealani could have called anybody in this village and things would have turned out just the same. It could just as easily have been Jerry McLeigh she called. Or maybe she didn't call anybody and Mrs. Tomoka found you when she was on one of her long runs across the island. Don't forget Mahealani herself. If she hadn't been concerned about you and made that phone call, you might still be laying on the hill. Donald, if you want to show your appreciation, then do things for some of the nice folks in the village who need some help now and again. You know as well as I do that we got plenty of those."

—⚅—

"How are you today, Mildred?" Kahuna reached out and gave her a hug, knowing that, on some days, Mildred was too timid to be the first to offer an embrace. "Happy to have the cataract surgery done, I'm sure."

"Oh, Kahuna, having vision problems is just *the worst thing*. This had near about ruined my golf game. And I couldn't see the pictures of my grand-nieces and grand-nephews that my brothers and sisters send me from the mainland."

"I'll be very happy to see you back out on the course. And I'm sure you'll really enjoy seeing those pictures."

"So, Kahuna, how is our new friend Donald getting along? Is there anything I should know about him?"

"Anything you should know about him? Mildred, do you want me to share personal details of his life? Isn't that *his* business?"

"I didn't mean it like *that*. I wasn't being nosy. I wasn't. Not at all."

"Mildred, I can tell you this. He offered me sincere and heart-felt thanks today for a time when I helped him out. And he called me *Kahuna* for the first time ever. I think I may be gaining his confidence and his friendship. I hope it means that he's on a good path."

"Do you think he's ready to accept Christ as his personal savior?"

"Mildred, no. He's nowhere near there. I don't think he ever will be."

"Well, there's no hope for him, is there? He's a doomed soul. Oh, how pitiful."

"Dear, I didn't say *that*. Christianity is a beautiful thing. But it's not the only path that will lead a person to become an enlightened and charitable soul who cares for those around him. I'm sure you can think of at least one other path to enlightenment and grace that doesn't involve belief in Jesus as our savior."

"Hmmm. That's really surprising, and funny. Because Donald doesn't *look* Jewish."

—⚅—

"You need money for *what?*"

"Teddy, the hospital sent me a three-thousand-dollar bill for a bunch of tests I didn't need and for the two nights it took them to figure out I didn't need to be there. Plus they charged me for a ride in an ambulance I didn't want and a ride in a thirty-year-old medical helicopter that ought to be scrapped. I don't have that kind of money. I told them I didn't even want to *go* to the hospital."

"What the hell happened? How could you spend three thousand dollars on medical care?"

"It's a long story. You don't want to hear it."

"Uh, *yeah*. I think I do. This story is going to be the most interesting thing I hear all day. Being a lawyer is boring and stupid, remember? Who was it that told me that? Um, who? … Oh, yeah. It was *you*, butt muncher."

"Oh, look, I had a car accident. That's all. The damn roads out here are just shitty little things. At night, there's no lights and so I ran off the road and rolled down a hill. I sprained my neck and got my ankle twisted under the car and got knocked unconscious. I coulda died out there if they hadn't found me. It was pretty awful. You shoulda seen it. Just awful."

"So how many drinks had you had?"

"Oh, fuck you, man. You weren't even there and you don't know what happened. Why do you have to go asking a question like that? You're a little twat, you know it? Your kids must really hate asking you for help with stuff. You're always there with your little value judgments. Teddy, lookit man, the roads here suck. That's all there is to it. Don't I ever get the benefit of the doubt with you? *Ever?*"

Ted paused for a breath and rolled his eyes. "Donald, don't bullshit a bullshitter. How many drinks?"

"Oh, go ahead with the moral superiority. Who do you think you are, Felix Fucking Unger? It was just a couple. Alright? Are you happy now? Do you feel all high and mighty and shit? God damn it to hell. You just won't give it up, will you?"

"So if the hospital wants three bills, why do you want to borrow four?"

"Well, the Suzuki needs tons of repairs. It's going to take almost a thousand to get it running again."

"Donald, you want me to give you money for car repairs? Douche bag, why don't you just fix it yourself? You've got the time."

"Have you seen this? Have you? Oh, wait. You're six thousand miles away so you probably haven't, *flounder face*. The body is all bent in and rubs against both wheels on the driver's side. The rear axle is bent beyond repair. It's got to be yanked off and replaced, which means major adjustments to the transmission since the vehicle is four-wheel drive. This is not just replacing a blown head gasket. This is major structural shit. And the only guy on the island who can do the work has got me over a barrel and he knows it. I'm screwed here. I need the money."

"You know, Donald, I *knew* this call was coming. I *swear*, I knew when you left for Lanai you would end up putting the touch on me for cash. I just figured it would take longer than seven months before you started to outspend your guaranteed income."

"Teddy, it's not like this is *my* fault. The roads here really do suck. They should be paved and lighted. If they were, this would never have happened. I told them I didn't need to go to the hospital and they took me there anyway and gave me a bunch of tests I didn't want. I've had a sprained neck before. I know what it feels like. I told them that. They're just looking to make a butt load of money from a *haole* who they think is a rich guy."

"Give me a *break*, will ya? You went out at night and got all liquored up and you rolled that car yourself. That's all on you, man. And any reasonable doc would have insisted you go to the hospital to get checked out. If they didn't, you'd be calling me up because you wanted to sue them for malpractice, you entitled little fucker."

"Teddy, c'mon. Don't start calling me names. Just help me out? Please? I'm in a bind here. I really need the cash. I can pay you back when my inheritance comes through. You know I'm good for it."

"Donald, listen. I'm going to do you a big favor here. I'm *not* going to lend you the money, I'm ... ."

"Holy irony, Batman. Hold the train. Where's the part where you do me a favor? Because I swear I just heard you say you were *not* going to lend me the money."

"You get to figure this one out on your own, little brother. You're a big boy. You don't have a wife depending on you that I find myself worrying about. You have everything you need to solve this problem. So go solve it. It's not my problem if you got your dick caught in a ringer."

"Teddy, you know I'd help you out if you needed it. You know that. I'm your *only brother* for chrissake. You can't leave me hanging. You just can't. Can you imagine what Dad would say? He'd totally kick your ass over this. You know it. I know it. *Everybody* knows it."

"Don't you bring him into this. Don't you even *dare*. He didn't fuck up his life and have to start fresh somewhere else."

"You know he'd want you to look out for me, the same way he looked out for Uncle Tommy. Things always worked out better for Dad. He had a job and he had money and Tommy didn't. He always said he felt it was his duty to help. He said we needed to look out for those not as well off as ourselves."

"And I thought lawyers were bad at selective memory loss. Donald, you're leaving out the part about how Tommy was a raging alcoholic with anger management issues. If Dad hadn't nursed him along with free money, Tommy would have had to clean up his act and find a job. Did you notice that it wasn't long after Dad died that Tommy started doing better? He had to depend on himself if he was going to pay for rent and groceries. So you, man? You need to clean up your act. You got a house and you got a car and you got money coming in every month to cover your expenses. You got everything you could possibly need. And look, you're still doing the same stupid shit you were doing in Glen Burnie. Just knock it off, *idjit*."

Ted stared at his bare feet on the kitchen floor, waiting for his brother to respond. "Donald? Donald? Aw, holy shit. Are you *crying*?"

"Teddy, I love you. But you're an asshole. You're killing me over here."

"Donald, you're an idiot. And I love you, too."

Donald honked into a paper towel. "Are you still planning on coming in the spring?"

"With all the money I've loaned you, would I dare miss out on the chance to get you to put me up in Hawaii for a free vacation? No way, slick. I'm calling in that marker."

16

Lanai, Hawaii
October 20, 1977

"Donald, I think it's time we took some wedges out to the golf course. Just you and me."

"Kahuna, my neck's still sore and Doc Arai says I need to keep this stupid collar on for a little while longer. He says I should rest and I'm starting to think maybe I should listen."

"I know what he said. He gave me permission for what I have in mind. This shouldn't hurt your neck one bit and you can keep your collar on. C'mon, let's get going before you think about it too much."

From Donald's back yard, the pair walked thirty yards past the green on number one where Bobby Joe pulled handfuls golf balls out of his pockets and scattered them around the fairway.

"Donald, what's the worst part of your game?"

"So who are you, Mister Fucking Rogers? You don't have to ask me questions that have obvious answers like I was six years old. My short game sucks."

"Listen, I'm getting ready to give you some advice you haven't asked for. Can you deal with that?"

"If it makes my short game better, I'll get on my hands and knees and scrub the pubic hairs off the floor around your toilet. Go ahead, already. I'm aging over here."

"So, Donald, do you have any idea why your short game gives you such trouble?"

"Oh, holy hell. Get to the point already, will you? Just tell me what you want me to know."

Bobby Joe tilted his head and smirked. "Do you see what you're doing here, smart ass? Do you *see*?" Bobby Joe stepped closer to Donald and plugged the tip of his index finger into Donald's chest. "This is why your short game stinks. This thing – you're doing it right now."

Donald stood tall and looked down on the elfin, yellow-skinned man who stood before him. "*What?* What am I doing?"

"You're impatient with the here and the now. You want to blow right past it. You're focused on where you expect to be and you just want to get there, already. You want to ignore the process of learning, of trial and error. You don't take the time to try and *enjoy* the process – the actions that will get you to where you want."

"Wait ... what?"

"Donald, when you line up over a wedge shot or a putt, you're all wrapped up in hoping the ball will go in the hole and how you can act all triumphant if it does. When you swing, you're not thinking about what it takes to hit the ball and you're not watching the ball. You're certainly not watching the *backside* of the ball at the spot where you hope to hit it. You keep looking where you want the ball to go. Cletus, if you ain't watching the ball, you ain't going to make a good shot. Ain't no way. Get into the here and now. Enjoy it. Savor it."

"Bullshit. The ball is the only thing I can look at. There's all this grass and then there's this little white spot in the middle of it. What can anybody look at but the white spot?"

Bobby Joe tilted his head again and smirked. "Alright, smart guy. Here. Take this wedge and line up over that ball like you want to put it on the green." Donald did as he was told. "So can you turn your head and look at your target?"

Donald stared straight down. "No, I can't look at the goddam target line. My goddam neck hurts too goddam bad for that. All I can do is look straight down. This is why I didn't want to come out here, remember?"

"Good. So make your shot."

Donald parked his feet so his face was directly over the ball, pulled the club head back about two feet and swung through. He enjoyed the satisfying click that comes from hitting a ball dead center on the club face. He stood up straight and turned his torso so that he could face the hole without twisting his neck. The ball had come to rest about six inches past the hole. Bobby Joe kicked a ball toward Donald's feet. "Here. Do it again." Donald set up and swung and breathed a happy little breath when he again heard the click. He stood up and turned to look at the result; the ball had come to rest even with the hole, leaving an eighteen-inch putt. "Here's another. Go again." Donald repeated his motion with the same results.

"Better?"

"Yeah, I think so."

"Better?"

"I said *yes,* already. What are you, deaf?"

"So you got a neck you can't turn, even if you wanted to. You got no choice but to look at the one and only thing that matters. You're forced to focus on the here and the now. And look what happens."

"So I make sure and look at the ball when I hit it. This is supposed to be a big deal that requires you to resort to the Socratic Method? Kahuna, you could have told me this when I was lying on my couch."

"Donald, there ain't no way you could have learnt this on your couch. You're the type who has to pee on the electric fence before you learn not to. You have to get burnt to a crisp before you get it that the sun burns your skin just the same as it does with everybody else. You're the one who has to get assaulted by Bradley before you get it that the rules of the worship center apply to you the same as everybody else. You're the one who has to flip your Suzuki and shit your pants and spend twelve hours getting closer and closer to death before you realize that life is a *gift.*" Bobby Joe paused and stared hard at Donald. He paused some more. "Is there anybody on this whole island who ought to be happier about being alive than you? *Anybody?* After what you've been through?"

"I'm grateful to be alive. I'm grateful in a way that I never was before."

"Are you grateful enough to spend your time thinking how lucky you are to be standing on a golf course right now?"

Donald resisted the urge to stab Bobby Joe with a sharp comment. "Of course. Your point being?"

"When you're lined up to hit your ball, I want you to think about how grateful you are just to be lined up to hit your ball. You're not dead and decomposing in the woods somewhere, waiting for strangers to discover your remains so they can use dental records to identify you. You're not in Glen Burnie dealing with a boss who hates your guts. *You're alive.* You're among people who love you so much that even when you fuck up your own life, they show up at your door with gifts of food to cushion the blow. You're on one of the most beautiful golf courses on the planet with a priceless view of the Pacific Ocean. You're working on your *third* chance at life. I want you to be so grateful for that moment before you hit your ball that you realize how beautiful it is, that you won't let it pass without recognizing it and giving thanks. A minute from now, you can do the same thing and it doesn't matter if your ball is in the hole or twenty feet past it. Two minutes from now, when you're teeing off for the next hole, do it again. Right now?" Bobby Joe clicked his fingers in Donald's face. "Right now is the only thing that matters. Right now is everything. Be happy you have right now. If you're thinking about thirty seconds from now or even ten seconds from now, you're not appreciating *right now.* You're not playing good golf. You're taking too much for granted."

17

Lanai, Hawaii
October 22, 1977

It was a joy to be able to get yourself out of bed so that you could walk to the bathroom, stand and aim your penis at the toilet, Donald decided. To be awake, alive and expectant was completely lovely. As he relaxed his gut and waited for the pressurized urine in his bladder to force itself past the fleshiness of his prostate, he imagined the pleasure of release that was waiting for him and, without warning, he found tears streaming from the corners of his eyes.

He leaned forward and flattened his palm against the wall, making it easier to hold up his torso, which was confined by a clamshell contraption that immobilized his neck, and he unexpectedly found relief from a crick that had caused two cervical vertebrae to feel stuck for God knows how many days.

His urine began to escape and found its way to the center of the toilet bowl. He began weeping and when he inhaled, he sucked in salty tears.

A good piss is such a beautiful thing.

18

Honolulu, Hawaii
December 1, 1977

"Mr. DuBrock, I think Lanai has tremendous potential as a golf resort. You can see that, can't you?" Tommy Banks' hope for a positive response was enough to make him hold his breath without even realizing he was doing it.

"That may be, Tommy. Can we can talk about that when I'm not getting ready to putt?" David DuBrock kneeled and eyed the eighteen feet of green space between his golf ball and the hole. He looked over his shoulder at Damien, his assistant and caddie, who was bent over and considering the same subject. Damien was shielding himself from the sun with a navy blue umbrella broader than a hula-hoop and made of dense sailcloth. "Right edge, Damien?"

"At least two balls' width outside right edge, sir. See the grain close to the hole? It will push your ball a touch left when it gets close."

"I'm not seeing that. Are you sure?"

"Yes, sir. See how the grass loses most of its sheen about four feet from the hole?"

"Your degree of confidence?"

"Extremely high, sir. Better than 90 percent." Damien paused so that he could choose his words carefully. He didn't want to impart any negative energy. "Just be sure to get it all the way there. The grain is gristly enough that it will probably slow the ball down."

David stood tall and approached Damien, a lean man with hair as red as tomato paste and skin lighter than cigarette smoke. He put his face into Damien's, their noses nearly touching. "You wouldn't want me to miss, would you?"

"Your success is my success, sir."

David wrinkled his lips and squinted at his employee. "Good answer. This will work. I can feel it in my gut." He picked a discolored blade of grass as his mark, set his line and practiced his stroke. He stepped up to the ball and tapped. It rolled a perfect end over end and looked certain to miss long right. When it got four feet from the hole, it made a supernatural turn to the left, gentle at first and then sharper. It dropped in the side of the hole, half-circling the cup on the way to its bottom. Damien took the putter from David, wiped the head with a damp towel and reinserted it into the golf bag lying at the edge of the green.

"See you on the next hole, sir. I want to study it before you drive."

David kneeled down, fingered his golf ball and, eyes closed, lingered over a long breath that brought calm to his center. *A birdie. How luscious.* "Tommy, you were saying?"

"I was saying that the remoteness of Lanai is a feature that many extra-wealthy vacationers will find appealing. It's removed from the common portions of the islands that attract middle-class vacationers. It has an exclusive air and it offers privacy and has amenities and activities that the nearby islands don't, horseback riding, skeet shooting and deer hunting, to name just a few. The rolling terrain around the west end of the island is perfect for a golf course. Dole has an extensive underground irrigation system already installed, which will save you a substantial sum on golf course construction."

"If it has so much potential, why isn't Dole doing this?"

"We lack the expertise, sir. It's not part of any of our core businesses. If it was, we might consider it."

"Is Dole willing to partner with me on this?"

Tommy stood tall. Dennis DeLorenzo told him to expect that question and he was ready. He gave the answer that David DeLorenzo had him to: "Under the right circumstances, and for the right price, yes, we would."

"Denny told you to say that, didn't he?"

Tommy clenched his teeth. That question wasn't in the playbook. "What makes you say that?"

"Denny and I have known each other since our sons were in kindergarten together. He knows me. I know him. It's a Denny kind of thing to say. Sending you here to open negotiations on the golf course instead of doing it himself? That's a typical Denny move. He knows I can read him like a book. His body language and tone of voice would give away the store."

"Seriously? *Really?*" Tommy cleared his throat. "I mean, how can you be so sure of yourself?"

"We've played poker dozens of times. I know every time he's bluffing, and he knows I know. I can tell if he's betting with a hand better than a full house. His face is like one of those large-print books they make for old folks."

David looked ahead and saw Damien, umbrella in hand, scanning the fairway on the next hole. He motioned and they began a walk to their next station. "Tommy, you tell Denny this: put any price on Lanai he wants and I'll pay seventy-five percent of that. Just name the price. I will need for Dole to give me an eight percent equity stake in their company at fifty percent of market cost and Dole needs to be in the resort project as a silent partner with a twenty-five percent stake. If the project should lose money, Dole has to cover twenty-five percent of the losses and it needs to keep a line of credit available to help cover twenty five percent of start-up costs. In five years' time, I will guarantee that I'll buy Dole's stake for what it was worth at the start of our deal. The deal will close only after I get all necessary permits and approvals for construction. You got all that? Or should I have Damien write it down for you?"

Tommy clenched his teeth again. *I may be someone you can intimidate. But I'm not stupid.* "Yes sir. I'll pass that message along. Of course, I have no idea how the board will respond."

"You know perfectly well how the board will respond. The board will do any damn thing Denny wants. If it flies with Denny, it will fly with the board. There's one other thing I need. Denny has to give me a seat on the board for as long as Dole has a stake in the project. The corporate bylaws have to be amended so they can't just boot me off. If Dole runs into trouble and can't afford to hold up its end of the bargain, I want to be in a position to know right away."

Once they arrived at the tee box, Tommy remembered something else Dennis had told him: lower DuBrock's expectations. He cleared his throat. "Mr. DuBrock, one thing – I'm doubtful that Dole can sell you an eight percent stake. The company may not be holding that much of its own stock and I don't know if we're holding the kind of cash necessary to go buy that on the open market."

"Tommy, watch this." David put his hand on Damien's shoulder. "Damien, how much of Dole's common stock does the company own?"

"A little more than eleven percent, sir."

"How much did Dole spend to acquire that eleven percent?"

"Most of that was acquired for virtually no cost when Dole's former CEO passed away in 1973. For tax reasons, his will and company bylaws both valued the stock at zero dollars and called for its return to the company so that his son, Dennis DeLorenzo, could acquire it for himself on whatever terms he wanted."

David looked at Tommy and nodded. "Now let's see, I think I have honors. Damien, what are we looking at here?"

Damien handed his boss a five wood. "Three hundred and ten to the front of the green, sir, which is sloped front to back. But there are bunkers at 215 yards out which are nearly impossible to avoid given your typical driving distance. If you hit this wood your typical 175 yards, you'll have a perfect nine iron to the front edge and the ball should roll almost all the way to the hole."

David beamed. "Damien? Whatever we're paying you, it's not enough. Remind me to talk with you next week about a raise."

"Yes, sir. Thank you, sir."

19

Lanai, Hawaii
December 20, 1977

What is a man supposed to do with himself on a Sunday night if there's no television? The question hung around Donald's neck like a boa constrictor that hadn't eaten in weeks. In search of an answer, he had looked under every piece of furniture, behind every closet door and even in the pockets of the jackets and pants Dixie had left in her closet. He had come up with a copy of *Playgirl*, a pair of crotchless panties, a half-full decanter of *Galliano* banana liqueur and several colored bottles in the refrigerator with unreadable Japanese labels and semi-gelatinous contents. Their insides smelled shockingly unfamiliar but edible.

There was a radio. The only station with a reliable signal, KONI, had seduced him with Jerry Lee Lewis and *Great Balls of Fire*. Dressed in boxers and socks, Donald sang along and thrust his hips hard enough to slide himself across the linoleum floor in the kitchen. But then KONI had repulsed him with the unctuous: Captain and Tennille's *Muskrat Love*. He yanked the plug out of the wall and withdrew to the lonely and black front porch where the near-complete absence of light created a mild euphoria. After a while, he took to leaning dangerously far back in the front porch rocker and to pressing his thumbs against his eyelids so he could enjoy the light show.

After sitting and staring into the darkness, he found he could quiet his mind completely – void it of all conscious thought – just by breathing slowly and staring into the night where his eyes were unable to find anything upon which to focus. Donald experienced an intoxication each time he reached a state of plainness and was able to set up the balsalight barriers to reentry of anything recognizable. It never lasted, though. Every blank moment reminded him of something and every something he imagined put words in his head and then he was back to where he started. He remembered the time when he and Teddy were small and went swimming off Ulmstead Point with their dad. Donald learned that if he held his breath and leaned his head back, he could effortlessly float and enjoy a sensation of weightlessness that resembled what he now knew as peace.

The sound of footsteps interrupted. From a distance he imagined he could see the faint outline of a person who was getting closer. It was only when the person got within arm's distance that he could see the outline of a head of curly hair and realized it was Tina.

He stood to greet his visitor, expecting her to say something. She stared at him, child-like, and deliberately climbed the three stairs to the front porch and took a seat in the rocker next to him. She sat for several silent moments, staring out into the night, as if she could see the trees across the road. Donald stood over her and slowly lifted an eyebrow.

"Well, hello."

Tina exhaled and winced. She felt like she was wrestling with a difficult concept – and losing. "Donald, here's the thing. I'm a woman. And I have a woman's *needs*. I don't need a relationship. I don't need baggage. I don't need obligations. I just have, you know, needs. And once a week or so, I'd like to come over and take care of my needs. Can you deal with that?"

"*Needs*? Are you talking about sex?"

"Yes. Needs."

"Um, yeah. I can handle that. So do you mean now? Right now?" Donald sat up.

"Have you ever heard of herpes?"

Donald slumped. "Yes."

"Do you have it?"

"No. Would you like me better if I did?"

"Definitely not."

"Hmmm. Alright, then. So, um, now?"

"Aren't you interested in knowing if I have herpes?"

"Now that you mention it, it might be a good question." Donald looked at Tina, who was staring at him blankly. "So do you have herpes?"

"No."

Donald sat up straighter. "So, like, *now?*"

"So do you have any problems with impotence or premature ejaculation or anything like that?"

"Nope. Mister Happy stands at attention whenever a woman tells me she's going to take her clothes off. He's never let me down."

"Good."

"So, like, now?" Donald gestured with his thumb toward the front door and slid forward on his rocker, hoping it was time to get up.

"Aren't you interested in whether I might get pregnant? Whether we need birth control?"

"So can you? Will you? You know, get pregnant?"

"No. I had my tubes tied when Toby was born."

"Hmmm. Ok." Donald scrunched up his forehead and squinted. "Are we getting closer?"

Tina leaned over and put her face as close to Donald's as she could without actually touching noses and sniffed. "You're still a heavy smoker, aren't you?"

"I smoke, yeah. Like a lot of people. Why, you want one?" He reached down to the porch deck and grabbed his pack of Marlboros and held them, open, toward Tina.

"I'm not going to sleep with you if you smell like cigarettes. That's a deal breaker."

"Hmmm. Ok. So now?"

"Didn't you hear what I just said?"

"So, like, you want me to go brush my teeth or something?"

"No. Cigarette smoke lingers for days. It's in your hair, on your clothes and on your skin, and it's probably all over your house. It's disgusting. You have to quit smoking."

"What? You just want me to quit? Just like that? What the hell is this?"

"Are you interested or not? I can leave if you're not."

"*Wait*. Don't leave. Don't do that."

"You want sex? You quit smoking."

Donald looked at the pack of Marlboros in his palm. He looked up at Tina. He looked back at the cigarettes and then leaned back in his rocker, his eyes narrowed. "So you think you can come over to my house unannounced and just start telling me what to do? Is that how you think this works? Just tell me how you expect me to live? Isn't that kind of shitty? *Oh, Donald. You can fuck me but only if you quit smoking.*"

"What I know is that most men will do anything if it will get them a piece of ass. You don't have to treat me like other girls and lie to me about how much you like me or if we'll get married some day or a load of crap about how pretty I am. You don't have to promise to call me or be interested in seeing me again. You don't have to take me out to dinner or spend money on me. You don't have to pretend that you're interested in what I talk about. You don't ever have to pretend you want to go out with me."

"And so I repeat: Do you think you can just come over to my house unannounced and just start telling me what to do? Is that how you think this works?"

Tina stood up, hands in her pockets. "See ya."

"*Wait*. Don't leave." Donald squeezed the pack of Marlboros that had been sitting flat in his hand and popped them over his shoulder and past the porch railing. "Done."

"I'll be back next Sunday about nine thirty."

"So you think you can just dictate my schedule? Just tell me when to be ready?"

"Do you have something better going next Sunday night?"

Donald sniffed and his chin got tight. "I guess I'll see you then."

Tina stood up and started down the front porch stairs.

"Hey, wait. Can I still sleep with other women?"

"*Are* you sleeping with other women?"

"Oh, Jesus Christ. What do *you* think?"

"I didn't figure that a man who spends his evenings in his boxers drinking beers on his front porch was doing much screwing around. The answer is no. I'm not going to have sex with you if you start to sleep with other women."

"Ok, then."

"And, Donald. If you start sleeping with other women, I'll find out. It's a small island."

"Ok, then."

"Oh, and one other thing. If you tell anybody we're having sex, it's all over. I don't want the village knowing my business. Do you understand?"

"Yeah. I think I'm getting the picture. If I do whatever you say then you'll sleep with me."

"Good. We understand each other. See you next week." Tina turned and headed down the stairs.

"Tina, are you always this blunt with people? You just tell them what you want and expect they'll deliver like Domino's Fucking Pizza?"

"Donald, I'm forty six and I've been through two husbands. Both of them did their best to ruin my life. I've got two nice children to finish raising. I'm too old and too jaded and too busy to be subtle. I want exactly what I want. If you can't give me that, then I'll just find someone else who can."

"You're not interested in having a relationship? For real?"

.

20

December 26, 1977
Wailuki, Hawaii

Some days, five o'clock seemed like a mythological flying creature with crooked wings whose existence was devoted to the false promise of rescue for those unjustly imprisoned behind a desk. For Dale, an employee of the Maui County Municipal Government, workaday life on a tropical island full of wealthy vacationers guaranteed cultivation of such delusions while he waited for quitting time.

He also liked to imagine curious events that might interrupt the quiet spells that left him feeling half dead. Months ago, there had been one interruption that required no imagination. It was the day he was behind the consumer service desk when Tony Orlando stepped in, expecting to buy a building permit for the Rococo manse he wanted to build at Uaoa Bay. It was to include a pool shaped like a pair of quarter notes, a guest house, a helipad and a subterranean screening room with a wet bar. Dale interviewed Tony O for an hour about his plans, taking notes as he talked, looking like a concerned public servant gathering essential information. He had started solely out of fawning curiosity. *Tony Orlando is standing right here. Holy shit.* But then Tony dipped his head and looked at Dale over the rim of his sunglasses and touched him on the forearm "I want to build on Maui so I can avoid all the riff raff around Honolulu – *if you get my drift.*"

Dale's parents were hotel workers and had raised four children in the shadows of Waikiki. He waited until Tony appeared annoyed with what seemed like an unreasonably long application process. That was when Dale let it drop: Tony O couldn't apply for a permit until he came back with plans signed and sealed by a licensed architect. Even those would probably get returned for revisions and have to be resubmitted.

This made Tony scrunch up his mouth behind his poufy moustache and scowl. *This is not how they treat A-listers in Palm Springs, you rube.* Some guys could go a lifetime and never have a moment nearly as grand, Dale knew at the time. He tightened his lips and nodded at Tony. *Do you know how many miles it is from here to Kansas, Toto? Do you know how many miles?*

The best part about a day like that is for the rest of your days, when folks talk about celebrity encounters, you've got the best story of all.

Dale's desk phone rang and it startled him. "Dale Sentua. Maui County Code and Zoning Enforcement. Can I help you?"

"Dale, this is Al Benanua. We worked together on the zoning reclass for the Hilton a little over two years ago. Remember me?"

"Yes, of course I remember. You sent me that beautiful gift basket full of liquor. I had hoped you would get me another at Christmas this year. I drunk up everything you sent over already. I need *more.*"

"Did I leave you off the list? That won't happen again, mate."

"Man, you know I'm kidding, right? This is a tight ship we got here. So what's up?"

"Well, I might have another project and I got a couple of questions I was hoping you could help me with."

"Go ahead, man. You're already the most interesting thing that's happened all day."

"Well, I have a client who's thinking of a hotel, spa and golf complex. You know for now, it's just a maybe, just a *what if.* Can we keep this just between you and me? I'd hate for rumors to get out that got people all juiced up and then the plan didn't go anywhere. Because for now, it's just an idea. That's all."

"Just you and me, Al. If word gets out that somebody's got a big project on tap, I suddenly got a whole room full of supervisors pumping me for long memos interpreting zoning code. I got concerned citizens standing in line and pestering me for information. Does that sound like fun to you?"

"Hey, thanks. Listen, just hypothetically, do you see anyone on the board of supervisors standing in the way of another big project? The Hilton project got two *no* votes even though it seemed like all of Maui was supporting us. I know the board membership has changed a little since then."

"I don't see any real problems here, Al. As long as you keep your plans to the west end of the island. The feds have complicated the regulations for lands all around Haleakala. You can't build an outhouse out there without approval of a team of cranky bureaucrats who pull the strings from six thousand miles away."

"Hold on. I'm not talking about Maui. I meant *Lanai*. If somebody wants to do a project on Lanai, do you think there are likely to be problems getting approval from the board?"

"Nobody has tried building anything there since before I was born. Why would anybody want to build there? Dole has the place all planted in pineapples. Lanai isn't a place for tourists."

"Well, part of the island might get a new owner. He's thinking of something different than fruit."

"The only member from Lanai on the board is Paige Paikai. If she's okay with your guy's plan, then the rest of the panel is probably fine, too. But most people on Lanai don't want to rock a boat. They got steady jobs and peace and quiet and it's been that way forever. This could be a hard sell."

"So who are the heavy hitters there? On Lanai, I mean."

"Heavy hitters?"

"In most places, there's a handful of people that everybody looks to for approval. You might call them community leaders. I call them heavy hitters."

"Well, I can only think of two people. The first is Jeanine McGovern. She lives in town and her husband is mayor of Lanai City. The old man is whipped. He does everything and anything his wife wants. People joke that she runs the city from her kitchen. If folks in town want something done, they don't go to City Hall. They go to Jeanine's back door with baked goods or home-grown vegetables. Then there's this other guy, Bobby Joe Hu. He's a minister or something in this super-rich golf community on the east end of the island. Almost all of the island's money lives there. If they don't want it, it definitely ain't gonna happen. So if you can't get Bobby Joe on board, you probably won't get your project."

"So, Dale, are you saying nobody in your memory has ever applied for a permit to build a commercial project on Lanai?"

"The only thing I remember is that a few years back, Dole applied to dredge around an existing commercial dock so they could use bigger boats to move larger shipments of pineapples. They wanted to dredge 300 yards offshore. They only could get approval for dredging no more than fifty feet offshore. The island is surrounded by coral reefs inhabited by protected species. The locals were all fine with whatever Dole wanted. It meant job security. But the feds in Washington at Interior had objections."

"The feds blocked a dredge permit? *A dredge permit?* You can't be serious."

"Ever heard of the snail darter? We must have about twenty species that are protected and they spend their days swimming around the reefs near Lanai. Every damn one of them is tons prettier than that little runt-squirt in Tennessee."

"Dale, you've been a big help, man. So tell me, do you like Myers's rum?"

"You're talking my language, bruddah."

Right after Al Benanua hung up, Dale dialed the phone. "Alberta? Are you sitting down?"

"Dale, I'm planking away at my typewriter on deadline. The Hulopo'e Surf Club is sponsoring its annual banquet and I need to get this typed up so I can have enough copy to fill next week's issue. Can we talk later?"

"Doll, I think you're going to want to talk now. I got a big tip for you. Only you have to promise you didn't hear it from me. Nobody can know that I'm your source."

Alberta leaned back in her armless secretary's chair. "Pinkie promise, Dale. Nobody will ever know. Go ahead. Just make it quick, will ya?"

"Alright, here's the thing: Dole is selling Lanai to somebody who wants to put in a hotel complex. It's supposed to have a golf course, a pool, a spa, all that stuff."

"Holy moly. Are you serious? This is happening now? Right now?"

"I don't know when. Only that it's planned. It could be right away. It could be two years. It could be ten years."

"How do you know this?"

"One of Dole's lawyers called me up to ask about whether the county supervisors would approve it."

"You got a name?"

"No, I don't got a damn name. If you call him up, he'll know it was me who told you. I'm probably the only guy outside of Dole who's allowed to know. Alberta, I'm serious, here. You can't do anything that would let on who told you this. I could lose my job. You got it? You just write it up like you know a couple of lawyers on Oahu and all will be fine."

"Dale, I got it. Nobody will know. Listen, can I call you later with questions? I gotta get this copy to the printer and the ferry leaves in twenty minutes."

21

Lanai, Hawaii
December 27, 1977

"Would you like a glass of wine?" Donald's voice box was shaking like a bed in a cheap motel.

"I'm not here for wine. You know that."

"I know, but would you like one anyway?"

"I'm a tequila girl. Got any Patron? I might take a drink of that."

Donald shook his head and feared right away he had disappointed his soon-to-be lover. His stomach growled. He knew Tina had heard it. "I think it likes you."

Tina scanned the room and lingered doing it. She appeared to be tallying available resources and considering options. She knew Donald was waiting for her to say something and was willing to wait for a while. She absorbed a dram of fortitude from the aroma of inferiority he was throwing off. She was in control and they both knew it.

She dropped her purse and kicked off her flip-flops just inside the door. She pushed the front door closed and made sure it clicked. She walked into his bedroom where she pulled tight the curtains and, only then, clicked on the light and turned down the sheets. As Donald watched Tina prepare his house for their encounter, he gulped from his glass of cold Chardonnay, part of a bottle that Dixie had thoughtfully left behind.

Tina took the wine glass from Donald's hand and plunked it on the coffee table and pulled on Donald's hand until he was standing. She stood back, thumbnail between her teeth, and scrutinized him. *Where do I start?* She attacked his belt buckle with both hands and before Donald knew it, his pants and his undershorts were down at his ankles. He thought he would step out of them and kick them aside but he didn't get the chance. Tina put her palms on his hipbones and pushed. He lost his balance and fell bare-assed onto the couch, arms flailing. She lifted his feet and, just like that, Donald was naked from the waist down. By the time she unbuttoned Donald's shirt, he had flipped up and was ready for business. Tina gripped him by the handle and pulled. "Come with me."

After laying Donald face up on his bed, Tina peeled down and crawled, cat-like, onto her prey.

"You know, for a thin, fit woman who has a tight body and firm tits, you're amazingly pretty."

"Shut up. You'll ruin the mood."

Donald blanched. "What the hell mood is *that?* You've only been here about four minutes and I'm pretty sure we don't have a mood yet. Anyway, I was being sincere. You really *are* beautiful."

"Just shut up, alright? It's not helping."

Tina flipped all of her hair to one side, straddled Donald's midsection, put her mouth on his and, with the tip of her tongue, searched for resistance. *Mmmmm. That works.* Tina spread out, squirmed and enjoyed the warmth of skin on skin. Donald's voice box and eyelids quivered as a warm and slippery sleeve glided around him. He reached out only to have his arms shoved above his head, flat on the mattress. He watched with fascination as his partner rocked on top of him, her head leading and her torso following and her front edge pressing hard into his underbelly. Tina grabbed into handfuls of shoulder flesh with fingers and fingernails. She groaned. She grabbed harder a – hard enough that Donald winced with a pleasant shot of something painful. He could feel the burn of spicy friction building. Then Tina groaned louder and then *louder.* She yanked on Donald's hair so hard he thought his head might come off. And then she curled up on his chest, her head resting beneath Donald's chin.

"Can I put my arms around you?"

"Yes. That would be good."

"Can I say something nice to you?"

"No. Just be quiet."

"Do you want to see my breast stroke?" He rubbed a hand against her left nipple.

"Stop. Just be quiet."

Donald embraced her and savored the slowing rhythm of Tina's breathing. *How long has it been since a woman curled up with me? Dear Jesus, have I ever missed this.* After several minutes, she went limp and her breathing turned epiglottal.

Donald lifted his head and shoulder to inspect the scene. One of Tina's arms flopped off of his belly and lay against the bedsheets. He whispered: "Tina? *Tina?*" No response.

The telephone rang. Donald looked at his purring kitten and then at the nightstand. It was within reach. He decided to pick it up.

Donald whispered again: "Hello?"

"Donald – hey, man."

"Hey, Teddy."

"Why are you whispering?"

"I have a new friend. She's sleeping on top of me right now."

"A new friend. Is this a pet? Or a friend of the human variety?"

"It's a woman, dorkmunder."

"Well, my timing is pretty good. When I get there in the spring, I'll have your divorce papers. They'll be finalized and all I need is to get you to sign them. Then I can file them and you and Kim are done. All done. No more marriage. I thought you might enjoy having that to look forward to."

Tina stirred. She lifted her head and a tenacious string of drool stretched from her chin to Donald's chest. She wiped it away with the back of her hand, her eyes still closed. "I have to go." She pushed Donald's heavy arm off of her shoulders and crawled away. He held the phone away from his ear and admired the shape of her body as she balanced on one foot at a time and stepped into her nearly transparent panties.

Tina palmed Donald's knee and blew him a kiss, and then she was gone.

"Teddy, I think I just had the worst sex of my entire life."

"Really?"

"Yeah, and I want more. Isn't that weird?"

"You're a man, and men are pigs. Given the opportunity, we will sleep with anything that gives us permission."

"I'll see you in a few weeks. It will be fun. Don't forget your clubs. Hey, can you bring me some Titleists? I'll pay you back. There's no place on this whole damn island that sells golf balls."

Donald dressed and retreated to his living room for another glass of wine. He sat in a canvas chair next to the open window and glanced out to see his neighbor, Alani, seated at her kitchen table, barely fourteen feet away. She realized she was being watched and looked up at Donald. "What the *hell* are you looking at?"

Donald pulled closed the shade.

22

Lanai, Hawaii
January 2, 1978

Bobby Joe, shoulders tight, trundled across the first fairway. He arrived to Village Meeting a shade on the late side, as was his intention. As soon as greetings were exchanged, the bomb dropped. Herb Kaopuiki, a tiny man who talked too fast and who was rumored to have earned a fortune in winnings as a jockey at Santa Anita, spoke first: "I was talking to Alberta when I saw her at *Shoppers* and she said that Dole Fruit is selling the island to this big real estate developer man from the mainland – DuBrock something. No, wait. His name is David DuBrock. He's going to turn the island into a cheesy resort with gambling and floor shows and hula dancers greeting people at the airport." He paused to inhale. "They're going to have cruise ships coming and going. Alberta is getting ready to write a big story about it in *Lanai Today*. I don't like it. This is a quiet island for quiet people. We don't need Las Vegas in the Pacific. That would be just ... just *awful*."

Bobby Joe, hands on the leading edge of the pulpit, scanned the faces in the pews.

Jerry McLeigh stood to be heard. "I heard that tuh-tuh-too. I was talking to a real estate lawyer on Oahu yesterday who ruh-ruh-represents Duh-Duh-Dole. The duh-duh-deal is almost duh-duh-done. DuBrock had surveyors staking sta-sta-staking out possible construction sites last muh-month on the north side of the island. He's got architects drawing up puh-puh-plans. We have to stop this. It would kuh-kill ... kuh-kill the island. Tha-the number of ha-ha-haoles cuh-cuh-coming here would be ruh-ruh-ridiculous."

Herb jumped. "Jerry, you can't go complaining about *haoles*, you weenie. You moved here from Chicago not even five years ago. You eat Twinkies and milk for breakfast for crying out loud. Bruddah, you as white and mainland as they get."

"We need to get our facts before we go off half-cocked," said Bobby Joe. "Lots of these things get planned and then never go anywhere. We don't want to get all worked up over nothing."

"Kahuna, according to Alberta, the deal is close to done," said Herb. "Dole Fruit is losing money on Lanai because their competitors are paying field workers in Thailand twenty cents an hour. Dole is already negotiating the date of settlement and the terms for a rent back of about two years so Dole has time to harvest the remaining crop and use up existing supplies for planting. We have to get busy while there's still time."

"I don't know how Dole could *do* this to the island," piped Kiki Kaopuiki, Herb's wife. "We have been so nice to Dole. They *owe* us better than this. Everything we do is for Dole. Almost the entire island works for Dole. What's going to happen to the workers?"

"Donald, you know a little something about business," said Bobby Joe. "Why don't you get in touch with Dole and see what you can find out for us?"

Donald shifted in his seat, inattentive and unready. "Wait. ... What?"

"Remember Steve Marsh, Dole's island manager? We played a round with him a few months ago. Call him up and see what you can find out. Come back and fill us in. But do it quick. It sounds like the process may have moved along quite a lot already."

The next morning, Donald phoned Steve and asked about DuBrock's plans. Steve told him to hold the phone and it made Donald wonder if Steve was avoiding the question.

"Hello, this is David DuBrock."

"Good morning, Mr. DuBrock ... Uh, sir. I'm Donald Gibson and I live in the village on the east end of the island. So is it true? Is it true that you're buying the island? The village is quite interested in knowing a little something about what's going on."

"The answer is yes, Donald. I am buying the island, or about ninety-five percent of it anyway. Are you selling? I'll buy your village too. I can offer a great price. You'll really make out."

"The village is not for sale. I doubt it ever will be. We hear you're planning a golf resort? Is that true?"

"Absolutely. It's going to be first class all the way. You'll just love it. Eight hundred guest rooms, four restaurants, several shops and two tournament-ready golf courses. We're going to have facilities for corporate retreats, PGA events, you name it. Kenny Rogers and Dolly Parton will perform at our grand opening in about two years."

"You're shooting to open in just two years? That soon?"

"I've got a few more details to work out with Dole before the date for a soft open can be confirmed, but yes. That's our plan. Maybe you'd like to come over and have a look at our civil engineer's site plan? Our architect has produced some partial elevations. You can look at those, too. This is going to be magnificent. It will put Lanai on the map."

"Sounds like you've really put a lot into this? You seem quite proud."

"This is my baby. She's going to be *special*. So listen, I've got to run. I'll put Steve back on the line."

"So, Don, what do you think?"

"Steve, is DuBrock still in your office?"

"Nah. He had to catch a helicopter back to his yacht. He said that Sonny Bono is coming over from Honolulu to have lunch with him. Can you believe it? *Sonny Bono?*"

"*Who* is this guy? Is there any way to stop this train? Or at least slow it down? A lot of the folks in the village are really nervous about this."

"Corporate has decided it's not going to grow on Lanai any more. It didn't matter if DuBrock came along or not. Dole was going to be pulling out. It's just not profitable anymore. They considered letting the land sit and maybe using it as a tax loss to offset gains from other business units, but DuBrock made an offer the company couldn't refuse and corporate has promised to relocate me and my family to Thailand when pineapple growing here is done."

"You're moving?"

"Look, don't be worried. DuBrock is a nice guy. You'll like him. He's straight up. Like, part of the deal here is that Dole can't stop working the fields until the resort starts hiring. DuBrock *insisted*. He didn't want to put the entire island out of work waiting for construction to finish. Like I said, he's a nice guy. He really is."

"Steve, it sounds like he's just making sure that he has hotel workers on site when he needs them. He doesn't want to have to spend extra money to bring them in and buy them housing."

"Maybe. But at least he's talking about preventing unemployment. A lot of guys wouldn't even do that."

"Oh that's an easy sell to the village. Hey guys, this DuBrock is worth getting behind. He'll give you exactly the lip service you are hoping for. Steve, can you even hear yourself?"

"Donald, he's in it for a profit. The guy is a very, very successful businessman. I heard he's worth a couple of billion. That's billion with a *B*. But he does good projects. Really nice stuff."

"So does he golf?"

"Yeah, it's one of his favorite things."

"How soon until Bobby Joe and I can get him out on the village golf course? Can you find out for us?"

"You could play with him next week. I am going to usher him around the island so he can see what he's buying. Until yesterday, he had only seen pictures and site plans and taken aerial tours."

"Guys, it's true," said Donald. "All of it. DuBrock's buying the island and he's got a massive resort planned. Cheesiness is on its way." The faces of Bobby Joe, Kiki and Herb Kaopuiki and Jerry McLeigh all showed signs of dread.

"Can't we talk to DuBrock and get confirmation? I hate to find out we had our story wrong," said Bobby Joe.

"I talked to DuBrock directly. He was in Steve's office when I called. Kahuna, I think we can take him golfing next week and have a chat."

Bobby Joe chewed on his lip. "Can we stop this from happening?"

"I don't think we want to stop it," said Donald. "I think our ammunition is better spent on having an impact on what the finished project looks like. Dole sounds committed to pulling out of Lanai. If that happens, all those pineapple workers will be out of jobs."

"We have to oppose this," said Jerry. "Th-This is just flat out wrong fuh-fuh-for the island. We have to stuh-stop it from happening. I've talked to all the members of the Buh-Board of Elder-Elders. They're in you-you-unanimous agreement."

"We can't go along with his plan. We just can't," said Kiki. "It would be so, so … just so *wrong*. This island has never been about tourism or crowds. It's about a spiritual connection to the land and the sea. This is one of the few places on the globe that a person can live away from crowds and away from all the crass commercialism that makes devotion and faith so difficult. I mean, would you ever open a souvenir shop in a church or in a shrine? *Would you*? Heavens, no. It would just be so, so … just so *wrong*."

"Donald, Kiki makes a good point," said Bobby Joe. "Can't we explore all possible avenues for preventing this before we start to consider how we might accept it?"

"Kahuna, have you spoken to Pat Arakawa's father about this?" queried Donald. "There certainly will be permits and approvals required before construction can begin. Usually, there are public hearings required."

"I called him last night. Most of the local approvals, such as building permits, are sewn up. Those approvals are less than thirty days old and he said we could raise a legal challenge if we think anything is in violation of zoning or land-use regulations. The few approvals still pending are for special exceptions and have to go through the public hearing process. So we can speak in public against them."

"So there's still time?" Herb looked around the room. "We can *win* this."

Donald shook his head. "Look guys, Steve tells me that Dole Fruit is pulling out of here no matter what. *They are pulling out. Period.* They aren't profitable and haven't been for a while and they're not going to get profitable. The Asian pineapple producers are killing them on price. So the alternative to the resort is Dole pulls out of Lanai and we have massive unemployment. We don't need the island in poverty."

"Buh-buh-But if we could find another g-grower, we might be able to keep the puh-plantations growing," said Jerry. "That would really be the buh-buh-best way, wuh-wouldn't it? Among the villagers, we have enough muh-money, I would bet, to start our own cuh-cuh-company. We know the islands. We know the puh-people. We could make this go. I could run some numbers and see if it wuh-would wuh-wuh-work."

"If Dole Fruit can't grow here profitably, there's probably *nobody* who can," said Donald. "Dole has all the boats and planes and trucks and contracts and personnel they need to distribute product. They've got an established brand name and fruit marketing experts and economists who can predict demand and project costs. That's how big business works. If anybody else comes in here, they have to start from scratch. If a herd of Thai pineapple pickers will work for nickels and dimes, I doubt there's anybody who could make an American operation work. We need to accept that pineapple growing on Lanai is coming to an end."

"Donald, you just want to *give up*," said Herb. "You don't understand what Dole means to the island. There's got to be away to stop this. There's *got* to be."

—⚹—

"David? Would you like honors?" asked Bobby Joe.

David DuBrock accepted with a smile and surveyed the first hole of the Wakea and Papa Worship Center and seeing a short, broad fairway, looked back to Bobby Joe. "Three hundred and twenty-five yards to the center of the green?"

"Three hundred and thirty-five, actually."

David held out a hand. "Three wood please, Damien."

"Not driver, sir?"

"No. A three wood should leave me with a perfect 110 yards."

Damien complied and David set the club head on the ground and inserted a tee right next to it with a Titleist mounted on top, its equator just below the top edge of the face of his club. He stood back, took measure of his line and noticed the faint movement of the tops of the trees on both sides of the fairway. He absorbed some air, sweet with the scent of pineapples growing in fields just a few hundred yards away. Then he set up and waggled. He took a sweeping backswing that went as far back as his shoulders would allow. He held his club perfectly still for a moment, hovering over his shoulders, and then his hips began to turn. An instant later, his club took an inside-out path toward the ball and his hands turned over slightly, leaving the club face partly closed on impact. His Titleist, which bore a red number one, started out sharply to the right and then turned back toward the center of the fairway. It landed 190 yards away and then rolled another thirty yards on the firm fairway.

Bobby Joe tightened the muscles in his temples and gave Donald a stare. *This guy is the real deal. He is patient and crafty.* He motioned. "You ready, young man?"

Donald bashed his tee shot 240 yards out in the middle of the fairway. Bobby Joe matched him for distance almost exactly and the foursome began their march, three with bags on shoulders. "So, David, have you ever developed a golf course before?" queried Bobby Joe.

"Oh, yes. Quite a few. My team has done dozens, some of them with Arnold Palmer. You've heard of him, right? My guys know their onions."

"Ever developed one on a small, rocky island three thousand miles away from civilization?" asked Donald.

David cocked his head. "Why do you ask?"

"You'll find most of the resources you need for a golf course are either unavailable or in very short supply. Power is crazy expensive, for example. Our island's small reserve of groundwater would be quickly exhausted if you used a conventional irrigation system. The excavation typical for a mainland golf course won't work here. Just a few inches beneath most of the surface of Lanai are dense layers of volcanic rock. To break that up would require machinery too massive to move onto the island, and you'd have nowhere to put the spoils. The Hawaiian waters for miles in all directions are protected by federal and state environmental law."

DuBrock arrived at his ball, held out his hand and, without a word, received the pitching wedge that he expected from Damien, holding his blue umbrella. "It sounds like maybe you don't want me to build here. Could that be?" He surveyed the green and kept an ear cocked toward Donald. *Pin back left on a nice, flat section of the putting surface. Shelf, slope and collection area to the right.*

"It's going to be your land. You can do what you want. I just wanted to share a few thoughts. Things on the island are not always what they seem. It wouldn't do you or us any good if your plans don't work within the limits of the island."

"Damien, I don't recall any one on our design team raising concerns about the cost or availability of power, do you?"

"No, sir. I would recall that if they had."

"I don't think they discussed the possibility of excavation being more difficult or expensive than we're used to. Did you hear them touch on that?"

"No sir. I did not."

DuBrock gently practiced his swing – back and forth, back and forth – then he stepped up to his ball. "Well, for every problem, there's a solution." DuBrock set up, swung and sent his ball high. It crested far above the green and then fell straight down, right next to the pin where it bounced once and settled.

"Ah, sweet shot. Don't you think? So, are there any other obstacles you can think of, Donald?" DuBrock held his follow through an unusually long time, his weight resting almost entirely on his front foot. "It sounds like the advice I'm getting from highly paid professionals might be incomplete."

Donald approached his ball and examined his line to the pin. "Yes. I can think of several. Shipping material and supplies to and from the island is more cumbersome than you might expect. We have no commercial wharf or dock. The water close to shore is too shallow to accommodate most large commercial vessels. We have no paved roads outside of a few on the interior of Lanai City." He took several low practice swings, making sure to turn his hips and to brush the bottom of his wedge against the grass. "We have only one small gasoline station that runs on a single above-ground tank that holds no more than four thousand gallons of ordinary gasoline, and no diesel. Some weeks, it runs dry and we have to wait several days for a delivery." Donald set up and swung. His ball flew high and dropped onto the front edge of the green, then rolled half way to the pin. "We have only one trained mechanic on the island. So importing the quantity of construction materials needed for you to build, to say nothing of the food, beverage and other supplies needed to keep it operating, would likely require some significant new infrastructure." Donald slid his wedge back into his bag.

"Damien? This all sounds new to me. Is it new to you?"

"Engineering mentioned the need for new roads. But nothing about the shallow water, limited groundwater or the limited supply of gasoline and mechanics."

Bobby Joe pulled out a seven iron and practiced a cut shot. Donald looked surprised. "Kahuna? A seven iron? It's not but ninety yards."

"Well, the fairway is soft from regular watering and this green is harder than most because it dries out so quickly. I'm thinking I'll run the ball up toward the pin." He proceeded to do just that, his ball ending near the center of the green, on the good side of the right-hand slope.

"Make a note for me, will you, Damien? When I'm in Omaha next week to have lunch with Warren and Charlie, I want to schedule a meeting with Leo Weekly to talk about engineering issues. His guys should have been all over this."

"Yes sir."

Two million in design fees and he doesn't mention basic things like this. "So Donald, if the island is made of rock, do you suppose we'll have trouble excavating a foundation for the hotel?"

Once on the green, David marked his ball and flicked it to Damien, who caught it. His receiving hand was enclosed in a damp, green towel. He manipulated it for several seconds and handed it, glistening and clean, back to his boss.

"I don't believe there's even one building on the island with a basement," said Donald. "The cost and time required to excavate are just too much."

David looked at Damien and made a motion like he was writing on paper and he whispered: "Make another note, will you?"

Bobby Joe eyeballed his putt for no more than two seconds and took a few practice strokes with his putter and, while he did so, Donald removed the flag from the pin and lay down his bag of clubs. Kahuna's putt tracked a gentle arc across the mostly flat green before finding the right edge of the hole and dropping in. Donald's putt, from closer to the left edge of the green, was dead straight. His ball found the center cut.

"You fellows know this course pretty well, it looks like," said David. "Two birdies on the first hole couldn't be an accident." He replaced his ball on the putting surface and picked up his marker. He kneeled to scrutinize the thirty inches of ground between his ball and the hole. "Straight putt?" he asked, somewhat rhetorically. After a moment he turned to his playing partners. "Straight putt?"

"Well, is that what it looks like to you?" responded Bobby Joe.

David's brow wrinkled up. "I was just asking for a bit of advice, that's all. Can't you help a guy out?"

"It looks straight," said Donald. "But it's outside right edge *at least* an inch. If you look carefully, you can see that the grain runs crosswise."

"*Outside* right edge? It's not even a three-foot putt. No way. It can't move *that* much." David stood over his ball and aimed his putter inside right edge and tapped. His ball started straight, took a left turn in front of the hole and passed close by its left edge. "Sheee-it. You were right. I shoulda listened." David reached across the hole with his putter and tapped the ball in.

At the tee box for the second hole, David lay down his bag and scrutinized the landscape before him. "About one ninety to the far side of the landing area?"

Bobby Joe quietly nodded, just once.

"So where's the pin? What are we shooting at?"

"Off to the right, out of sight. The green is raised by about sixty yards, notched into the side of a steep rock bluff."

David hung back, waiting for his partners to take honors. Bobby Joe swung outside in with a three iron, the club face left open and his ball

"He says he's all about the money. But it seems like what he really wants are accomplishments that will make others admire him as much as he admires himself."

"Yeah, but do you think he'll listen to me? Do you think he'll actually modify his plans to the project to make it more compatible with island life? Or is he just blowing sunshine up our asses?"

"I believe he'll listen and for the reasons you've already talked about. He's a crafty businessman who wants to make a buck. He wouldn't offer you fifty thousand a year if he was blowing sunshine."

"How does that translate into I'll work with folks on the island?"

"Well, you made a compelling case for him. He seems convinced that the same things that will avoid spoiling Lanai are the things that will save him money and make his project more profitable."

"How do you think the villagers will take the news that I'm working for him?"

"I have no idea." Bobby Joe toweled dry the handle of his putter and slid it into his bag. "Village Meeting is coming up. I guess we'll find out."

"Was it wrong of me to agree so quickly?"

"That was a good thing. DuBrock was annoyed by the fact that I was remaining distant and not kowtowing to him, and there you were giving him info that he needed to make an unprecedented eagle on number two. He's really eager to have you in his corner. He thinks you can help him and he wants you to look at him as some kind of amazing business wizard that you'll look up to and want to emulate. It all feeds his desire for self promotion."

"You get all this from a round of golf?"

"When a man plays golf, he puts himself on display."

Donald fidgeted with uncertainty for several moments while Bobby Joe continued his work. "Do you think I'm on the right track here? Lots of people think we should hold out for somebody else to come in and farm pineapples."

"I don't know if you are. I'm not a businessman and I don't know business, but your thinking makes more sense than anybody else's. So I'm putting my bets on the Donald."

Bobby Joe checked the arrangement of his clubs. His putter and his wedges were in one compartment. His woods and irons were in another. "So Donald, when did you learn so much about real estate development?"

"I took all these classes on development in business school. Plus, I once planned a Ford dealer from the ground up. The owner was a compulsive tight wad and believed me when I told him I could coordinate the whole project on a budget. I surprised us both when I actually did it."

Bobby Joe wiped off the grip of his gap wedge, the last to be cleaned, and slid the club into his golf bag with the rest of its brothers and sisters. "This bucket of soapy water shouldn't go to waste. It will clean quite a few more grips. Do you want to take it home with you?"

23

Lanai City, Hawaii
January 22, 1978

Kahuna disliked moments like this. He was tempted to say that he hated moments like this but he knew that hate was a waste of energy.

At moments like this, his gut felt tight and his life force felt weakened. He found himself thinking of reasons to avoid doing what needed to be done. He found himself tempted to make choices he knew he would later regret. So he forged ahead.

"Karen, Doc Arai says he thinks I have a heart condition called afibrillation. I need to go to the hospital in Honolulu to get it checked out."

"You need some funds?"

This was it. This was the moment. Kahuna inhaled slowly. "Yes, I will."

"How much?"

"The round trip shuttle to Honolulu is seventy bucks. Doc says the testing at the hospital will probably run between $300 and $500."

"How about I give you $700? If you have any change, you can keep it."

"If I have any change, I'll give it back to you, Karen."

"Kahuna, is this serious?"

"Probably not. Doc says that usually they put afib patients on daily medication and everything is just fine."

Karen pulled out the checkbook for the village's operating account. She wrote out a check payable to Bobby Joe Hu for seven hundred dollars and no cents.

24

San Francisco, California
February 2, 1978

"Mr. DuBrock? Do you want to talk to Nick Winters? He's calling again."

"He won't give up, will he? Yeah, put him through." David extracted his legs from beneath his antique desk and reclined on a couch. He extended his hand and pushed the speaker button on the phone, which was sitting on the nearby coffee table. "Nick? What the hell is up with all these phone calls? You're driving my people crazy. We have an agreement." David adjusted the pillow beneath his head, closed his eyes and settled in.

"David? I can't get your people to give me a signed contract for performing at the Hukilau. This is completely unfair. I'm not some nobody and I don't perform for free. Don Ho doesn't do that and I don't do that. You *know* this."

"Nick, did you suffer a closed head wound? Have you totally forgotten all that I've done for you?"

"David, that's ancient history."

"Nick, you wouldn't have that little hotel in the Adirondacks and you'd be in the East River with concrete shoes if I hadn't paid off what you owed to Tony Bananas. The note you signed says I can foreclose any goddam time I want and leave you with nothing but your P.F. Flyers and your collection of Matchbox cars. So I own you. *I own you.* You're going to perform at the Hukilau during Christmas week and New Year's Eve. You're going to tell People magazine that you're performing for free. And the reason you're doing it, because we both know they're going to ask, is that David DuBrock has done so much for you and is such a stand-up guy that you didn't have the heart to ask him for any money. It's your way of saying *thanks*."

David paused, pleased that he could impose a silence. "When the reporters come to me asking for my reaction, I'm going to tell them that you're one of the few people in this world who understands the meaning of friendship. And after that, maybe you'll get some phone calls from people who will actually pay you something."

"David, please. Don't make me do this. This is humiliating."

"Nick, do we have an understanding?"

"David, no – don't … ."

"*Nick*, do we have an understanding?"

"Screw you, David."

"Now you're talking sense. You can expect a call from the booking agent to work out all the details. When I talk to him next week, I expect him to tell me what a easy-going person you are." David hung up the phone and smiled.

He yelled into the next room. "Doris? Call Tom Matthews in Los Angeles and tell him Nick Winters is on board."

25

Lanai, Hawaii
February 2, 1978

Toby's drive flew low and barely cleared the rough on its way to the fairway. "So how do I tell her I like her? How do I make her like me?"

Donald injected his tee into the soil and balanced a Titleist on top. "You see her in school every day?"

"Yep."

"You're in almost all the same classes?"

"Yep."

"Do you guys already know each other?"

"Sorta kinda. Some of her friends are friends with my friends. She knows who I am and stuff."

Donald put his feet at shoulder's width and waggled. *Whoosh. Pawhunk.* He picked up his bag and the pair began to walk.

"I'm not really sure about this one, Toby."

"Oh, come on. Just tell me what to do and what to say. I know you know. Mom says you were a total pussy hound on the mainland."

Donald checked up and put a hand on Toby's shoulder. "Hold on, little man. Did your mother really say that? She said I was a *pussy hound?*"

"I heard her say it when she was on the phone with her sister. Mom can be pretty direct, if you hadn't noticed."

Donald nodded with a purpose. "I noticed."

"So?"

"Toby, what makes you think you like this girl?"

"What do you mean? I like her. *I like her.*"

Donald motioned and they started walking again. "Have you tried talking to her?"

"Yep."

"How did that go?"

"Not so good. I got confused. I had to pee really bad so I ran away from her and into the boys' room."

"Oh, this is bad."

Toby set down his bag next to his ball and slid out a five wood. "What do you mean?" The young man assessed his line to the green and settled in. *Whoosh. Pathunk.*

"Toby, you're in love with a girl you don't even hardly know. I been there. It's bad."

"So what do I do? What do I say? Tell me, already. I want her to like me."

They started walking. Donald took in a deep, slow inhale. "You can't make her like you. It can't be done."

"I don't believe you."

"You can't *make* anyone like you. You just can't. But you can make nice with her friends. That way, when you try and talk to her again, it won't seem so out of the blue and it won't feel so weird. Maybe at a lunch table or something in the cafeteria when everybody's hanging out you can start up a conversation."

"What do I say? How do I do this?"

"Just pretend she's another guy, like one of the guys you're already friends with. When you first got to be friends with them, how did it start?"

"What do you mean? We just started talking and then we were friends. This is different. This is a *girl*."

Donald set down his bag and assessed his situation. "What do you think, Toby? A hundred and sixty?"

"I'm pretty sure it's one sixty to the front edge. Probably another ten or twelve to the center."

Donald eased out his five iron. *Whoosh. Pawhunk.* "Toby, girls and guys aren't all that different. It just feels different because the reasons that you make friends with girls is usually different than the reasons you make friends with guys. ... Look, you're a nice guy and you have a good heart. This is why your friends like you so much. Just be friendly with her, and don't be in a hurry. If you start to talk to her and get all flustered, back away and try again later. After you talk to her, see if she makes the effort to talk with you. If she's a good person, she'll recognize that you're trying and she'll try too. Just have some faith, little man."

26

Lanai, Hawaii
March 20, 1978

"We can't possibly trust you. You're working for *the man*." Tim McLeigh's nostrils puffed out, coarse tufts of grey and black hair exposed for all at village meeting to see. His talent for creative hyperbole had found an outlet. "He's your boss for crying out loud. He wants to turn the island into his own medieval fiefdom. He wants to basically control the entire island. He wants everybody on the island to be his little minions and Stepford slaves. *Wave at the nice tourists and smile, folks. They pay your wages.* Give me a break. What are *we*? Chopped liver?"

"We already have a medieval fiefdom," responded Donald. "Our master is named Dole Fruit. The island is just going to get a different master. Get used to it. This is going to happen whether you want it or not. By the way, you know that DuBrock is not paying me anything, right? You know he's paying my salary to the Lanai City Library? I don't owe him one damn nickel. My whole reason for working for him is because I can influence him. Like, DuBrock is already focused on the fact that if he doesn't redesign plumbing and sewer that he'll quickly exceed the island's resources. He's abandoned his idea of expanding irrigation systems on the golf course."

Tim smirked. "Oh, so we can just assume you'll take care of everything? Just put our faith in Donald and *everything* will be fine?"

"Donald, Tim's being annoying, like usual, but he's right. You act as if it's all going to be fine and dandy," said Kiki Arakawa. "But nobody can give us any assurances that any good will come out of this. It's just one big question mark. What about all the people who would be on the island *all the time*? The noise and the trash and the traffic and the hustle and bustle? It would just be so *wrong*."

Donald swallowed slowly. "Look at the facts. We know that Dole Fruit is leaving the island. They don't believe it's profitable to grow pineapples on Lanai. Dole won't let this land sit untended if they can get something for it. They're going to sell it or rent it to *somebody*.

"Suppose we could stop Dole from selling, and suppose we could prevent DuBrock from buying and building. What would happen? Everybody on the island who isn't receiving Social Security or who isn't independently wealthy would be out of work and unable to buy groceries. Imagine what that does to our way of life." He paused for effect. "No grocery stores. No bank. Hundreds and hundreds of Lanaians would flee for Oahu or Maui and leave behind a village full of empty houses surrounded by weeds and trash and feral dogs. Paradise gets uglier than my ex-wife's mother."

Tina stood. "Donald, there's so much change and so much uncertainty involved here. You can't blame us for being concerned. Our way of life is at stake. I heard DuBrock talk about being *a good steward of the environment*. He wants to control the environment and suck profit out of it. He's going to screw it up."

Donald stood to respond and opened his mouth. Bobby Joe, pulling rank, quieted him with a wave of his hand and a tilt of his head. "Folks, the more Donald talks the more I think he makes sense. Unless we want to hire a team of lawyers to file an injunction in court, there's no stopping this. Even if we do file, there's little chance of success. Karen Nakamura tells me that once an administrative agency has issued a decision, it's almost impossible to get the courts to change it. Dole *is* moving out. I talked to their Lanai manager and he confirmed it. I have copies of stories from The Wall Street Journal that Dole has invested big in Vietnam and Thailand for its pineapple farms. Anybody who wants to can come by my house and I'll show you.

"I was there when DuBrock offered Donald a job. Donald had the man eating out of his hand. Big, complex and expensive issues that DuBrock's mainland architects and engineers hadn't even considered, Donald shoved them right in DuBrock's face. It's obvious that DuBrock is looking for ways to make his project work within the island's limits."

Donald seated, looked up to Bobby Joe and offered up a quiet smile. *Thanks, man. I needed that.*

After Village Meeting, Donald stood outside the chapel and waited for Tina. Wendy Walker walked up to him and didn't stop until he could smell her Coco Chanel. "You have a lot of nerve. You really do. You come in here and throw your weight around like you own the place and you've hardly been here twelve months. This is not over." Before Donald could say a thing, Wendy and her blonde hair walked away.

27

Honolulu, Hawaii
April 1, 1978

"David you're a sonofabitch. You're putting me in a real box."
Denny DeLorenzo was practically foaming at the mouth.

"All's fair in business, Denny. Like sending me an insecure lieutenant to float a proposal worth sixty million dollars when you could have done it yourself. Did you think I was going to feel sorry for the guy and roll over?"

"Be careful what you say about him. He's a terribly bright young businessman. So how soon can we close this deal? We want to get Lanai off our books. Our institutional shareholders aren't going to be happy if the island operations keep cutting into profits."

"Denny, on the front end of this project, Dole is going to take on some debt. We still have some approvals to secure, which will take several months. Construction will take two years. You'd better be ready for some negative earnings."

"Like I said, you're putting me in a box. You know me too well and you're taking advantage of me."

"I'm doing no such thing, Denny. I'm giving Dole a substantial stake in a business that will grow. Dole has the chance to make a lot of profit and to acquire equity in a project that's likely to become quite valuable. I'm just making sure Dole has an incentive to give me a fair price on the deal and to help this project succeed, which it will."

"So can we talk about how to get this deal done?"

"Denny, there are a couple of threads still hanging loose. Like, in the foreseeable future, I'm going to need a work force. So I need Dole to keep growing pineapples. As soon as I need people, you can announce you're cutting back production and announce layoffs. As the need for workers increases, you can cut back more until eventually you're not doing any farming at all. Lanai will be off your books. I won't even be charging you rent to use the fields that you've sold me."

"So you want the field workers to go straight into the hotel business? One day a field worker and the next a bellhop?"

"I want them to be unemployed for about three weeks before they get job offers from me. They'll come in to fill out an application hungry for work, and feel grateful when they get hired. I'll even give them signing bonuses about equal with the pay they would have had for the weeks they were out of work."

"Are you being kind or manipulative? I can't tell."

"It's neither, Denny. It's *business*. I want employees who are grateful to have work. Our wealthy guests want clean cut, deferential and well-spoken waiters and maids and front desk personnel. These people have been field hands who could go to work unshaven and unshowered. They won't be able to do that in the hotel industry. Not if they want to keep their jobs."

"What else do you want?"

"We're bound to encounter local opposition to the project. This kind of change will scare the pants off of them. Dole has to talk up this project and help make it look good. You need to publicly present Dole as a partner in this venture."

"That's easy enough. Anything else?"

"Yes. After phase one of the hotel opens, future plans will probably increase building density above zoning limits. When the time comes, I need to use your law firm to usher through the requests for special exceptions to zoning. I need them to convince the county supervisors to keep in place the agricultural tax breaks on the hotel property until we're actually open. Maui and Lanai are both beholden to Dole and they already seem to have a certain comfort level with your lawyers. So you need to get your lawyers to agree to represent me on this even though they will probably find there's a conflict of interest present. I'll be happy to sign whatever they want, going along with the arrangement."

"Done. Anything else? Or do we have a deal?"

"We have a deal."

"Alright then. I'll have my guys talk to your guys and get the paperwork all finalized. Can you come to Honolulu for the closing? I'm thinking maybe three or four weeks ought to do it."

"That'll work. Have your girl call Damien when you think you have a date and he'll put it on my calendar." David motioned to Damien, who was seated on a nearby couch and, unbeknownst to Denny DeLorenzo, was listening in on an extension.

"Excellent, then. So when you come out, do you want to bring Dolores with you? You can stay in our guest house and the four of us can have drinks and play golf like in the old days. It will be fun."

"Dolores will love that. I can't wait to tell her. We'll see you in a few weeks."

David and Damien both hung up their phones at the same moment. "You got them to give you everything you wanted. Very good, sir."

"Thank you, Damien. Call over to Jeff in legal and give him the details. Tell him I want him to get in touch with Al Benanua right away. I want this done."

28

Lanai, Hawaii
May 8, 1978

Bobby Joe always liked the seventeenth hole mostly because it featured a drive across a rocky inlet with a view of the Pacific that, most days, included whales that breached. After he and Donald teed off and started their walk, Bobby Joe figured he'd better speak his mind before the round was over and the chance was lost. "Donald, could you lose the f-word? It really bothers folks to hear it so much. You say it all the time."

"Lose the *fuck*? Stop saying *fuck*? Emily Fucking Post, lookee here. *Fuck* is maybe my best friend of all time. *Fuck* is the family dog that loves you and sticks by you when you're on the outs. *Fuck* is the bond between brothers who just got busted by their mom looking at the dusty stack of dad's Playboys that were stashed in the attic."

Donald snorted and stared at Bobby Joe. "Lose the *fuck*? How could you possibly console somebody who just had their new car plowed into by some dickhead who drove off and didn't leave a note without the *fuck*? It's *Oh, fuck, my man. That's the worst.* When you're at the bar buying the guy a drink to make him feel better, you tell the bartender *Johnny's car got fucking tagged in the fucking parking lot by some fucking idiot.* And Johnny feels better because he knows there's people who feel his pain and identify with him. I mean, how do you boost a pal who just got a big bonus without *fuck*? A moment like that is *Eight fucking thousand dollars? The man gave you eight fucking thousand dollars?* Your buddy is on top of the world because in his pocket he's got eight *fucking* thousand dollars. He shares that with you because he knows that when he gets home, his wife is going to pinch that *fucking* wad for something like a new *fucking* powder room in pink *fucking* tile. But he knows he's got friends who know exactly what that *fucking* means and they want the moment to be *fucking* special.

"So no more fuck? Stop saying *fuck*? No fucking way. No. Fucking. Way. This is who I am. You might as well ask Salvador Fucking Dali to stop drawing clocks that look like they got poured out of a soda bottle. You know what I'm saying, right? You know? I'm saying you're being fucking ridiculous."

"Have mercy, Lord. Donald, I think you're away."

29

Lanai, Hawaii
November 24, 1978

Bobby Joe's arms came down fast and ahead of his torso. When the head of his seven wood struck, the ball sailed low and weakly to the left and then sliced high across the fairway and got pushed backward by the wind. He wondered if the rules of physics had been suspended by a malevolent deity amused by the despondency of a vulnerable human. He clenched his teeth and held on. *How in the hell did I do that?*

He shuffled back to his bag. He shoved in the grip end and chewed on his cheek. *This ain't working out so good.*

On the day, there had been little to celebrate. Bobby Joe had three-putted the submissive green on number one. His shot to the elevated green on number two had sailed high, bounced off the pock-marked wall above and then rolled off the edge. It returned to his feet where it taunted him, knowing he would be unable to think of anything but failure when he swung again. He had chunked his approach on number nine and his ball landed in a two-inch depression that had probably been left by the heel of the wide man in plaid pants who had come from Oklahoma to visit with Mr. Aoki. There was the tee shot on number ten that he had whiffed. That was when his back began to feel like a Snickers bar that had been left in the freezer. And how many wedge shots had he hit thin today? He drummed his fingertips on the top edge of his bag and tried to think of something happier.

Jerry McLeigh, Karen Nakamura and George Burdell grabbed their bags and started their so-happy-to-be-golfing walk up the short grass. Bobby Joe put his hand on his bag and started to pick it up. Just as quickly, he set it back down again and slumped. *Do I really have to finish this round?* Karen did an awkward stop mid-step and turned back. From twenty yards away, she motioned. *Come on. Pull it together. Nothing can be as bad as all that.*

After a short march and a little poking around, Bobby Joe located his ball, sunk into a depression filled with dense growth. With a seven iron, he hoped to muscle the ball. Mid-swing, he straightened up, rotated at the waist and slapped the toe of his iron at the ball's center. He watched in silent distress as his shot darted into a line of trees. A few seconds later, an unseen hand threw the ball into the center of the fairway. *Oh, Bradley, bless you. I needed that.*

As Donald waited for his playing partners to putt on the twelfth green, he stared at a spot on the thirteenth fairway, 360 yards away, where Bobby Joe picked up his ball and put it in his pocket. George, Jerry and Karen simultaneously turned their attention from their putting to their friend. He waved his hands low in front of him. *No, no. It's alright. I'm done.* Karen reached out and put a hand around Bobby Joe's neck and pulled him close. *C'mon. We love having you with us.*

Bobby Joe picked up his golf bag and exited the course on the right side of the green, through the pine path that lead to Puu'nali Lane, past the shack where Bradley ate and slept, and then around the corner where there stood a monkey pod tree, believed to be the oldest living thing on the island, and then to a familiar pale house with peeling paint which was home.

An hour later, he was sitting in his kitchen, a Primo in hand and listening to *Astral Weeks* when Donald let himself in.

"So what's bothering you?"

"Who says *anything* is bothering me?"

"Well, you got all lackadaisical when you had to poke your ball out of the dip on the thirteenth fairway. Then you muffed an easy approach to the green that I've seen you make a hundred times. You picked up your ball and bailed out in the middle of a round. And here you are drinking alone and listening to mood music written and performed by a man who, according to you, is a little over the top with his devotion to Christianity. Yeah, I'd say there's something bothering you."

"Relax, Donald. There ain't nothin' to be worrying about."

"Somebody once told me that you golf the way you live. A guy who doesn't even want to finish a round with the lovely Karen Nakamura? You look like a guy who's tired of being alive."

"Donald, don't worry about me. I'm fine."

"Bullshit. That's complete and obvious bullshit. Something has burrowed deep under your skin, chief. Something nasty. Come on. Spill it. It will make you feel better."

Bobby Joe sniffed at the air and then dug his tongue in between his cheek and gum where, decades ago, he used to enjoy working on a chaw of Red Man. He took a deep, last slug from his beer and swished it around. He pushed his toe at the little spots of sunshine that had been lucky and persistent enough to make it from eighty six million miles away right here into the kitchen of the most beloved man in the village.

"Hello?"

"What?"

"What the fuck do you mean *what*? Kahuna, this is not some wing nut you're talking to. This is *me*. This is the guy who defends you to the fundamentalists in the village who think you're immoral because you're not Christian. The same guy who owes you for pulling his sorry ass out of a near-fatal car crash. Man, you can't just sit there and hope I'm going to give up and go away."

"Donald, I need to tell you something. It's … well, it's not what you might expect."

Donald nodded.

"You need to promise me you'll keep this to yourself. Nobody can hear about this."

Donald nodded again. "This is just us."

"See, Dixie and I were a couple. We were practically married. She was the best friend I ever had. Donald, when you minister to a village, you start to carry around other people's problems. Some days you even look at people as foolish because they can't solve problems that seem minor. She was the only one I could talk to when I found myself getting annoyed or irritated by people who I honestly care for. The only one. She knew just when to shut me up because I'd been going on too long. Lately, she's been showing up in my dreams at night like she's still alive and everything's just fine and I can just walk over to her house and she's sitting on the couch and I can lay down and put my head in her lap and she'll play with my ears and call me *goober*."

Bobby Joe sucked down a mouthful of beer. "When I wake up and she's not here, I feel like the loneliest, most tired man in the world. It's a feeling that lasts for a whole day. I just miss her. I really miss her. I have buried myself in what I do for the village to make up for her not being here, just to keep busy with something positive. It's coming up on two years since she died and I've gone as far as I can on that. Donald, I'm out of gas. I feel like I have nothing left to give. Just … nothing. I just can't get over that she's gone. It's killing me. Some days, I can't hardly drag myself out of bed. It's just too much. Without Dixie? I just can't hardly manage." Bobby Joe looked straight on at Donald. His eyes were glistening. "You wanted to know what's wrong? Well, that's what's wrong. I'm having a crisis of faith and I don't have anyone I can talk to about it."

"Wait … what? You and Dixie? You were married?"

"Practically married. We spent almost all our time together. We cared for each other. We had a relationship."

"But you each had your own house."

Bobby Joe sucked in some extra air, hoping it would impart enough patience so he could politely answer what seemed like a stupid question. "Donald, Dixie was very smart about these things. She said that if we lived together, we would get tired of each other, and she was right. She didn't want us getting all pissy with one another because I was the neat freak in our relationship and I couldn't stand that she always let things get so messy. She didn't want us arguing over money or home repair jobs or whose turn it was to scoop shit balls out of the litter box for the whiny cat she used to have. She figured if we each kept our own house, we could have a place where we could retreat sometimes to deal with our own stuff. She didn't want us becoming an old married couple who got terminally riled at each other.

"So we lived in separate houses. More than half of the year, we were sleeping at her house or at mine. We were making breakfast together. All the time, we listened to Van Morrison together. We went on trips together. Like, once a year we would go to San Diego and play Torrey Pines. All the time, we loved each other. I've never had a friend who understood me like Dixie. I think she felt the same about me. We were totally simpatico."

"You and Dixie? *Really*? I would never have guessed."

Donald stared awkwardly at his feet, not sure what to say. His fascination with learning that Dixie wasn't gay had overcome his desire to assuage his friend and he was struggling to find a way to get back on track. All those years in Glen Burnie bringing up him and Teddy and she never mentioned interest in a single man. Donald had foolishly assumed it was because she harbored a secret. There she was faithfully waiting for the day when she could get back to her man, the one waiting for her six thousand miles away.

"Donald, I think I'm just going to go take a nap. I'll see ya. Thanks for coming by."

"You know, if Dixie was here she would tell you that you were being silly. She would say that you're a big enough person to walk on your own two feet, that you need to go out into that big world and just be happy. That's what she told me whenever I got to feeling sorry for myself because my parents were dead."

"She wouldn't say I was being silly."

"Oh, no? You don't think so?"

"She would say I was being an asshole. She couldn't stand for people to go around feeling sorry for themselves, especially if they ran on about it. Donald, I *know* this. I know all of it. I've run it through my head a hundred and fifty eleven times trying to get back to feeling normal. But I got them walkin' blues. Every day, I'm further away from remembering what Dixie's voice sounded like and what it felt like to have her laying next to me. This is just the worst old feeling I've ever had. It's taken over and I probably just need to rest." Kahuna emptied out the dribbles from his nearly empty beer bottle into the sink and chucked it into the trashcan. He turned to go into his bedroom.

"Kahuna? Rest up. I hope it makes you feel better. But as you run things through your mind, remember this: There's a reason that everybody here loves you and wants to be close to you. There's a reason that you could go shit on everybody here and they would still love you. There's a reason that a fuckhead like me has managed to get over himself and learn a little humility. *That reason?* That reason is you being devoted to the needs of others. You have lived a life where the most important thing is kindness to the people around you. You don't push one religion or one supreme being down everybody's throat like if we don't believe in a special and specific one, we're going to burn in hell for eternity. You keep together a community of people, some of whom fervently believe their friends and neighbors are going to hell because they worship the wrong god. They all believe in different shit and yet they hold together. Do you know why this village … "

"Donald, enough. Please? That's enough."

"No. It's not enough. It's not even close to enough. You don't deserve to feel shitty. You got no business moping around like this. You're better than that. Do you know why this village is the place it is? It's because you are the one we all hope to be like. You're the one everybody uses as a yardstick to measure themselves against when they wonder if they're living right or wrong. You're the one. *You.* Do you know why an uber-Catholic control freak like Tim McLeigh can get along nice with a profane agnostic like me? It's because we both know you would be disappointed in us if we didn't find a way to get along. Neither one of us can stomach the idea that we might let down the man we both respect. Neither one of us wants to feel like we don't measure up."

Donald considered stopping there. Bobby Joe's morose expression convinced him he'd better keep going. "Forty years from now, this village will still be here running along the same happy way it is now. It's all because people like Toby and Ramona and even folks like Tina and me, if we're still alive, know the beauty and the importance of kindness and tolerance. That's not me being nice, that's me being honest about how important you are to the people in this village. If you're going to sit home and hide your loneliness, people won't understand. They won't understand why the guy who always reached out to them didn't let people reach out to him. They won't understand why the guy who prevents each of us from pulling into our shells in our weak moments is doing exactly that. Don't do that. The village can't afford it. People around here would feel cheated and closed out if they knew. The people who feel close to you, Toby and Ramona for starters, would start to wonder if that had been the real you they thought they were dealing with all those years."

"Thank you, Donald. I'm going to sleep now. It's escapism, I know, but I can't help but feel right weary." He put a hand on Donald's solid shoulder and offered a face that sagged at the edges. Then he hesitated. "Donald, you know, those are exactly the kinds of things Dixie used to say to me. So *thank you*. Really. I mean it. Thank you. I think I'm starting to see in you what Dixie admired so much."

"She admired me?"

"Absolutely she did. She said that when you were at your best, it always seemed to bring out the best in others."

"Wow. Who knew? I always thought I had disappointed her. She always seemed to act like I had fallen short." Donald turned to go, and then he turned back. "Kahuna, after your nap, why don't you come over? Toby went fishing yesterday and caught him some really nice papio. It's home marinating right now. I'm going to grill it up for dinner. A little company and a few laughs would do you some good. You can relax. No cooking to do. No dishes to do, and you know how much you enjoy being with Toby and Ramona."

"Donald, that sounds right nice. I'll be there. What time?"

"Kahuna, see, here's the thing. People around here don't wear watches or watch the clock. When you see the sky starting to get a little dark, it's dinner time. Seriously, man. Are you *tense* or what?"

Donald reached out his arms and absorbed Bobby Joe. "You crazy little Chinaman. I love you. I really do." He took a knuckle and knocked it gently on the small man's shiny head. "Here's a noogie for your troubles, goober. We'll see you at dinnertime."

30

San Diego, California
April 20, 1979

In the early days of summer at Torrey Pines South, the greenness and the freshness of the surroundings have brought callous geezers to tears. The idea that they get to spend one of their last days on earth on one of the most beautiful golf courses on Earth can be too much to bear. On the sixteenth hole, a par three, the view of the green is framed by a Pacific so effervescent it reminds most adults of the first time they sipped champagne. There is no horizon; the off-coast San Diego mist makes it look like the sea and the sky are a Zen-like one. It's enough to make you forget the deep bunkers that wait for any ball that strays just a little left or right.

"Ramona, do you want your seven?"

"Kahuna, I want my six. The air is heavy today and seems to be slowing my shots and the wind from the ocean is blowing toward us. Plus the flag is way back."

Kahuna handed Ramona her seven. "You probably want this. You're only looking at 151 yards to the center." He nodded with a purpose.

Ramona tightened her bottom lip. Do I say anything to the guy who taught me to play? Who volunteered to caddy for me in a tournament that might win me a college scholarship? Because this is not enough club. She waggled and took her club back as far as it would go. She turned her hips hard, hoping it would get her extra distance. Her ball settled on a slope on the front portion of the green and rolled backwards, ending up twenty yards away from the putting surface. If I had hit my six, I'd be putting for birdie.

Ramona pitched from the short grass and left herself a six-footer. She read the break correctly but hit it light and missed saving par by three quarters of an inch.

On the seventeenth, she waited for the twosome playing ahead by praying for peace of mind. She refused to look at the leaderboard visible in the distance. She thought it was bad luck to check it in the middle of a round. "What do I want to do here?"

"You're tied for the lead with your playing opponent. You probably want to push for a birdie on one of the remaining holes, unless she bogies."

Ramona blasted her tee shot 255 yards and left herself an approach of just over one 150 yards. Bobby Joe handed her a six iron and Ramona shook her head. "I need my seven."

"You just hit your seven on a 150-yard shot and came up short."

"Yeah, but the wind was against me. The wind here is behind us." Ramona yanked out her seven. She avoided Bobby Joe's gaze, which she feared would disclose the notes of judgment running through her mind. She focused on her ball and the brush of the heel of her club against the turf as she rehearsed her next shot. *Why can't he just give me the club I asked for? Does he think he knows better than me?*

Ramona set up and swung. She hit the turf just ahead of her ball, which slowed her club head and pulled it open. Her shot went high, short and right. It landed in a greenside bunker shaped like a diseased kidney. *I let myself get angry. I have to calm down.* After digging her feet into the sand, Ramona skimmed the sand with a wedge and lofted her ball to within two feet. She tapped in for a par save. Her playing opponent hit the green with her approach and two putted. *Still tied.*

On the eighteenth, a 485-yard par five, Ramona striped a drive 258 yards down the middle. Her playing opponent could manage only 230, not her best drive of the day. With her second shot, Ramona's playing partner laid up short of a pond that fronted the green.

"Three wood, please."

Bobby Joe blanched. "You want to go for the green? Are you sure? That's 275 yards."

"I came to win, remember?"

"That's a long poke, sister."

Ramona reached over and yanked out her three wood and gave Bobby Joe a hairy eyeball.

She set her line and imagined her shot. She stood at address and waggled. *Why does he have to say things like that? I'm not a little kid.* Ramona backed away and took a deep inhale. *I have to calm down.* She closed her eyes and prayed again for peace of mind. When she found it, she stood at address. Her swing and her follow through happened as if somebody else was holding the club; it was all muscle memory. After her follow through, she balanced on her left foot, club resting on her shoulder and watched as her ball flew high and straight. *Come on, be the number.* Her ball touched down in a small band of rough grass and bounced onto the green. It followed the left edge of a ridge that bisected the green from front to back and then turned left toward the pin. It came to rest just four feet from the hole on a triangular platform of bentgrass. The tiny gallery exploded in applause. She extended the grip of her three wood in Bobby Joe's direction, expecting him to take it from her. She refused to look at him.

Ramona's playing partner was a high schooler from Knoxville, Tennessee, named Christy. She liked argyle golf shirts and had her name sewn onto her staff bag in raised stitching that matched the color of her shoes. Neither she nor her big brother, who was working as her caddy, had uttered a word for the entire round. Christy pulled out a fifty-six degree loft wedge and stroked her ball two feet past the hole. Right after Ramona felt her heart leap with joy, it sank again. Christy had launched her ball with enough backspin that it spun backward and dropped into the hole. Christy jumped on her caddy's back, put a fist in the air and screamed. "Yes!"

Bobby Joe handed Ramona her putter. "Don't miss."

Ramona closed her eyes. "You don't think I know that already? Can you just be *quiet?*" She knew right away she had acted poorly. "I'm sorry Kahuna. I guess I'm feeling the stress."

As she stood over her putt, she noticed her hands were trembling. She backed away and found that she couldn't draw in a smooth breath. She kneeled and closed her eyes and prayed for more peace of mind. She couldn't find it. All she could think of was Bobby Joe's message of desperation: *Don't miss.*

Ramona rechecked her line. She stood at address. She drew back her putter. Then she pushed her ball left and four inches past the hole.

—⚡︎—

"Mom, he kept doing stuff that made me mad. Like, he kept talking to me as if I was still just nine years old. I could have won that tournament. I could have *won*."

"Ramona, you wouldn't have been in that tournament if Kahuna hadn't taught you what he did. Next year, you'll just have to try and do better."

"Do I have to take Kahuna as my caddy? Do I *have* to? He's smart and everything and I love him. But he doesn't know how to deal with competition. He doesn't know what to do to make me win."

"Ramona, the only one who makes you win is you. *You.* Don't try and pass the buck on this. You have to take responsibility for your own actions."

"Oh, mom, you don't understand. You don't understand tournament golf. You just don't. It was *me* golfing out there, but being in a competition is different than just playing a round. Kahuna doesn't get that. I love him and he's my friend. I just don't want to use him as my caddy. That's not so terrible, is it?"

"You *have* to take him as your caddy. He would be insulted if you didn't."

31

Lanai, Hawaii
April 21, 1979

"Who does this guy think he is? He acts like all righteous, like he's Jerry Fucking Falwell."

"What guy? Who?"

"Bradley. Who else? He just stole another ball. It landed right here, I'm sure of it."

Donald clomped around the woods adjacent to the fairway on number six and could not find the Titleist he had hit with a perfect draw so that it tracked the curve of the banana-shaped fairway. He pulled another from his pocket and dropped it on the turf. "I've apologized twice already." Donald stroked his ball flush with a six iron and watched it fly the green. *Damn. He's screwing with my head.*

"What did you say, exactly? When you apologized, I mean."

"I told him I was sorry that I had upset him so much. I was sincere. I really was sorry."

"That's not an apology."

"Yes it is."

"No, it's not. All you're saying is you're sorry that he's upset. You're not apologizing for the things you did. If all you do is apologize for making somebody mad, you're missing the point. An apology is saying here's what I did wrong and I shouldn't have done it."

"That's screwy. Totally screwy."

Karen looked Donald square in the eye. "Screwy is trying to play here while Bradley is mad at you."

32

Lanai, Hawaii
April 22, 1979

The 1944 Ford GPW was a field mechanic's dream. Designed for military use, the engine compartment was spacious enough to house a soldier who wanted to crawl in, pull the hood closed and get out of a rainstorm. Removing the cylinder head to change the gasket required removal of only six tall-headed bolts which fit pleasantly into the receptacle of a three-quarter-inch socket wrench. Underneath, the car had nearly twenty-four inches of clearance, which made it a cinch for an ordinary man to slip in with a bucket and open the drain plug when it was time for an oil change. He could also take cover if mean people with guns were trying to kill him.

"Kahuna, you could not have picked a better car for Lanai. Where in the hell did you manage to find one?"

"Over on Oahu, they had a surplus auction back around 1960. The Navy used to keep tons of them."

Donald slid out from under and began wiping down his greasy forearms with a faded shred of towel. "I got your head gasket changed and I swapped out both your anti-freeze and your oil. Plus I put in new plugs. The old ones were fouled from the engine fluids leaking into the cylinders. You shouldn't be blowing blue smoke any more and it will run a lot smoother."

Later in Kahuna's kitchen, Donald shoveled in food from a paper plate. "Kahuna, where did you learn to cook so good?"

"My mama, God bless her, because I was her only child, she always kept me close to her, even when she was cooking. She learnt me how not to make some awful Chinese food."

Donald dug a pair of chopsticks into a mound of stir-fried ingredients, most of which he couldn't identify. "What is this – bananas?"

"Plantain."

"What is *that*?"

"A starchy fruit that looks like a banana but is usually not quite as sweet. When you cook it, some of it converts to sugar and it gets sweeter."

"What's this stringy stuff?"

"Samphire. It's like seaweed."

Donald's head popped up. He stopped chewing.

"It grows near the ocean. It likes salt water. It goes very well with the abalone that's mixed in with the rest of that stuff on your plate. Much better than Spam, wouldn't you agree?"

"I'm probably better not knowing everything you put in here."

"Next time, I'll not hit you with so much all at once. So listen, I need to ask you something. How would you feel about traveling to the mainland with Ramona and caddying for her in the national amateur? I'm talking about after your third anniversary, of course."

"Kahuna, that's something you do."

Bobby Joe shook his head. "It doesn't have to be. I believe you might have certain talents I don't. You have the killer instinct. You know how to focus on winning, and you have a salesman's gift for making people feel at ease. Not many folks have both. You'd be perfect for this."

"Are you serious?"

"Serious as a Baptist missionary. I know you still count strokes even when you're playing for fun. You try daring shots late in your rounds when it looks like you're trying to break some number. You are a *competitor* – and why do you think Toby comes to you for advice? It's because he feels comfortable talking with you. You've got the salesman's gift. He doesn't talk to anybody else on the island like he talks to you. His mother has been a little worried about him, like he was getting all closed up inside."

"How do you know this?"

"Donald, come on. How much do you know about other people on this island, some of whom you've never even met? Word gets around, slick."

"So do you think Ramona wants a new caddy?"

"I can sense it. This year, she lost by a whisker and I think she was put out with me. She's a good, balanced kid who is all about kindness, but put her in a tournament and she's all about winning. I've seen how you two get along on the golf course. You guys are ham and eggs."

33

Lanai, Hawaii
April 30, 1979

"Ramona, why don't you go first?" Donald waved her onto the tee box. Donald motioned to Ted and pulled him several steps away. He quieted his voice: "Teddy you need to watch this girl. Her swing is *amazing*."

Ramona found her target line and took a few moments to compose herself. She set up, took a flowing backswing and then uncoiled with a muscular flourish. Her shot flew like a tiny cannonball on a nearly straight path toward the flag. It touched down almost 200 yards away and then bounced for another 40.

Donald raised his eyebrows. "Ever seen a girl hit like that?"

"There are some PGA pros who can't hit like that. Holy *shit*."

"Grab your driver, Ted. Fire away, man."

Ted dropped his shoulders and squinted. "You want to wait until after I hit before you go? Are you feeling okay?"

"You've been drooling about playing in Hawaii. Go already."

Bobby Joe nodded with approval. "Ted, go ahead. This is the kind of afternoon that makes a feller want to take his time."

Ted surveyed the hole, teed up a Wilson and aimed to the left edge of the fairway. He hit an outside-in slice that put his ball on a nice piece of short grass 200 yards out.

Donald and Bobby Joe looked at one another. Donald yielded with a shrug of his shoulders and a tilt of his head. Bobby Joe took a moment on the tee box with his eyes closed before he tagged his ball and rifled it 220 yards.

Donald set up with his manly stance. He drew his club back as far as he could, the muscles in his gluteus tensing. Then there was an efficient downswing that sounded like a hummingbird flitting past your earlobe. Before anybody knew it, his Titleist, one of two dozen that Ted had brought him from the mainland, was 235 yards away, patiently waiting for its master.

After hiking to his ball, Ted pulled out a nine iron and tried to imagine how to get his close to the flagstick. "Bobby Joe, any tips?"

"Take it high and see if you can land it on the front edge of the green. It should roll to the back edge and turn right, close to the hole. Keep it center or center left."

Ted practiced a half-swing, hoping for nothing more than a 100 yard shot. He set up, prepared to swing and then, feeling incorrect, stepped back.

"Teddy, you got this, man. I've seen you make this shot a thousand times."

Ted grinned quizzically. *Is he softening me up? Is he going to ask for money later?* "Thanks. Thanks for the encouragement, brohawn." He stepped up and gave his ball a pop. It landed on fairway grass, just shy of the green, bounced once and then rolled right. It stopped on the right edge of the green, about twenty yards from the flag.

Bobby Joe made the shot he had recommended to Ted, leaving himself with a two-foot putt for birdie.

Donald extracted a pitching wedge and practiced a smooth takeaway and a stiff-armed quarter swing. He looked to Bobby Joe. "Positive thoughts?"

"Absolutely. And breathe."

Donald stepped over to Ted and gave his brother a hug and then pointed straight at his face with an index finger that was backed up by authority and energy from sources unknown. "I love you, man. You're the best." He beamed. "OK. I really feel *positive* now. I'm basking in the beatific glow of unconditional love and acceptance."

Ted shook his head and blinked. *What the hell is this?*

Donald returned to his ball and, with a swing as smooth as a pair of satin panties, carried his ball high and long enough that it bounced on the hairy front edge of the green and rolled long and right, leaving him a six-footer.

Ted pulled off his cap and ran his fingers through his hair. His mouth wide open, he looked to Bobby Joe and uttered one-third of a syllable. He looked to Donald and then back to Bobby Joe.

Bobby Joe believed for a moment he night need to summon Doctor Arai. "Ted, are you ok?"

He inhaled and then exhaled and then waited for the wheels to stop spinning. "Yeah. I'm fine. Just fine."

On the sixth hole, Donald gently sliced his drive, trying to get around a bend in the fairway. After flying over 200 yards, his ball plopped down and dribbled up to the edge of a line of trees.

"Oh, nice shot. You're made it past that stand of plumeria. I been there a hundred times. There's a patch of short grass over there. You'll have a nice line to the green," said Bobby Joe.

Donald arrived at the landing spot but decided his ball had vanished. He searched about in vain, wondering if he had bounced further into the trees than he had first thought. Then came the heavy footsteps in the shadows. *Is that Bradley? Holy shit.*

Donald pulled an extra out of his pocket and took a drop. *This is for you Bradley, you little prick.* He stroked a six iron and released early, leaving a divot ahead of the ball. His ball flew a measly fifty yards. "Aw, you little *motherfucker.*"

Bobby Joe approached. "Tough luck, Cletus. Looks like Bradley's still mad at you."

"He *still* can't let go? That was a lifetime ago."

"Apologize. Get it over with."

Ted pondered it all. "Who is this guy? What's his story?"

"Bradley is not like you or me," said Bobby Joe. "He has a really hard time talking with people, even being around them. When he does talk to someone, it seems like he always says something that don't fit the conversation. His mama was a sweet woman who lived near the fifteenth green. When she got cancer and knew she was going to pass, she asked me and a few other villagers to look after him. So we make sure he has what he needs. He thinks of himself as the enforcer of the rules of the community. It makes him feel useful."

Bobby Joe put a hand on Donald's shoulder. "Apologize. He'll be happy. You'll be happy."

"I've tried. I wrote a note and left it on his door. Karen said it probably wasn't good enough."

"What did you do that you have to apologize for?"

Donald bit his lip and sighed. "You don't want to know."

"Yeah, I do, dickweed. Spill it."

"I went out and played a round on the village course before the board of elders gave me permission to play alone. Bradley saw me on the course. We had us a little scuffle."

Donald pulled a small container of seed mix out of his bag and filled his divot. He collected the small bits of grass and soil he had distributed with his club head and tamped them on top of the bruise. "Apologize. *Sheesh.*" He clenched his teeth. "It frosts me when I make a good shot and I have to worry about crap like getting my ball stolen."

Ramona set up and, with a delicate swing of her seven iron, dropped her ball on the middle of the green.

Donald brightened. It was time to move on. "Little sister, that was *gorgeous.* Your short game is a beautiful thing."

On the seventh tee, Ramona started waggling in preparation for her drive. "Hold on, sugar," said Bobby Joe. A familiar figure in a top hat approached, goose stepping, followed by a caddy in white coveralls, carrying his bag. Ted looked at Donald and wrinkled his chin. *What the hell is this?*

"Ted, this is King Kalakaua, supreme ruler of the Hawaiian islands. It is customary to bow when he approaches." Donald winked. Donald, Ramona and Bobby Joe bowed at the waist. Ted hesitantly followed their example. "Would you like to play through, your Tremendousness? We would be honored if you did."

Donald motioned and into Alani's living room they went, Fumi following close behind.

"Get the hell out. Get out of my house. I don't want you. I don't need you."

"Alani. You please to let me examine. You have bruise on forehead. You need doctor. Maybe hospital."

"I don't need anything, especially from a bunch of *men*. Get out." Alani stood up, intending to make her point more forcefully. She lost her balance and fell back on her couch, arms flailing.

Fumi kneeled and took Alani's hand and waited for the woman to show signs of calm. "Relax and breathe. We love you and want to make sure you are healthy."

Ted scratched Beauregard under the chin and enjoyed watching the mutt close his eyes and hold perfectly still while sweetness and peace reached his core. "Your dog is a nice fellow."

"Beau is the best company there is. He ain't never once complained about nothin'. Not once in his whole life. You couldn't say that about anybody you ever met, now could you?"

Beauregard settled between Ted' knees, chin on his thigh.

"Bobby Joe, thank you. I mean it. Thank you."

"For what?"

"For giving me back my brother. He's back to being the kid I grew up with. I think you had a little something to do with that."

"All I've done is try and be good to him. Donald decides how he wants to live his life."

"I've tried for a long time to bring him back to reality. There's been no talking to him. Just none. Until now, anyway. So thanks. I feel like I have my brother back."

Bobby Joe sucked on his bottle of Primo. "I can't believe that a smart guy like Donald hasn't yet figured out who gets Dixie's estate if he fails to stay for the full three years."

"He still doesn't know? Has he even asked?"

"Nope."

"That would explain a few things. He has seemed strangely unappreciative of my efforts to help him make good use of his time here."

"Under the circumstances, I would have expected that."

"Maybe we should tell him. Do you think?"

"If we tell him that you and I are next in line to get Dixie's wealth, he might take it the wrong way. It would seem manipulative. If he figures it out on his own, he's a mite likelier to appreciate what his brother has done for him."

Ted nodded. "Bobby Joe, I can see why Dixie liked you so much."

—⧜—

Ted and Donald propped their feet on the dashboard while waiting by the runway for the plane that would take Ted on the first leg of his trip back to Maryland. Donald fished in his pants pocket and pulled out a slip of paper.

"Teddy, take this. It's a down payment on the money I owe you."

Ted scrutinized the paper. "A check for *two thousand dollars*? Right now, somewhere in hell, they're ice skating."

"Can you please not be a farthead? I'm trying to do the right thing."

"This is awesome, Donald." He folded the check in half and inserted it into his shirt pocket.

"Come back again soon? It's been great having you visit."

"Cathy and the kids will want to come. You know that, right? Getting a pass to go to Hawaii and play golf by myself wasn't easy."

"Bring 'em. We can take them to the Hagood sisters' house and do the hokey pokey."

34

Lanai, Hawaii
May 1, 1979

Alani put her grocery list in her purse and put on her hat, the faded purple one with the brass grommets around the headband. She took several steps toward the front door. *I need groceries. I am going to the market. I am and I will.* She reached for the doorknob, the last milestone on her way into the fishbowl of judgment that surrounded her domestic cocoon. Her hands began to shake.

So she sat and waited.

Then she got angry. *There's no reason I can't just go out this door right now and drive myself to the market. To hell with all those people out there and their value judgments.*

She stood up, opened the door, walked out and saw her Jeep elevated on jack stands with a pair of legs poking out from underneath.

"Who the hell are you and what are you doing to *my* car?"

The long legs began to slide out from under. They were attached to a long, male torso which was attached to a neck which was attached to a face. The face belonged to Donald. He sat up and pulled a rag from his waistband and began wiping his hands. His face was streaked with a slippery mixture of sweat and black grease.

"I fixed your brakes." Donald stood and rolled a floor jack underneath the middle of the front axle. He pumped the long handle and lifted the chassis several inches and, while remaining safely outside the frame, reached in to remove the jackstands. He then lowered the Jeep to the ground. "Your drums and pads were bad on all four corners. I was afraid you were going to run into my house next time you tried pulling into your driveway. That would be *bad.* So I fixed them. You know all that nasty screeching you used to get when you stepped on the brakes? That should be all gone now. It will stop when you want it to."

Alani stood and found herself feeling frozen. *What the hell is this all about?*

"I also replaced the line feeding brake fluid to the master cylinder. It was old and ready to crack. That meant I had to bleed the system and add some brake fluid. Your other brake lines are still pretty good."

Donald began collecting the detritus from a long morning of work: several empty boxes bearing a bright red *Raybestos* logo, dead brake pieces, desiccated bits of tubing and two empty Pepsi cans. He dumped them in Alani's trash can, which was parked next to her side door. "The next time you are having any problems with your car, just ask. I'm only twelve feet away."

Alani forgot to close her mouth and she let it hang as she slid in behind the wheel, started the engine and backed away on her way to town. Donald watched her disappear around the bend in the road.

Donald shouted after her, certain she could not hear: "*You're fucking welcome.*"

Standing at his kitchen sink, Donald worked up a satisfying lather that covered both forearms to the elbow. He scrubbed with his fingertips and whistled.

*Well, rave on
it's a crazy feeling,
And I know, it's got me reelin'...*

35

Lanai, Hawaii
July 2, 1979

Donald liked sitting on his front porch after dinner because of the feeling he got when the onset of night caused the world to turn black and to become nearly silent and everything, including him, was forced to yield. When that happened, he imagined he was being absorbed by something peaceful and much larger than himself.

Also, it was always nighttime when Tina would show up for a booty call.

All at once there was a presence. A person climbed Donald's front step, sat in the rocker next to him and put something heavy in his lap.

"Donald, these are brownies. I made them myself. There's a thank you note on top. It's made of paper so don't eat it."

In the dark, Donald stared at where he knew his lap was. *Well, this is awkward.*

"Um, who are you, exactly?"

"Donald, it's me. *Alani.*"

Donald exhaled. "Why are you bringing them to me?"

"You fixed my brakes. I'm supposed to say *thank you.*"

Donald's mouth sprang open. In the dark, he didn't have to worry about keeping a straight face. *That was two months ago.* "Alani, I was happy to help. I hope you feel safer now."

Alani left her hands in her lap and stared into the void. *I should probably say something now. But what?* Donald lifted the brownies to eye level and tried to examine them. In the night, he could see nothing. He could hear Alani breathing and thinking.

"Thank you for not putting any more cigarette butts on my lawn."

"You're welcome."

It got quiet again and stayed that way.

"Okay, bye."

37

Lanai, Hawaii
July 14, 1979

"Alani, you used to teach English, right? Can you look at this thing I wrote and tell me if it looks okay?" Donald handed her a sheet of paper and waited as Alani perused it.

"Grammatically it's fine."

"Yeah, but is it a good apology?"

Alani's head retreated. "Why do you need to make an apology?"

"You don't need to know that, do you?"

"How else can I tell if the apology is any good?"

Donald released some anxiety through pursed lips. "Here's the thing: I went out and played alone on the golf course before the Board of Elders gave me permission. Bradley saw me and we had a little, you know, *scuffle*. Now he won't leave me alone. He keeps stealing my balls on the course."

"Who's Bradley?"

"Bradley Spackler. Seriously, you don't know who he is?"

Alani shook her head. "Never heard of him."

"Bradley thinks of himself as the enforcer of the rules on the golf course. If you obey the rules, then he'll be nice and do things like find your golf ball in the woods when you hit a bad shot and toss it back onto the fairway for you. But if he thinks you're not following the rules, he'll hound you. He'll steal your balls off the fairways and mess with you."

"You're apologizing to *him*?"

"I broke the rules, and now he won't leave me alone. Almost every time I play, Bradley steals my balls."

"Then your note looks fine. It says you made a mistake by breaking the rules and you're sorry you did it. You even promise you won't do it again."

38

Lanai, Hawaii
September 8, 1979

With the underside of her wrist, Tina pushed aside the curly, red wisps sticking to her sweaty temples. She splooted two more shots of neon yellow dish soap into her sinkful of hot water, plunged in more dishes and began sponging them forcefully to remove a coating of dried pancake syrup that she had demonized. The dried syrup was named Rodney. Rodney was a pathological womanizer. Rodney had to go.

In the side yard, visible to Tina through a window just above her sink, Toby and Ramona were competing with sand wedges to see who could land a ball closest to a flagstick stuck into an open patch of grass.

"*Toby!*" she said, "I haven't heard you practicing your cello since Wednesday and you have a recital coming up. Mozart in B sharp is not going to learn itself, is it?"

"Mom, don't be so lame. There's no such *thing* as B sharp."

"Toby, you're missing the point. You need to practice."

"*Alright*, mom."

"Ramona, have you finished your homework? Don't you have a bio test?"

"Can't you be like a normal mother and neglect your kids sometimes?"

The pair shuffled in from the yard.

The sound of Bruce Springsteen floated out of Ramona's bedroom along with the commotion of shuffling papers and three-ring binders clacking open and closed. "Ramona? Please don't study with your stereo. It distracts your brother when he's playing his music, and it keeps you from concentrating."

"I'll just use my headphones."

"No music. Not until your homework is done."

The screen door at the back porch rattled. It was Donald. "Tina? Hey baby."

Tina leaned back from her steamy work station to glance out the door.

"Oh, hi." She turned her attention back to the sink.

"I tuned up your Toyota for you and cleaned out some gunk that had built up in the carburetor. It shouldn't sputter anymore. Here's your keys. I think it still needs a ring job because it's burning some oil. The parts will be in next week and I can put them in if you can do without your car for two days. I can, you know, let you borrow mine if you need it."

"Oh." Tina paused. "Um, thanks. Just drop the keys on the table there."

Donald stepped in and dropped the jangly bits. Tina kept at her dishes, her back turned to him.

"Here you go, Tina."

"Okay. Thanks again."

Donald glanced at the back of Tina's head and passed through the doorway. Just as soon he was back, his nose pressed against the screen.

"Tina? What the hell? Couldn't you at least act like you appreciate what I do for you?"

"I said *thanks*, didn't I?"

"Oh, come on. I would get better treatment if I was a stranger and had shown up hungry begging for food."

"You're exaggerating."

"You're avoiding the issue."

Tina's head dropped. She picked it up again and turned to face Donald. With the back of her hand, she motioned for him to back away

"Maybe. Maybe not. If I do it will be at ten thirty. Don't be asleep. It totally kills the mood if I have to get you warmed up." She stood up and dug her greasy fingernails into Donald's jaw, scowled and walked back into the kitchen. She let the screen door slam behind her.

39

Lanai, Hawaii
September 10, 1979

Benny Keahale always stood close to Wendy before prayer circle and they both knew why: Benny was sweet on her and wanted to hold her hand. He loved that Wendy's perfume smelled like a geisha girl he'd visited in Tokyo when he was in the Army and how the blue powder that went from her eyelids to her eyebrows made her face light up.

Wendy pretended that she didn't notice Benny's interest. It seemed nicer than saying what she really thought about a man with crooked teeth who was always hiking up his saggy corduroy shorts because he was too cheap to buy himself a belt.

"Let us pray." Wendy raised her arms and everyone joined hands. Benny's palm had grown sweaty in anticipation, as usual. Wendy grimaced as they joined hands.

Almighty and merciful father, we pray that you will guide us and sustain us as we come together to plan for the future of Lanai and its people. Father, give us your blessing and help us to find what is best for our beloved friends and neighbors. In Jesus' name we pray, Amen.

"Let's everybody have a seat and we can get started."

Benny looked around. "Wendy, shouldn't we wait for Donald? I thought he was planning on sharing some information with us tonight."

"He's late. We can't wait on him. He's only one man."

"Yes, but he's the man with the information."

"Benny, we're not waiting, not on *him*."

Wendy stood near the podium in the Chapel of Balance and made eye contact with several of the forty-plus village members assembled in the pews. She offered appreciation for their presence. And then she dove in: "So how do we avoid this train wreck? What can we do to keep David DuBrock from ruining Lanai?"

Benny was eager to agree with her. "If Dole leaves, it will kill the island. Dole is a tradition, it's our heritage. Our entire way of life depends on the peace and quiet that surrounds us."

"Pineapple growing has worked just fine on Lanai for over a hundred years. There's no reason it shouldn't work fine for the next hundred." Several members of the group applauded at Tim McLeigh's assessment.

Wendy liked the tenor of the comments and dared to take the conversation in the direction she had in mind. "I think the better question is how do we convince Donald of these things? He's the one who has David DuBrock's ear. He may be the only one on the island who seems able to get DuBrock to listen."

Tim took the bait. "Yeah, but he's in DuBrock's pocket. DuBrock has bought and sold the guy. And Donald doesn't understand Lanai. He doesn't get it. We're supposed to figure he knows better than we do what's right for the island? When he's been living here, what? Two years?"

Other comments from the back of the room left Wendy feeling like she had accomplished what she had hoped to.

"We all know he doesn't speak for us. Donald wants to destroy our way of life. He has no idea how much it means to the island to keep Dole. I mean, Dole built Lanai City. They laid the water pipes and built the streets. Dole is *the* reason people live on Lanai. We can't lose them. We just can't."

"Is it fair that Kahuna has thrown his weight behind this guy? I thought we were supposed to be able to trust him."

"Wendy, I think we need to find someone who *can* speak for us. I think we're agreed that Donald is a loser. Personally, I don't trust him and I don't like him. We need to ditch him. What's so special about him that he gets direct contact with DuBrock? We have to put a stop to this."

In the dark, outside the chapel door, Donald was clenching his teeth because of what he had heard. Then he pulled his foot off the first step, released the handrail and backed away, relieved that he had not been noticed.

—⚓—

"Kahuna? Why did you get me in this mess? Half the people in the village hate me. You should have heard what they said about me at prayer circle twenty minutes ago."

"You're a businessman. You know business and you know sales. I thought you could have an impact."

"I didn't bargain for all these people who can't stand me. When I go to community, nobody will sit with me. I'm a pariah."

"Don't you think you're exaggerating? And overreacting?"

"They called me a loser. You should have heard them. They think I'm destroying their way of life. They're mad at you, too."

"Is that right? Well Donald, welcome to my world."

"How do I get them to stop hating me? I can't stand this."

"You could stop working for DuBrock, and you could stop urging people to accept the idea that Dole is leaving. Just withdraw completely from the situation."

"But that would be stupid. Dole *is* leaving and DuBrock is coming. There's no stopping it. DuBrock might have ruined the island if I hadn't stepped in. You saw it yourself. Like, he hadn't given any thought to how little groundwater he had to work with. Our water supply would have dried up if I hadn't got him to focus on that."

"Why do you care? What does it matter?"

Donald tilted his head. "It matters. *It matters.*"

"Maybe the question is how you communicate with people in the village. How do you convince them that you're right and they should agree with you?"

"That is the question. But what's the answer? What do I do? You're good at this kind of thing. *Tell me.*"

"I don't know the answer, except that it's probably a different answer for every person. Consider how people view you and how they react to you. What is there about you that people will find convincing? There may be something in there that helps."

Donald squeezed his face until it hurt. "I *hate* this. I can't sleep, even. You know, I could be out golfing every day and lounging on the beach and completely ignoring this whole complicated ball of shit. I could just go through with blinders on and instead, I'm making an effort to get this right. I'm really trying to help here and people just don't appreciate it. They don't understand I'm doing this for *their* benefit."

"Don't get selfish here, man. You sound like you're more interested in getting people to like you than you are in getting something done."

Donald shook his head.

"You can make it easier on yourself if you don't let yourself get all rattled just because people don't like what you say. You have to consider it and deal with it. As long as you honestly believe that what you're doing is right, you have something positive to focus on that will guide you."

"Yeah, but what if I'm not right? *What if?*"

"How willing are you to reconsider your opinions?"

"All you got is questions. I need answers."

"Donald, relax. Breathe. All you have to do is separate the pepper from the fly shit. It's simple."

"You're killing me. Do you know that?" The stillness of Bobby Joe's kitchen was nearly overwhelming. "Do you think you could call a village meeting? Could we get everybody together to talk on this?"

Donald stood on the edge of the eighteenth green, three feet from the hole, his hands wrapped around the grip of his putter.

"So you're one putt away from carding a fifty-nine. Just one putt and you set the course record." Bobby Joe pulled the flag stick. "Go ahead and make it."

Donald took a practice stroke and examined his line. He set up and prepared to take his putt.

"You know, Donald, you're a complete jerk. Who in the hell are you that you ever thought you could develop a decent golf game? Who? You're a complete loser. You suck at golf and you always will. Why don't you just give it up?"

Donald stared at the back edge of his ball as his putter came through. His putt was two inches short and tailed to the right and the end of its path. He shook his head. "Try it again?" He pulled his ball back with the nose of his putter and picked a new spot to work from. He took a practice stroke and examined his line. He set up and prepared to putt.

"Donald, every time the people in this village find a reason to like you, you give them a reason to think they're wrong. You come from far away and right away you try and tell them how they should live their lives, how business on the island should be done. Pure arrogance. And what do you know? What, exactly?"

Donald stared again at the back edge of his ball as his putter came through. His putt ran three inches long and burned the left edge of the hole. "I think I almost got it. Can we try again? Louder this time." He retrieved his ball and set up on the opposite side of the hole, about four feet from his target. He took a practice stroke and examined his line. He set up and prepared to take his putt.

"Donald, can't you just accept that you're too much of an idiot to figure out the village? How dare you try and speak for the village when so many people here flat out don't like you?"

Donald's putter came through and he *ahhhed* with lightweight pleasure as he heard his ball rattle around in the bottom of the cup. He swiveled his head and looked sideways at Bobby Joe. "I got this. Let's go."

Bobby Joe stood on the tiny ledge in the corner of the pavilion and raised his arms. Immediately, it got quiet. "Because so many in our village have grown so concerned about our island's future, I thought it would be wise to come together and have Donald address us. He has spent a great deal of time with the developer's engineers and has more knowledge about the project than anyone else in the village."

Donald rose and tried twice to stand on the ledge but found it too small to fit even one of his size fifteen feet. After almost falling over, Donald decided he had no choice but to stand flat on the concrete floor to address his audience. *Well this is starting out all shitty.* A packet of flesh underneath his left eye quivered as he opened his mouth.

"Uh ... uh, I know that many of you – of *us* – are worried and anxious about what may happen since plans for development were put on the table. I wanted to share what I've learned and to give people the chance to ask questions. While the fact that people are concerned is obvious, it's not clear what specific problems people are concerned about. Other than the fact that swapping out a pineapple plantation for a resort is a *change*, what specific effects are people worried about?"

"They want to change the entire island. *Isn't that enough for us to be concerned?*" Anita Bentley stood bolt upright in the front row and started talking without an invitation. "Donald, many of us are concerned that a person who doesn't understand the island's heritage and history is dictating what the island is going to look like. Every week, you're working with the designers and meeting with DuBrock and telling those outsiders what will work and what people will tolerate, when you really have no idea. We are not on board with the idea of losing Dole and leveling the pineapple fields with a high-rise hotel that serves alcohol and brings in thousands of people who will leave behind nothing but their trash and their sewage. These are people who will be causing accidents on the road to town. They will have no idea how to drive Lanai. They're going to *ruin* Lanai. Our entire way of life will be gone."

"Anita, that's just not *true*, that's ... ." Donald stopped himself. *Don't argue. Just listen.* "Anybody else?"

Benny raised his hand like he was afraid his arm would get stolen. Donald pointed to him and nodded. "Come on, man. Stand up and speak your mind."

"If the village opposes the change, if we are unified, we can stop this from happening. The board of supervisors won't go along with this if

"Maybe you should talk to Ted about this. Dixie put together her will based on conversations she had with him."

"They conspired? They did this behind my back?"

"Donald, don't go jumping to conclusions. Talk to Ted."

—∿—

"So Ted, when were you going to tell me?"

"Hmmm. Alex, I'll go for *Clues to the Hidden Meaning of your Faraway Brother* for six hundred. Help me out here, boner boy. What's this all about?"

"It's about Dixie's will. When were you going to tell me?"

"I'll have to go back to *Clues* for eight hundred. Wisenheimer, what the hell are you talking about?"

"I'm talking about the fact that if I don't meet the terms of Dixie's will, you and Kahuna split Dixie's estate. You forgot to mention that little detail."

"I figured if it mattered, you'd ask."

"Ted, you're a goddam *lawyer*. People pay pointy headed little dorks like you thousands of dollars to save them the trouble of reading contracts. This is the kind of crap you *volunteer* to people."

"You're acting all pissed off and entitled. How is this even possible? Did you forget that the whole plan was to put four million dollars in your pocket? Plus it got you out of a bad marriage and a bad job and a pile of debt."

"I've been toyed with, Ted. It's underhanded. It's dishonest. It's *stinky*."

"Donald, do you remember when you said you felt like the punch line in the cruelest joke ever told? Do you remember when your life was in the crapper? And you begged for somebody to tell you what to do? Did you ever wonder why it was that you had to spend three years removed from all the things you hated so much before you got the four million?"

"Ted, how can you not get this? I can't face the people on the island now. They all know this. I'm a patsy to them. You remember Phil Connors from Sunday School? He was an asshole unless he knew the teacher spotlight was on him and then he was goody two shoes. He was so goddam transparent. Well, now I'm Phil Connors. I'm just a dorkazoid who has turned into a patsy. How can I show my face around here?"

Ted felt the burn of acid in his gut. It pressed against the folds of his esophagus before it created a caustic gas that slipped north and passed through his sinuses and made his eyes water. He steadied his head with the palm of his free hand. *Where's this coming from?*

"Donald – I thought we were past this Oh, poor little me bullshit. Aren't you better than this? How about Oh, Ted, thank you so much for encouraging me to be a better person when you could have been a dick and kept the money for yourself? Don't you have even the littlest bit of appreciation? How many people would have tried to make sure you got four million dollars instead of them?"

42

Lanai, Hawaii
January 19, 1980

The nape of Tina's naked neck carried the cinnamon-like aroma of carnations. As Donald sucked at it, she clutched the bedcovers, pushed in her face and moaned. "You found my favorite spot. Oh, that feels *good*." The sucking moved south an inch at a time, along the bumps of her spine and down to the small of her back where it turned into the kneading of flesh – pale, gluteal and compliant.

Tina's hips tilted. She found his hands and pulled them onto her belly. Donald grabbed and pulled and the body of his partner popped up like a pup tent with a tiny, pink door. Donald moved closer and, in an instant, the colors of the world intensified; the pleasure center in his brain lit up like the neon sign outside the Gayety Show Bar on East Baltimore Street. He surged and retreated and surged and savored the spongy feel and sound of moistness begetting moistness. From his gut came an exhale that sounded like a hungry bear.

"You're such a good boy, Donald. *So good.*"

"Baby, you say the nicest things."

The pair rolled sideways and spooned, slowly slithering, Donald nibbling Tina's neck, his hands tracing the slimness of her center.

Then came a voice: "Donald? *Donald?*" The screen door rapped against the front of the house. It rapped again. Then a pause. The spring that held on to the flimsy frame creaked long, shrank back then snapped closed. The voice came into the front room. "Donald? Are you here?"

"Holy shit," Donald whispered. "That's Alani. Baby, stay right here. Please? Don't move?" Donald jumped up and pulled on a pair of underpants. "Alani, wait there – I'll be right out." He slid into a pair of blue jeans and a t-shirt, opened the bedroom door only the few inches necessary for him to slip out, stepped into his living room and was careful to pull the bedroom door tight behind him. Right in front of him stood a pair of inflamed eyes. A starchy slab of Alani's midsection had escaped from beneath her t-shirt and hung over the waistband of her beige sweatpants. *This does not look good.*

"Come sit. Here." Donald motioned toward his couch and they both sat. "What's wrong? What's going on?"

"Donald, I'm not sure. I ... . I was sitting at home and I was all alone and then I realized that I was *all alone.* Then I felt alone and lonely. *And old.* Really, really old." Donald tried to study her face. Alani stared at her knees and sniffled. "Donald, will you be my friend? I'm almost seventy years old and I don't have any. Really. Not a single one. I just need a friend. One friend. I promise to *try* and be nice."

"Alani. Yes. Yes, I'll be your friend. Honestly, I already thought I was your friend."

"Thank you, Donald."

"So, if that's *all,* well, ..." Donald stood. Alani's face remained wrapped in her palms.

"Donald?"

"Yes?"

"Can we talk? I need to tell you some things. If we're friends, we can talk, right?" A thin stream of clear liquid pulled down from her left nostril.

Donald sat back down.

"See, for my whole life I have found talking to people to be really, *really* stressful. It's just awkward. *I'm* so awkward, I don't know what to do or what I should say to people. And yet, I have this aching need to be with people. It's like I need to eat but I don't know how to chew. Do you know what I'm saying? Do you *know?* Every so often, I find a somebody

44

Lanai, Hawaii
February 5, 1980

In a wooden desk by the front door, there was a chunky box of vellum note cards. Each of the cards was produced by a native Hawaiian artist and had been embossed with the image of a cross and a harmless-looking, four-legged blob that was probably a lamb. Dixie bought the box and cards at a shop on Molokai and used them to write lovely messages to people when they needed encouragement or if they had done something to make her feel special. Donald lifted the hinged lid, extracted a blank card and uncapped a fountain pen. *I will call you later and explain. Please don't be mad. This is* <u>*not*</u> *about you.*

Donald's suitcase was covered in two years and eleven months' worth of dusty neglect. He slid it out from beneath his bed where it had been hiding with a never-used leaf for the kitchen table and two boxes of never-used Christmas decorations. He flopped the suitcase open on top of the sheets. In went the underpants, the socks, the shaving kit, the pants and the shorts. He corralled his four pairs of flip flops, then wrinkled his lips and pitched them back into the dark corner of his bedroom closet. *Toby would probably like to have these.*

In a towel, he wrapped the framed photo of Tina and her kids that had been sitting on his nightstand. He inserted it between pairs of pants where he hoped it wouldn't get damaged. He enveloped his golf clubs in a vinyl zip bag with a Braniff International Airways tag.

The cutest cottage on the island, the white one with the lavender echinacea blooms bunched by the front railing, was the little haven that Tina created to give Toby and Ramona a place to feel ordinary and happy. Donald found it still and quiet. He slipped in the back door and propped his note card against Tina's pillow. In the bathroom, he opened the patchouli lotion that Tina spread on herself at bedtime. He splurted some into his palm, then worked his fingers together. He covered his face with his hands and inhaled. *I want to remember this.*

At the Bank of Lanai, Donald stepped up to a writing desk, filled out a withdrawal slip and passed it to the teller. She slipped him a bulging envelope of bills. As she did, she asked if he wanted to keep a few dollars in the account to prevent it from being automatically closed. He declined. "Are you making a special purchase, Donald?" she asked.

"I guess you could say that." Donald let the envelope settle into the bottom of his pocket then he reached out, took her hand, pulled the hand close and kissed it. "You look lovely today, Kini. Quite lovely."

Kini Polamalu closed one eye and squinted with the other. "My husband would be quite jealous." She didn't pull her hand away. Donald didn't let go, either.

"He should be."

He parked the Samurai on a grassy stretch, just outside the airport fence and killed the engine. He pulled the keys out of the ignition and started to put them in his pocket. *Somebody else could use this.* He reinserted them.

A Piper Cub, its engine laboring and its wings spread wide, blasted past, barely twenty feet overhead and directly between Donald and the sun. The large shadow that passed left Donald feeling like he had been photographed or that maybe he was being watched. He imagined for a minute that the Donald up above was observing. After a vigorous head-shake, the Donald up above was erased. The Donald on the ground looked around and decided he was alone.

Donald shouldered his golf bag and lugged his suitcase up to the padded bench inside the terminal building where he dropped them both.

"Danny, can I get a ticket for the four thirty to Honolulu?"

again. Donald looked up and saw Bobby Joe on the tarmac, walking away.

"Harry, can we go now? *Just go.*"

Harry stood up and faced Donald. "You know this stuff already, I imagine. But I have to say it anyway."

"Oh, Harry – you? *You?* Please save it."

"Donald, I ... "

"Harry, c'mon. Just quit."

"Donald, I ... "

"Harry, I'm not having it. I'm not."

"Donald, you don't understand. I ... "

"I understand just fine, Harry. Just shut up already and fly the plane."

"Donald, this plane is not taking off until I say what I have to say."

Donald's jowls lost altitude. He leaned his head back against the seat and stared at the airplane's ceiling. "Go ahead. Get it over with."

"Our flight to Oahu will last approximately thirty minutes. During that time, we will be over water. In the unlikely event of a water landing ... ."

Seven minutes later, the propellers were turning so fast they couldn't be seen. Harry pushed forward on a throttle lever and the aircraft began moving toward the runway.

Donald took deliberate and slow breaths. In and out. In and out. He could feel his heart racing. Then he sat up and leaned forward. "Harry," he shouted. "Stop the plane."

45

Lanai, Hawaii
March 30, 1980

Cleaning is therapeutic. It feels so good when it's done. This is what Bobby Joe kept telling himself as he scrubbed dried particles of food from the floor tiles surrounding the base of his kitchen cabinets. After rinsing and squeezing his sponge in a bucket of blue chemicals, he poured the mix into the sink. Rather than wash it right down, he used it to clean the sink, mashing down hard on a scrub brush that had been a housewarming gift when he first moved to Lanai in 1944.

He pulled out the drain plug and the sound of water swishing around and down kept him from hearing the footsteps of the tall man who entered through the front door and walked purposefully to the kitchen. Bobby Joe sensed the presence of another and looked up.

"Donald. What a surprise." Bobby Joe reinserted the brush into the plastic holder where it lived and then washed his hands. "What brings you here?"

Donald extended his hand which contained a rectangle of paper. "Here. This is for you."

Bobby Joe leaned in to examine what he deduced was a check. It was made out to him in the amount of two million dollars. He raised an eyebrow. "You'd better explain that one, chief."

"This is yours. It's for you."

"Donald, that's the last thing in the world I want."

"There's no reason I should have Dixie's whole estate. It's not right. I want to give you half. It would make me feel better if you would take it. You'd be doing me a favor."

Bobby Joe shook his head. "I told you before, the only way I know how to be is poor. I'm pushing 80 and it's way too late for me to figure out how to be a rich man. You're still young enough to figure it out."

"Take it? Please?"

"There ain't no way I'd do that. Do you know how many other people there are who could use some of that? Who really need it?"

"Kahuna, this money is making me miserable. I hate having it. Help me out here."

"Find somebody else. Me taking that money would be like trying to put gas in a car with a full tank." Bobby Joe watched Donald fiddle with the check, like he was still thinking of ways to put the money in Bobby Joe's pocket. "Donald, tell me something. What possessed you to decide to leave the island and jump on that plane? That made no sense."

"I got to feeling sorry for myself. Whenever that happens, I do things that make no sense. Thank you for talking some sense into me."

46

Bethlehem, Pennsylvania
June 15, 1980

"Do you want me to keep you updated on the score of the other golfers while the tournament is going on?"

Ramona pulled her eyeballs out of her chemistry textbook and let her head flop. *Please tell me you're not for real.* "I'm still kind of a kid, Donald. Shouldn't you decide that for me?"

"You're not a kid. You're seventeen. There's places in Africa where they have grandmothers younger than you."

The cabin of the airliner overflowed with white noise so spongy that Ramona felt like she could rest her head on it. The din felt better than listening to crazy talk from a new caddy who was tripping on his shoe-laces in his quest for a clue.

"All I know is that the good caddies seem like they can figure out stuff like that."

A stewardess brought a ginger ale and a small foil packet of nuts for each. Donald raised his hand. "Hey, can she get more nuts? She loves those."

The stewardess complied. Donald sipped his ginger ale and winked at Ramona. "See? I got the concept down cold. It'll be great."

Out the window, he noticed a small spot on the surface of the Pacific. *How do those little fuckers on the deck of that ship not get lost in the middle of an ocean as big as that?* Donald turned back. "Ramona, should I read every green for you? You know, like *every* green?"

Ramona slapped down her highlighter in the middle of a long paragraph about potentiometric electrodes, the essence of which was eluding her. *He's killing me.* "Didn't we practice stuff like this? Like a lot of times?" Donald's lower lip curled tightly around his bottom teeth and he bit down. "Look, if I need a read, I'll *ask* for one, okay?"

—ɯ—

"Mom, we've not even played a practice round yet and he's already asking really dumb questions and acting all fumbly." Ramona sat on a paisley bedspread with her bare feet curled up under her. Across the room, on a muted television, the CBS Evening News showed film of autoworkers in t-shirts with bellies, round and large, carrying protest signs in front of an oily building made of cinder blocks. Next to the television were an empty ice bucket and two drinking glasses sleeved in wax paper.

"He said he's never been in a tournament that counted before. In some ways, you have more experience than he does. He's probably just a little nervous."

"He's going to be my caddy. He's not allowed to be nervous. He's supposed to know what to say so I don't feel nervous. The tournament hasn't even started yet and already I'm nervous. He's making me that way."

Without wanting to, Tina remembered the day when she discovered her dead husband and his suicide note. The sad man's face was purplish. A puddle of drool speckled with pink had spread out around his mouth where he was kissing the garage floor, his eyes wide open. Her first thought after finding him was to wish that things could be undone, to ponder the steps necessary to put the pieces back together. She shook her head to get rid of the image. *There are some lines that once you cross them, you can't go back.* "Ramona, get out on the golf course. See what happens. Some people thrive in competition. I think Donald might be one of those people."

"Is it too late to call Kahuna and have him fly out?"

"Don't you *dare*. Shame on you for even saying that. Donald has spent a lot of money for your travel, your hotel and your custom-fit golf clubs and everything. He's put a lot of time and heart into this. You would hurt him deeply if you didn't let him caddy."

"I know, Mom. It's just that this is my last chance to win the junior national. If I hope to get a scholarship to Pepperdine, I have to win. *I have to*. That's what the man from the athletic department told me."

—⁓—

On the first day, there was no wind. The sky in Bethlehem was concealed by a low, grey blanket. It was so low, it looked like you could reach up and grab a handful of it. Ramona thought the conditions were ideal. By the time she and Donald reached the turn, she had two birdies under her belt and was feeling confident. *I can do this. I can win.*

The eleventh hole at Saucon Valley was an unusually long par three fronted by a line of pot bunkers deep enough to make a hiding place for the kind of goblins that hide in the corners of a child's closet when the lights go out. Donald pulled out a six iron and offered it up. Ramona sniffed. "That's not enough club. It won't get me there."

"You don't want it to get you there. You want to get almost there so the bunkers are out of play. Then you can do your pop shot, get it close and one putt. See how the back of the green slopes away behind that plateau in the middle? Just about everybody who makes the green from the tee will have to chip back on, hoping to save par."

"I don't know, Donald. I don't get a good feeling about this."

You little shit. Just do what I tell you. I've been playing this game for thirty years. Donald took a cleansing breath. He relaxed his grip on the six iron and let his arm hang. *I'm calm. That's better.* "If you want what you've always got, then do what you've always done."

"*What?* What are you … ."

"If you want what … ."

"I know what you said. What does it mean?"

"It means if you want to come in second place, you should play the game the way you played last year. If you want to win, you have to try something different." Donald dangled the six iron in front of her.

Ramona looked especially cute with a curly ponytail poking out of the hole in the back of her red cap. She held out her gloved hand. "This had better work."

I'll talk to you about being snarky after the round. "Have a little faith. Tell yourself that before you set up."

The hopeful girl stood behind her ball, teed up and ready, and considered her line. She closed her eyes. *This is good. This will work. Donald knows what he's doing. I hope.* She set up and swung. Her ball flew high and straight and landed four yards short of the closest bunker. When she looked at Donald, he had an eyebrow cocked and his head was tilted at her as he nodded.

Both of Ramona's playing partners went for the green. One of them had her ball tail to the right and roll into a pot bunker just off the putting surface. The other landed her shot on the plateau in the center. It rolled down the slope on the back side and disappeared before settling into a depression where rainwater gathered in heavy storms.

The girl whose ball rolled off the back, a quiet kid from Sandusky, Ohio, bit off pieces of her fingernails and spit them out as she considered options. She chipped out of the drainage swale with a nine iron. For a minute, it looked like her ball wouldn't clear the slope and that it might return to her. "Don't you dare roll back. Don't you *dare*." Her ball listened and took her instructions literally. It traveled a few inches past the top edge of the slope and came to rest near the center of the green, leaving her an eighteen-footer. The other player was a dark-skinned girl from Puerto Rico who idolized Sam Snead and played barefoot. She looked and sounded like a pro when she *whunked* her ball out of the bunker on a thin layer of dry sand. But her shot landed on the fringe, just short of the green, and stopped dead.

Donald remained quiet for a moment to allow the girl from Puerto Rico to gather her thoughts, then leaned in toward Ramona's right ear. "Do your pop shot. It's perfect for this."

"You *think*? If I don't hit it right, ..."

Donald interrupted her with a sand wedge. He put a hand on Ramona's shoulder, the tip of his thumb under her collarbone and silenced her with an index finger placed against her chin. "You got this. You know you got this. This is your *thing*. Just like you practiced. Be committed." He retreated seven paces and out of Ramona's view with the staff bag, a soldier at attention.

The leading edge of Ramona's wide-open wedge scuffed the ground half an inch ahead of the ball, as intended. The ridges on the graduated face of the club slid under the ball while Ramona accelerated her swing, sending her missile on a nearly vertical path. It hopped high over the sand trap and landed about five inches shy of the hole where it bounced once before it landed into the center of the cup. *Birdie.*

The parents and siblings of Ramona's playing partners, watching from a respectful distance, clapped politely.

Donald stepped up, grabbed the wedge and whispered: "This is where you tip your cap and acknowledge the crowd. It's not so easy for those folks to applaud for a kid who is making it look like their daughters won't make the cut."

On the eighteenth, a golfer standing on the tee looked at a short par four. The green was nearly invisible for all of the bunkers that fronted it. Ramona felt around for her three wood and found it wouldn't come out of the bag. She looked down and saw Donald's hand holding the shaft.

"What? *What?* I should go long? You see those traps in front of the green that are kinda close right?"

"Yes, but see the finger of fairway that runs up the right side of the green? If you hit it two fifty and put it there, you take lots of sand out of play for your approach."

"So you're thinking driver?"

"I'm thinking driver with a fade."

"I saw the scoreboard. I shouldn't have looked, but I'm already leading by two whole strokes. Do I need to risk putting my drive in a trap?"

"You got three more rounds to play before this is over. You need every stroke you can, and all that sand is very close to the green. If you land there, the worst you're looking at is par."

Ramona swooshed her drive onto the peninsula of short grass next to the green. Two minutes later, she stood behind her ball and saw nothing but grass between her ball and the flag. "I can do a nice bump and run. The sand is out of play, just like you said."

"Bump and run, sister. We're on the same page." Donald handed her a seven iron. Ramona placed her ball in the back of her stance and, with a stiff-armed, one-quarter swing, gave it a polite bump. It flew twenty yards to the edge of the green and rolled halfway up the steep slope until it was even with the flagstick.

"You need to mark that ball right away. That's a one putt right there but not if it gets to rolling back down the hill."

A few minutes later, Ramona wiggled her fingers and squealed a little when her putt went in for another birdie. She was just loud enough to be heard by the players on the green. Donald reached in and took her putter. "Keep it under control. Act like you been here before."

After her playing partners putted, Ramona removed her cap and shook hands with them and with their caddies. She surrounded Donald's middle with her arms and pulled in close. "I'm going to win. I just know it."

"Confidence is good, but don't forget there's three more rounds before this is over."

"Mom was right. Competition brings out the best in you."

Pasta salad or fried chicken? Mixed fruit or French fries? Ramona considered lunch options, the worst of which seemed more alluring because they were illuminated by infrared lamps.

"Just get what tastes good. That's what matters." Ramona looked over her shoulder. "Hi. I'm Tammy. I'm from Arizona."

"I'm Ramona. I'm from Hawaii."

"You live in Hawaii? Really? You're *so* lucky. I've never even been there. Is it paradise? Everybody says so."

By the time they had filled their plates and sat down together, Tammy had asked Ramona if she had ever scored a hole in one, if she could

"Yeah, I know. We both know. You made that quite clear on the first hole this morning. How about *you* be the boss of *you* and *you* get up and win this fucking tournament. Work with me. Give me an F." Donald blew again with this lower lip and his front teeth pressed together.

Ramona's left eye almost closed up thinking about it. "Donald, this is weird. What are you doing exactly?"

Donald's buttocks pressed into the grass and he draped a forearm over one knee. "Have you ever noticed how some golfers say *fuck* a lot? Mostly men golfers? Have you? That's a man's secret weapon. Most women don't like it because they think it's all coarse and offensive. But it's the word that makes everything better. If you hit a bad shot, it's *fuck you motherfucker*. If you hit a good shot, it's *so fucking right*. If your pal hits a good shot, you tell him he's *having a fucking great day*. If you're late to the golf course and you miss your tee time because the starter is a jerk, well *that's so fucking wrong*. Every time it works, it makes things better. *Fuck* is your friend. It will rub your shoulders and speak your name when things go wrong. It enhances the flavor of great moments, sort of like the MSG they use at Chinese restaurants, only *fuck* doesn't make you feel all spacey half an hour later. And right now, you need this. You really do."

"I need this? *I* do?"

"Yeah, you need it you little shit. Stand up and stop being all slobbery and look me in the eye." He grabbed her by the arm and pulled her to her feet. "Poke me with your finger and tell me to fuck off. Do it."

"I can't say that. I can't. ... I ... ."

"*Do it.* Just do it already."

The girl pursed her lips and looked at her shoes. Then she poked Donald in his left nipple with an index finger. She opened her mouth and invested effort. But nothing came out. "I can't."

"Fuck you, Ramona. Fuck you. *Fuck you*."

She lowered her shoulders and closed her fists.

"Fuck you. Fuck you. Fuck you. ... Fuck you. Fuck you."

"Stop it, Donald. You're making me mad."

"Fuck you, Ramona. Fuck you to hell."

"Donald!"

"Fuck you."

"Alright. Fuck off."

"That's good, but louder. Much louder."

"Fuck off!"

"Fuck off, *Donald*. And when you say my name, say it quieter than when you say *fuck off*. It works better that way."

"*Fuck off,* Donald."

"See? *You aren't the boss of me* doesn't really work. I can tell that the reason you're mad has nothing to do with me trying to be the boss of you. It's too ambiguous. You and I both know it. So when you say *you aren't the boss of me*, your anger is still yours. It doesn't go anywhere. It probably feels worse because it seems like you can't do anything about it. You know, *darn* or *aw jeez* or something is lacking in horsepower. There's no force behind it. Those are words you use to tell the world something is wrong but in the back of your head you're thinking *I must be polite. I don't want to be profane and offend somebody.* But the thing is, if something is bad enough to mess with your game? It's bad enough to make your knees buckle and make you get all teary and shit? Then *sassafras* or *golly Ned* is just a waste of time. Why even bother? Why not just keep your suffering to yourself? But *fuck off, Donald?* That's undeniable. That's clear. That's cutting at a thick rope with a blade of blue steel. *Fuck* says you're mad as hell and you're not going to take it any more. You say *fuck* and some of your anger is gone. You've hurled it at me – a rock at my head. I feel it and I get it. It's not yours anymore. You have bought yourself distance from what's got you pissed off. You've asserted yourself. You feel better. And maybe you can play a little better."

"Really?"

"Really."

"Well fuck it. I think you're fucking right. Because I do feel better. I feel *fucking* better."

"Now go hit. And yes, the driver's a good choice. You need the extra distance if you want to get your second shot close to the hole, and your control with the driver is usually good enough to keep you safe."

Ramona wrapped her long arms all the way around Donald and pressed her face into his cushiony pectorals, a move that turned out to had to yell for Cathy to rescue him and when she tried to get serious and calm things down Ted pulled her in too.

Later that evening, Cathy sounded like she meant it when she told Donald that it was really sweet of him to come and visit and then headed upstairs to put herself and the kids to bed.

"Donald, do you think you'll see Kim while you're here?"

"Why would I do that? She hates me."

"I'm not so sure. I saw her just a couple of weeks ago. She sold me that Mustang convertible that you saw in the garage."

"Wait. … What?"

"She took your old job. Apparently she's good at it. They had her picture up on the wall. She made *salesperson of the month* twice in the last year. She asked me to thank you."

Donald uncrossed his legs and leaned forward. "Seriously? You wouldn't kid about this, would you? Why would she want to thank me? I made her miserable for twenty-five years."

"Kim said that she learned everything about how to do that job from listening to you. All those years you bad-mouthed Charlie Chasanow and complained about customers who wasted your time are paying off. Donald, she's a whole different person. You would hardly recognize her. She said she's quit drinking and she looks great. She seems really happy. You know, she's the only woman selling cars over there and all the men coming in want to deal with her because they think she's hot. I think she's making some good money."

"Teddy, I don't think seeing Kimmy would be a good thing. It's probably better for her if she thinks I'm an asshole and she pats herself on the back because she put all that behind her."

—⚒—

At Friendship Airport, which is what most people were still calling BWI, they offered direct flights to Honolulu with a single stop in Los Angeles. While waiting for his plane, Donald saw several people eating fast food at tables along the concourse. He studied their faces and spotted a guy with a salt-and-pepper beard and a *Terps* hat who was eating alone. *Perfect.*

Donald sauntered over and helped himself to a couple of French fries. The bearded guy stood up, read for confrontation and then relaxed. "Great balls of fire. I recognize you. You're … ."

Donald shook his head and waved his index finger in front of the man's chin. "Don't tell *anybody* about this. Really – don't. They'd *never* believe you."

49

Lanai City, Hawaii
January 2, 1984

After a whisper-quiet walk across a field of dense wool-blend carpeting, the waiter brought the coffee and the lunch check at the
same time, which was as Wendy Walker had requested. She was hoping
that she and her niece, Jennifer, could get to the first tee by one thirty.
His feet at shoulder width and his hands clasped behind him, the waiter
stood at Wendy's elbow while she fished in her purse for a turquoise
wallet full of credit cards. "It's lovely that we finally have a nice sit-down
restaurant on the island. But it shouldn't have to come at the expense of
growing pineapples."

Jennifer sipped coffee from a delicate teacup as she recalled mother's
complaints about her intransigent older sister

"Maybe in a few years, this resort will seem like the island's heritage,
Aunt Wendy. It seems to be rather popular."

"Nonsense. The Hawaiian Islands are perfectly suited to growing
tropical fruit. It's what they were *meant* for." She clicked an American
Express card onto the tiny bamboo tray that held the lunch check.

The waiter's chin dipped. "Ms. Walker? You know, Lanai was an
unoccupied desert when Dole bought it. Nobody thought it was good
for anything. People thought Dole was crazy for buying it. The only
reason it looks green now is because of extensive irrigation. When Dole

completes its withdrawal and the irrigation stops, most of the island will turn brown."

"That can't be true. The village golf course is quite green and it has almost no irrigation."

"It's on the windward side of the island and is one of the few places that gets regular rain. The point at Puhi'elelu Ridge stands high enough that it divides the approaching clouds and prevents most of the interior from getting regular rain."

"How could you know all this? I've been on the island my whole life and I don't know this. You're making this up."

"I was a supervisor of Dole pineapple pickers for almost twenty-five years. If we had problems with irrigation equipment, I had to pull men out of the field to go fix it. Honestly, this resort is the best thing that could have happened to the island. Most of the pickers I used to supervise are working indoors and making better money. Most of us have health insurance for the first time. Two months ago, my wife and I could finally afford to buy our home from Dole." The waiter held out his clean hands for Wendy's inspection. "See these? They used to be scabbed up year round from getting stabbed by the tips of leaves on the pineapple plants. I used to couldn't put anything in my pockets because it hurt too much to put my hands in."

51

Lanai, Hawaii
May 2, 1984

Trying to wipe the ass of a feeble man who has shit two layers of brown slurry into an adult-sized cotton diaper is unpleasant. There are more acute ways of describing the job but Donald found that it works better if you don't think about them, at least while you are doing the wiping.

He could hear Kahuna's voice from a long-ago golf lesson: *You can't make good choices about hitting out of the woods if you're feeling sorry for yourself. Clear your head. Give yourself permission to be happy.*

Donald decided to make the work more pleasant by singing.

There she was just a-walkin' down the street
singing doo wah diddy diddy dum diddy do
snappin' her fingers and shufflin' her feet
singing' doo wah diddy diddy dum diddy do

When Donald sang *She looked good*, he could count on Bobby Joe for a double grunt response that meant *looked good*. And when Donald sang *She looked fine*, Bobby Joe would give a slightly different double grunt and they both knew what it meant. It meant *looked fine*. Most days, that's all it took to get them through a stinky little job.

Finding that little bit of joy was enough to make a man feel blessed as he watched his handiwork swirl down the toilet.

And I nearly lost my mind …

—⚬—

Tim McLeigh was tainted, having grown up in the big city of Chicago. It left him feeling impatient at anything that made him wait. He knew he struggled with impatience but that only helped a little. His impatience persisted even though he had lived the last several years in a place where reasons to hurry were less common than traffic lights. He thought about this after he knocked on Donald's screen door and became aware of seconds ticking by while he listened for noises that meant Donald was going to respond.

Donald appeared from inside and held open the door. "Come in and sit down, Tim. How are you, man?"

"I'm doing well enough, but I'm having real troubles. Is there any way I could try and talk to Kahuna?" The screen door slapped its frame when it closed. Tim sat on the couch.

Is he trying to be funny? Then came the plain look on Tim's face. "Tim, I don't think so. Kahuna can manage only about one or two good words in a day. Sometimes, from the way he grunts or from his facial expressions, I can tell what he's thinking, but that's about as good as it gets."

"Could you talk to him for me? I'm really having trouble. I mean, I need help with my swing."

Kahuna is trying to avoid aspirating his oatmeal and this guy wants advice on his golf game. Donald exhaled. "What kind of trouble are you having, exactly?"

"My approach shots and my chip shots have gotten really inconsistent. Some days, they're everywhere. I'm in the woods or over the green, anyplace but where I'm trying to go. Like my five wood off the fairway? I'm topping it all the time. That shot's been money in the bank for years."

Donald chewed on the inside of his lip and nodded. "Give me a minute." As he stepped into Kahuna's bedroom and closed the door, Donald fought against a wave of irritation rising from his gut.

The memory of Kahuna's voice came to him again: Don't go getting riled at people who seem inconsiderate. It won't do nothing but screw with your game. Chances are, you've pulled the same crap.

After closing the bedroom door, Donald parked on a stool at Kahuna's bedside, the same spot where he read aloud from books and newspapers to his friend. With a hand on the old man's shoulder, Donald looked him in the eye. "Tim McLeigh is here for golf advice. Do you have anything for him?"

A mild palsy had set in, making Kahuna's head move back and forth in a jagged, diagonal motion. His eyes appeared to focus on Donald, but never for more than a few moments at a time, and he was drooling onto a bib.

"Tim's spraying and topping his approach shots and his chip shots. He's probably hurrying around the course, don't you think? Probably he should find a way to slow down and calm down. Like maybe on the golf course, he could sing some songs the same way we do together?" Donald smoothed a hand across the forehead of his charge. "Thanks, my brutha. I knew I could count on you."

Donald bent and kissed Bobby Joe on the forehead and then held his cheek against the man's temple. *You're in good hands, dear friend.*

In the living room, Donald sat on the coffee table so he could stare down Tim from close range. "You're lucky. You got him on a good day. Tell me, do you still find yourself feeling rushed all the time?"

"Yeah, pretty much. I'm sure that has something to do with my problem."

"What sort of things have you tried to make you feel less rushed? You know, sometimes if you just give yourself permission to relax, it can help."

"Kahuna told me that several times. He also suggested I breathe slowly and look at the tree tops while I imagine my next shot. I already do both those things. Sometimes, I even close my eyes and remember what it used to feel like when I was little and it was summer and I didn't have to go to school or anything and I just had all this free time."

"And?"

"That used to work, but it's gotten stale. I need something new."

Donald let several moments pass. He wanted to create the appearance that he was deep in thought. Then he leaned in. "Tim, do you like music?"

"Doesn't everybody?"

"Well, some folks more than others. What is some music that makes you feel at peace?"

"That's easy. Debussy's Claire de Lune."

"Wait ... what? Boxcar Willie's bass player? He had a solo career?"

"I think Debussy was a little before Slim's time. He was a French composer of classical music."

"Kahuna says that when you're getting set up and before you decide how to hit, you should hum some Debussy for about a minute. Whistle it if you think it helps. Get it in your head. Feel the flow and the rhythm. Let it push everything else out of the way. A little music will give you peace of mind. If one song gets stale, try another. You'll find that your game gets better almost right away."

"Kahuna said that? All that?"

"Like I said, you got him on a good day. It helps that I spend so much time with him. I can understand some of his grunts and groans."

—⁂—

In the afternoon, somebody from the resort always came by Donald's house to drop off a drawstring sack full of clean sheets and clothes and to pick up a sack of soiled. On weekdays, that somebody was usually Marianne Cope who lived in town and worked in housekeeping. Back when Marianne worked days in the pineapple fields, her mother passed from pancreatic cancer. That left her without care for her daughter, Victoria, whenever school was out. Bobby Joe spent lots of hours with the girl, mostly on the golf course. She looked up to Bobby Joe and thought it was extraordinary that so many people came to him for advice. When the girl grew up, she went to divinity school. She found work ministering to a Unitarian Universalist congregation east of Minneapolis.

Marianne approached her manager, Kalia, to see if the resort could take care of Bobby Joe's laundry. Kalia agreed right away. She remembered one time when her Jeep was running rough and Donald had adjusted the carburetor and the timing. He refused to accept any payment and said car service was free for all the pretty girls on the island. It was the first time anybody told her she was pretty since the days in junior high school when her math homework was still simple enough that her granddaddy could help.

When David DuBrock came through unannounced one day and found out about the arrangement, he grew quiet and it made Kalia become concerned for her job. She needn't have been. David suggested that a resort employee drive the hotel's Range Rover out to Donald's house each day to pick up and drop off. After the resort was up and running, David had accounting run some numbers and they concluded that Donald's ideas were saving the resort owners nearly $500,000 a year.

—⚹—

Karen Nakamura had played all her rounds alone since Bobby Joe couldn't be her partner any more. After a lackadaisical front nine late on a Thursday afternoon when nothing seemed to be working, she sat on a bench by the tenth tee waiting for the fairway to clear. *Maybe I should quit this game for a while. It doesn't feel right at all.*

"Can I join you?"

Karen's head whipped around. There stood a mushroom-shaped woman in snakeskin pants and orange cotton flats with a haircut that looked like it had been given in a dark closet. "Alani. Well, hello. Of course you can join me. I didn't know you played." *Alani couldn't make conversation with a bible salesman. This will be awkward.*

"I had never played and then talking with Donald convinced me I needed to get out here and try it." When she teed off, Alani used a five wood. After a flourishy half-swing that was no more kosher than a bacon cheeseburger, her ball flew 140 yards straight out and settled in the middle of the fairway. "I love this game. I can't believe it was right in my back yard all this time waiting for me to find it."

Karen's drive faded right and disappeared into a line of pines. Her lips got forcibly wrinkly and her arms fell down at her sides. *Dammit. Again with the slice.*

"Wait, I think you're going to hit the Bradley tree." A pause. Then again, much louder: "The Bradley tree. I think you're going to hit it. *Oh, Bradley tree? Where are you?*"

A figure jumped out from behind a clump of rocks and fished Karen's ball out of some rough grass and hurled it into the center of the fairway. "Oh, look at that, you ended up in such a beautiful spot. Perhaps you can teach me how you do that."

"How did you even know he was down there?"

"We have an arrangement. I make him dinner and he comes golfing with me. He's the only reason I can break ninety."

"He talks to you?"

"Sure he talks to me. Why wouldn't he?"

"I didn't think Bradley talked to anybody but Bobby Joe."

"He talks to Donald, too. Donald introduced us, so now he talks to me. Hey, do you know why golfers wear two pairs of socks? In case they get a hole in one. Bradley told me that joke."

"And it's *almost* funny. That's incredible."

"Bradley is a very funny man." When she got to the fairway, Alani took an eight iron and after another flourish with high elbows and jiggly hips, she whacked her ball about 100 yards, still ninety yards shy of the green.

"You didn't want to go with something a little longer than an eight? You hit it nice and straight. You could be on the green already."

"I go through stretches when my longer clubs don't work and I'm in one right now. Donald told me if that happens, I should scale it back and use shorter clubs, that I should set my sights lower for a little while. You know, take baby steps. Plus, when I use shorter clubs, I make more shots and get more practice. It keeps the game from getting too frustrating."

"Donald told you that?"

52

Lanai, Hawaii
February 2, 2002

The thunder, the rains and the scary commotion of atmospheric in-stability that had stomped around during the night lifted before first light. By breakfast, it left behind a cleansed slate that was hardly dry to the touch. From the inside of Tina's elfin-cute kitchen window, Saturday morning looked like it was all greenness, inviting niceness and clarity. It smelled of coffee and cinnamon-raisin bagels.

Tina, who had been dressed, fed and ready for nearly twenty minutes, waited patiently at the kitchen table, legs crossed and hands in her lap, until Donald took a big swallow and emptied his second cup. She raised her eyebrows and tilted her head toward the back door. Donald nodded and slipped on his broad-brimmed hat and his favorite pair of flip-flops and out they went, past the garden with the daffodils that tossed their heads in sprightly dance and into the open where the golfers liked to roam free. In the up-above, the Cook pines whispered a chorus that some say was in honor of those who had once played here but could no more.

When they reached the tee box for number eighteen at the top of Puhi'elelu Ridge, Donald and Tina sat cross-legged, facing one another with their eyes closed and their hands joined. There they remained for several minutes, under streams of clouds that collided with the high point of the island where they divided and opened a window to blue sky.

"Shall we get busy?" Tina stood, her ropy twirls of silver and red nearly glowing in the haze, and held out a hand. Donald took it and rose slowly and unevenly, his free arm extended for help with balance.

"Ever since I turned seventy, my knees have been screaming at me. Getting up is painful some days. Aw, hell. Listen to me complain."

"Well, fortunately, you have other parts that work reasonably well. Good thing, too." Tina grabbed Donald's package and tugged. "Because I'm a woman. And I have a *woman's needs*."

"Sweetie? *Baby*? I'm an intelligent and sensitive man of the Twenty-First Century. It's demeaning that my woman values me only to satisfy her carnal desires. I want to be judged by the content of my character. You know, I have a brain. I have talents. I have *feelings*. I need to be treated with respect and dignity."

"Sugar, I need respect, too, and there's nothing that says respect like taking your woman on a little trip to Shangri-la. You are a man who is as respectful as anyone alive. I am so thankful. I totally respect you for that."

"Tina, I knew there was a reason I made you my best friend. You're awesome." Donald kissed her forehead and wrapped his arms around her. He then opened the nearby gardening shack and pulled out a hand mower, its blades blackish with a grassy residue. After adjusting the setting to medium-short, he began to mow the tee box. Tina took a pitchfork, stepped carefully down the golfer's path and began aerating the soil on the fairway grass, punching holes over and over into the ground.

After mowing the entire circle, Donald grabbed a container of seed mix and began spreading it on thin patches on the fairway, a few spoonfuls at a time. He took a moment and stared uphill at the headstones mounted into the grassy portion of the slope just beneath the tee box. "Have you noticed how the headstones for Dixie and Bobby Joe have started tilting downhill? Maybe it would be a good project for us to reset them. I hate to see them like that."

"Can we do that next weekend? Remember when we reset Wilbur's stone last summer? Those little fuckers are *heavy* and my back is sore from gardening two days in a row."

"That would be fine, baby. Speaking of which, next weekend it's my turn to lead discussion at vespers and I'm having trouble coming up with a topic. What do you think, maybe short-game philosophy? I thought maybe I could tie it into a discussion about how positive regard for others calms us at times of stress and makes us better people."

"Oh, that's been done to death. Plus, I've always thought that topic was too broad. We had that very same discussion the week when you and the other men in the Old Testament study group went golfing on Oahu. It started out fine but then Wendy Walker got all *inspired* and droned on. Did you know that if you don't accept Jesus as your personal savior, you can't play good golf? God gave his only son so that we could chip and putt like champions."

"Sweet old Wendy. She has a hard time figuring out what people will find interesting, doesn't she? She just needs a little help. She'll get there."

"Oh, *gawud*. Can't you just come out and say she's a boring and myopic old fart? I mean, that's what she is, right? Do you always have to be so dang nice?"

"I'm not being nice, baby. I'm being self-interested. If I want to keep peace of mind, I can't go putting people down. The thing is, it's true. Wendy has trouble knowing what to say to people that won't put them off. People see her coming and they want to be going. You got me thinking. Maybe this is my topic: how to deal with folks who are conversationally challenged. I know quite a few people who could stand to give that subject a little attention. Like our round on Tuesday with Colleen and Denby. They were trying to tell you about how your putt was going to break even as you were setting up over your ball. I could see you clenching your jaw."

"Omigod, that would be perfect. I'll take them a pie and make sure they know they're invited and are planning to attend. Oh, if you could get through to them, the whole village would be so thankful. They're the *worst*."

"They're not the *worst*, baby. Don't be so critical. They just haven't come as far as you have. They haven't learned the same lessons you have.

They think they're being helpful and they have no idea it upsets people. If somebody could be sincere and direct with them, they might take a different approach."

"You ask anybody on the island and they'll tell you the same thing, they are the worst. Not everybody can be as tolerant as you."

"Well then it's decided. Y'know, I've got the annual *Golf and Spirituality* address in about a month when Butch Harmon's coming in for his workshop. I was thinking of lecturing on the value of telling folks about any criticism you have right to their face and not, you know, *behind their back.* I'm afraid I knew a couple of people who seem to have trouble with that one." Donald elevated his eyebrows and gave Tina a stare.

"Hey, not me. No way. You can't tell me that I'm guilty of that. It's just not true. It is not. *It is not.*"

"Feeling a little defensive?" Donald stood erect, hands on hips and pushed out his chest like he had boobs. "*Can't you just come out and say she's a boring and myopic old fart?*"

"Oh, come on. I was *just saying.* That's all."

"Would you say it if Wendy was here? Right here? Suppose somebody heard you saying that and they didn't know you like I do. They would probably think you were judgmental and small. And what were you *thinking* before you said that? Nothing nice, I'll bet."

"Well, damn it, Wendy is a fundamentalist gasbag. She is. Everybody knows it." Donald remained silent and lowered his chin, still staring at Tina. "Oh, alright. Maybe I could be a little kinder. I will try and work on that."

"I know it would make the *whole village so thankful.*" Donald clasped his hands beneath his chin and grinned beatifically.

"Oh, shut up you old coot. Be nice to me or *I'll cut you off sheckshually.*"

"That's about the emptiest threat I've ever heard. You couldn't stand to cut me off. You love riding the Zamboni more than anybody I ever saw."

Tina gave him a shove and held up her pitchfork, its tines pointed at Donald's midsection. "Perhaps I should just threaten you with carnage."

"Hey, don't point that thing at me. I'm on a mission from God."

Just then, a red-headed gnome carrying a saggy golf bag on her shoulder marched out of the woods. She had an off-center ponytail mounted near the top of her head and her bicuspids were kneading a fluorescent orange wad. "I'm done with my gardening. I'm *playing*. You two better watch out so you don't get hit. Okay? You got me?"

Tina glanced at Donald and then back at the disarming mixture of cuteness and impudence standing before her. She stood Grantwood tall with the pitchfork in her hand. "Dixie, you know darn well that nobody plays on gardening day until after lunch. There's plenty of work to be done and you need to do your share, just like everybody else."

"But, Grandmother, I have been weeding and picking up rocks for *hours*. I'm tired of gardening. I just want to play. Mama said I could."

"Oh, Dixie. Puh-lease. Should I go and ask Ramona if that's what she said? We both know what she would say, don't we? Listen, why don't you come help me with my chores? We can make up some stories while we work. I know you love that."

Dixie demurred. "If I do some work, will you play a round with me after lunch? I asked Mama, but she's too busy."

"There's nothing I would like better, sugar. Now come on over and give us a hug." Tina wrapped her arms around the girl, held her close and smoothed out her red curls. "You are my little love bug. I just can't get enough of you. And your mama, too. Now, drop your bag and take this pitchfork. You can poke some holes in the ground to give the grass some air. It needs to breathe just like you do."

Tina took a shovel from the shed and walked down the fairway and began to straighten the edge of the flower garden that ran along the right side of the fairway. When she had completed a sweaty thirty-minute lap around the garden, she took off her gloves, kneeled and took a handful of soil. She took a deep inhale and absorbed its loamy essence and then released slowly. "Thank you for everything, old friend. We miss you so," she whispered.

From over the hill, above and beyond the tee box, came a signal. *Clang. Pause. Ca-clang. Pause. Clang. Pause. Ca-clang.*

"Lunchtime!" squeaked Dixie. "Let's go eat. Then we can play. I want to play! I want to *play!*"

"Slow it down just a little. We'll get there in plenty of time," said Tina. The trio gathered up their tools and put them into the gardening shed and began the walk to the pavilion. Tina looked down at Dixie, who was walking with her hands in her pockets. "Bug, you forgot your golf bag. Run get it now. We'll wait for you."

"Can't I just get it later? I want to eat right now. I'm so hungry. Please?"

"Dixie, how many times have you left your golf bag lying on the course? Do you know? Because I've lost count."

The girl shrugged her shoulders and looked at her feet.

"How many times has this lovely man found them and brought them back to you?"

The girl stood motionless, her little bare feet on the ground.

"Little sister," said Donald, "today's your lucky day. I'll be right back."

He disappeared down the hill and then scampered back up with the golf bag on his shoulder. "Here you are, sweet stuff."

Donald kneeled down so he was face to face with Dixie and took her free hand. "You have always been so kind to me, little Dixie. Thank you for that. After lunch when we're on the course, can you show me how you hit your tee shots so far? It would mean a lot to me. It really would."

At the pavilion, the happy chatter of hungry villagers resounded. Billy Dundee, who had recently moved from Sydney, Australia, into the Hagood sisters' old house, entertained Wendy Walker, seated in her wheelchair, with stories about having the confidence to wrestle alligators because he knew his faith in God would keep him safe. Jerry McLeigh was stuttering and waving his hairy forearms through an enthusiastic account of a recent round at Pebble Beach while Alani and Bradley pretended to listen.

Donald stood in the corner of the pavilion, in front of the ledge where Bobby Joe used to stand. When Donald raised his arms, quiet spread in an instant. Everyone joined hands and spoke in unison:

Lord, grant us compassion so that we may inspire others to happiness;
Lord, grant us the strength and courage to love and to be loved;
Lord, grant us the faith to be optimistic and to encourage optimism in others;
Lord, grant us wisdom so that we may know and speak of what is best.

and then,

Lord, grant us peace and good health so that we may have fun.

As he prepared a lunch plate for Wendy, Donald's mind wandered back to the days when he felt as if he was watching himself from above. He wondered how long it had been since the Donald from above had popped in, uninvited.

He set a lunch plate, a drink and silverware in front of Wendy. She reached out and grabbed Donald by the forearm. "The food looks good. Thank you, Kahuna."

THE END

Postscript

Who among us has ever accomplished anything without owing someone else a debt of gratitude?

My wife, Catherine, has patiently put up with me while I wrote 'Church of Golf' and has helped tremendously with reviewing the manuscript and listening politely as I talked endlessly about possible plot twists, character development and so on. That's true love, right there. Darling, I love you.

My daughters, Caitlin and Meredith, have been incredibly supportive. In some cases, they inspired bits and pieces of dialogue that they may recognize. I love you both. Thank you for being awesome people.

Mary Dattoli, my assistant, reviewed the manuscript more times than either of us can count and has helped with extensive work on research and planning. She has done so much and all with good cheer, intelligence and determination. Bless you, dear. And thanks.

A number of people reviewed and commented upon my manuscript. Every one of them has added something valuable. Alan Mairson and Lynda DeWitt both served as book editors with insightful comments on matters both minute and grand. Book editor Jack Adler was likewise helpful and highlighted dozens of things that made 'Church of Golf' a better read. All three of them were crucial in development of this book. My deepest appreciation and humblest admiration is offered to each of you.

Thanks also to Jim Steele, William Farneth, Ki Jun Sung, Dave Ryner, Diane Teague, Howie Reitz and Michael Geffroy, who read the manuscript and offered terrific comments.

I have to add a special extra note of appreciation to Alan Mairson and to Howie Reitz who, combined, inspired this book and may not have even known it.

Over the years, I have had numerous conversations with Alan about theology and religion. In one of these, while we were drinking, Alan expressed his belief that a kid couldn't grow up with a strong moral code if he/she wasn't brought up in a synagogue, church or other house of worship. I told Alan that he was wrong – the lessons that lead to development of a moral code will come no matter where a kid spends his time, even it it's a golf course at a country club. That sparked a lively little debate that ended only after spousal intervention.

Just a few days later, I was having lunch on a bench at Dupont Circle in Washington, D.C., with Howie and a couple of other guys and we got to talking about golf. Howie said that some of the most important things he had ever learned came from time spent on the golf course. He said that he learned the importance of humility and balance because he had gotten frustrated with golf and remained intent on getting better at the game. When Howie said that, a light bulb turned on. I right away realized there was a great story to be told about lessons learned on the golf course.

Finally, I want to acknowledge my boyhood friend Donald O'Neill who is the model for the main character in this book. The Donald I knew was one of the most remarkable people I've ever known. He was whip smart. He was creatively profane. He was a wizard with a lacrosse stick in his hands and seemed able to quickly master any sport. When he walked into a room of strangers, they became friends right away. He had keen insight into human nature. Everywhere he went, unfamiliar women approached him and flirted.

Donald was also terribly narcissistic. Because he was so funny and so decent, people didn't seem to care. When he was sober, Donald was a joy to be around; he was a great and loyal friend.

Unfortunately, Donald had problems with addiction. Drugs and alcohol caught up with him and lead to his death at age 37. Growing up, we were as close as twin brothers and I have missed him terribly for what feels like years and years.

'Church of Golf' is not Donald's story, but it could have been. I found myself wondering once what Donald's life would have been like had he overcome his addictions. That was when it occurred to me that he'd make a good model for Donald Gibson.

As I wrote 'Church of Golf,' I imagined Donald O'Neill whenever I wrote dialogue or sketched out activities for Donald Gibson. I heard his voice in my head when I wrote or reviewed Donald Gibson's dialogue. It felt very much like Donald O'Neill was alive and that we were communicating. It was valuable therapy. Now, instead of imagining my lost friend laying in a cold graveyard, I picture him on a remote Hawaiian island, out of reach. He has conquered his demons and he is thoroughly happy.

- Spencer Stephens
  October 2014

Made in United States
Orlando, FL
30 March 2022

16299536R10202